A big
fat rain-
drop fell on
the windshield. I
watched it, that single,
fat, glassy blob of rain; I
watched it splat and slide. Then
another came, and another, and
another. "Lock the doors," said Simon.
I couldn't think how; which button?
"Your side," said Simon. "Your lock—" He
reached right over me and hit the lock on my door.
SCHTOMP! The doors locked. The people in the
parking lot were screaming, running for cover—running
back to the supermarket, where other people were trying to
get out. Screams, shouts, gunshots. People running all over.
BLAM! A woman—a little trail of blood running down her
face—slammed against the car. She saw us inside; she tried to get
in the backseat of the car on Simon's side, a baby seat there. "Let
me in!" she screamed. "You do not open the doors," shouted Simon, his voice hard and cold. The woman scooted round the
car—BLAM! Her palms slammed down on my window; her
face pressed close—the look on it, the terror, the pleading. She could have been my mom. "Please!" she
screamed at me. "There's nothing we can do
for her," shouted Simon. "Ruby, there's
nothing we can do."

PRAISE FOR VIRGINIA BERGIN'S *H2O*
A *VOYA* PERFECT TEN BOOK OF 2014!

"[*H2O*] brings life and humor to an otherwise dark situation. Reminiscent of classic post-apocalyptic and dystopian novels, from Michael Crichton to Stephen King to Lois Lowry to Suzanne Collins. A great, high-interest read for contemporary teens."

—*VOYA*

"Creepy and realistic. *H2O* left me thirsting for more."

—Kristen Simmons, author of *Article 5* and *Breaking Point*

"Ruby's candid, addicting narration brought this terrifying and wholly plausible story to life. This is a book you'll devour all at once—from the safety of your umbrella!"

—Jessica Khoury, author of *Origin* and *Vitro*

"It's a gripping concept, and there's something particularly terrifying about the end of the world coming in something as sweet as a misty drizzle. Ruby's narrative voice is exceptional."

—*The Bulletin of The Center for Children's Books*

"Watching Ruby draw strength from her ability to tell her own story is as inspiring as it is harrowing."

—*The Horn Book Magazine*

"Attention to detail, coupled with a very strong main character, will draw readers in and make them think twice about leaving the house—at least not before checking the sky for signs of rain."

—*School Library Journal*

ALSO BY VIRGINIA BERGIN

The Storm

VIRGINIA BERGIN

sourcebooks
fire

Published by Sourcebooks Fire, an imprint of Sourcebooks, Inc.
P.O. Box 4410, Naperville, Illinois 60567-4410
(630) 961-3900
Fax: (630) 961-2168
www.sourcebooks.com

Originally published in 2014 in the United Kingdom by Macmillan Children's Books, an
imprint of Macmillan Publishers Limited.

Library of Congress Cataloging-in-Publication data is on file with the publisher.

Printed and bound in the United States of America.
WOZ 10 9 8

For Karen, Sue, and John

As soon as I'd gotten the first warbling word out, I knew I'd made yet another horrible mistake. Not because of the not-being-able-to-sing thing, but because the song was the song my mom sang to me when I was little, the one she wouldn't sing that night when she sat outside the door—"Dream a Little Dream of Me."

Every lovely, pretty thing in it felt wrong.

There were no stars. (YOU COULDN'T EVEN SEE THE STARS BECAUSE IT WAS CLOUDY AND IT WAS RAINING KILLER RAIN.)

There was no breeze. (THERE WAS JUST KILLER RAIN WHISPERING, "I WANT TO KILL YOU.")

There was no birdsong. (BECAUSE THE BIRDS WERE TOO BUSY PECKING OUT HUMAN EYEBALLS.)

The next part is supposed to be really sweet, about how you'll dream of the people you love. It doesn't say anything about "EVEN THOUGH THEY'RE PROBABLY DEAD." I couldn't go on. I got all choked up. I wanted my mom.

Genius, Ruby. You really are a genius.

The killer rain applauded me, drumming down harder on that thin plastic roof.

H2O

I f this was a regular story, like the kind you'd read for fun, it would have such a great beginning. Probably they'd want to make it into a movie—it'd be that good. It would start in Mission Control—or maybe deep in space, where a massive hunk of rock—an asteroid—is whizzing through the stars on a collision course with planet Earth.

We cut to Earth: all over the world, everyone is terrified. They crowd around their TVs, weeping and praying. Probably there's also a lot of hugging and kissing and hand-holding, that kind of thing. Lots of deep and meaningful conversations—but not too many; we don't want to spoil the action.

The final countdown starts, and back in Mission Control some old guy in a uniform stands aside to let some hot young dude—a misunderstood rebel genius who's masterminded the operation— press the button. His girlfriend is there—or maybe she's at home, watching on TV, whispering, "I love you, Brad," as he launches the super rocket that's Earth's only hope.

Now all everyone can do is wait and hope and pray.

You'd have to speed up the next part. Apparently in real life it took hours and hours, days, for the missile to reach the asteroid. In the movie of the book, it'd take just enough time to let the buff dude and his girl find each other, so they can be kissing when:

KA-BOOM!!!!

The asteroid is blown to smithereens. (It looks really pretty too: a shimmering starburst in the sky. Everyone on Earth goes *ooh* and *ahh* and does some more hugging and kissing.)

The buff dude has saved the planet! The hot guy triumphed! Hurrah!

See?! What a great story!

Except, as I said, this is just the beginning…and in any case, I was too young to remember the asteroid and all that. Me and my friends, we'd seen the stuff about it on the Internet, and honestly, it was boring.

Simon, my stepdad, heard me say that once, and he went crazy.

"Are you telling me," he said, "are you telling me"—

Here we go. You knew, you just knew, when he repeated stuff like that he was going to repeat a whole load of other stuff. On and on and on and…

—"that you find the near destruction of the planet Earth, on which you live, boring?"

I have to say that when he got on his high horse like that, I couldn't help it: I saddled up my own. Yee-haa!

"Well, yeah," I said.

I was telling the truth. I hate it when you get into trouble for stuff like that, for just saying what's true. It's like THEY—the parental types and about 99.911 percent of all known teachers—want you to lie about what you think. You get into trouble for lying about everything else—who you were with, what you were doing, whether you've done your homework or not—but they don't care when you lie about what you think. They actually *want* you to do it. It's called agreeing with them, and that's what they want, all the time, even if they're totally wrong.

"Unbelievable. Did you hear that, Becky? Are you listening to this?"

That was another thing he did; he tried to drag my mom into everything.

"Simon," she said. "Let it go. She's just trying to irritate you."

The truth about *that* was half the time I didn't know myself whether I *was* trying to irritate him. I couldn't help myself. He annoyed me. My mom said we were two peas in a pod, which made me really angry because he wasn't even my dad. Like I would ever share a pod with Simon—being forced to share a house was bad enough.

"I'm not," I said. "It *is* boring. Something really bad *nearly* happened. It's, like, so what? There are a lot of really bad things that are actually really happening."

"Ruby," said Simon, borderline total rage-out, "what you are failing to understand is that"—

I forget what else he said, what it was I was failing to understand. Same old, I expect—with same old results. He'd get madder and madder, I'd get madder and madder, and my mom would get drowned out. Or else we'd both end up going after her. It probably ended up with me getting grounded—that happened a lot—or being told to go and clean my room, or do the dishes even though we had a dishwasher, or clean out the stupid guinea pigs' cage.

The thing is, I would give anything to be back there in the kitchen having that fight. I would just agree with him or say sorry or something…but there will never be another argument in the kitchen. There will never be another argument anywhere in this house.

My name is Ruby Morris, and this is my story. If you are reading it, you are very, very lucky to be alive…but you already know that, right?

CHAPTER ONE

There's really no point going on about how things used to be. For one, I can't stand to think about it—even though I do, a lot, and it makes me want to throw up with sadness. For two, it kind of doesn't matter, does it? It's over. And for three, I'm not writing this because of how things used to be—I'm writing this because of what happened. So I'll start right there. This is what happened:

I was sitting in a hot tub in my underwear kissing Caspar McCloud.

Ha! That also sounds like a great beginning, maybe from some kind of kiss-fest romance, or maybe Caspar would turn out to be a sexy vampire. But the truth is—and this is the one thing I will do, for sure. I will try to tell the truth, even if it hurts me to say it, even if it shocks you to hear it (and I doubt it will, because if you're reading this you've probably had about a gazillion shocks already)—the truth is, it wouldn't be right to pretend that kissing in a hot tub was the kind of thing I usually did on a Saturday night, because it wasn't.

It soooooooooooooooooooooooo wasn't. Don't get me wrong: I'd kissed boys before (two); I'd been to parties before (like, since I was five years old or something). I'd even sat in that hot tub in my underwear before (with Lee—that's Lee as in Leonie, my best friend). But that night, that party...it was the best, the most amazing—scarily amazing—time I had ever had in my life up until that point. (Not difficult.)

That night—that one, glorious, hot Saturday night—I was becoming a new me, one who was going to have a boyfriend named Caspar and do stuff like kiss in hot tubs at wild parties all the time. Yes, from the nagging jaws of the THEY, I was about to snatch complete, amazing greatness and total brilliance. And a boyfriend.

What can I say? It happened. It really happened! Zak, who lived in this massively cool, rambling old farmhouse, and whose parents were so laid-back you could basically do whatever you liked, pulled the speakers outside the barn where we—that's me and all my lovely friends (exception to be named shortly)—had been hanging out drinking LETHAL cider punch, and a bunch of us stripped down—to our underwear—and climbed into their hot tub.

We sort of danced where we sat, doing so-slick-yeah-check-it mini arm moves. It was totally hilarious, but it was also totally cramped…until people started getting out again, moaning that the hot tub was too hot.

It was like some dreadful slow-motion countdown. With every person that got out, the water in that tub got stiller and stiller. I kept wishing it was one of those Jacuzzi tubs with bubbles, but it wasn't; unless you kept trailing your hands around on the surface, you could see everything. So I sat there, casually fanning my hands around…because across that pool of steaming water sat Caspar *Swoon* McCloud.

And in between us sat Saskia, who wasn't fanning her hands about at all.

I do want to say that, even before that night, I wasn't really sure how much I actually liked Saskia. Not that I really knew her; she'd just started hanging out with us lately—even more lately than Caspar, who'd transferred to our school from the artsy hippie school, and was cool and wild and was in a band, and I'd once told Simon and my mom I was babysitting with Lee so I could go see Caspar's band play at a bar. And it was there, while Caspar was onstage at The George, doing his guitar thing, that he'd looked up and looked at me, and I'd looked at him and—

KA-CASPAR-BOOM!
(PART ONE)

I realized I was in love with Caspar McCloud.

And this is too much information, isn't it? This is exactly what I said I wouldn't do, which is go on about how things were. I can't stand it. I'll shut up.

Back in the hot tub, Lee came to my rescue—or tried to. She came up and asked Saskia where the gin had gone (I told you that punch was lethal), and Saskia said she didn't know, and Lee said she thought she'd seen her with it, and Saskia said she hadn't had it, and Lee said maybe she could just come and help her look for it, and Saskia, who SO knew all along what Lee was trying to do, sighed this enormous bored sigh and stood up and climbed out of the tub with her *chest* practically in Caspar's face and then turned to me and said:

"Don't do anything I wouldn't do."

Then there really was nothing but a steaming hot tub of water between me and Caspar McCloud.

I was so shy. I nearly died of shyness. Also, I was slightly worried that I was going to cook to death or perish from an exploding bladder because I really, really needed to pee. I tried not to think about that, and it wasn't difficult because I was in a state of pre-kiss terror. For sure, any second now, there was going to be a kiss. There HAD to be a kiss.

"Hey, Rubybaby," said Caspar.

That's what he called me: Rubybaby. From the lips of anyone other than a divine being, it would have sounded cringe making and vomit worthy. From the lips of Caspar McCloud, it was utterly thrilling, as if an electric-lipped angel was kissing your soul. You know: hot and crackly.

"Hey, Caspar," I said, crackling.

"Why don't you swim on over here and keep me company?" he said.

I fixed him with this sultry model's stare (deadpan but pouty) that I'd been practicing at home. "Well, why don't you swim on over *here*?" I said.

It was the pre-kiss terror that made me say that. Basically I would have swum the Atlantic to get to him. *Genius, Ruby.* All I'd done was prolong the agony.

Slowly and sexily, we both scooted toward each other. Actually, I'm not sure if you can scoot slowly and sexily, but that's what it felt like. Also, it felt like it took an eternity, when really it was probably about ten seconds or something.

I looked into his eyes. Then I had to look away because it was just too, too intense. I could see all my friends, dancing and messing around like idiots, and behind them, this gorgeous red sunset blazing in the sky.

If I'd looked the other way, I would have seen something else. I would have seen clouds gobbling up the night. Maybe I would even have seen the clouds reflected in Caspar's eyes, but when I got a grip enough to stare into them again, I wasn't there to admire the view.

BOMF! I practically head-butted him as my lips mashed into his. His lips sort of opened a little, and I kind of pushed my tongue into his mouth. I thought that was what you were supposed to do, to show how passionate you felt or something. Like I said, I'd kissed boys before, and that's what we had done. It had been fairly disgusting. Kissing Caspar like that wasn't disgusting; it was scary, and it felt all wrong. Until…I dunno. It just changed. One minute it was tongue-on-tongue combat, the next minute…

If this *was* my blockbuster movie, we would pause here. It would be worth a whole scene all by itself, that kiss. We would linger on it for as long as possible. That kiss. Those kisses. Where does one kiss end and another begin? We just kind of melted into one another. I know that's the kind of stupid thing they say in cheesy romances, but we did. That's what happened! One minute I was my own clumsy me-being, freaking out, and I could feel this divine Caspar-being (was he freaking out too?), this Caspar-being's tongue, and the next minute…I dunno…it was total—

KA-CASPAR-BOOM!
(PART TWO)

We didn't hear the yelling.

Fingers dug into my arm. My lips disconnected from Caspar's. I turned and—

"GET OUT!" Zak's dad shouted into my face, hauling me from the tub.

And that is when it all began.

CHAPTER TWO

L ike most people in the country, Zak's parents had gone to a barbecue that night. That's the thing about Britain, isn't it? First glimmer of sunshine, first sign of heat and everyone goes nuts, puts on their shorts, and has a barbecue. Doesn't matter if it looks like rain; we go out and we stay out until the first drop falls. No—it's worse than that: it actually has to start pouring before people give up and go inside. You add to that a holiday weekend—a whole extra day for sunburned people to lie around wishing they hadn't drunk ten zillion cans of beer and/or that they had cooked the hot dogs properly on the grill—and you get…well, you get what happened, don't you?

Zak's parents weren't supposed to be coming home, so it was obvious right away that something was wrong because they were back, but it was even more obvious that something was wrong because they were freaking out. Normally, they wouldn't have cared at all about whatever it was we were doing. That was what was so cool about Zak's. OK, he had the hot tub and the barn and woods and fields and everything to hang out in, but the really cool thing was that his parents were completely chill. They smoked joints in front of us—hey, they even gave Zak weed! That's how chill they were.

Tonight, they were not relaxed. They basically went all Simon on us. They herded us all into the kitchen. The only thing that was un-Simon was that Zak's dad, Barnaby, kept swearing.

OK, so this is going to be the only other rule about this story: I will try to be honest; I will try to tell everything as it was, but I will not swear. My mom hated me swearing—the word *God* included, despite the fact that (1) she said it herself all the time (but denied it) and (2) as far as I can tell, everyone else on the planet says it all the time too. "There's no need for swearing," she'd tell me. Even with the whole world in the grip of a death-fest mega-crisis, she'd say, "Ruby, there is absolutely no need to swear."

Actually, there *is* a huge need for it in this story, and a lot of swearing did happen, but out of respect for my mom, I will not write those words. If, like me, you curse all the time anyway, you can go ahead and add your own swear words, but I hope you'll understand why I can't.

I'll write something beautiful instead. I'll write "🦋." For my mom.

"Oh 🦋! Oh 🦋! Oh 🦋!" Barnaby kept going.

(The thing is, Zak's parents were always into some pagan-y religious thing or another, so it's possible that Barnaby really was calling on some specific god and wasn't just generally ranting.)

He locked the kitchen door.

"You're frightening them," said Zak's mom, Sarah, but Barnaby wasn't listening. He closed every window in the kitchen, and when he'd finished doing that, he started closing all the other windows.

You could hear him, banging around all over the house.

We weren't frightened at all. It was a little weird, but the hardest thing was not to get the giggles—although in my case I had nothing to laugh about, now there wasn't even any water to cover me. I did my best with dish towels. All our stuff, everyone's stuff, was in the barn.

"Mom, what's going on?" said Zak.

"We're not really sure," said Sarah. "Someone Barnaby knows called him and—"

Thump, thump, thump—bang!—thump, thump, thump, went Barnaby upstairs.

"Mom?" said Zak.

Bang! Thump, thump, thump. Barnaby came back down the stairs.

"You'd better ask your dad," said Sarah.

See now, that *was* kind of weird, wasn't it? Zak didn't normally call his mom "Mom"; Sarah didn't normally call Barnaby "your dad." If I didn't know Zak was practically immune to a whole lot of stuff that really bothered other people—like being embarrassed by your parents—I would have thought he was freaking out too. But his parents did crazy stuff all the time, and everyone knew they did, and usually no one laughed about it much because everyone understood what Zak had to deal with…and also because Sarah and Barnaby were so kind to us.

This latest crazy thing, whatever it was, it was just bad timing, party-wise.

"Turn the radio on," Barnaby told Zak.

"*Dad?*" said Zak, but he turned it on anyway.

They didn't have a TV. Zak's parents didn't even have a digital radio; they had the old-fashioned crackly kind. Guess what was on? *Gardeners' Question Time.*

They were discussing the best methods of tackling blight on roses. Someone lost it and giggled. The giggling, it spread.

"This isn't right," said Barnaby quietly. "It should be the news."

I laughed too; it was impossible not to crack up with Mrs. Fotheringay-Flytrap describing the spots on her Rambling Rector rose…but you want to know something weird? While I certainly wouldn't in a million years have thought, *Oh no! This must mean the world as we know it is about to end*, I kind of *knew* it wasn't right too. I didn't know what was *supposed* to be on, but I knew *Gardeners' Question Time* shouldn't have been. My mom LOVED that program and listened to it every Sunday—every Sunday. Not on a Saturday night. Never on a Saturday night. Not exactly scary, though, was it?

"Go and put your clothes on!" Sarah snapped at us.

I shivered. Caspar hugged me close. Leonie grabbed my hand.

Sarah *never* snapped at us.

"They're in the barn," said Saskia—in a really horrible way, like Sarah was stupid.

"Take ours, then," said Sarah. "Take whatever you want. Just get dressed."

Someone muttered something and headed for the kitchen door.

"Don't go outside," said Barnaby. Loudly, angrily. "You do NOT go outside."

We shuffled out of the room, the whole herd of us. On the stairs, someone cracked up, and we all had to make a mad dash for Zak's parents' bedroom so we could laugh our heads off in private, without hurting their feelings.

"What the 🦋 is up with your parents, man?" said Caspar.

"Got me, dude," said Zak. But he didn't sound OK; he still didn't sound OK. "C'mon," he said to Ronnie—my techie-est friend—and they went off to Zak's room.

The rest of us, we played dress-up with Zak's parents' clothes. It was so funny we forgot all the weirdness. Caspar pulled on a kaftan.

"Ohhm!" he said, doing this prayer thing with his hands.

I laughed so hard I almost—

"I need to pee," I remembered.

Lee followed me to the bathroom. I went first. I had to—I was bursting. Then Lee went while I surveyed myself in the mirror: 🦋. So much for the model look. The big, baggy hippie dress was the least of it. My lips, which felt puffy-bruised and tingling from the kissing, looked kind of normal, but I had mascara zombie eyes, and where I'd had bright red lipstick on earlier, it looked like it had sort of smeared itself all over my chin; even my nose had gone Rudolf. No hope Sarah would have makeup remover, so I wet a piece of toilet paper, dabbed it in the soap, and wiped at my chin.

It wasn't really lipstick at all; it was my first ever full-blown kissing rash, and it stung. It *really* stung.

Nothing I could do about it, so I quickly scrubbed at the mascara disaster. Their soap—which wasn't like the soap we had at home but some organic, lentil-based, gray-green thing—was useless. It didn't even foam up, so that was it, then: I was half black-eyed zombie, half human cherry. Mortifying. Seriously mortifying.

"C'mon, get out!" shouted Caspar through the bathroom door. "Molly wants to puke!"

Great. I had to face him knowing what the face I was facing him with looked like. We opened the door, and Molly burst in, about to be sick. Under normal friendship circumstances, it would have been our duty to stay with her—but, honestly, just listening to her made my own stomach start to heave. It was bad enough looking like a mutant in front of Caspar—I definitely did not want him to witness me spewing my guts out, so I grabbed Lee's hand, and we went back downstairs.

We passed Zak's room on the way, where he and Ronnie were bickering for control of the computer. ("Why's it so slow?! Just click there," Zak was saying, trying to grab hold of the mouse. "Just click on it!")

In the kitchen, the radio people had moved on to discussing plants for dry, shady borders—which is a serious problem, apparently, and was not nearly as funny as the earlier part of the broadcast. Barnaby looked as if he was in a trance, staring out the kitchen window at… OK, so now the party had been totally spoiled; it was raining. None of us had noticed. Why would we? We'd been too busy laughing our heads off.

"I think you all need to sober up," said Sarah, handing out glass after glass of water. "Leonie, can you please put the kettle on?"

"YesSarahYes," Lee slurred, glugging her water.

Barnaby grabbed his cell phone and started jabbing at it, trying different numbers.

"🦋. 🦋. 🦋," he said, having trouble getting through.

Then *Gardeners' Question Time* stopped. It just stopped.

Then *it* started.

"This is an emergency public service broadcast…"

"The rain—" That's all I remember hearing to begin with. "It's in the rain," and everyone staring at the radio as if it were a TV. That's how hard we all stared at it—everyone except Barnaby, who dropped his cell and went out to try the phone in the hall.

Lee shoved the kettle on the stove and came and held my hand, the one that wasn't gripping Caspar's.

"Ru," whispered Lee. "Do you think we're gonna die or something?"

"No!" I said.

Of course no one was gonna die!

My mom was out at the neighbors' barbecue.

It's in the rain.

I felt as if I was the last person to get what was going on. I stood in that kitchen, shivering—I leaned into Caspar's body, but even that felt cold—and finally I sort of started to get it. See, for days there'd been stuff on the news about some new kind of epidemic—outbreaks in Africa, in South America. Then reports from Russia. Some new kind of disease thing, deadly, but, well, it wasn't here, was it? Not like the bird-flu thing when Simon (who was probably more worried about the birds) had gotten all worked up. So had a lot of people. (OK, so had I; it gave me nightmares.) But this? It was so… *remote*—that's the word—that we never paid any attention to it. Ronnie had tried to tell us about it, I remember that, and we had all rolled our eyes and told him to shut up, because it just seemed like another thing for Ronnie to blabber on about.

"The rain," they kept saying on the radio. "It's in the rain."

"I told you so," said Ronnie, stomping down the stairs into the kitchen.

He had. He had said, "There's something in the rain." And we'd all gone, "Yeah right! Shut up, Ronnie!" because we knew just what kind of website he'd have read that on—probably the same one that claimed the Pope had been replaced by an alien (that's why you never see his legs; they're green and spindly)—and Ronnie had gone, "No! There is! There's something *in* the rain. Look!" and tried to show us this eyewitness video thing on the Internet, but it had been taken down, which Ronnie said proved it was true.

"Shut up, Ronnie," someone said.

Lee stared at me. "Ru," she said. "I really am scared."

She started crying. Other girls were too. I hugged her. I hugged my lovely best friend.

It's in the rain.

Saskia swept downstairs wearing one of Barnaby's shirts like a minidress. For a moment, she stared at the radio like we'd done. Sarah tried to hand her a glass of water, but Saskia shook her head.

"I wanna go home," she announced.

She's such a…not a drama queen, but a… She's not even a spoiled brat. I suppose the best way to describe it is Saskia always finds a way to get what she wants. It's not even because half the boys in school drool over her… OK, ALL the boys in school (because they like her or want to be like her), pretty much all the teachers (because she's cunningly polite to them and makes a showy effort to understand whatever it is they're talking about), and a seriously shocking number of the girls (because they also like her or want to be like her) drool over Saskia, and that should be enough to explain why Saskia always gets her way, but it's not. It's something weirder and darker. Seriously, she's like a hypnotist or something, sending out invisible mind rays that zap her victims into doing whatever she wants. But not tonight, Sask! Seemed like no one else but me was even listening to her anyway because everyone was staring out the windows at the rain.

It just looked like rain normally looks. You know, drippy.

You could hear Barnaby on the phone in the hall, dialing, slamming the handset down, and redialing. He wasn't calling on a god anymore; he was just plain swearing his head off.

"I said I wanna go home," Saskia re-announced.

"Whatever," someone said.

She stormed into the hall to try to get the phone from Barnaby, and Zak bounded down the stairs, Molly drifting down after him, looking sick as a dog.

"The Internet's down!" Zak said. "Like the WHOLE of the Web just crashed."

"Told you so," murmured Ronnie.

"It's probably just a local thing," said Sarah.

Ronnie shook his head in that way that he did to look like he knew stuff no one else did. Molly heaved again, and Sarah looked at her in panic.

"It's the punch, Mom. She just had too much punch," said Zak.

People kind of nodded sheepishly, same way you would if someone else's parents had caught us.

"Barnaby," Sarah called, rummaging in a cupboard, "do we have any coffee?"

Coffee. Even then, even at that moment, I thought that was kind of random. Like that would solve everything. Barnaby wandered in from the hall. He looked…grim. That'd be the word. *Grim.*

"I can't get through," he said. "To *anyone*," he added, looking straight at Sarah like she'd know who that *anyone* was.

You could hear Saskia back out in the hall; she had the phone to herself then, and was dialing and redialing and swearing her head off too.

"DO. WE. HAVE. ANY. COFFEE?" Sarah asked Barnaby.

That seemed to sort of snap him out of it—and a lot of other people too. Girls who'd been crying (because girls are allowed to under extreme circumstances) stopped; boys who'd looked like they were going to cry got a grip. For a moment, it was just all so normal. A bunch of late-night people getting late-night snacks and drinks. Barnaby found some ancient coffee beans in the freezer and started pulverizing them in an electric grinder. Zak sawed into a loaf of their heavy-duty homemade bread. He handed the slices to Sarah, who put them into a wire thing to toast them on the top of the stove. I got mugs out; Leonie got teaspoons; other people got other stuff, all the stuff you need: teapot, sugar, knives, jams, plates, butter, milk.

I saw Caspar edging away from us all. I saw Caspar staring mournfully out the kitchen window.

I went to him.

"It's OK," I whispered, hoping the darkness by the kitchen door would hide the hideous mess my face was in so we could share a romantic moment.

"No it's not," he said. "That's my MP3 player out there."

He pointed at his jeans, out on the grass, getting rained on.

"🦋 this," he whispered.

"Caspar!"

I was so stupid. I whispered it, so no one noticed.

"Chill, Rubybaby," he whispered back and kissed me.

I don't know whether that kiss was meant to shut me up, but it did. Even with all the freaky horribleness of it all, I still had the hots for him, and I still couldn't believe that we'd actually kissed—and in front of everyone, which basically meant that as far as the glass mountain of being cool was concerned, I had now developed spider-sucker climbing powers and had effortlessly scaled to the top. Best not to blow it now by blurting, "Ooo! Caspar! No! Zak's dad said we really shouldn't!" at the top of my voice.

He unlocked the door. He grabbed a towel. He held it over his head. He dashed out. I saw him do that. I saw him go out, barefoot in the rain in Barnaby's kaftan. He dashed back in again. Slipped the lock back shut. Dumped the towel.

No one else had noticed. And me? I dunno what I thought was going to happen, like he'd just go up in a puff of green smoke or something. He didn't. He rummaged in his jeans, pulled out his phone and his MP3, wiped them on his kaftan, and waved them at me, grinning.

I felt like an idiot.

"Cool!" I whispered. I didn't know what else to say or do, so I gave him this quick, casual peck on the lips and went back to the snack making, so I'd look like *I* was cool and hadn't even thought about angsting about anything. Tea! I had to make tea! I had to make a whole lot of tea right now! But the tea was made! OK! I had to casually butter toast …That was good, that was better…casually buttering toast.

Barnaby switched the coffee grinder off. It made a racket, that thing. That was fine, because it meant you couldn't hear the radio. It was also why no one had heard Caspar.

He was sort of groaning, but not like a Molly pukey groan. It was some other kind of groan. He stepped out of the darkness by the kitchen door.

"✴," he said, scratching at his head, at his face.

He looked at his fingertips, at the blood and pieces of torn-up skin that coated them. There was blood running down—not tons of it, but trickles and smears—from his scalp, from his face—where there were sores, red marks, like burns, but bleeding. He looked like one of those gory Jesus pictures, minus the crown of thorns. Wherever the rain had touched him, wherever it had seeped through the towel, there was blood...even his shoulders, even his chest. Soaking through the kaftan. His naked feet looked like he'd walked a mile on broken glass.

Saskia flounced back into the room and screamed.

Sarah rushed over to Caspar—"Don't touch him! Don't touch him!" said Barnaby—and she hesitated.

It's the first thing you do when someone is hurt, isn't it? You go to help them. Even if they're in a really disgusting mess and the sight of all that blood makes you feel like you're going to throw up or pass out, you go to help them.

"It might be contagious," said Barnaby.

So here's the thing; I suppose I could say this later or not say it at all. That's how much difference it made. As I said, Barnaby and Sarah were very, very good to us: dream parents, totally chill (and nightmare parents because of being off the scale in terms of embarrassment). Thing was, as Simon pointed out to me when I was going on about how awesome they were one day, they could afford to be. I huffed on about it, but I knew, annoyingly, he was right. Zak's parents never seemed to work; they never seemed to have to do anything but fiddle about in the garden or show up to naked yoga classes (oh yes!)...and the reason Zak's parents could spend all day growing weirdly shaped organic cauliflowers and doing dog pose naked (DO NOT imagine this!) was because they were rich. They were old-school rich; probably they'd started stashing cash the day coins were invented. Zak's godfather was some kind of lord. His uncle was another kind of lord and sat in the House of Lords. His grandma had been a lady with a capital *L*, not a small one like everyone else's grandma.

Barnaby and Sarah "knew people." That's what the other parents said, and like the whole grandma deal, it didn't mean they knew people the same way everyone else did. It meant the kind of people they knew owned the country or ran it or both. Someone Barnaby "knew" had called him and warned him. How many other people got a warning?

But this is not a Hollywood movie. The warning counted for zilch.

"Dad, they're not saying that," said Zak. "They're not saying it's *contagious.*"

They weren't. That word never got used.

But you know what? No one did go to help Caspar.

It's the rain. It's in the rain.

I'd kissed him. My lips, my chin…they tingled. They stung. They'd been stinging anyway. They were just stinging, normal stinging. It *had* to be normal stinging.

The smell of burning filled the room.

"Oww!" said Molly as she grabbed the wire thing to rescue the toast, dumping it onto the table. "Ow!"

Caspar groaned—louder and harder. It was horrible to hear.

"I'm sorry," he moaned, one hand clawing the other raw. All of us were thinking, *Don't do that! Stop doing that! Please, stop doing that!* "I'm so sorry," he said, and he sort of sank down, crouching against the door.

"Right," said Sarah. She went into the hall to get her coat.

"*Sarah,*" Barnaby called after her—but wearily, almost, like they were going to have some regular kind of a fight.

The effect on all of us, despite the circumstances—and apart from Caspar, who was groaning in agony—was we all sort of looked at the floor a little, like you do when someone's parents are having an argument in front of you.

"I'm taking him to the hospital," Sarah said, pulling on her rain-coat, patting pockets for her keys, scanning the kitchen for them.

"They say not to," said Barnaby.

They hadn't said that either, actually. All they'd said was that victims should be given Tylenol. Ha.

"I'm going," she said, reaching into Barnaby's pocket for his keys.

He grabbed her wrist—and held it.

"*Sarah*," said Barnaby. "There is no point."

If he'd been Simon, the next thing he'd have said would have been, "*Be reasonable.*" But Barnaby didn't say that; Barnaby didn't say anything like that. Sarah extracted her hand, and the keys—

"It's fatal," said Barnaby.

Whoa! There's harsh and there's… At that moment, everyone in that room hated Barnaby. You could feel it. They hadn't said THAT on the radio. They DEFINITELY HADN'T said THAT.

Caspar groaned again. He was shaking quite a lot. I didn't know what that was. Pain? Shock? Fear? I touched my lips, my chin…stinging, sore—but normal, right? Just normal. I didn't—I couldn't—have *that thing*.

For a moment, Sarah stared at Barnaby in a most un-kaftan-mom-like way.

"Get up!" she said to Caspar.

Somehow Caspar stood. Everyone kind of pulled back a little.

"Sarah!" shouted Barnaby, sounding most un-kaftan-dad-like. "I am *begging* you!" But his voice had gone all wobbly, like he couldn't choose between raging or pleading.

Or something else—that's what I think now. Fear, probably. Maybe despair.

"Come on," Sarah told Caspar, handing him the towel.

They went out the back door, Sarah in front, Caspar stumbling after her.

I let go of Leonie's hand.

"Wait," I said.

I ran out into the hall; I shoved my feet into a pair of someone's rain boots. I looked back at everyone in the kitchen. For a second, if you ignored the looks on everyone's faces, it looked so cozy—big pot of tea, mugs waiting; even the burnt toast smelled good.

"Ru! Don't!" sobbed Leonie.

And I swear, if someone else had said a single other thing, I would have caved.

"See you later, hon," said Ronnie.

"See you later, babes," I said.

Just like we always did.

CHAPTER THREE

It wasn't like I was about to run out into the rain. There was a kind of carport thing outside, a place where they stored all sorts of (hippie) junk and chopped wood. Their cars—a little zippy thing they used to get to yoga classes (hopefully wearing clothes on the journey) and this other beat-up big one, a station wagon—were parked there. So it'd be wrong if you in any way thought I was being brave. I really wasn't. I don't even know what exactly I was thinking. I wasn't thinking.

I suppose I felt bad, for not having tried to stop Caspar going outside.

I got into the front seat. Sarah didn't say anything. She didn't even look at me, not to begin with; she just drove. To this day, I'm not sure why she didn't send me back to the house. Maybe she wasn't thinking straight either; maybe she needed someone with her; maybe she thought Caspar and I were a serious item and not just two friends who'd only started making out about an hour ago. Or maybe she thought I might need to go to hospital too. Maybe she'd seen the state my chin was in; maybe she'd seen how I couldn't stop touching my lips, checking. I wasn't sick; I *couldn't* be sick.

Sarah had put Caspar in the back so he could lie down, and I was glad because it meant I didn't have to look at him. I'd been kissing his face off, and now I couldn't even bear to look at him. What *it* does to people is disgusting.

You could still hear him, though, panting and shaking and groaning and moaning.

Zak and his family lived way out in the sticks, down miles and miles of country lanes. Do you know what the lanes are like in Devon? They're tiny. They twist around all over the place. On either side are high banks. On top of the banks are hedges. You can't see where you are. It's bad enough in the daytime; at night it's like being stuck in some crazy maze. Up and down and left and right, twisting and turning—all you can see in front of you is a little patch of road, to the sides of you walls of grass and stone and brambles. I started to feel even sicker, which made me panic, which made me feel sicker.

"Don't," said Sarah when I went to roll the window down.

It had stopped raining then, but she was right. Water dropped onto the car from the trees. Every now and then, Sarah turned the wipers on. I watched the silvery, dark drops smear across the screen. It was kind of impossible to get your head around it, how something so ordinary could…how they were saying it could do that, make someone sick like Caspar was sick.

Fatal, that's what Barnaby had said. *Fatal*.

I shut my eyes and tried not to think about that. I tried not to think about anything except not throwing up. I breathed deeply, waiting for us to get to the main road. At least then, we could speed up; at least then, the car would stop weaving about.

Neither of these things happened. We didn't speed up and we didn't stop weaving about. When we hit the main road, there were lots of other cars on it, some heading out of town, most heading into town. The traffic was moving still—not a crawl, faster than that but slower than it should be. The road was really busy.

At first, when I saw that traffic, I closed my eyes again. I didn't want to think about what was in those cars, whether we were just part of a long line of cars carrying people like Caspar, suffering. I didn't want to look at the traffic. I didn't want to think about how long it was going to take for us to get to the hospital, which was miles and miles away, in Exeter. There was a hospital in Dartbridge, but it wasn't the emergency kind; my mom said you couldn't even go there to get a sliver taken out.

Fatal.

I breathed. I tried to just listen to the engine. When I felt the car weaving again, I thought maybe Sarah had taken a shortcut and we were back on the lanes.

My dad took me and Dan on a boat once. Dan's my half-brother; he's twelve and he's a pain, but I love him—brother-brat beloved. My dad's not with Dan's mom anymore either, so Dan and I, we've got the whole smashed-up family thing in common. It's kind of bonding. Anyway, we'd gone on this boat on a river with my dad, just for a weekend, and when we'd gotten off, I still felt like I was on the boat, for hours after—as if the ground was water and I was bobbing about on it.

That's what it was like in that car; I felt like we were back in the lanes, weaving. It made me feel so sick I opened my eyes. I wasn't imagining it; we *were* weaving about. For no reason. I looked at Sarah; even though it was so dark, I could see there was sweat on her forehead—but sweat, not blood. I dunno what I thought—that she was nervous, that she was panicking… It wasn't until there were streetlights that I noticed her hand. She kept flexing it, like it hurt. Flexing it, then rubbing it against her raincoat. I saw her look at it. I looked too. Her palm was bloody.

"The towel," she said quietly. "It was wet."

I looked around at Caspar.

"Don't touch him," whispered Sarah.

He'd rolled over onto his side; in the orangey bursts of street-lights, his face looked shiny, dark with blood, ragged from scratching, his eyes staring at the seat in front—so still, his gaze, while his body shook and shook, and he groaned and groaned.

I looked away. I tried not to panic.

The traffic ground to a halt.

"🦋," said Sarah. She was grimacing with pain now; her jaw started to shake a little, as if she was freezing cold, but sweat ran off her face like she was boiling hot. "We'll have to go another way," she said.

I saw her look at her hand. "I'll drop you at your house," she said.

I didn't argue. I wanted to be there. I wanted my mom. My chin hurt. It kind of throbbed.

She banged the car down a gear, then jerked the steering wheel left. We bumped up onto the curb. Car horns went crazy, honking at us as we drove—at an angle, half the car on the pavement, half in the road—until there was a car so tight against the curb we couldn't get past. Sarah pounded the horn; they wouldn't budge—and now, behind us, other cars were trying the same trick, tooting at us to get out of the way. There was a bump—the car behind actually tried to push us on.

"There's nowhere to go!" I shouted at them, even though I knew they couldn't hear.

"🦋," cursed Sarah.

She turned the wheel hard and slammed down on the accelerator. I screamed because it felt like we were going to roll over, but we steadied, and that's how we did it. That's how we got down as far as Cooper's Lane—at a crazy angle, the car now half on the side-walk, half up on the grass median where there were tons of daffodils in spring.

"All right?" said Sarah as, just missing a streetlight, we cleared the end of the lane and bounced back down onto the road.

And she looked at me then, and somehow she smiled.

"Yeah," I said. Somehow I managed to smile back at her.

Five minutes later, we pulled up outside my house. I sort of felt like I should say something, but I didn't know what to say. "Thank you for giving me a lift home" just didn't seem to cut it.

"There's your dad," said Sarah.

Simon was standing at the den window, watching. Stressing, by the looks of it.

Know what I said? What I always said to anyone who said that: "He's not my dad."

I turned to look at Caspar. He had his hands clasped over his face. I couldn't see his eyes, only his lips.

"Caspar?" I whispered.

His lips, the lips I had been kissing, moved a little.

Maybe he was whispering, "Rubybaby…"

Maybe he wasn't saying anything at all.

"Go on," said Sarah.

"Don't touch the outside of the door," she said as I opened it.

I stood in the road to wave her off, all around me alarms, screams, shouts, panic.

Then I turned. Simon wasn't in the window anymore, and the curtains were shut. So was the front door.

Huh?!

I ran up to the porch and banged on the door.

"Simon? Mom? Mom!" I shouted.

The lights were on, and through the frosted glass of the door I could see them, the shapes of them, moving around. I could hear them too—talking low and angry to each other, like they did when they were fighting and didn't want me to hear.

"Mom!" I shouted, banging on the door. It was nearly a scream.

There was a Ruby Emergency Key stashed in the garden, but

I could hardly go rummaging around in the poison-rain soaked shrubbery to get it, could I? I banged on the door again.

"MOM!"

I felt this horrible stab of fear…then Simon's face loomed up at the glass.

"Ruby," he instructed through the glass, "you need to take those boots off to come in the house. Carefully. You mustn't touch any water. Do you understand?"

"Yes," I said. It was the right thing, I knew, but I felt angry.

He opened the door then. My mom was standing at the end of the hall. My mom!

She kind of gasped at me.

"Ruby! Oh my 🦋! Your face!"

You know, for a moment I actually thought it might be easier to make out like I had *that thing* rather than fess up.

"It's from kissing," I said.

"You're OK?!"

"Yes!" I wailed.

She sort of smiled at me—this soppy, sobby smile of joy. And I did too! She looked like a mess; she'd been crying, but at least she wasn't covered in blood or anything. I suppose she might have been thinking the same thing about me.

I stepped out of the rain boots easily enough—they were massive—and into the house—onto a garbage bag. Simon, who'd been standing by the door, blocked my path. He had a broom in his hands, and he actually put it in front of me. I looked up at him in total disbelief. The look on his face was terrible—and weird, not his usual angry face, all grim-jawed but shaky somehow. Upset. *Scared.*

"You need to go in there," he said, pointing at the den.

He was wearing rubber gloves. Ha! I thought he'd been cleaning.

"*What?!*" I said.

"Oh, Ruby…" said my mom. She came a couple of steps toward me.

"Becky, stay back!" Simon told her. "Go in there, please," he said to me.

I looked at my mom. "Are you OK?! Is Henry OK?!" I couldn't work out what was going on.

"Just go in the room, darling," said my mom. "Please?"

I went in, thinking Simon would follow. I suppose I was so used to being in trouble, getting told off, that a part of me kind of thought that was what was happening. The party I'd been at? Maybe I hadn't exactly mentioned I was going to it.

Simon shut the door behind me and locked it.

CHAPTER FOUR

O ne little rainstorm. "Only a shower." That's the kind of thing my mom said all the time because it rains a lot in Devon. Where I used to live, in London, where my dad still lived, it hardly ever seemed to rain, and even if it did it hardly mattered because you could always hop on a bus or a subway that would take you exactly wherever you wanted to go without getting a drop of rain on you. In Devon, you had to walk places—or kill yourself biking up hills. If I moaned that I didn't want to go and do something or that I wanted a ride because it was raining, that's what my mom would say: "It's only a shower!" It meant, "Get on with it." Simon, on the other hand, could never leave it at that.

Example No. 1
Simon: If you were going to a music festival, you wouldn't be bothered by a little rain, would you?
Me: Well, as I'm not allowed to go to festivals, I wouldn't know.

Example No. 2
Simon: So, Ruby, how come you don't mind spending hours in the shower, but you're bothered by a little rain?
Me: I have to spend hours in the shower because the shower is useless.

(This is me taking a dig at Simon because he refused to get a new shower.)

You get the idea.

Then there were the historical ones, which were his absolute favorites; he had millions of them.

Example No. 3
Simon: Supposing Sir Edmund Hillary had looked outside his tent and said, "You know what? It's raining. I don't think I'll bother conquering Everest after all."
Me: It doesn't rain on Everest—and anyway Sherpa Tenzing got there first.
(I didn't really know whether that was true, about the rain—it just seemed it should be...but the Sherpa Tenzing part? Ronnie had told me that. Some things he said were true.)

Example No. 4
Simon: Imagine if Winston Churchill had said, "You know what, it's a little rainy in Europe. Let's just let Hitler get on with it."
Me: Actually, this country is part of Europe, and, anyway, I'm not going to war, am I? It's only a stupid guitar lesson.
Simon: Which you asked to go to and which we're paying for.
Etc.

That one ended up with me grounded for the rest of the week—*after* I'd been forced to go to the guitar lesson (in the rain).

I just want to tell you one more.

Example No. 5
Simon: Imagine if the Americans and the Chinese and the Russians

had said, "Oh no! It's raining! Let's not launch the missile that's going to blow up the asteroid and save the planet until it's nice and sunny."

Me: Great! Then we'd all be dead and I wouldn't have to live with you!

I really did say that. My mom heard me, and she was really upset. She told me, for the zillionth time, that Simon did have feelings. I didn't believe her. I hated him. I thought I meant it, what I said, but I didn't *mean it* mean it; it was just how I felt at the time.

Since then, there have been times I've felt that way and I have meant it. Not the part about Simon, but about how it might have been better if the Earth had been blown to smithereens. At least it would have been quick. Less suffering.

◆◆◆

That night, locked in the den, I thought I was suffering. I didn't ask what was happening or why. I went nuts. I really went crazy. The Henry Rule went right out of my head.

Oh. Oh no.

I do not want to have to do this. I need to tell you who Henry was. My own sweet liberator.

My babiest brother-brat beloved. Only one year old.

When my mom told me she was pregnant with him, know what I thought? I thought that because of the secret-y way she said it—when there was just me and her in the kitchen—and in spite of the fact that she and my dad had been divorced for centuries and despite the fact that my dad had had Dan with Kara, and they'd split up too, and he was now dating "floozies"—that's what I heard my mom tell my Auntie Kate—when she said she was going to have a baby, I thought she meant that she was having a baby with my dad.

DUH.

When I realized she meant Simon, I went up to my room and cried my eyes out.

BUT!

If I had understood what a wonderful thing Henry would be in my life, I would have jumped for joy. Because Henry, dear Henry, set me free. It's true; even before he was born, Simon and my mom got so obsessed with him that they got less and less obsessed with me. I was given my OWN set of keys to the house (although, luckily, we still kept the Ruby Emergency Key) and best and most fantastic of all: MY OWN CELL PHONE.

So: *the Henry Rule*. It was a total, complete, and utter no-no any day—possible global-disaster days included—to make any sort of noise that might wake him; that was the Henry Rule—for which, up until that moment, I was fully, totally, completely, and utterly signed up because once Henry got going…he could bawl for England. Yes, my babiest brother-brat beloved was a bawling beast.

I would have just texted Lee immediately, but—MY CELL! I DIDN'T HAVE MY CELL! IT WAS IN ZAK'S BARN WITH THE REST OF MY STUFF!—so I pounded at the den door. I screamed and shouted all sorts of terrible things, and all of them at Simon. I couldn't believe it—what I had just been through and now this. Then I started throwing things around a bit. Yup.

There was plenty of stuff to choose from, because that room was basically a dumping ground for all the stuff that wouldn't fit in the rest of the house. There was a computer in there, surrounded by junk, which was where I was supposed to do my homework—but there was usually so much junk dumped around the place, I used that as an excuse to borrow Simon's laptop and work in my room, i.e., surf the Net, IM, and not work at all.

I didn't rage randomly. I picked out Simon's stuff. I threw

whatever I could lay my hands on…and then, I started breaking things. His laptop wasn't there, or I probably would have smashed it. I snapped some of his stupid CDs, dropped this hideous pottery vase thing he said he'd made when he was in school.

Simon, doing art—can you imagine?!

All the while, he stood outside the door, going, "Ruby, calm down. Ruby, calm down."

I suppose my mom must have gone upstairs; I could hear Henry crying.

I told you I would tell you everything, except the swearing. But it's hard telling this part. I'm not proud of how I acted. I am the opposite of proud. In my defense, all I can say is that it was all too much. Do you see? One minute my life had been the best it had ever been, kissing Caspar McCloud, the next minute it was…

Ka-boom. I snapped the stupid walking-stick thing Simon took on country rambles. It was hard work snapping it, but I was ultimately doing him a favor because it made him look like an old man and a nerd. Then I saw his binoculars. His new binoculars. His nerdish pride and joy. Simon liked to watch birds, you see. Can you imagine anything more deeply boring?

"Ruby, calm down. Please, calm down."

I tried to snap them, to bust them in half. The walking stick thing had been hard, but these were impossible. And then I thought of it: I'd throw them out the window. I yanked back the curtain. And then I stopped.

One little rainstorm. Only a shower.

"Simon," I called. "It's raining."

"It's OK, Ru. It's OK."

"Please let me out!"

"Ruby, you have to listen to me. Please, calm down and listen."

"I'll listen! I'll calm down! Please, Simon, let me out."

41

I heard my mom's voice then, Henry fretting. "Ruby, we can't."

I pressed myself against the door, and I listened to them. All the while I watched the rain falling. I did get it, right away, when they explained it to me. I had been outside, hadn't I? For Henry's sake, for my mom's, they couldn't take any chances.

Then I talked, and they listened. Every word I said—about what had happened at Zak's, about Barnaby saying it might be contagious, about Caspar, about Zak's mom, about the cars going to the hospital—all of it seemed to prove that right, that I should stay in that room until we knew.

"I don't have it," I said. "I know I don't."

My chin, my lips, my mouth, my nose throbbed. *That's kissing. That's just kissing.*

"It happens really quickly. It does. I've seen it."

My stomach churned. *That's gin and cider. That's just gin and cider. And* fear.

"Yes," said Simon. "I believe you…but we can't take any chances. Do you understand?"

Yes, but—I thought.

"Do you understand, Ruby?" asked my mom.

"Yes, but—"

"So please…just until tomorrow morning?" said my mom.

"It'll have to be longer than that," Simon muttered at her—I heard him.

"Just for tonight," said my mom.

I could hear Henry gurgling.

"OK," I said.

I got up then and closed the curtains.

"Mom?" I called.

"Yes, Ruby?"

She was still there; I knew she'd still be there.

"I'm thirsty," I said.

I heard them, not what they said, but the murmurings of a discussion. It wasn't an argument. I could imagine it: what to give me, how to give it to me, perhaps, also whether I could be trusted not to freak and break out the second they opened the door.

"Ruby?" said my mom. "I'll get you something. I'll be back in a minute."

♦♦♦

And I thought about how it was then—that, really, we had been double lucky. That I'd had Barnaby drag me out of the hot tub, and my mom and Simon... They'd gone to the neighbors' barbecue as planned and taken the babiest brother-brat with them—not in some hideous child-abuse way, keeping him up all night, but because he had kept them up all night the night before, teething, and had slept all afternoon and was full of energy, and just when my mom dared to pick up a glass of wine, Henry decided it was time to start keeping them up for another night. So she took Screechster Boy back home. She put the radio on. She rocked my baby brother to sleep, trying to listen to *Gardeners' Question Time*.

She was so dog tired, she said, she didn't even bother wondering why it was on.

Simon would have stayed out, but apparently one of the neighbors had said something nasty ("an inflammatory remark") about the Royal Society for the Protection of Birds. It was probably a joke, but Simon, after being warned by my mom after the last time he'd flipped out at someone for making fun of bird-watching, had downed his drink and stormed home—seconds before the rain began.

I might be exaggerating a little, but that's basically what happened.

A short while later, there was a knock at the door.

"Ma?" I said.

"It's me," said Simon. "Ruby, I'm going to open the door. I've got some things for you. I want you to stand back, away from the door. Will you do that?"

"Yes," I said.

He opened the door. His face looked closer to normal—not shaky, not angry either, not even when he saw the mess in the room. He threw my duvet in, then—one, two, three—cushions from the sofa.

"Sorry," he said. "The air bed's in the shed."

My pillow came next. Then my bathrobe, my snuggliest pajamas, and my winter fluffy fake-fur slippers.

"Your mom doesn't want you to get cold," he said.

Then he threw a bucket in, on top of the pile.

"What's *that* for?" I asked.

"Guess," he said, slinging in a roll of toilet paper. "And—"

He tossed in my mom's toiletry bag, but carefully, so it landed on the duvet. There was a new toothbrush sticking out of it; mine was in the barn at Zak's…WITH MY CELL. DID I MENTION THAT ALREADY? I DID NOT HAVE MY CELL PHONE!

He slid a tray into the room. Tea and toast. With peanut butter. I thought we'd run out of it.

Finally, he reached round the corner and put two big glasses of water down on the floor. I suppose he thought I'd been drinking.

"I guess you have to lock the door now," I said.

"Ruby…" said Simon.

I thought about Caspar lying in the back of the car. I thought about Henry.

"It's OK," I said. "Lock it."

"Night, Ru," he said. He shut the door and locked it.

I probably would have just cried my eyes out then or something. But—

"Ru?"

It was my mom.

She sat on the other side of the door while I ate my toast. I leaned against the door, and I felt as if I could feel her on the other side, sitting and leaning against it too. I felt as if I could feel the warmth of her through the wood. I rattled on, asking her stuff: about whether my dad had called (he hadn't; I already knew no one could call anyone, didn't I?), about whether she thought everyone would be OK... And the more people I thought to ask about— family, friends, friends of family, families of friends—the worse it got, like how it is when you are little and they teach you to pray and to ask God to bless everyone, and you get really worried about remembering everyone, thinking if you don't, something bad will happen to them, and it'll be your fault.

"Shhh! It's OK, Ruby...shhh," she said when I started up again about Nana and Gramps. "Now, do you need anything else?" she asked.

"Sing to me," I said.

I wanted the lullaby song she did every night when I was little.

She sighed—so loud I could hear it through the door.

"Mom, please..." I tried.

"Ru-by, it's bedtime," she said.

Please don't leave me. That's what I thought. "OK," I said.

"Night night, darling."

That's what my mom said.

I made a bed nest like Dan does, switched out the light, and crawled into it. Under normal—*normal?!*—circumstances, I would have texted Lee then. No, I would have forgotten how many minutes I had left and called her. I could picture her, with the others, sitting around the big old table in Zak's kitchen. I wondered how Caspar was, whether Sarah had gotten them both to the hospital.

He'd be OK. *Fatal.* He'd be OK. *Fatal.* He'd be OK.

I couldn't stand it anymore, so I got up and turned the computer on.

The Internet was down, just like Zak had said, but maybe Simon had disconnected me. That was possible. That was very possible.

Nothing to do but go back to bed.

Normally, at night, it was dead quiet. Not like at my dad's, where there was noise 24/7. Tonight, Dartbridge sounded like London. You could hear sirens, alarms, car horns. Also, sometimes, shouting. Sometimes shouting…sometimes screams.

And another sound: so quiet, so soft. The rain. *It's only a shower.*

💧💧💧

I didn't realize I'd fallen asleep until I woke up because someone was banging at the front door. I was up and trying to get out of the room…until I realized I couldn't. Simon must have been asleep too, because it took him a while to get there. The hall light came on, but he didn't open the front door.

"Hello?!" he called.

"Help me! Help me! Help me!"

I pulled back the curtain a little. Our neighbor, Mrs. Fitch, was standing in the rain. In her nightie, not even a bathrobe on top.

I heard my mom thump down the stairs. I let the curtain drop.

"Simon?" whispered my mom.

"*Simon? Rebecca?!*" cried Mrs. Fitch. "Help!"

I heard Simon, plain as day, which it nearly was—the light had gone gray, the way it does when dawn is coming through the rain. "We can't," he said quietly to my mom.

46

"Please!" cried Mrs. Fitch, almost as though she'd heard him.

"We can't help," shouted Simon. "Go to the hospital."

"It's my husband! I can't move him!"

"We can't help," said Simon.

"It's the baby," cried my mom. "We've got to think about Henry."

"Please!" screamed Mrs. Fitch.

"Come away," I heard Simon whisper to my mom.

The hall light went off. I heard Henry starting to fuss upstairs. I heard my mom go to him, already saying, "Shh! Shh, shh, shh, shh," in her lovely lullaby voice as she rushed up the stairs.

"Ruby?" whispered Simon. "Are you OK?"

I didn't answer. I wanted him to think I was asleep.

"Please!" screamed Mrs. Fitch. She banged at the door.

I didn't hear Simon go back into the living room, but he must have; the TV got turned up.

"*Now urging people not to panic—*" I heard.

He must have shut the door then; I couldn't make out what they were saying anymore, just the scary, bossy sound of it going on and on about how bad everything was. But at least it did sound more like normal TV, different voices chipping in, and not the same thing over and over.

"*Help me! Please!*" screamed Mrs. Fitch.

I stood in the dark. It went quiet. I could hear the rain, still, but not Mrs. Fitch. I peeped through the curtains. She was standing in the front yard. She was clawing at her face, at her head. I couldn't look away, somehow. Something white landed on the grass next to her; I saw it was a box, a small white medicine box of tablets, the instructions, loose, fluttering down after it. My mom must have flung it out. I saw Mrs. Fitch pick it up. She looked up at the window—not the one I was peeking out of but the upstairs one— Mom and Simon's room. She looked up, and in the gray light, I saw the ghostly red running on her face, the skin torn away already where she couldn't help but scratch.

I let the curtain drop and buried myself in my bed. I tried not to listen to it all: the murmur of the scary, bossy voices on TV; the sirens—not so many now—and the car horns, also not so many. Mrs. Fitch, groaning again. Why didn't she just go away? The pitter-patter of the rain. Such a quiet sound you shouldn't have been able to hear it, but once your ears caught it, they couldn't seem to let it go. Then Henry started bawling, throwing a massive tantrum—and that was a good thing. It drowned out every other sound, and it was a noise I knew how to deal with; I wrapped a pillow round my head to muffle the brother-brat out and fell asleep.

CHAPTER FIVE

When the next morning began, it began like a lot of mornings have begun since then. For a moment, I thought everything was fine. For a moment, I'd forgotten.

And then I remembered.

I woke up thinking about Caspar. I'd been dreaming about him, but not how I'd seen him last, lying in the back of Zak's mom's car. I dreamed we were playing a gig together. It was brilliant. We were brilliant.

I've got to tell you now that even if the entire world hadn't totally ka-boomed, this could only ever have been a dream. That guitar lesson I didn't want to go to? It wasn't just because it was raining—it was because I was terrible. I'd only started doing it because I thought it would impress Caspar. OK, and I thought I'd turn out to be terrific at it, but I wasn't. I was terrible.

And, by the way, I was terrible at singing too, but I sang all the time (in my room or with Lee), hoping that if I practiced enough, I'd suddenly, miraculously, become fabulous at that too.

Dreams—good ones—are beautiful things.

(And sometimes they come true. I should know: I kissed Caspar McCloud.)

Anyway, for a couple of moments before I opened my eyes, I was in heaven. And then I woke up in hell.

I stretched and felt floorboards under my legs where my bed should have been. The cushions had slipped around. I dunno how Dan manages it; he's like a hamster or something, building his little nests. I'd had the worst night's sleep ever, tossing and turning—and even before I attempted to get up, I kind of knew I felt like crap, and then I remembered *why* I felt like crap.

Caspar. Oh my 🦋: Caspar.

I reached up and felt my chin—yeurch! Seemed like over-night it had turned into a kind of giant scab. I felt my nose; that didn't feel scabby, but I'd need a mirror to be sure. If I didn't look like too much of a horror, I'd take the train to Exeter and look for Caspar at the hospital—or get Simon to take me. I had some wicked foundation to deal with the face situation... No, I didn't. That was in the barn with—MY CELL! I HAD TO GET MY CELL PHONE. Get my cell phone—which would mean seeing my friends too, which was great—get my founda-tion. Go see Caspar. Get a shower first—no, check the Net, then shower. Figure out my outfit, do temporary emergency makeup with items from the reserve makeup supply. Possibly have to do emergency mascara borrow from mother; definitely emergency perfume borrow (a.k.a. "steal"; she had a bottle of this really nice stuff I wasn't supposed to use, and the last time I'd borrowed a little, she'd gone mental—even for my mom—when she'd sniffed and figured out I'd used it). Ask, then borrow, or just borrow? Just borrow. It was an emergency.

MY CELL: priority mission. Yeah, that's what I was thinking. That and I was thirsty—but the glasses of water were gone—and I was bursting, so I had to pee on top of last night's pee in the bucket, and when I'd finished peeing, I checked the computer; it was still on from last night, and everything was still down. It still showed the time though. I tried to remember when I had come in, wondering how much longer I might be forced to stay in that room if Simon got his way. It made my sore head muddle.

Then I opened the curtains. It was raining.

Surrounded by narrow beds of plants that sprouted crazily, there was a little square of grass outside; "the front lawn," Simon called it. He mowed it, lugging the mower up the garden from the shed and through the house—dropping grass cuttings everywhere—for the two and a half seconds it took to cut the patch. Then he lugged the mower back through the house—dropping grass cuttings everywhere—and back down the garden to the shed. My mom said the front lawn wasn't worth the trouble—the grass didn't even grow properly, the way the shrubs muscled in on it—but Simon did it anyway.

If I felt anything about it, I felt that front lawn *was* Simon. The order in the chaos, something like that.

The front lawn, that small, tidy square of mown green, was muddy, torn up—clawed up, like an animal had been at it.

Mrs. Fitch was lying on it. She had her back to me. The box of tablets lay next to her.

It was raining hard. It was raining on Mrs. Fitch. Mrs. Fitch wasn't moving. I watched. Mrs. Fitch didn't seem to be breathing.

You know what? Even then I thought… I dunno, that she had stayed out in the rain too long or something? That she was old anyway, so she could have just had a heart attack. Died of hypothermia. Or had a stroke, like Grandpa Hollis.

I drew the curtains shut. I'd never seen a dead body before, and I didn't ever want to see another one. It was horrible, just horrible… and the curtains weren't enough. I shut ten thousand doors in my head and even then I couldn't keep it out. I had no words to say to myself to make it OK; instead, it was my body that started to shout. *I'm thirsty! I'm thirsty, and I'm hungry, and I feel really grubby and…I am so not going to poop in a bucket. I want breakfast. I want a shower. I want my cell phone. I want OUT.*

Before I said anything, I turned the handle of the door because you just would, wouldn't you? The door opened.

"Simon?" I called softly. You see, the house was quiet, and I didn't want to wake Henry. Come to think about it, the world was quiet. I could hear a few stupid alarms still, but no sirens, no car horns, no shouts—or shouts that could have been screams. That was all I could hear: a few stupid alarms. And the rain.

I listened *hard*.

"Simon?" I whispered.

Henry had to be asleep. I peeked my head around the door. The door to the living room was open. The TV was still on, sound down. You could see the reflection of it in the glass of all the family photos on the windowsill—Grandma Hollis, smiling, TV flickers on her face.

Maybe Simon was crashed out in front of the TV?

"*Simon?!*" I hissed.

I tiptoed a few steps down the hall, tiptoed to not to wake Henry. I knew I wasn't sick like killer-rain sick, so I kind of felt OK about it. Only, actually, I wasn't that sure that I wasn't killer-rain sick. I wasn't all covered in blood and groaning, but I knew how much I definitely didn't feel right. I felt really, really thirsty, and my head hurt. I was hungry too, but I felt sick at the same time—and a little dizzy. Not good…but I couldn't be sick *that way*. Surely? Could I be? No. Maybe. No.

The maybe made me scared.

"Simon?" I whisper-called.

Yeah. My head felt really swimmy and swirly.

I tiptoed further down the hall. I stood at the bottom of the stairs; I listened.

It was so, so, so quiet.

I peeped round the corner. There was no one in the living room, but for a moment the TV caught me there because I saw the pictures for the words I'd heard the night before. Now there were no words, but because I had heard them already, I thought I knew what they would be. I thought I knew what they'd be saying. The pictures… These, I had not expected. Not even because of what they showed, but because, well, it just wasn't how they do stuff on TV, not even when something really serious is happening and they're probably all freaked out. It was *amateur*. You know what it reminded me of? When me, Lee, Ronnie, and Molly had done our media studies project together: a news report on a zombie outbreak. We should have given it to Zak to edit, but Ronnie insisted. The costumes, the makeup, the location—the woods at Zak's place—were awesome. The edit was 🦋 crap.

(For your information: We got a B. Zak and Saskia teamed up with some of the others and got an A+ for a spoof washing-detergent ad. Zak was supposed to be the producer, but somehow Saskia seemed to end up doing most of that and most of everything else (voiceover; lead role glamorous housewife; bespectacled-but-hot washing-detergent scientist), but, still, can you believe it? Wasn't the whole zombie thing, even with a 🦋 edit, a whole lot more creative? Ronnie said they didn't care about that, and that's pretty much what the teacher said too—but I ask you, which project turned out to be more relevant, huh? How to survive a disaster situation versus how detergent gets sold? I'm regrading us to an A+.)

Anyway, the TV. They were cutting in and out of a studio, where a woman behind a desk was talking to two men on screens behind her; it said they were in Manchester and Edinburgh. In between, they cut to stuff they'd filmed earlier—a hospital; a corridor filled with people, bloody, writhing, groaning. You didn't have to hear it to know, just like Caspar. Back to Studio Woman. Then shots of lines of cars. Back to Manchester Man. Then a clip of a politician. OK, I'm not all that up on political stuff, but it could have been the prime minister; it was some man in a suit, trying to look like he really, really meant what he was saying and totally looking like he didn't. Then a clip of the American president—him I knew—doing the same thing. Then back to the studio.

And then a graphics thing—a lousy graphics thing—of the world. As it rotated, weird red raindrops splopped onto countries until it went back to the Europe part—splops already in place—and zoomed in on Britain. Splop, splop, splop. The whole of the south-west got covered in one big, red tear-shaped splop.

Underneath, a stream of words said nothing much different from what I had heard the night before: STATE OF NATIONAL EMERGENCY DECLARED...PUBLIC ADVISED TO REMAIN INDOORS...DO NOT CALL 911...NO TREATMENT CURRENTLY AVAILABLE...

You know how normally when they do that ticker-tape stream of headlines along the bottom of the screen, they move from one subject to another? They didn't. Same subject, it just kept coming and coming, on and on...

...SCIENTISTS CLAIM BACTERIUM IN RAIN IS CAUSE...SYMPTOMS INCLUDE BLEEDING, SEVERE PAIN, NAUSEA...

And then they showed it: the thing. They put up this picture of this microscopic *thing*. This thing that looked so pretty: a little round sun with these wiggly rays—a little blob of a thing with squirming tentacles.

I had felt sick before; I felt even sicker now. I didn't want to look at it. I wanted a cup of tea.

I went into the kitchen.

The house was so quiet I didn't expect anyone to be there. Simon was at the table. Except for the stove and the table, every surface in that kitchen—and some of the floor—was covered with some kind of container, all of them filled with water. That was weird, but I didn't want to go there. I saw; I did not want to discuss.

When I walked in, he lifted his head up. His face…it was not normal. It was not stiff or shaky either. It looked all collapsed.

"Hey," he said really quietly.

He looked at me. Whoa! That look! What was *that?!*

It was too weird and intense—and I guess it was for him too, because he went back to his list. Yes, he was *writing a list*. That would have been a bad sign on any normal day—plus he'd never, ever said "hey" to me in his life, so that was pretty weird as well. But from the way he looked, you could tell he must have been up all night, so his brain was probably completely scrambled. That's what I decided to think; Simon had been up all night (with Henry!), so I'd better be careful because, as well as the list, the laptop was on the table. If I could just get him to let me use it, just for a second…

"Hey," I replied, ready to be told to get back in my cell. "I called—"

"Yeah," said Simon.

"Um…Mrs. Fitch is—"

"I know," said Simon. "Try not to look."

"It's horrible," I said.

"Yes," he said.

"Simon, can I please just use the bathroom? And then please could I get some breakfast? And…" I stopped, thinking now didn't seem like quite the right time to raise the cell phone thing. I'd have to work up to it—plus there was the laptop. I wanted to ask about the Internet, but I couldn't without revealing I'd already been on the other computer without permission. (That's how strict he was.)

"I'm really sorry about last night," I said, thinking that might get me one step closer to my phone, to my friends, to normal. To the things that counted.

"It's OK," he said.

Huh?!

"You don't have to stay in the den anymore," he said.

HUH?! That was tricky, because I knew I didn't feel OK even if I didn't feel *that* not OK, but I knew I didn't want another zillion hours waiting on my own with Mrs. Fitch dead outside, and…then I thought about my mom and Henry. I couldn't make them sick.

"I don't really feel OK," I blurted. "I don't feel *bad* bad, not like…you know. I just feel a little bad."

"Ru?" he said. He looked at me, worried, freaking me out. "What feels wrong?"

I told him. It annoyed me that he smiled when I said it. He smiled—not some massive grin, but a definite flicker of a tired, "oh you, you're so young (and stupid)" smile. Only it was sad-looking somehow too—and not the usual, "I'm so disappointed in you (oh you, you're so young and stupid)" sad look.

"What did you drink at Zak's?" he said.

Yee-haa! I was just about to saddle up in outrage, deny I'd had a thing to drink and yell at Simon for even thinking such a thing, when—

"Zak made some punch," I said. Double blurt. At least I wasn't to blame.

"Punch? Oh dear! What was in it?" he asked.

He was really weirding me out now, because normally if he even slightly suspected illicit activities, he'd flip out, and that'd be it: me grounded and scraping poop, pee, woodchips, and hay out of the guinea-pig hutch. I could just see it… Except I'd actually confessed, and he wasn't going ballistic. Weird.

"I dunno," I said. "Cider?"

He was looking at me so strangely I voluntarily blurted out more truth.

"And gin," I said.

Quadruple confession. (A record!) Any minute now, I'd be telling him I'd tried pot, had lied about the babysitting, and was in love with Caspar McCloud, so I searched my brain for something that would make it sound like I wasn't as bad as some people.

"Molly got sick from it," I said.

Sorry, Mol. Normally that would have been a great rage-deflection tactic, but Simon didn't seem to care.

"I think you've probably just got a hangover, don't you?" he said, super calm and gentle. "You need to rehydrate—and eat."

On that, we agreed. I grabbed the kettle. It didn't seem like there was enough water in it for the eight hundred cups of tea I was needing, so I turned to the sink.

"Stop," he said before my hand was on the tap.

I looked around at him.

"I don't think we should use the water anymore," he said.

I looked at the tap—dripping like it had been for weeks, waiting for Simon to fix it—and then at the thousands of containers full of water all over the kitchen.

"Not those either," he said. "You'll have to get by with what's left in the kettle. There's orange juice and milk in the fridge."

I put the kettle back. I kind of stared at it and then the tap, and then the sea of containers. *What?!* Was that disgusting little tentacle-y space thing in the house?!

"Don't touch any of that water," said Simon. "I'll get rid of it."

I was too thirsty and muddled to start thinking. I flicked the kettle on, poured myself a glass of orange juice, and glugged it down. My stomach gurgled horribly.

"I'm just gonna go to the bathroom," I mumbled.

"You'll have to use the bucket," said Simon, staring at his list.

"*What?!*" I said, but not a yee-haa "*What?!*" It was just a "*What?!*" kind of what, the kind of "*What?!*" that comes out of your mouth when your brain doesn't get it.

"We don't know whether the water's OK anymore. It's too risky."

"But…I need to…" I wasn't going to put my rear end *in* the toilet, just *on* it.

"Sorry, Ru. Use the bucket." He added something to the list then.

I pooped in the bucket (too much information?). I thought I wouldn't be able to, but I was desperate, and anyway I told myself it was just like one of the terrible camping trips Simon took us on before Henry came along: rain pouring down, squatting on a plastic toilet thing. (We didn't go to the kind of campsites where there were showers and toilets and swimming pools and entertainment. Or even other people. We went to cold, windy fields in the middle of nowhere.) I piled layers of toilet paper on top of my poo, and even though it was my own—and you can't smell your own like you can smell other people's, can you?—I felt so embarrassed. I felt…so…humiliated. Like it was so unfair—for me.

Bristling—that's what you call it, when you're trying to not be angry even though you're furious—I went back to the kitchen. Simon was making scrambled eggs.

"I suppose I can't even wash my hands," I said, *bristling*, as I sat down at the table and poured out the last of the orange juice.

"Or have a shower," Simon said, pointing at a pack of Henry's baby wipes across the table.

NO SHOWER?! ARE YOU KIDDING?!

Cell phone, friends, Caspar. Priorities, Ruby, I thought, *priorities*. I wiped my hands, *bristling*.

Simon put a pile of toast and eggs in front of me, plus butter and jam and the secret stash of peanut butter. He'd also made a cup of tea.

"Last cup in the kettle," he said as I slurped.

"Thanks," I mumbled, feeling totally, bristlingly depressed.

Simon didn't eat. He just kept staring at his stupid list. He didn't add anything to it; he just kept looking at it.

When I had finished, I got a glass of milk.

"Feel better?" he asked.

It was harder to bristle; I did feel better.

"Yes. Thanks," I said.

"Good," he said.

I glugged down the last of the milk—well, almost. I did what you always do, which is leave this little bit in the bottom of the carton so you're not forced to rinse it out and put it in the recycling. I felt about ready to tackle it: how I was going to get Simon to take me to Zak's—though I figured it would be pretty hard to persuade him until the rain stopped. I looked out the window; it was coming down in sheets, pouring down, from the kind of low, gray sky that's got no hope of sun in it.

That's nimbostratus; I know that now. I didn't then. All I knew was it looked like the kind of gloomy total cloud-out that means: forget it, you're going nowhere.

But I could in a car. If we could just get into the car without getting wet—like if we took that huge umbrella my mom used to keep her and Henry in his stroller dry—and then we could just drive into the carport at Zak's place...but maybe I should try for the laptop first, check email, and see what had been going on and—

"Ruby," said Simon. "I need to talk to you."

CHAPTER SIX

H ere we go. *Now I'm gonna get it.*

That's what I thought, you see. The whole world was in some kind of hideous death-fest space-bug meltdown, and I was still on the page before, still stuck in yesterday. I still thought… I dunno what I thought! That everything—well, if it wasn't exactly the same right now, that it would still be the same… later? Tomorrow?

I'm not stupid; I knew something really bad was happening, but at that moment in time, I just wanted to see my friends. I wanted my cell phone back so I could call Caspar, which I'd never actually done before—we'd just texted and done the whole virtual flirtation thing a little—but felt I could do now on account of the kissing and the suffering. I just wanted to call him, almost as much as I wanted to call Lee…but did Caspar even have his phone, or had he left it at Zak's? I could get it and take it to him and—

"Ruby! You need to pay attention," said Simon.

I sure did! I was going to have to charm my way out of there. I helpfully grabbed my plate and had my hand on the tap before—

"No!" Simon bellowed. "Don't use the faucet!"

I sat back down with my plate and smiled sweetly at Simon. *Look contrite*, I thought—which means looking really sorry, even if you're not. He sighed—not in a nasty way, in a sad way—and pulled his chair around next to mine.

"I need you to really listen," he said.

OK, I thought, *humor him*. I nodded contritely.

"No one really knows what's going on," he said. "Not for sure. But until we know, we need to stick to these rules."

That's when the list came out. It was basically a to-do list from hell. A hideous, death-fest mega-crisis do-this-do-that checklist, only it was all don'ts and no dos. You can imagine what was on it: all the stuff that had been on the radio. All the stuff I'd been trying to block out, plus a few things I hadn't even remembered hearing and that, later on, I realized was stuff Simon must have thought of.

DON'T GO OUT IN THE RAIN.

(*Duh!* I thought.)

DON'T TOUCH ANYONE WHO'S TOUCHED ANY WATER. OR ANY ANIMAL. OR ANYTHING. DON'T TOUCH ANYTHING THAT'S TOUCHED ANY WATER.

It felt like his list was already losing it a little, but I did get what he meant. I could imagine that horrible microscopic bug thing creeping about everywhere.

"Zak's mom said not to touch the car door," I said (to pick up some Brownie points).

"Good," he said. "That's exactly what I mean."

Maybe he'd just let me use the laptop; it was sitting right there, right in front of me, and—

"Ruby! Please! You need to concentrate."

I peeled my eyes off the laptop and focused on the list. The next item was the freakiest:

DON'T TOUCH ANYONE WHO'S SICK. OR DEAD.

"That's horrible," I said.
He grunted.

DON'T TOUCH OR DRINK ANY TAP WATER.

He rattled on for a while then, about how although no one had actually said the tap water was bad already, it probably was or would be very soon because people had probably panicked like he'd panicked and emptied their water tanks, which would just speed up sucking the bad water into the pipes unless you could shut the water off, which he couldn't because he'd have to go outside to do that, so even though the water he'd filled up every last container in the house with was probably OK, you couldn't be sure, could you?

"No, Simon," I said, and before he could go on about it anymore, I read the next part out loud.

DON'T USE THE TOILET. NO BATHS. NO SHOWERS. DON'T EAT ANYTHING THAT'S BEEN OUTSIDE. NO FRESH FRUIT, VEGETABLES, FISH, MEAT.

The meat part annoyed me; technically, apart from eating fish, I was a vegetarian. It was just that it was a little hard to keep it up sometimes, and there'd been lapses—that Simon knew about and never let me forget.

"Yup. Got it!" I said brightly.

"And, Ru, this is the most important thing."

At the top of the list, he wrote one word, in capitals, underlined. Then he wrote over it again and again. One word:

THINK

"Do you understand?" he asked.

It was too much; I just wanted to get this mini-lecture/test thing over with, but I knew "OK!" wouldn't cut it.

"Like filling the kettle?" I said.

"Like filling the kettle," said Simon.

Phew. Comprehension test passed. But no—

"Do you understand, Ruby? You have to think. You have to stop and think, whatever it is, whatever you feel, you have to stop and think."

"I get it," I said.

"What?" he said. "What do you get?"

"That I've got to think," I said.

"About what?"

"About… I dunno, about the water and stuff."

"Yes," he said.

He turned and held my face in his hands; it scrunched the Caspar-kissing sore patch a little and made it hurt, but I was too freaked out to even say "ow."

"Ruby," he said. "You have to think."

It was the worst eyeballing he'd ever given me.

"You have to think about yourself," he said. "You have to put yourself first."

Huh?! My whole life, I'd been told I was selfish. Simon, he'd just say, "Will you please stop being so selfish?!" while my mom would say something like, "Oh, Ruby," and I just knew she meant the same thing. And now?

"You have to think about yourself first, Ruby. About your *survival*."

Yup, he'd gone from weirding and freaking me out to full-blown scaring me out. He wouldn't let up.

"Before you do anything, what are you going to do?" he asked.

My chin hurt.

"Think," I said.

"About what?" he demanded.

"About me," I said. Said? Any second now, I could feel I was going to be forced to shout a little, just to make him lay off.

"What are you going to do?"

"Think."

"About?"

"ME. Leave me alone, Simon—I've got it, all right? I have to think!"

"About?"

"Survival!"

"Whose?"

"MINE!" I shouted. I hated him then, more than I had ever done. "MINE! ME!"

He let go of my face.

The house was still quiet. I'd shouted and the house was still quiet.

"*Mom?!*" I shrieked.

Shrieked—that's a word for a kind of scream, isn't it? Not some great howl of a scream, when you know, but the kind of scream you make when—

"Think!" Simon shouted, trying to grab my arm.

I was too quick for him. I stormed up the stairs; I flung open the door to their room.

Oh…oh…oh…I saw my mom.

She was just lying there, curled around Henry, like she might be asleep. The bedsheets were all rumpled up. I didn't fling myself at her, in case she was just sleeping. Yes, I still thought that was what it could be.

"Mom?" I said.

The way she was lying, on her side, she had one arm stretched out across the pillow. Her hand was all bloody. The blood had soaked into the pillow. Her other hand, not bloody, lay on Henry's tummy. He was lying on his back, completely still. Only the tiniest little red sore on his cheek.

"*MOM?!*"

Simon's hands snatched around my middle and pulled me back. He pinned me to him.

My scream died in the air; it died and joined all the other screams. They live like ghosts, like echoes in the minds of the living.

My scream burst out and died, and my lungs refused—*refused*—to suck in air. I wanted to stop, to die with that scream.

"Breathe, breathe, breathe," Simon kept saying. He was crying. He would not let me go.

Then it comes. Your lungs suck in air; your body decides for you. You will live.

You're one breath away from her, then two, then three, then four, then five.

Mom, I am still breathing.

CHAPTER SEVEN

I don't know how we got back downstairs. I was sobbing, that I remember. Wailing, so I could hardly breathe. But I did breathe.

What I kept trying to say, over and over, was that I knew why. I knew what had happened. Hadn't I seen the tablets fall? My mom must have reached out into the rain to throw the box to Mrs. Fitch. Poor, stupid, 🦋 Mrs. Fitch.

Why hadn't I realized? Why hadn't I shouted? Why hadn't I thought?

And then what? Had she known right away? No…or else she wouldn't have touched Henry. Oh, she would have stroked his little face. Not even enough to wake him. Just the softest touch on his cheek. She did it to me still—even if we'd fought, I'd pretend to be asleep just so she'd do it…the softest touch and a little kiss.

For the rest of that day, it rained. Simon and me, we set up camp in the living room, made Dan nests there. I guess neither of us wanted to be alone.

I'll tell you the parts I remember, but, really, how it all went, what we said and did, it's kind of muddled.

What I do remember, more than anything, was stuff about sound, the torture of it. To begin with, he turned the TV off. Fine, because who would want to see that? Even though it had been on

mute anyway, those pictures… I dunno. They kind of made noise…
because of how horrible they were, I suppose. But when the TV was
off, all we had was the rain. I couldn't listen to that, but whatever
we tried to stop it with—music, a DVD—none of it was right.
Cheerful stuff, sad stuff, silly stuff—whatever we tried seemed so
wrong, so angry-making. And unless you had the volume up, deaf-
eningly up, you could still hear it: the rain.

So we watched boring stuff. Simon had tons of it. It's almost
enough to make me laugh—but not quite—that I sat through a
boxed set of bird-watching DVDs and this history series he'd bought
and been trying to force me to watch for weeks because he thought
it would help with my studying.

Ha. I thought history was boring, and now here I am writing
my own.

Simon would be pleased, I think.

We talked—not much, but also a lot, if you know what I mean. We
talked in little bursts, about Mom, about Henry, about what had happened. And then we'd have to stop for a while, because it hurt too much.

The whole time, everything we said and did, I kept thinking about
my mom and Henry upstairs. I couldn't stop seeing them in my head.

I got angry with him. I wanted to know why he hadn't called me,
why he hadn't let me say good-bye. He told me he hadn't known.
He'd heard Henry. He'd thought it was the teething. He was about
to go up there with one of Henry's teething rings from the fridge,
but then it had stopped. After that, he'd heard nothing, thought it
best to let them sleep. He'd stayed up the rest of the night, watching the news, trying to get back on to the Internet, trying to phone
people. When it got to seven a.m. and Henry still hadn't piped up,
he went upstairs to check on them. It was too late.

But why had he left me to sleep and then sat me at the kitchen
table with his stupid list when—

"I was trying to think about what your mother would have wanted," he said.

How she had kept quiet, I don't know. I just can't even imagine. Most people I've ever heard with the sickness scream and groan and…

"Why didn't she call you?" I said.

I said it in the middle of a thing about wetland birds. Marsh warblers.

"She would have been worried about giving it to us," said Simon, staring at the screen. Then he looked at me. "She would have been worried… If I got sick, there'd be no one to look after you," he said.

♦♦♦

He did shout at me a few times. Just "RUBY!" Mainly for going to turn the tap on. Once for nearly knocking a jug of water over. When that happened again, he put on rubber gloves and carefully shifted all the jugs and bowls and pots and pans of water into the corner of the kitchen and fenced them off with chairs and the trash can. I don't know why he didn't just chuck it all down the sink; too splashy, I guess. Or because that would somehow feel like setting it free. So there it sat: our little poisoned sea. I hated the sight of it.

I wanted to call my dad.

"Everything's down, Ru." That was all Simon said. He passed me the phones anyway: the landline, his cell, my mom's cell.

I tried my dad; I tried Leonie. I didn't know anyone else's number by heart; that wouldn't have mattered because my mom and Simon had pretty much all our relatives and most of my friends' parents' numbers on their phones, but there wasn't even a dial tone. No sound at all on both their cell phones, and just a single endless beep on the landline.

"What about email?" I said. "We can email people."

He gave me the laptop too. He hadn't shut the Internet off. The Internet was down. I kept trying the laptop, the phones. I don't know how long I tried—a long time—while the TV guy rattled on about the Tudors and Stuarts. They weren't even on our syllabus. Nor was the Civil War, which is what the TV guy was going on about when Simon took the computer and the phones from me. I didn't put up a fight. I was crying.

"They might be trying to get through to us too," he said.

He laid his cell, my mom's cell, and the regular phone on the windowsill, in front of all the family photos. The laptop he put on the coffee table.

"We'll try every hour," he said.

We did. We took turns. We ended up not even telling each other that nothing had changed.

Sometime during the afternoon, there was a really loud bang—like an explosion, I guess—in the town. We both jumped up and ran to the kitchen window. You could see nearly the whole town from our kitchen: the castle, the church, the housing development that spread up the hill east of the river where Leonie lived.

There were flames and smoke coming up from the High Street. A fire in the rain.

Simon opened cans of fruit, poured out the juice, and gave one to me.

"Where do you think that is?" he asked me. "The George?"

You could see, working it out from the rooftops, that it must have been.

"Such a shame," muttered Simon.

Dartbridge is jam-packed with old buildings, medieval stuff—even the dentist's has got gnarly old beams on the ceiling. (I've spent a lot of time looking at them.) Probably if it had been any other old building in town, I might have thought a stupid build-ing didn't matter, not now, but it wasn't any other building. I wanted to tell him that The George was where the second most amazing moment of my life had happened prior to the all-time number-one kissing amazing moment that had happened at Zak's party. I wanted to tell him that was where Caspar had looked up at me, when he was playing his guitar, and that I had felt myself fall in love on the spot.

We stared out at it. There were no sirens.

I said it then: "Simon, I'm really scared."

He led me back into the living room. I sat in my nest; he sat on the sofa.

"Should I make us something to eat?" he asked.

"No," I said.

This is a thing to know, a thing I have learned, about what fear and grief and horror do. They mash you up from the inside out. They twist you, and they break stuff inside you. They tear stuff out. They get whole brains, whole hearts, in their hands, and they crush and crush.

"Can I come and sit with you?" I asked.

"Yes. Of course," he said.

And for the first time ever, I snuggled up to Simon on the sofa.

I thought how pleased (and shocked) my mom would be, and I cried.

I felt *so small*. Littler—younger—than even before I knew Simon. I felt as tiny as Henry. Tinier. I didn't want to cry. I wanted to bawl. For my mom.

When it was dark, Simon did make some food.

"I'm going to make a stew," he said.

He made stews when we went camping. "Comfort food" was what he called it. They were horrible—and, as I once pointed out, if we went on the kind of vacations everyone else got to go on, you wouldn't need comforting. Even my mom had laughed.

"Do you want me to help?" I asked.

You can imagine how often I would have voluntarily helped Simon make one of his hideous stews, but I sat and peeled vegetables. I didn't want to be away from him.

Normally, even on a campsite, he'd drain and wash the kidney beans or whatever, but now he slopped the whole can into the pot.

"Won't that taste disgusting?" I said.

"No choice, Ru," he said. "I'll spice it up with something."

He had his back to me as he opened the cupboard where the herbs and spices were. He rummaged, opening unlabeled jars and sniffing, and his head turned a little. I saw tears on his cheek; one slid down, and I saw him lick it from his lips.

"I could kill for a cup of tea," he said, turning back to the stovetop to dump random stuff into the pot and stir it. He wiped his face on his sleeve.

I saw the list he had left on the table:

THINK

I went to the freezer. I got the ice cubes and popped them into the kettle. It didn't look like enough, so I chipped off ice from inside the freezer, crammed that—my hands numbed dead with cold—into the kettle.

I plugged the kettle in and flicked it on.

"Earl Grey, peppermint, or black?" I asked. Like my mom would ask.

It took three boils to make it. All that ice and just enough for one cup. Simon chose Earl Grey. We both knew why; that's what my mom liked.

The stew was horrible. Simon stopped me from pouring salt all over it and onto the baked potato that went with.

"It's dehydrating," he said. "And it's bad for you, anyway."

I gave him a look.

"It's what your mother would say."

I couldn't really eat it. I mean, you wouldn't really want to, but I sort of knew I must be hungry, even if I didn't feel it.

"She'd also say, eat up," said Simon.

"I can't," I said.

From the looks of his plate, he couldn't either.

"Simon, are we going to die?"

He didn't answer for a while, then he laid his knife and fork down. He said, "I don't know."

That was how we came to turn the TV back on, to find out. He said if it upset me, I should just say so, immediately, and he'd turn it off. I knew what he was expecting—the same thing I was expecting: hospital shots of people dying, the TV people going on and on about it. In a way, what there was instead was worse. I just didn't realize it at first.

The scary pictures had gone, so had Studio Woman and the Manchester and Edinburgh Men. Everyone had gone. Instead, there were just words on the screen and someone reading them. For a second, I thought it was some kind of documentary thing, the sort of thing that bores me stupid, until Simon flipped through the rest of the channels. They either came up blank fuzz or showed the same thing: EMERGENCY PUBLIC SERVICE BROADCAST. But it was different from the first one. Were we having ANOTHER emergency?

(No, we weren't. It was just what they should have told us in the first place, but I'll get to that.)

You know what Simon said? "If only we had satellite…"

Know what I nearly said? "Like I asked!"

I had. I'd asked about a million times if we could at least just get a package with the music channels, said it would help me learn guitar. It might have.

He got the radio then, plugged it in and crept across the dial—yes, that's right: about the only thing we had in common with Zak's family was we weren't even allowed a digital radio. It was crazy making, the sound of the radio, with the TV going as well. Then he hit a crackly station playing that "It's the End of the World As We Know It" song and turned it off.

"I'll try later," he said, looking all anxiously at me.

"It's OK," I said. "I get it. It's really bad, isn't it?"

But I didn't really get it. I think I thought… I dunno, that Studio Woman and the Manchester and Edinburgh Men had all gone home—because you would, wouldn't you? You'd want to be with your family to check that they were OK and stuff, or help them or just be sad like we were if they weren't OK and you couldn't help them.

Thinking that made me choke up. Thinking that made me think how my mom was upstairs and—

"Should I turn the TV off as well, Ru?" Simon asked.

"No," I said. "It's fine."

It's fine. Can you ever imagine such a stupid thing to say?

Nothing was fine.

If you're reading this, you know what they were saying on TV and on the radio. Unless you were some kind of really strict hippie, without even a radio…or a nun or a monk? I'll bet they're not allowed TVs, not even for educational purposes, just in case they're tempted to switch channels, watch wannabe talent shows, and spend the collection money or whatever voting on rip-off rate phone lines. (Like I did.) (I don't even really watch those programs, not really.) (I was

bored.) (It was almost an accident.) (The guy looked like Caspar.)
(Mom and Simon were out.) (Every time.) (Including when I also
voted for that girl.) (She kept crying and stuff, and not realizing she
was brilliant, so I practically had to give her a vote—even though I
knew there was zero chance she would win.)

(The phone bill—which I cunningly, scaredly intercepted—is
still under my bed.)

I am going to write it down anyway, what was said about the
rain. I am going to write down everything I know about what was
happening, because maybe someone should…and because maybe I
need a break from thinking about what that was like: me and Simon
in the living room, and my mom and my Henry upstairs dead.

THE RUBY MORRIS
KILLER RAIN SUMMARY

So, this is the Ruby Morris Killer Rain Summary. This is what they said on the TV and the radio. This is what I heard, plus what Simon told me he'd heard, plus the things Simon figured out all by himself…plus a little of the stuff that I got to know and hear about after. This is, I think, as much as anyone knows.

To begin with, they said they didn't know—*really* know, for sure—what was causing it, but some people—not just any people, scientists—thought it had to do with the asteroid. That when it had been blown to smithereens, it had made kind of a mess. Tons and tons and tons and tons of rocky mess. After a while—like, nearly seven years—the mess got to Earth. It got sucked here by gravity and— *Pop! Pop! Pop!*—the mess of rocks got into the Earth's atmosphere, making a really gorgeous firework display that you could see pretty much everywhere on Earth—except boring old Dartbridge, where it was cloudy and no one got to see a thing. A few big chunks did fall to Earth, and before there was no one left alive to fight about it, some of the scientists and politicians were having a big argument about what exactly had happened to those pieces of asteroid. I don't suppose it really matters. You see, the rest of the mess had been blown into even tinier smithereens of dust that got spread around, all over the sky.

Everyone knew about the dust. It was the dust that made the

sunsets everyone had been ooh-ing and ahh-ing about, the kind of heavenly sunset there'd been on the night of Zak's party. Yup, doom was written right across the sky and everyone was going, "Ooo! Isn't that lovely?" and probably taking pictures of it.

Selfie with sunset and sausage. Having a lovely holiday weekend.

What no one knew (Ronnie would probably disagree) was that there was something in the dust: a tiny, weird space thing. A bacterium. A thing that had lived inside the asteroid for millions— maybe billions?!—of years. They didn't know how it did that, but apparently even some bacteria on Earth—*extremophiles*, that's what they said they were called—can survive for endless centuries—for, like, forever. Can survive how and where no normal living thing could, gobbling sulfur in boiling hot springs, for example, or at the bottom of the sea, or in the armpits of certain boys.

They said the space thing was a kind of *polyextremophile* because, unlike your regular extremophile, there were tons and tons of things it couldn't care less about: heat, cold, radiation... But what it was really, really pleased to see after all that time stuck in a hunk of rock in space was water. It likes water A LOT.

It breeds in water. Not breeds, exactly; it likes itself so much it just makes more of itself. It replicates. It replicates *really* fast. Like— ka-boom—one minute there was a smashed-up asteroid's worth of bacteria, and the next minute, the whole sky, our beautiful sky, was teeming with them. Riddled with them. Swarming with them. The clouds were poisoned.

I never really thought of the rain as being beautiful. If it ever got clean again, I would go out and dance in it. I would love every single precious drop.

It's only a shower. *It sure is, Mom! Why, I just adore the rain!*

78

Get on with it. *Yes sir, Mr. Simon, sir! No problem!*

Every single precious drop of rain got contaminated. And every single precious drop fell to Earth.

When the rain touches human skin, there are a few moments when nothing happens—when, perhaps, you might even think that you will be OK. Then it starts: a rash that burns…that burns so bad you will want to scratch the skin from your own body. Do that—and you won't be able to stop yourself—and you're just helping it along. It starts to chow down into your flesh. It doesn't care about the pain if it gets snarled up around your nerve endings. It is *very* aggressive. It attacks anything in its path; it is up for a fight. It is determined to get what it wants—and what it wants is to burrow its way into your veins, into your arteries, into your blood.

That's what it's after. Your blood. They think it's the iron; that it likes to snack on iron—and, boy, after all that replicating, it was starving.

Depending on how much you've been exposed—if, say, you got drenched with water from head to toe—the first blast of pain as the bacteria elbow their way past each other to the all-you-can-eat buffet inside you can be enough to send you into total catastrophic shock. If so, you will die very quickly. If that happens to you, you're lucky—same as if you go and drink it. That's just like flinging open the front door to your insides and saying, "Come on in!"

If you just get a few drops of water on your skin—like my mom—you will die more slowly. Though, if you are tiny, like Henry…the beloved…it will still be quick.

It's a really fussy eater; it only likes your red blood cells. It's so happy to be inside you, gorging, after millions and billions of years of hungry thirst. It helps itself to the most juiciest parts of you, replicating super-fast as it gets its strength back, barging its way right into your blood cells, making more and more and more of itself until—POP! Your cells just burst.

The inside of your body is exploding, cell by cell.

There is nothing—NOTHING—to be done. It laughs in the face of antibiotics. No medicine on Earth can save you; there is no cure. They advised acetaminophen for the pain. Aspirin, apparently, just brings on more bleeding. So they advised acetaminophen.

HA! It does nothing.

And, when it was all too late, they said victims—or anyone suspected of sickness—should be quarantined for twenty-four hours. This is a joke, and in two ways:

1. "Quarantine" makes it sound as if you might come out alive (you won't); and
2. I've never seen or heard of anyone who lasted longer than three hours. Max.

I suppose the other way in which quarantine is a joke is that you can't get it from having a sick person just breathe on you or something. It can't get into you through your lungs. Incredibly, I'm with the space bug on this one; before I dropped biology, we studied the respiratory system, and I didn't get it either.

To get sick from a sick person, you have to actually get the sick person's blood on you, on your skin. Or a dead person's? I don't know. Who *would* know? That, like a lot of other stuff, isn't exactly the kind of thing anyone's going to be in a rush to test out.

(I mean, really, what kind of an idiot would think, "Hmm, I wonder if this lovely fresh apple I just picked is OK? Maybe I'll take a great big bite and see…")

In fact, there's plenty of stuff people don't know (even if they say they do), so my advice would be… Well, Simon said it on his list. Don't do this, don't do that. Otherwise, basically, you're dead.

◆●◆

To anyone living in the future, my recommendation would be that if there's an asteroid heading toward your planet, either blow it up when it's NOWHERE NEAR your gravity, or else move to another planet.

Is there anything positive to add? Apart from no one is ever going to find that phone bill under your bed or make you walk anywhere ever again when it's pouring?

Yes! IT COULD BE WORSE!

It could be, apparently. There's moisture in the air, isn't there? There are teensy droplets of water everywhere. I don't just mean when you get dew or condensation or stuff like that; I mean really, really teensy droplets that you can't even see. Simon showed me a picture in a newspaper once: *Dew on a damselfly*. I remember precisely which kind of tiny winged creature it was because, although I just said, "Oh wow, yeah," or something like that when Simon showed me, it was so OH WOW! YEAH! I looked it up on the Internet myself after. It was ah-may-zing! This little boggle-eyed alien-looking critter covered—COVERED—in teensy-weensy globules of water.

A while after this whole thing started, I remembered that picture. I remembered it and it made me paranoid for about five minutes, but then it made me understand what Simon said the scientists had been going on about: that you've gotta get hit by a certain number, a certain volume, of bacteria to get got; otherwise, your body *can* fight back. But what that certain number is? You can add that to the list of things only an idiot would try to figure out.

Drip. Drip. Drop. Dead.

That's it. That's all I've got to say.

Hold on. If there's one thing they tried to drum into us at school—and actually there were about five million things they tried to drum into us, day in, day out—it's that it's no good just repeating facts. No, for good grades, it is important to not just bleat what someone else has told you, but to show that you are capable of actually thinking about what it is you have learned.

Sooooo, in conclusion…

What I think, really, is that this should have been the moment in human history when teenagers should have taken over the Earth (a little like they said cockroaches would do in the event of nuclear war, but obviously we're a lot nicer than cockroaches).

Think about it: we don't like to go outside when it's raining; we don't like drinking water (it's boring); we don't like eating fresh fruit and vegetables (because the THEY are always going on about how we should).

We'd have had to get over the need to shower, but frankly, I hadn't used soap on my face for at least a month (since Lee read an article that said it gave you premature wrinkles), and I can fully vouch for the cleansing properties of baby wipes. The showering: we would have gotten over it. We would have had to. We are, actually, very capable of adapting.

If this sounds like a joke to you, read on and think on because the other thing about us teenagers is that we're much, much nicer people than most adults (*see Footnote 1*). Our world would have been a better world.

OK, that's my take on it. It's probably not quite right, but mainly it probably is. I'm giving myself another A+.

Footnotes
Footnote 1: With some exceptions.

CHAPTER SEVEN
PART TWO

W e watched the broadcast thing a few times. There was a pause
when it got to the end, and then it would start over again.
I asked Simon some stuff; he answered—when he could answer.
There was so much stuff he didn't know, that no one knew. The
main question, I guess, was what was going to happen next.

I'm glad no one could answer that. I wouldn't have wanted
to know.

You know what it reminded me of, though, Emergency Public
Service Broadcast Number Two? It reminded me of how, when
you're in trouble and you know it, the way you kind of go easy on
the basic facts. That's Emergency Public Service Broadcast Number
One; you're cornered, so you've got to fess up, but it's much better
to keep the fessing to a minimum to avoid a full parental freak-
out. You want to hold off blurting the further details—well, for as
long as you can, really. That's Emergency Public Service Broadcast
Number Two: what you confess when there's no longer any point
in denying stuff. The worst example I can think of is this girl at
my school who basically got caught with a boy, so she had to
admit they'd done the deed (when they'd actually been doing it
for months). Her parents went nuts about EPSB No. 1; they went
so nuts she didn't actually get around to telling them the second

part (EPSB No. 2) until they found the pregnancy-testing kit in the trash…

Let's just take an easier example:

EPSB No. 1: "OK, so I've just come home in an outfit I didn't leave the house in…so I might as well tell you I went to a party."

("OK, you'll have noticed anyone who got rained on has become sick, so we may as well tell you: it's in the rain.")

EPSB No. 2: "I think I might be sick in a minute, so you may as well know that at that party I drank some punch—with gin in it."

("You may have noticed some people are dead, so we may as well tell you it's fatal. Oh! You've got it too? Shucks! We may as well tell you: it's contagious.")

You'd think you'd get your head around it, hearing the same thing again and again—there's an initial freak-out, then people get over it—but somehow Emergency Public Service Broadcast Number Two got worse the more times you heard it. And it wasn't just because my mom and my Henry were dead—that was bad enough. It was because it made you start thinking about…stuff you couldn't even begin to start thinking about—say, like, whether the world was ending. So I tuned out.

It must have been too much for Simon too because, not long after, he put the DVD back on. The history thing had made it up to World War I. I told Simon we weren't doing that at school, so he put the bird thing on instead, but really it was because it was too horrible to look at: all those people dying. He left me watching a thing about woodland birds while he went and messed around with the radio in the kitchen. He kept it so quiet I couldn't hear whatever it was people were saying. There was music sometimes. I don't know what. I wasn't even listening for it. I wasn't listening to the bird thing either, and not even to the rain. I was thinking about my mom and about Henry, my dearest, babiest, brother-brat beloved.

CHAPTER EIGHT

In the morning, it was sunny, like it had been for so many days before the rain came. It was sunny, and the sky was blue—the kind of blue that makes you forget there's even such a thing as rain. The kind of blue that made you think it was all over.

Before I remembered it was supposed to be a vacation day, I had this one random thought—really so stupid and silly but also kind of almost funny—that Simon was actually going to say I had to go to school. Really, I could almost just imagine it! *Look, Ruby, I know you're upset and some terrible things have happened, but we have to get on with things* ("It's only a shower")—*plus you've got your practice exams coming up* (he was obsessed with exams) *and, after all, what would your mother want?* Etc., etc., etc.: GO TO SCHOOL.

But that didn't happen. So we put the radio on. It wasn't over.

The same emergency broadcast played over and over. Simon turned it down, but I'd already tuned out, same way you would if it was some blah-blah thing about politics (or *Gardeners' Question Time*). That was how to deal with it.

The thing that was less easy to deal with was the thirst. The day before, I hadn't really noticed it so much, not after I'd seen Mom. That next day…best way to describe it is: you know how it gets when you really, really like someone, when you're basically totally in love with them? Well, it was like a horrible version of that. I COULD NOT STOP THINKING ABOUT HOW THIRSTY I WAS.

(And you know how if you can actually SEE the person you like, it makes it even worse and you keep wanting to look at them? I felt like every other second I found myself staring at the little poisoned mini-sea of pots and pans and jugs of water in the corner of the kitchen.)

I had to close the fridge door quickly to avoid the terrible sight of Henry's teething rings. There was nothing to drink anyway. The orange juice was long gone; that last tiny drop of milk had gone bad, and I'd already scraped the freezer clean of ice—completely. I'd even found a pizza—they never bought pizza—stashed (as in *hidden from me*) under the peas and the fava beans in the freezer drawer that had all the vegetables in it, where no one in their right mind would go looking. Through the little plastic window they put so you can see they're not lying about how good the pizza is, I saw it had gathered a giant layer of frost on top, so the sneaks must have had it stashed for a while. I picked off the frost and boiled it in the kettle with the tiny bit of melt-water I'd thawed off the peas. The tea, Simon had said, savoring the taste like a chef would, tasted of oregano…with a hint of fish. He was right; I'd also found half a box of frost-furry fish sticks and carefully scraped the little spikes of ice off them.

We had one can of fruit left: peaches. Simon wanted to give them all to me, and even though I wanted them all, I made him split it. He gave me more though. I saw him do that. I mashed mine up in a cup. I slurped as slowly as I could, pretending I was having a smoothie, as we watched the town from the kitchen window, taking turns to zoom in on the action with his binoculars.

In some ways, the outside world looked normal. Mainly that was because what you can see from our kitchen window are rooftops and trees; when all the leaves are out, when all the plants are grown, you can't really see down into the streets (where there were dead people); you can't see down into the patios of pubs (where there were dead people); you can't see into people's homes (where there were dead people); and you can't really see into people's backyards. If you could have, you would have seen what I've seen a million times since: dead people sprawled around barbecues. So, yes, it all looked normal. The trees and plants seemed to be OK. Nothing looked withered or sick or dying. Birds flew in the sky. It looked like a nice, normal day... except, even with the windows still shut tight, you could *hear* it wasn't right. There were alarms going off all over the place and...you could see the parking lot behind the library. Cars were coming and going; not tons like there'd normally be, going around and around looking for spaces, but there were some cars. *People* were coming and going. That was where the normal part stopped.

The people in the parking lot—they weren't just your regular shoppers; they were staggering back from town with bags and bags of stuff, shopping carts even. Not just food, either; all sorts of tons of stuff, like it was Christmas or the January sales. A man and a woman had a massive flat-screen TV in a cart; it tipped over in the parking lot and the TV smashed. They went off again with the cart, but I didn't see them come back. Then a couple of guys got into a fight, and this woman started jumping around all over the place, waving her arms—screaming at them to stop probably, or screaming for help.

And all the while, the radio was on, the emergency broadcast quietly telling people, over and over, to stay home and remain calm.

Remain? Doesn't that sort of make it sound as if people were calm and had to stay that way? When exactly did they think people had been calm?!

"Oh, for crying out loud," said Simon, disgusted.

He put the binoculars down and went out of the kitchen; I heard him tramp upstairs to use his bucket in the bathroom. I picked up the binoculars.

From a distance, the fight had just looked a little silly: tiny men scrapping; tiny lady jumping. Close up, it was fascinating—in a nasty sort of way. I almost cheered when the smaller guy managed to knock the bigger guy down—but the bigger guy didn't get back up.

That parking lot, didn't Simon always go on about how it was a disgrace? Full of potholes that were now full of water. Water that was now full of death.

You could see the big man clawing at his arm, then wrenching his whole shirt off, his body bloody where he'd hit the ground.

It turned out the woman was with him and not the other guy; she ran to him.

Don't touch him! Don't touch him! Don't touch him! I thought, even as she slumped down and cradled his head like it was a baby.

Don't touch her! Don't touch her! Don't touch her! I thought, even as the big man reached up his hand…to push her away? She grabbed his bloody hand in hers. She—NO! NO! NO!—kissed it.

Stay home, remain calm.

The woman bent over the man, kissing and kissing his lips; not making out, not one long kiss, but kisses and kisses and words in between, saying stuff, her body rocking, her hand going from his head to rake at hers—at hers, where her face had turned bloody—and back to his, stroking his cheek. Kissing him, rocking him, saying stuff.

Love is stronger than pain. In the parking lot behind Dartbridge Library.

"We need water," said Simon, bustling back into the kitchen. "I'm going out."

I put the binoculars down.

We kind of had a fight then. It wasn't one of our old fights; this was a very new kind of a fight.

There was no shouting, for starters. There had been no shouting (except about the faucet and that) since I'd seen my mom. The high horses did get saddled up, but very quietly, with no yee-haa. Simon didn't want me to go with him because he was worried it wouldn't be safe. I didn't say I knew it wasn't safe because I'd just seen two people dying (probably) in the library parking lot. In any case, that was other people. That wouldn't happen to us. I point-blank refused to stay home alone.

You can't leave me, you can't leave me, you can't leave me—that was all I had to say about everything he said.

Also, even then—maybe especially then—I still thought that if I went with him, I might be able to get him to take me to Zak's. I would see my friends. I would get my phone.

I really did think this. I really did think all my friends would still be at Zak's, wondering whether they should go out or not—although stuck in the country like that, they wouldn't know that no one seemed to be paying any attention at all to what the broadcast was telling people. And maybe they'd know how Caspar was. I had seen what had happened to my mother and to Henry, and to the parking-lot people and to Mrs. Fitch, and still I had this thought that Caspar would still be alive. I suppose you could say it was more of a hope.

By the time me and Simon had finished having our new not-a-fight fight, clouds had begun to appear in the sky—not big clouds, not rain clouds, but gangs of little raggedy clouds.

Some kind of altocumulus type I now think they must have been, but I can't remember whether they were castellanus (raggedy at the top) or floccus (raggedy at the bottom). Little, raggedy clouds.

"Ruby," said Simon. "I have to go *now.*"

"You can't leave me," I said. For the zillionth time.

Simon caved. He had to: I would not be left alone.

"Don't look," he instructed as he opened the door.

He didn't say what at; I knew. I looked anyway. There were flies all over the mess that had been Mrs. Fitch's face. I felt…what I would come to feel a lot, for a while—this thing I didn't even know what to call back then, this wave of grief and shock and horror—not so much for Mrs. Fitch, in truth, but because Mrs. Fitch made me think about my mom.

Not even out of the garden gate and all I wanted to do was go back and hide under my duvet and watch *Birds of the British Isles* until it all stopped.

The gate banged shut, and I heard them: the neighbors' dogs. Alarms screeching and squealing up from the town and still you could hear them. Dogs that wouldn't normally be bothered by the bang of a gate being bothered by it.

We got in the car and got as far as the end of Cooper's Lane. It was like the traffic jam that had been there on the night Zak's mom drove me home hadn't budged. In fact, most of it probably hadn't. It took a few moments to realize that most of the cars heading into town weren't moving at all, were just stopped still, abandoned—or worse… there were people in those cars and the people weren't moving. In between the stopped cars came the cars of the living, horns honking pointlessly as they tried to find a way through. There were cars stopped on the other side too, coming out of town, but fewer of them.

"Perhaps we'd better walk," said Simon, jamming the car into reverse.

We went back home.

We had one last not-a-fight fight, a mini one, right outside our garden gate.

"Ruby," he said. "I really want you to stay home."

You can't leave me, you can't leave me, you can't leave me, and all the while the alarms going, the sirens going, the neighbors' dogs barking, the buzz of flies...the little gangs of poisoned clouds snuggling up together, getting just a little thicker and fatter and sinkier.

I won the fight that wasn't a fight, but I paid a terrible price for it. Even though it was totally obvious it wasn't going to rain anytime soon, Simon made us go back into the house and get dressed in rain boots, waterproof pants, and double raincoats. He told me to put the hood up on my raincoat, then produced one of his "Indiana Jones goes bird-watching" hats.

"No," I said. "No way. I'd rather die."

I didn't mean I'd rather die as in killer-rain die. I just meant... whatever it was I used to mean when I said stuff like that. He slapped the hat on my head, then cruelly tightened the hood of the raincoat.

I was outraged by the horror and shame of it, but I couldn't say anything, could I? Yes I could! I loosened the hood from my mouth and scabby chin.

"Well, what are we going to do about our hands?" I said.

I only said that to point out the pointlessness of it all, not so he'd go and get dishwashing gloves for us both.

He dangled them in front of me.

"If you'd rather not," he said, "we can both stay home and die of thirst."

I did feel that was somewhat unnecessarily brutal, but I put the awful gloves on and retightened the hood of the raincoat. The less you could see of my face, the less likely it'd be that someone would recognize me—with any luck. Simon handed me Mom's massive umbrella.

"I'm not putting it up," I mumbled through the raincoat.

"Right," said Simon. "But if I say you need to, you do it."

"'K," I mumbled.

We marched back out the gate, and he opened the trunk of the car and handed me the shopping bags; you know, those big "green" long-lasting ones people use—"because they fit so well in the back of a car," Ronnie said, meaning there was nothing eco about them.

"So you do what I say, when I say, young lady."

"Yes," I said. It came out all loud and wobbly, so it sounded about a micro-millimeter off a yee-haa yes…but, truth is, I was scared.

It was baking hot, and I was sweating by the time we'd walked about three steps. When we got to the alleyway that led from right by our house into town, I was sweating even more—and I got more scared.

What you might need to know at this point is that Dartbridge is basically the hippie capital of the universe. It is drowning in tie-dye and organic vegetables. People walk barefoot through the streets not because they are poor, but because they want a closer connection to the Earth (despite the fact that there's a ton of asphalt on top of it). Even the graffiti, which looks kind of cool, is hippie; this squiggly symbol for peace gets spray-painted everywhere. Dartbridge, Ronnie said, was "a place so laid-back it was practically comatose."

Below the alarms and the sirens and the car horns, you could hear…not just shouts and screams, but the sound of things—glass—smashing.

"Is it a riot?" I asked.

I'd seen stuff like that on TV before. It happened in other countries mainly, but also in the UK when people were annoyed about stuff the government was doing—which Ronnie said would happen a lot more often if people knew what was really going on.

"A riot in Dartbridge? I don't think so," said Simon. "People are just panicking a little, I guess."

We didn't go the way we'd usually go, straight into town via the library parking lot. Simon went to the right, along the back road, South Street. Fine by me, because I didn't want to go anywhere near The George. Not so fine was…there was a guy slumped up against a wall. He looked as if he'd just fallen asleep there, like a drunk guy might, snoozing in the sun.

"Don't look," said Simon, but I did.

He wasn't snoozing. His face was all bloody, and his eyes were gone, holes where they should have been. I didn't know it then, but that's what birds do, peck out the pieces that are easiest to get their beaks into. Nice.

In all my life, up until the day before, I'd never seen a dead person. Not counting the parking-lot people—which I didn't like to do, because I hadn't actually seen them die, had I? Like Caspar, it had to be possible that they'd be OK—I'd now seen four dead bodies. *Four.*

Ha ha ha. That's pretty funny, huh? Do you see? I was still counting.

And…does it sound too weird to say it? I felt glad that my mom was at home with Henry, not lying in the street—or in her nightie in someone's front yard, like Mrs. Fitch.

Simon was wrong. It was a riot.

South Street goes along next to the High Street, then curves in to meet it. As we walked toward the noise, you had this little view—a tiny street's width—of the High Street. And across this little gap, people—not tons of people, but little flurries and spurts of them—were going back and forth, some walking, some running, some shouting. Some with scarves tied across their faces like it was a real riot or something. Some pushing carts, most carrying all sorts of stuff.

So what we'd seen in the parking lot, it wasn't just some random thing—it was what was going down.

"We'll go to the other supermarket," said Simon, staring at the little snippet of riot.

That was another moment when I (sort of) realized how serious it was. We basically never much went to "the other supermarket," a.k.a. "the good one." In my house, if there was something from "the other supermarket" in the fridge—or snuck into the freezer like the pizza—it was unusual, as in Shocksville unusual, and also a cause for deep joy. Lee's family went there all the time and always had tons of awesome stuff to eat—like ice cream, for a start, and snacky things you could microwave in seconds, french fries included. Pretty much everyone else's family shopped there too, at least sometimes. Even Zak's.

We backtracked and cut around along Snow Hill, weaving our way along the back streets until we'd nearly reached the river. Up ahead, you could see the junction where the end of the High Street meets a bunch of other roads: the bridge road from the east end of town where Leonie lived, the road that led into town from the seaside places like Paignton and Torquay, and the road that led to the hospital and the supermarket.

That junction was rammed with dead cars, with live people, with rage—you could hear it from where we stood: screaming, shouting, fighting, and the police, in a car, stuck in the middle of it, lights flashing. There was a policeman on the roof of the car with a megaphone, telling people to *Go Home, Go Home, Go Home.*

Simon looked…like he looked when he got handed Henry having a bawling fit. Upset, confused, and panicked. Stressed out but trying not to show it.

To get to the supermarket, we'd have to get through all that. Or—

"We could cut across the High Street further up," I said. "Just cut across. It'll be really quick."

Basically, I'd have marched across the Sahara if I'd thought there was something to drink on the other side. I could feel this disgusting layer of sweat building up inside the waterproof gear, and I'd already wondered if I'd have to survive by licking the inside of my raincoat.

"Where?" snapped Simon. Yup, stressed.

That's the thing about being a teenager, I guess. You know about stuff, you know about places, about shortcuts that adults don't. They get to drive everywhere; you get told, "It's only a shower," i.e., get on with it; go. So you find the quickest way… OK, so you also find secret ways… OK and places to lurk. Places where you won't be seen by parents cruising past in cars when maybe you're supposed to be in French class or PE—or a super-expensive private guitar lesson, for example.

My shortcut, it was down this little alleyway. At the end of it, you had to cut across the High Street, but not just straight across; you had to turn left, go along a ways, and then cut right to get into another alleyway. I guess Simon must have been thirst-crazy too, because we went for it. He gripped the umbrella like it was a club and took hold of my hand.

When I was small, when we first came here, when I first went out anywhere on my own with Simon (which wasn't for a long time), he'd try to get me to hold his hand to cross the road. I wouldn't do it. I'd fold my arms and march across the road alone. If you'd told me one day I'd cross the High Street in broad daylight holding his hand…I wouldn't have believed you for a second.

I held his hand so tight.

There. That's a thing I've said for my mom. And for Simon.

But honestly—and this is the weird thing—it wasn't as bad as I had thought it would be. The riot, I mean. Yes, it was like nothing you'd ever seen (well, certainly not in Dartbridge); there were people running around and smashing windows and stealing stuff and shouting at each other (plus alarms going off), but what you realized in about ten seconds is that although it's really scary and about as far from anything normal you would ever expect to see—especially in the hippie capital of the entire universe—no one is paying any attention to you at all. Everyone is just doing their own thing; they couldn't care less about you...unless you tried to take their TV or their tennis shoes or their bags of food or something, I bet. (So that was fine by me, because it wasn't like anyone in the middle of a riot was going to see me holding "Daddy's" hand and stop and say, "Ruby?! Oh my 🦋! What ARE you wearing?!")

Those people there, rioting, they looked like the kind of people you saw every day in Dartbridge. Some of them were just ordinary people; some of them looked like the sort of people who probably spent a lot of time going to basket-weaving workshops or worshipping crystals in woodland glades. Point is, the hippies and the townies, *everyone*, had gone nuts. If it had been organized by the school, it would have been what they called a "group activity," which meant you weren't allowed to just stick with your friends, but you had to actually "participate" with the sorts of people you'd really rather *die*—I must stop saying that—than participate with.

We cut back down, onto the hospital road, which was jammed with stopped cars. On the other side of that was the supermarket.

I guess we'd gone too far to turn back, so we went forward.

You know how a supermarket parking lot normally is? Everyone circling around like pizza-eating vultures just to try to park one space closer to the doors? Well, it wasn't like that at all. Cars were parked all over—not neatly in the spaces but jammed in everywhere, none of them moving, no one even packing stuff into them or honking and tooting to get out. Only dead cars, abandoned cars—and car alarms, going on and on.

"Come on," said Simon, dragging me through it.

Up ahead, the supermarket looked nuts. There were a lot of people going in and out of it, but it was the biggest supermarket for miles around, so that wasn't unusual. You didn't really get how bad it was until you got closer. Then you could see the front doors were all smashed in. And I do mean all smashed in—not just the glass in the doors broken or something, but the actual doors were gone. A truck was right inside the shop, smashed into the flower display.

Do I even need to say that there was no one at the registers, no one trying to stop or control anything? No, it was a grab-what-you-can job: people laden with stuff, but lots of mad, crazy, what-do-you-want-that-for? stuff. I saw a guy with a cart full of toilet paper, two women with a cart full of washing detergent, a kid lugging a basketful of ketchup and cake frosting.

Sounds like crazy fun, huh?

Simon and I, we wandered into all this, and it was obvious, right away, that we'd come too late. Somewhere in that shop a dog was barking as we roamed the aisles, realizing how bad it was. Where the fruit and vegetables should have been, it was bare. I mean stripped clean, bare-naked bare, nada. Not even a single bunch of beets left. (Boo hoo.) The dairy section: the milk, the yogurt—all of it gone. He took us to where the bottled water would have been: all the drinks, all the juices, everything, gone. From the looks of it, the booze was also pretty much cleaned out, I noticed. We went to the canned fruit; that was cleaned out too—even the prunes had been taken.

"I can't believe this, I can't believe this," Simon kept muttering.

I could. Inside my mouth it was as dry as when you go to the dentist's and they put that sucky thing in your mouth, so they don't have to work in a pool of spit. Bone dry. When I stared at those empty shelves, it was like they'd put that sucky thing right down in the middle of me and sucked up every last drop of moisture in my body.

We didn't even get to the ice cubes. They would have all been gone anyway. In the freezer section, there was stuff—frozen stuff, melting, thrown all over the floor. Small groups of people were bent inside the freezers, hacking away at the ice, shoveling it into garbage bags that leaked precious water. A woman was on the floor, mopping the water up with kitchen cloths and wringing it out into a bucket; two little kids stood near, sucking on kitchen cloths, each clutching a jumbo-bag of candy, and over them all, tough-looking men stood guard. One had a frothy-mouthed, mad-eyed, barking pit bull…one had a shotgun.

"We'll go somewhere else," said Simon.

He grabbed my hand and started walking me out, fast. From a display of bargain stuff he snatched up a steak and kidney pie, the kind in a can.

"Love these," he said.

I never knew that.

As we walked out, past the crashed car, I pulled away from him and picked up the biggest, most expensive bunch of flowers I could see. Just like I'd never seen Simon buy a canned pie even though he said he loved them, my mom—who totally swooned about flowers—never bought them. Not for herself.

"For Mom," I said.

Before I realized I might have done a very stupid thing, it turned out I might have done a very brilliant thing.

CHAPTER NINE

S imon stared at the bunch of flowers; water dripped from the stems.

"You watch out for me," he said, swapping his shopping bags and the umbrella for the flowers.

He shoved the flowers back into some random bucket. He did the same with other stuff, shifting flowers around so he had a free bucket. I got it then. Without making any kind of a fuss about it, Simon worked around the display, collecting water. Some of the flowers were dead already, sitting in empty buckets; some were wilted, with just a dribble of water left. Some looked pretty perky and fresh. He worked really slowly and slyly, watching what was going on around him, standing back and looking around from time to time, so he just looked like some dumb, confused, scared man, wondering what on earth was going on. Thirsty people, desperate people, walked this way and that, straight past him. When he was done with one bucket, he started on another.

And all the while I had this argument going on in my head, like, *How could he know that water was OK? But it must be OK, or he wouldn't be taking it.*

"You watch out, Ru! You watch out!" he hissed.

I was gasping to drink. *Pull yourself together*, I thought—in Simon's voice.

I don't know what made me do it—too many movies I guess, too many scenes in which people need to make a getaway, fast. Duh, we were going to have to walk for it anyway, but I backed up and looked outside.

Our exit was as clear as it could be; all that was in our way was just people, coming and going. I took my Indiana Jones bird-watching hat off and fanned my face with it. So hot, so thirsty. And then I looked up.

I don't know what made me do that either. I wish I could say I'd learned already how important it is to keep a watch on the sky, but—like using the faucet—it's the kind of thing I forget about a lot more than I should. I looked up…into a sky festering with death.

It was the beginning of a storm sky. The raggedy clouds had pigged out and gotten bloated: cumulus congestus, fat with rain. Below these big guys, little sneaky fractus clouds hung around, probably wondering which side to choose…and, in the distance, but already towering miles into the sky, big momma cumulonimbus calvus, puffing herself up to make an entrance.

She was what I would have called a thundercloud—but actually, she hadn't quite worked herself up enough for that. It's when she goes into bad hair day mode (seriously bouffant, with a streaky, icy flat-top) that you know she's going to lose it big time. Big? By then, she's the tallest thing on Earth: cumulonimbus capillatus, the thundery queen of all clouds.

That's what I know to say now; then, all I saw was: it really looked like it was going to rain.

I went back inside. I was going to tell Simon about the clouds, but—

"Give me the bags!" he shouted.

Other people were shouting too; you could hear it, down where the freezers were. It sounded like a fight breaking out. The dog was going berserk. The men were shouting, women too. A kid screamed.

I gave Simon the bags; he set the buckets inside them.

"Go carefully," he said. "Stay calm."

We picked up the bags, and we walked out, away from the shouting and the screaming. A few steps into the parking lot, Simon looked up at the sky.

"🦋," he said.

I thought he'd say we had to go back inside, but you could hear things were really going crazy in there. For a second, Simon wavered in the grip of a mind melt, then shouted, "Run!"

I thought we were heading for home. I ran, the precious water from my bucket slopping everywhere.

"Ruby!" yelled Simon.

I looked behind and saw him standing at the open door of a car.

"HERE!" he shouted. "COME HERE!" like I was a dog.

I turned and dove for the car, ended up in the driver's seat; from the bag on my lap, stinky water leaked all over my waterproof trousers—which weren't actually waterproof at all. I could see the material darkening, the water just soaking on through. The fight that had gone on inside my own head came screeching out of my mouth, louder than the racket of the alarms:

"*What if it's poisoned?!*"

I looked at Simon, who was glugging from his bucket.

"Aaah!" he shouted and wiped his mouth, as though it was the best thing he'd ever had to drink. "Ruby, I really don't think this water has been changed in days, do you?"

"*But how do you know that?!*"

"Because with everything that's *gone on*," said Simon, shouting very slowly, "I don't think anyone would have thought they needed to go and break into the supermarket and give the flowers some water. In fact, I'm sure of it."

He didn't know that for sure; he couldn't know that. I stared into the bucket in the bag on my lap; it looked worse—so much worse—than pizza, pea, and fish-finger melt-water. AND it stank. AND it was probably teeming with millions of wiggly little space bugs, all waving their tentacles at me, going, "Have a lovely drink, Ruby!" AND I thought I'd go mad with thirst just looking at it, AND I thought Simon had already gone mad. That's what thirst does; it gets to a certain point, and you'll drink anything just to make it stop. You just don't care anymore. That's why people go crazy in deserts and drink sand, thinking it's water, or why shipwrecked sailors stuck in lifeboats crack and glug down buckets of seawater (then go mad and end up bumping off their shipmates to gnaw on their bones). All I could do was stare into that bucket of stinking water thinking, *I JUST WANT TO DRINK.*

"And I feel fine," shouted Simon.

I drank.

Yes, OK, I can say how disgusting that water tasted. Horrible—and also very, very, very good. For just a few moments, the world was wonderful. You see, nothing happened. The whole world—the whole gone-mental world—just carried on around us; people scurrying through the parking lot—but you know what? We were OK. That feeling, that gorgeous feeling when you're thirsty—so thirsty—and you finally get to drink…aaah!

Then… I'd never heard a gun fired, not in real life, but I knew right away that's what it was. There was this massive shattering, crashing sound of glass breaking, followed by another gunshot.

What happened next, it was pretty bad.

People ran from the supermarket, zigzagging through the parking lot, fresh car alarms bursting out all over.

A big fat raindrop fell on the windshield. I watched it, that single, fat, glassy blob of rain; I watched it splat and slide. Then another came and another, and another.

"Lock the doors," said Simon.

I couldn't think how; which button?

"Your side," said Simon. "Your lock."

He reached right over me and hit the lock on my door. SCHTOMP! The doors locked.

The people in the parking lot were screaming, running for cover—running back to the supermarket, where other people were trying to get out. Screams, shouts, gunshots. People running all over.

BLAM! A woman—a little trail of blood running down her face—slammed against the car. She saw us inside; she tried to get in the backseat of the car on Simon's side, a baby seat there.

"Let me in!" she screamed.

"You do not open the doors," shouted Simon, his voice hard and cold.

The woman scooted around the car—

BLAM! Her palms slammed down on my window; her face pressed close—the look on it, the terror, the pleading. She could have been my mom.

"Please!" she screamed at me.

"There's nothing we can do for her," shouted Simon. "Ruby: there's nothing we can do."

All I could do was look at her, tears streaming down my face, mumbling, "I'm so sorry, I'm so sorry, I'm so sorry." Tears streaming down her face: "Please, please, please…"

She howled with rage, right up against the glass, then smashed her fist against the window. She spat at me—at the glass between us—and stumbled away.

"Get in the back," said Simon, grabbing the bucket on my lap and shoving it down next to his. "Get in the back!" he shouted, yanking me up and pushing me through, onto the backseat. "Lie down!"

He squashed down on top of me, the two of us crammed in next to the baby seat.

"Act dead."

That was what he said, "Act dead."

The gunshots went on. The screaming went on. The alarms, on and on and on. You could hear people pushing past the car; a couple times someone yanked on a door handle. It was all I could do to stop myself from screaming out loud when that happened.

"Don't think this gets you out of your studies," Simon bellowed in my ear.

My nose was pressed against the back of the seat. I could feel his breath in my ear. I heard the fear in it, smelled the rotten-egg stink of that water.

I thought he'd gone mad.

"Let's start with the reasons why Britain's empire declined in the twentieth century," he shouted. He jabbed me, hard, his thumb in my rib. "The decline of the empire was caused by…"

I was crying—or trying to. No tears would come.

"The decline of the empire was caused by?" he persisted.

He jabbed me again.

"Things that happened in Britain and things that happened in other places." I sobbed into the seat.

"Other places?"

"Like India!" I wailed.

"What happened in India? Come on! I know you know this, Ru."

"Gandhi," I shouted into the seat.

"Gandhi? Gandhi who? What? How? Why? This is an essay question, not a multiple choice." Jab. "Please, Ruby! Think!"

"The Indian…the National Congress was…founded in 1885…"

We went through it all: Gandhi coming along, Nehru, Mohammed Ali Jinnah. Simon didn't know it like I knew it, but that didn't stop him asking tricky questions, and he knew a lot more about what Churchill and the British government had been up to.

In time, all the people noise stopped. All you could hear were alarms, alarms, alarms…and the rain, drumming down on the roof of the car. *Hammering* down—so loud you could hear it over the rest of the racket. If it had been some old beater, like my dad's, we would have been done for. My dad's car leaked where you wouldn't think a car could leak.

It was best not to think about that.

Eventually, the rain stopped—for a while—but we didn't dare leave the car. Directly above us, the sky was groaning with clouds. Always hard to tell what kind when you're cowering underneath it. The sun managed to poke through a little before it chickened out completely and gave up for the night. The world was soaking wet… and people quiet. The car alarms, they went on.

We climbed back into the front seats. For a moment, we just sat.

This is a thing I learned about alarms. It's sort of based on Henry's crying. If you go on hearing it, tuning in to it, feeling it, you will go nuts. So you have to find a way to tune out, to not hear it. If you can, you put a pillow over your ears and just pretend you're crashed out at a really noisy party—but you've had a great time, right, so you don't mind the noise. If there's no pillow, stuff whatever you can into your ears.

"Is there any tissue or something?" I shouted. Parenty people, even in times of extreme crisis, always have that kind of thing.

The parenty people who'd owned that car did. Simon ransacked the glove compartment and found baby wipes and candy. He handed the baby wipes and candy to me and used his penknife to open the canned pie. He cut his hand doing it.

"Ru, would you like some of this?" he shouted, holding out the soggy, uncooked pie.

"It's OK, thanks," I shouted, even though my stomach was growling. I was stuffing strips of baby wipe into my ears.

"I respect your position on vegetarianism," he shouted.

Huh?! I pulled the baby wipe out of my ears just to be sure I'd heard him right.

"I said I respect your position on vegetarianism," he repeated.

What?! He'd never said that before, not once.

"Thanks," I shouted. I stuffed the baby wipe back into my ear and offered him some. He stuffed some into his ears.

"But, *honey*," he practically screamed, overcompensating for the earplugs.

He'd never said that either, not once. *Honey.*

"I think right now it would really be OK to eat this. I mean, I think it would really be OK. And I, for one, will never mention it again."

I hesitated; I was so hungry…

"Even though you wear leather shoes," he shouted.

Tchuh! For one microsecond, I thought we were teetering on the brink of an old argument. I dunno how I even had the strength left to do it, but I flashed a yee-haa look at him. He was smiling— gently—holding out the pie, streamers of baby wipe hanging from his ears.

"I think all that doesn't matter much right now," he shouted. "If you're hungry, please, eat?"

I peeled off a strip of raw, soggy pastry. It tasted great.

We ate—candy from the glove compartment for dessert—and I told him my noise-survival theory.

It got dark. It got cooler. There were lights on in the hospital, lights on in the supermarket. You just never saw anyone.

"Can we go home now?" I shouted.

Simon leaned over my seat to peer at the sky. Pointless, really, but I'd been doing it too. There were no stars, and the darker it got, the harder it was even to guess how thick, how heavy the cloud was that hid them, i.e., how likely it was that there would be more rain.

"Can't we just at least put the heater on?"

"We'd need the engine on," shouted Simon, peering across me.

"Well, would it be OK to do that?" I shouted.

Simon turned his head and saw the keys.

"Well done, Ru," he sighed.

He turned the key. The dashboard lit up. It looked extremely beautiful.

In the end, Simon decided we couldn't start the engine. The noise would be a risk. The sound, even among the alarms, might attract people, he said. I didn't disagree; if there was any chance that lady might come back...

And we couldn't drive off, could we? We were completely boxed in, stranded in a sea of other stranded cars. Simon said he thought maybe the cars had been left by people trying to get to the hospital that first night, not caring—or not knowing—that it wasn't that kind of hospital. I wished he'd shut up, because of the baby seat in the back of the car. That was a terrible thought... It also freaked me out, thinking how Caspar had been, but I'd seen no blood or anything smeared around the car. Maybe the car had belonged to someone who was just visiting someone, and they'd left the baby at home. Someone visiting someone in a hurry, forgot they'd left their keys in the car, and didn't come back.

So we froze, but we had the radio. And when we realized there was nothing to be heard but what we'd heard before, we had music. That is to say, we listened to *The Carpenters, The Greatest Hits Collection*, Disc One. It was the only CD they had.

In the night, Momma Cumulonimbus finally flipped out. There was a huge thunderstorm, a massive scrap in the sky. I hoped those little blobby micro-bugs were getting a battering, getting zapped by lightning and thrown around all over the place, but they probably loved it.

I won't go on about what it was like that night; you can figure it out for yourself. Add it all up in your head: mother dead + Henry dead + supermarket shoot-out + killer rain pounding down + car alarms blaring on + thunder + lightning + "Top of the World" =

If you don't know that song, "Top of the World," check it out. Play it over and over and over. Enjoy.

CHAPTER TEN

I woke like you wake when you're camping: too early and already too hot. And you haven't slept a wink, and you're all bent-up funny and aching from lying on the crappy, ultra-thin, might-as-well-not-be-there-at-all foam "mattress" thingy through which you could feel every last little hilly grass/weed/thistle clump on the SLOPE Simon said wasn't a slope but which definitely was a slope because you've been rolling down it all night, freezing to death, before you were cooked awake by the burning sun—if you hadn't already been shouted awake by the 🦋 birds singing.

Only that morning it wasn't birds; it was car alarms.

How long—I mean really—HOW LONG do those things go on for?!?!?!

(Oh and you know what else? We had to empty one water bucket into another, so I had one to pee in, in the back of the car. Lovely.)

Simon had gotten the baby seat out, and that's where I'd been lying, "sleeping," on the backseat. If I hadn't been trying to at least pretend to sleep, if I'd been freaking out like I wanted to freak out, I'm pretty sure there would have been more quizzing me on history, so I kept quiet. Somehow I had, finally, fallen asleep, and now I had woken up.

I sat up. Full grump, I admit it. I'm not all that good in the mornings anyway.

"Good-bye to Love" ended and "Top of the World" started over. Simon was just sitting there.

"Morning, Ru," he shouted.

He didn't exactly sound cheerful either. He didn't even turn around. I grunted back; that was definitely all I could manage.

The windows were misted up on the inside. I wiped one with my sleeve.

"It's OK to do that," Simon shouted. "It's just our breath."

That's when I remembered it: *Dew on a damselfly.*

And if it hadn't been OK? Would he have said in time? Everything that was awful and scary flooded back into my head. I looked out the window. The world outside looked dry, more or less. The sky looked blue, more or less. (Only some cirrus fibratus, most likely: fine streaks of cloud, flicked about on high winds—like Queen Cumulonimbus Capillatus had raked her nails across the sky as she stormed out.)

"I think we can go now," he shouted.

He clicked the handle back, then poked his door open with the umbrella. A few droplets of water fell from the door, from the roof. Rain? Dew? Poisoned? No way of knowing. He made us wait and wait—the alarms, now able to get through fully, blaring—watching each drop until he was sure it had stopped.

The parking lot—it wasn't nice. There were a lot of dead people there. Bodies, bloody, lying about all over. As we picked our way through it, you could see what had made that shattering, crashing sound when everything had kicked off: one of the massive supermarket windows was now a pile of glass.

"Ru," he shouted at me, "we could go home now, or we could look and see what's left."

I really, really, really wanted to go home, but I shouted, "OK."

Simon got the bags, in one of them the precious tiny bit of water he'd managed to leave in his bucket, and we picked our way through it all.

I didn't think; I just followed. I could do that because Simon was thinking for me.

At the smashed-in doors of the supermarket, we stood and listened. You couldn't hear anything with the alarms going. What you could see, though—that was terrible.

"Wait here," shouted Simon.

"You can't leave me," I shouted.

You can't leave me, you can't leave me, you can't leave me.

"If anything happens," shouted Simon, "you run straight home. You just run."

So we shopped. Normally, if I got forced to go shopping, I moaned like 🦋. I kind of skulked around the supermarket after Simon and Mom, sighing at all the stuff there was no point even picking up because you knew you wouldn't be allowed to get it. Not even one thing as a treat—and definitely, under no circumstances, any kind of cereal with chocolate in it. I picked up two boxes of chocolatey cereal, one the ordinary kind, one with teeny marshmallows. I got those jam-filled things you can shove in a toaster too.

Simon wasn't watching me…but I saw him. He was rummaging in dead people's shopping carts.

"Look for water, Ru! Look for stuff to drink!" he shouted, waving a carton of soy milk at me.

Yes, it was a shopping trip like no other. Stepping over bodies to get stuff kind of puts you off a little.

In the freezer section, the pit bull lay quietly by its master's body. Maybe that man had been shot… And those kids, with the bags of candy, they looked like they must have run out into the rain, then run back to him. Their mom looked the same.

The dog didn't even lift its head but let out a little sad growl when it saw me.

"Come away," said Simon.

There was only the bakery section left to visit. The bread was as much use as bread from a toy set: rock hard. You could have killed someone with one of those baguettes.

While I was loading up on chocolate flapjacks—hey, they're practically healthy, aren't they? All those oats—Simon made the discovery that ended our shopping trip. Like all good customers, we had kept to the parts of the shop that we were supposed to, but Simon pulled open the doors that led to the storage part.

It was all dark. He flicked on the lights: *flick, flick, flick, flick.* Enough lights to see it had been trashed, cleaned out. There was even a truck still parked in there. Someone, somewhere inside that warehouse, groaned.

"You 🦋!" snarled a man's voice. He sounded done-in, though, weak and broken...then screechy: "You 🦋🦋!"

"Let's go, Ru," said Simon, flicking off the lights. *Flick, flick, flick—*

There was this clickety-slide-click sound that you only ever hear in movies.

Just like I'd never heard a gun fired from a distance but knew right away what it was, I double-knew what a gun sounded like getting ready to be fired.

And so, again, we ran.

On the way out, without even pausing, I snatched up the best bunch of flowers I could see. Simon, without even pausing, grabbed up our bucket with the measly bit of water left in it.

I wouldn't want you to think this took any more than a trillionth of a second. There was no discussion. We grabbed and ran. We so ran.

Simon said later it had been a professional job. That's what he kept saying, that the whole supermarket thing had been a professional job, how ordinary people like us would have left something for other people. I didn't say what my entire body, kicking up for water, water, water, something, anything, to drink wanted to say: NO I WOULDN'T. But he might have been right. There was the truck in the entrance, the truck in the storage area, and, right where we ran out, weren't the flowerbeds flattened, the mud churned up, cars pushed out of the way? Before people trundled out with carts full of toilet paper, before people had started hacking the ice out of the freezers, you kind of knew someone else had come and taken the good stuff…because I never saw a single person leave that supermarket with even a single bottle of water. I never even saw anyone leave with a cart full of beets and prunes, not even a plastic bag full of them. I never saw anyone leave that supermarket with anything much you could drink. It was gone. It was all gone.

We ran along the whole of Jubilee Road, all of it jammed with cars, alarms bleating and honking, but there wasn't a single person in sight. No one alive, anyway.

There's a thing I want to say—once and not say it again. I want to say it just in case you think I didn't care or even that—*how?!*—I didn't notice. There were bodies—human bodies—everywhere. I don't even want to talk about them again, how there's nowhere you can go without seeing them. So they get to be like lampposts or doors or trees; they get to be THINGS that are just there, that you wouldn't even bother mentioning (unless they get in your way or are especially important). And that sounds awful, and I wouldn't ever want anyone to think that about my mom, but also…that is how it is. There are bodies everywhere, and they are just there. They're just there.

They're the dead people. You breathe. You still breathe.

As we turned into the High Street—walking now, gasping—there was this young guy standing outside The Sun and Moon with a pint of beer in his hand. The kind of guy me and Lee would have gone all giggly about (before I was in love with Caspar). There was music— some rock thing so loud you could hear it over the alarms—coming from the open door of the pub behind him. He raised his glass at us: a toast.

Simon looked at me, a look that asked, "OK if I talk to him?" I shrugged. I shrugged when really I wanted to say, *What are you, crazy?! You want to stop and talk to this guy?! Are you really seriously crazy?!* LET'S JUST GO HOME!

But this guy…we were close enough to see that he was crying.

"All right, buddy?" called Simon in this "guy" voice he used to talk to contractors, etc., like he was one of them and not an accountant who liked bird-watching.

"Not really, buddy," called the guy.

There sort of wasn't anything else to say.

"Don't bother with the supermarket, eh?" said Simon. "It's bad there."

That guy, he nodded.

"We'd best be off, then," said Simon.

"Come down for a pint later?" said the guy. "If you fancy it. I'll still be here."

"Thanks, buddy," said Simon.

The guy raised his glass to me and winked—not a letch-y wink, like guys like that normally did, but a sweet one, like Grandpa Hollis used to do.

"Wait!" he called as we walked away. He sat his pint glass down on the doorstep and disappeared into the pub.

I looked at Simon; he shrugged. *Uneasily,* that's what I'd say—he shrugged uneasily.

Do you see what had happened already? Where you'd just say

hello to another person, or maybe chat with them a little, this fear thing came. Not even a specific "you've got a gun" or even a "what if this person is sick?" fear—and anyway that guy definitely wasn't sick and probably, surely, couldn't have been going to get a gun… It's a "what is this person going to do?" fear.

That was the first time I felt it too: I felt *uneasy*.

The guy came back out with a bunch of little bottles of cola.

"For your girl," he said, loading them into Simon's bag.

His mouth, it twisted up—but tight, so tight, like he was tying a knot in his lips to stop himself from crying.

"I had a girl," the guy managed to say. "Just…a little girl."

Simon took my hand. He gave it a squeeze. We walked away.

"Don't forget that pint, then," the guy called to Simon, his voice gone all sobby now. "Later. If you fancy it. Or another time."

The High Street was a tad trashed—and it was completely deserted. We avoided it anyway, turning into South Street, going home the way we had meant to come.

A crow was pecking at the body we'd passed on our way to the market, at his belly, where some other creature—a fox, maybe?— must have stopped for a nibble. The crow flew off as we came close.

"At least the birds are OK," said Simon.

I would have gotten pissed, like—how could he say such a thing? But it was true: we hadn't seen a sick or dead animal anywhere. It was only people that had been destroyed.

"Uh-huh," I said.

The sightless eye sockets of the man who was now bird food stared back at me.

And I remembered: he had officially been my fourth dead body. Less than twenty-four hours later, I had lost count.

My first dead body, Mrs. Fitch, was waiting for us in the front yard. Flies buzzed.

"🦋!" said Simon, gagging as he pushed me past her and unlocked the front door.

The second he opened the door, you noticed it. It wasn't our pee buckets—they smelled a little but we'd put bleach in. It was another kind of smell altogether—the beginning of a stench I know so very well now, but had never smelt until then. It is strangely sweet. Strangely...almost spicy. That makes it sound nice, but it's not. It was like Mrs. Fitch but stronger. Mrs. Fitch and no fresh air.

We bustled into the kitchen, shutting the door behind us, dumped our haul down on the table, opened the garden door and all the windows.

I stood there, holding the flowers.

"Ruby, I don't think you should go in that room," said Simon.

That was good; I didn't want to go in that room.

"I'll just put them outside the bedroom door," I said.

I didn't move.

"You don't have to go up there if you don't want to," said Simon. "I could do it."

"No," I said. "I want to."

I didn't move.

"Do you want me to come with you?" he asked.

I nodded. I felt like I'd felt when we were going to cross the High Street, like a small person.

I followed him up the stairs with the flowers. The smell got worse every step you took. I laid them down by the door, and we stood there, mouth breathing.

This random thought about a kid I knew, a kid in school we laughed at a little for doing that, drifted into my head. Then came this other thought that really me and Simon must look like we were shocked, that we had our mouths open in amazement, which was about right. Then came another thought that maybe this was what the world was like for that kid, shocking. Or that it all stank or something. And I felt bad for having these thoughts, all these wrong, random thoughts, but they came into my head because I wanted to think them more than I wanted to think about my mother. I did not want to think about my mother.

"Should we pray or something?" I asked.

There was a hundred-year pause before he replied.

"I can't," said Simon.

There was another hundred-year pause. In it, I tried to think something nice about God or heaven…but my brain felt as numb as my heart.

"I can't either," I said.

We went back down to the kitchen. We got all the food out, and we actually did eat a little, picking at the kind of junk that normally tastes delicious, the kind you'd cram your face with until you felt sick…but I already felt sick, and that food tasted of nothing but thirst and death.

"We can't bury them," said Simon suddenly, his face grim.

We hadn't even been talking about them, but we had been thinking about them. That is to say, I wasn't—but I was, if you know what I mean. Every thought I had—like why wouldn't the kitchen faucet stop dripping, like would I ever be able to have a shower again, like how long would the supplies of baby wipes last, like whether I'd end up with crusty dreadlocks from not washing my hair—every non-them thought I had was about *them*.

"I would like to," said Simon, "but I don't know whether it's safe—you know, to dig."

I cried then. Sitting at that table, I cried.

"I'm so sorry, Ru. I'm so sorry," Simon kept saying.

"It's not your fault," I said. I'd never said that before, not once.

CHAPTER ELEVEN

I knew what was coming.

Basically, I never wanted to leave the house again. I wanted to curl up, eat junk, and wait for the whole thing to be not happening—so I didn't say a word about it: not about what had happened, not about what would happen. Not about what we should do, about what we could do, about what on earth we were supposed to do.

After I'd cried in the kitchen, we went into the living room and closed the curtains and slept for a while. Or I did. When I woke up, Simon was still sitting there in the same place, and it was still the same day, and it was still the morning, not even the afternoon.

As soon as I woke, my hands twitched and—I swear—all on their own, they reached for the laptop.

"I checked everything again," said Simon, shaking his head.

I put the laptop down. This time, the pause was a thousand years long.

In it, I felt as if Simon was watching me and waiting for me to say something, and I knew if I did, it would be the start of talking about things I didn't even want to think about. I could have gone on like that for days and weeks, ignoring even the smell—the smell that you noticed even though you'd think you might get used to it and not notice it anymore. I could do that, be the Ostrich Queen of the Universe about things I didn't want to think about. Studying, for example. Only where normally it'd be Simon or my mom that finally brought stuff up, this time my own body was going to have something to say about it, because we were going to run out of stuff to drink.

The thing is, when we emptied out our haul on the kitchen table, there was nothing to drink. Well, there were the colas and one carton of soy milk. And the last festering, grimy inch of water in the flower bucket, which I would rather die than—I won't say that again. Ever. Unless I truly mean it.

I shuffled out to the kitchen and got myself a cola. The last cola. I got my toothbrush and the toothpaste from the den and shuffled back into the living room.

Simon shook his head a little, pursing his lips at me, as I cleaned my teeth with little precious sips of cola, spitting out into the empty bottle that the cola before the last cola had been in. In the old days (the day before the day before the day before yesterday), that head shake would have been the start of a yee-haa and a half. Yes, well, maybe I'd care about my teeth a little more if I didn't have to wear these train tracks and if you'd just let me get them whitened, etc.

Instead, I just smiled back a tiny bit—nervously. I knew what was coming.

Well, not the specific thing that Simon was about to say, which was hideous and appalling.

"Did you know," he said, "that you can drink your own urine?"

"That's disgusting," I said, spitting toothpaste froth into the empty cola bottle.

"No really," he said, "you can. It's just not recommended."

I wondered how come Simon would know such a thing, but pee drinking is probably exactly the kind of thing bird-watchers know about, in case they get thirsty on a long stakeout in a bird blind. "The Royal Society for the Protection of Birds does not recommend…"

I gulped my cola. I caved. "What are we going to do?" I asked.

"What do you think we need to do?"

"Get water," I said, because I had no choice. It sounded so simple.

"Yes," said Simon. "Where from?"

It felt like a massive trick question. Also not. It felt like…like he was nudging me toward what I didn't want to do more than anything, which was to think.

"I dunno," I said, i.e., I don't want to think about it.

Simon, he just looked at me, waiting.

"I don't wanna go to another supermarket," I said.

He nodded.

"And anyway, there's no point. Because all the good stuff is gone anyway."

I stopped there. I drained my bottle of cola. I couldn't help myself; I burped.

"Pardon me," I said.

"I do, Ruby. Always, for everything," said Simon.

The room filled with a sticky candy ooze of emotion. There was another of those pauses we'd been having; this one was shorter— maybe only fifty years—but it was long enough for me to think *NO NO NO NO NO NO. PLEASE don't start saying stuff because I NO NO NO NO NO NO cannot bear to be hearing stuff.* It was like when your grandma has had too much sherry and goes on about how much she loves you (and just so hopes you'll be OK because it was a terrible thing, your parents splitting up), or when your dad has had too much wine and goes on about how much he loves you (and never would have abandoned you, but your mother had made her decision) (conveniently forgetting to mention that it was the discovery of HIS secret "love child," brother-brat Dan…beloved

that admittedly might have kind of forced her to make that decision) or when your best friend gets trashed and wants to talk deep
and meaningful (and just so isn't sure that Caspar is really right for
you), and they get all gushy and you just want...to not be deep and
meaningful. NO NO NO NO NO.

"Well...eventually," said Simon, and grinned. "So what are we
gonna do, Ru?"

"Get stuff from other places," I said.

"Like?" said Simon.

Stop it, just stop it, I thought.

"Like other people's houses," I said.

I burped again, deliberately. It was all I had left—to show I
wasn't freaked and to keep the NO NO NO NO NO wall of shut-
up strong.

There, I've said what you wanted me to say, I thought...but for
half of a half of a second, I thought he was going to say no, that
he'd come up with another plan...that although he, like me, hadn't
seen any of our neighbors since Day One, he was sure they were
all fine and there was no way we could just go breaking into other
people's homes.

"Good thinking, Ru," he said. "I think that's the best thing we
can do right now."

So that was it, then. Without actually saying the words, we had
both admitted—what? That a lot of people, and maybe even most
people, must be dead. Because all our neighbors were...and why
should our road be any different to any other road? And we'd admitted that we were desperate and didn't know what else to do, without
actually saying that either.

"But we'll knock first, right?" I asked, feeling utter dread about
the whole thing. "You know, because maybe there'll be people
at home..."

"Yes, of course," said Simon, and he went off to get the crowbar from the shed.

For what happened next, I blame myself.

Simon did say I could stay home, and I did think about it. "You can't leave me," I said.

We got geared up all over again (about which I didn't say a word, even though it was blazing hot and sunny). We stepped out into a kind of silence. That was the most shocking thing. While we'd been inside the house, the car alarms had been stopping, one by one. To begin with, there'd just been this yowling chorus of them—most of them far from us but carrying, with the air so still and no wind to beat them back or other noise to fight them. When they started dying off, it got so you could hear the individual ones: a fast, high-pitched spaceship *weep-weep-weep-weep-weep*; a deep *honk-honk-honk* that came in a pattern, stopping then starting again; a *woop-woop, woop-woop* that sounded like an American police car. I got to know a whole bunch of those alarms, all of them different—and all of them trying to remind you of what had happened, and that there was a supermarket and a parking lot and a town full of dead bodies.

It's not like you ever give any thought to what a town sounds like—you don't; why would you?—until it stops sounding like a town. When we went outside, there was no people noise whatsoever. There was just birdsong, loud like you never hear it.

A second later, when the gate clanked shut, there was another sound, which was dogs barking and whining. Dogs barking and whining inside houses. I heard the howling of the terrier that lived at the end of the terrace; I could see Mrs. Wallis's grumpy shih tzus, Mimi and Clarence, at the living-room window, a low line of nose slime smeared on the glass where they had been running back and forth next to the windowsill, yapping. Her Siamese cat was upstairs, calmly watching us from the bedroom window. (She was called Ruby, which freaked me out when she went AWOL at night and Mrs. Wallis wandered up and down the street going, "Ruuuu-by! Ruuuu-by!") You couldn't see Whitby, the golden retriever at the corner house, but you could hear his big boomy bark somewhere inside.

What you could not hear—or see—were any of their owners.

The part of me that knew their owners were dead wanted to say to Simon, "Stop, let's rescue the poor pets!" But I wanted to believe those people were still alive, that even if they weren't there right now, they'd come home and be really upset if their pets were gone, so I said nothing.

We walked on, backpacks on our backs. I felt like a criminal, and we hadn't even done anything yet. I said I didn't want to go in our neighbors' houses; I didn't want to go in any house that belonged to anyone I knew, not even people I didn't *know* know, but just knew from seeing them about. That pretty much ruled out the whole of our road. There were other houses we could go to, down at the town end of our road, but I didn't want to go there. I didn't want to go anywhere close to the shops, where there might be other people around—people going crazy, people with guns. So we went the other way.

Simon stopped outside a house toward the end of our road.

I shook my head. "Not this one," I said.

I didn't know the people there at all, but I could picture them: this un-Dartbridge-like couple with stylish suits, shiny cars, and no kids. So we headed off our road, up another road. He stopped outside the next house. I didn't know who lived there. There was no car outside; no dog barked, no cat watched. I'd run out of reasons to say no.

We went up to the front door. Simon knocked.

We stood for a while, the afternoon heat baking us. Simon knocked again. No one came.

Simon got the crowbar out of his backpack, put on a pair of super-tough gardening gloves.

"Can't we just say something first?" I whispered. I was so worried there would be someone in that house. Someone alive. Or dying but alive. "I mean, they might be in. They might just be scared."

"OK, Ru," said Simon.

He bent his head down, lifted the letterbox, and shouted.

"*Hello?*"

When there was no answer, he gripped the crowbar.

"Once more?" I said.

Simon bent his head down to the letterbox and opened it. He peered in.

"*Hello?!* We're neighbors!" he called.

No reply.

He looked at me; I nodded. He smashed the glass in the door.

That smash—it was so loud. It felt like the whole of Dartbridge would hear it.

"If someone comes," he said, "you run home."

It seemed a little late to be saying that kind of stuff, but maybe that smash had freaked him too. It felt like you could still hear it, echoing across the whole town.

He reached his hand in and tried to open the door. He couldn't.

I'd been learning a lot of stuff about Simon, how clever he was; what he wasn't clever at, at all, was breaking into houses.

"We'll go around the back," he said.

Really, that was what we should have tried first. We went around to the side of the house. We tried the back door—it was locked, so we peered in through the kitchen window.

It was easy. He smashed it, he opened it, and he climbed in.

I hated that, him being in there and me being outside. If something happened to either of us...

I tried not to think about that. Without being told to, I kept watch while Simon ransacked.

He handed me a can of fruit salad and a bag of ice cubes. At this rate, we'd have to break into about fifty houses just to get through a single day. And if we ever wanted to do something hygienic— like get enough water to actually ever wash again—we'd probably have to break into the whole of Dartbridge. I was just about coping with baby wipes, but although something told me Simon wouldn't consider it a priority, I was dangerously close to running out of that spray-in dry shampoo stuff. I'd actually had to move on to the blonde glittery stuff, which was strictly reserved for nights out because if I wore it in the daytime it looked kind of... "You look like you've got dandruff," was what Dan said, doing pantomime choking after I'd sprayed it. Brat. (And I probably wouldn't have had to use it in the first place if my mom would actually let me dye my hair.) (And which I suspected she would have caved on if Simon hadn't gone and agreed with her the first time she said no.)

Thinking about all that made me completely depressed. In every way.

"Shouldn't we leave a note or something?" I asked.

"No," said Simon, climbing back through the window.

I think I kind of glared at him. It could have turned into a fight, but, honestly, I was too depressed to bother.

"Ru," he said. "I know this feels awful, what we're doing now, but it's what we have to do. I don't think these people are coming home. I think a lot of people are dead, Ru."

There: it had been said.

♦♦♦

The next house was more difficult but had much better pickings. It wasn't more difficult to get into—they'd left the back door open—but…it smelled like our house smelled: sweet and spicy. Thing is, what was in the fridge and the cupboards was so good, you didn't even care: juice, soy milk, sparkling water, and *vino collapso supremo*, said Simon, stuffing a fancy-looking bottle of wine into his backpack as I glugged down juice.

The third house and the fourth? I got over myself. Yes, we still knocked and shouted, but you kind of knew no one would come. And though I felt that dread about what we would find (dead people), I sort of also felt this weird thrill thing, this weird hungry energy to get stuff—the buzz when you find something, the triumph as our backpacks filled up.

At the fifth house, it wasn't so good. The TV was still on, for a start; the same stay-home, remain-calm broadcast playing. That was freaky. We had to shoo the cat out from the kitchen, from where it was… The cat seemed absolutely fine, so I guess nibbling on that body on the floor hadn't hurt it a bit. We didn't take stuff from there. We just left.

How stupid we were. How stupid I was. You need to just take stuff, whatever you can get. People who are dead are dead; they don't care… Maybe, even, they'd want you to take it. That's what I'd want: take it and live. And good 🦋 luck.

We stepped outside into the lovely warm evening. I felt sick—yes—and I felt something else. I felt angry.

"Let's go there," I said, pointing at a big house up on the hill.

We had enough stuff, really; there was no need.

"Well, I suppose we might as well," said Simon. "Unless you'd rather—"

"No!" I said. "I'm fine."

I assumed Simon was going to say "Unless you'd rather go

home—" but maybe he wasn't. Maybe he was going to say, "Unless you'd rather wait, just sit here in the sun for a moment, listening to the birds sing, and then we'll go home" or, "Unless you'd rather go let Whitby, Mimi, Clarence, and that terrier out." But Simon, who always told me what was what and what I had to do, or else droned on at me until I was forced to say it for myself, did not, on this occasion, this one occasion, tell me what I had to do.

"OK," he said.

I don't know why he said that. Maybe he'd gotten into the weird thrill of it too—I sort of felt like he had—or maybe he was thinking that we should just get as much stuff as we could while we could. I don't know.

The big house was detached, no cars around. No dogs barking. I had no clue who lived there, but they must have been rich. It wasn't just because it was a big house—I've got friends, like Zak, who live in big houses and they're as scruffy as our little one—it was the way it was: crisp. You know, all primped and prim and proper. A house without a hair out of place.

We crunched up the drive. We rang the doorbell. They didn't have a normal ding-dong battery-type doorbell—they had a *bell* bell. A real bell, hanging outside the door. We clanked on that; then we knocked. What we didn't do was call through the door. We didn't say, "*Hello?* We're neighbors!"

It was the first house we had come to where the front door was open. We went inside.

The smell was there to greet us. So was a cat, a little tabby. It came running up behind us from the garden. It didn't even hesitate; it just purred around us, like we were its owners, come home to feed it. We stepped inside the house, and Simon closed the living-room door—but not before I saw… There was a body in the den with a sheet over it.

We crept through into the kitchen.

It was a super-bonanza. There was a walk-in pantry. Inside it: tons and tons of stuff.

They must have been at the supermarket or somewhere like that, because there were boxed packs of water bottles, still plastic wrapped. Juice, long-life milk, soda water, tonic water. Tons of it. I felt the thirst kick right back in at the sight of it, and I swear I could have drunk every last drop. I tell you: looting, fear, rage, and grief make you mad with thirst.

"Bingo," said Simon.

As he loaded up our backpacks and every other bag he could find, I fed the cat. I found the cat food under the sink; I got a plate and dumped the whole can of food onto it. I mashed it up a little with a fork. I set it down on the floor, and the cat scoffed.

That's what I remember: the cat scoffing and me thinking I'd done a good deed. Then thinking the cat might be as thirsty as me.

There was a bottle of water on the table and glasses. I picked up the bottle. I unscrewed the lid; it had been opened already. And then I thought, *Yeurch*.

I didn't think the water might be bad, that wasn't what I thought at all. I just thought that the bottle of water had once belonged to that dead person, and it creeped me out.

It was a half of a half of a half of a second; that's all it took. I put the bottle down; Simon snatched it up. He'd just hoisted his backpack onto his back. He snatched up that bottle and glugged the water down.

"Let's go," he said.

He stared at me. I stared back—like he knew; like we both knew. Instantly.

And then he sort of grimaced.

A trickle of blood ran down from the corner of his mouth.

"Ruby," he said. "I need to go home now. I need to go home to Becky and Henry."

He turned and walked out to the front door; he steadied himself on it. He let out a roar and propelled himself off, out, down the drive, toward home. He went like…like I've seen marathon runners go, when you can see their whole body yelling *stop, stop, stop* but they're just gonna get to that finish line.

I dived back into that kitchen to grab my backpack. I think a part of me thought he would be OK, so we'd need all that water and stuff that we'd worked so hard to get. I grabbed the bag. I looked up. There was someone standing there.

A rich-looking man. Gray haired. Primped and prim and proper, like his house. Some weird look that was almost like a slow, astonished smile creeping onto his face at the sight of me—and then he looked at that bottle and that weird look curled up into a miserable frown and turned to stone. Gargoyle face.

You 🦋. I got it; even right at that moment, I got it. He had known the water in that bottle was bad. He had put it there. It had been a trap.

I plunged out of that house and ran after Simon.

At the end of the drive, I looked back; that man was on the doorstep, the cat in his arms.

💧💧

I followed Simon home. I followed him because whenever I tried to get close, whenever I called out to him, he kept waving me back, to keep me behind him, and I was too scared to disobey. I followed him, whimpering with fright like a dumb dog. I kept looking behind, but the gray-haired man didn't come. Simon cried out loud; he spat blood, he choked up blood, he threw up blood as he went. Halfway along, he stopped, dumped his backpack, pulled out the bottle of fancy wine, and smashed it open on a wall. He swigged from it.

Glass! I thought. *But there'll be glass!*

He raised the bottle to the sky, roared, then flung that bottle against the wall so it smashed into a million pieces, then he staggered on; I heaved his backpack up...then ditched it—the weight was just too much to bear.

He got to the house; he got up the stairs; he got to my mom and Henry.

I stood outside their bedroom door. That bunch of flowers I'd left outside, they were wilting, dying. Simon howling in agony. I opened the door. The smell punched me in the heart.

"GET OUT!" spluttered Simon.

I won't ever forget seeing him like that. At least I didn't have to see my mom and Henry too. Simon had covered them with a sheet.

I closed the door. I sat outside. The fright in me bit so hard in my guts that I felt I could puke too.

"Ru," he called, his voice all twisty with pain. "Help me. Get tablets. Get painkillers—get whatever you can."

I had instructions. I could do something. But tablets? All we had in the house since my mom had thrown the acetaminophen to Mrs. Fitch was indigestion stuff, hay fever stuff, and Henry's teething stuff. I knew; I'd looked when I still believed what the broadcasts said about acetaminophen.

I went downstairs; I went out the back door. I climbed over the fence that separated the Fitches' tidy garden from our messy paradise.

The back door was open. I went in. The TV was on, loud, filling the house with advice that was too late for the Fitches. I went through the stink, up to the bathroom. Unfortunately, Mr. Fitch was in there. He was the stink. I had to step right around him, thinking that if I touched him, I'd die right there with him in their horrible green bathroom. I yanked open the medicine cabinet, and I looted it. There was a lot of stuff in there; stuff I knew—acetaminophen, aspirin—stuff I didn't. Stuff prescribed for Mr. Fitch, who had a bad heart; stuff prescribed for Mrs. Fitch, who got worried about Mr. Fitch's bad heart. And a small bottle of brandy, which she told me and my mom she took a sip of every night.

"For medicinal purposes," she said. "Just a drop, before you clean your teeth."

("But she doesn't have any teeth!" I whispered to my mom. And my mom stepped on my toe to shut me up.)

I took all of it; Simon would know what was what.

◆◆◆

I knocked on the door. He didn't answer. I opened the door. His eyes rolled open as I dumped my offerings on the bed. He waved me off. He clawed open boxes; he popped pills, swallowed, slugged brandy. More and more and more pills. Simon wasn't going to get better. I wasn't helping him to live; I was helping him to die.

"Go away, Ru," he managed to say. "Go find help."

I thought he was going to say something else, about what I should do.

"I love you," he said.

CHAPTER TWELVE

Simon fell asleep, and he didn't wake up.

I sat in the kitchen, and I glued together that stupid, hideous pottery vase thing he'd made. My hands were shaking so much it kept going wrong. When it finally stayed together, I put it in the sink.

Since that first morning, when I'd gone to fill the kettle and Simon had told me to stop, he'd told me the same thing most times we were in that kitchen, because most times I forgot.

I forgot. I turned the faucet on. Water gushed into the vase for too many seconds before my brain screamed and my hands did something about it. I turned off the faucet and backed away from the sink. The tap dripped into the vase.

Disgusting. Disgusting, vile, filthy—I grabbed my rubber gloves and I threw every last container full of water out the kitchen window. I didn't empty them out; I threw them out—pots and pans and everything. I poured the last of the bleach all over the floor— but I could not bring myself to throw away that vase. I emptied it and filled it up with a bottle of tonic water from my bag. I carried it up the stairs. I put it down and put the flowers in it, willing them to live.

"Simon?" I called, standing outside their bedroom door. "Simon?"

There was no reply. From the vase, the dark ooze of a leak spread across the floorboards, and I stared at it, wondering how many of those disgusting little things were crawling about in it.

The panic I felt, it was the worst kind of panic. *Blind panic*, that's what they call it, when you stop thinking completely. I had never, ever felt so alone and so frightened in my whole life. My brain had no say at all in what happened next, which was probably the stupidest thing I've ever done—apart from the thing I'd just done, filling the vase with water, and the thing after the thing that happened next.

I couldn't stay in the house another second.

I got my bike from the shed, and I set out for Zak's. I had no water. I had no waterproof gear. I had no "Indiana Jones goes bird-watching" hat... I didn't even have a 🦋 umbrella. Ha ha.

I never normally biked anywhere if I could help it. Leonie and me, we'd biked over to Zak's once, the summer before, and it had nearly killed us. The plan was we'd bike back, but Zak's mom ended up taking us home, the bikes in the back of the station wagon. Simon and my mom didn't see her drop me off and thought I'd biked back...and I didn't set them straight; for weeks I moaned on about how exhausted I was so I could get rides to other places. And after that I moaned on about how dangerous it was. That part was completely true. Those Devon lanes, they look so lovely, but some serious crazies drive along them—and with those high banks and hedges, there's nowhere to get out of the way if you're on a bike.

That day, that evening, it was not a problem. I didn't see or hear a single soul. Not one car passed me. I guess if you actually liked biking, it would have been lovely: a beautiful summer's evening ride in the country. I didn't really notice that, same way as this time I didn't really notice the hills me and Lee had had to get off and walk up (moaning). I didn't really notice anything until I got to Zak's and saw the station wagon wasn't there. The little zippy car wasn't there either. What was there was Zak's dad. It looked as if he had been there for a long time. Like maybe he had coming running out after the car that night. Best not to think about it, best not to look. Poor Barnaby.

I guess you know what's coming next. I guess you can guess it. My darling Lee and most of my other friends were in the kitchen, but not how I had pictured them.

It looked as though most of them had died the way Simon had died. The cups of tea—half-drunk, festering, spilled—were still on the table. The coffee never did get made. Flies that weren't busy on my friends checked out the toast, the butter, and the jam.

💧💧💧

I remembered something Simon had said—or rather something he had not said. I'd questioned the thing about the tap water, you see. "Yes, but…" They didn't say anything about that on the TV, but Simon had said he thought it was an obvious risk. How could it be safe? I felt terrible, thinking there must be tons and tons of people like me, who wouldn't have even thought about it, people who didn't have a Simon to think for them. But I wasn't even worried about my friends; I told Simon we'd drunk water from the tap that night.

"And it was fine!" I'd said.

And Simon didn't say anything. I guess he knew.

You didn't have to be some kind of detective to work it out. Those glasses of water we'd drunk that night, the water I'd scrubbed my face with, those must have been the last drops of good water in the pipes. What we had filled the kettle with would kill us.

And later, when I thought about it, it taught me another thing: this space thing, you can't kill it by boiling it.

The radio was still on, telling my dead friends to stay home and remain calm.

If, that night, instead of going live to here and live to there, and "Ooo! Look who we've got in the studio!" if, instead of guessing and going on about other things, they had just said DON'T DRINK ANY WATER (AND, BY THE WAY, IT *IS* CONTAGIOUS), maybe my friends, maybe a whole load of other people, would still be alive. If Simon had thought of it, I couldn't understand why the government or the TV and radio people or whoever hadn't. If they'd just said that, even if they weren't sure. If.

I turned the radio off; I could have smashed it.

"Lee?" I said quietly, standing as still as she lay.

It wasn't like she was covered in blood or anything. There were just flies, buzzing. Other than that, Lee—my sweet, darling Leonie Lee—looked like…like maybe she was just messing around. Like we'd done tons of times when we were little. "Pretending to be dead." Like any second, she'd just crack up and lose it and laugh.

"Lee, please get up," I said, waiting for the smile to erupt on her sunken cheeks, for her to burst out laughing.

She didn't. Lee didn't smile. I was never going to see Lee's smile again.

I howled.

Still howling, sucking in air like a person with an asthma attack gasps it, I made myself look. I made myself check for everyone. I made myself see…what I had missed…just like you'd want to know about a party you'd had to leave.

You would never, ever have wanted to know about this. This'd be a thing you'd have been glad to miss.

Zak and Ronnie, they'd made it back upstairs. There was dried gore all over the keyboard, so it seemed like someone—Ronnie, for sure—had got back on the computer, still trying to look for answers where he always looked for answers, on the Web. And then? They were curled up on the bed together.

I found bodies all over that house. I found everyone...except Saskia. I checked in every room again. I called her name. I went outside and called—I could hardly bear to look at the hot tub, to think about me and Caspar, and how we had kissed...on a beautiful evening just like this and so totally not at all like this. On a beautiful evening when it looked like my life was finally going to be wonderful.

I wandered into the barn. There was all our stuff. My bag. My clothes. My makeup. My stupid cell phone, battery dead.

I gathered up everyone else's phones too. I had this idea that people would call to speak to my friends—mothers, fathers, aunties, uncles, brothers, sisters, cousins, other friends—and that it was somehow my duty to tell all those people that all my friends were dead. Like those people—mothers, fathers, aunties, uncles, brothers, sisters, cousins, other friends—would still be alive to tell that to.

There was only one person whose death I wasn't going to have to explain to anybody: Saskia. Her stuff wasn't in the barn. Her stuff had gone.

When I went back through the kitchen, I saw Caspar's phone and MP3 player on the floor next to his jeans. I took them too. And then I did what really was the most stupid of stupidest things I have ever done.

I biked home.

Hardly any distance from the house, I realized I was dying of thirst—and it felt like I really was. What I had seen at Zak's, it was so dreadful, so stomach-churningly sick-making in every way, that I hadn't thought to look for anything to drink. So, so stupid. I'd had nothing but some juice and a few ice cubes; I'd biked miles on a boiling hot evening, and now I had yet more miles to bike on a boiling hot night—which was the other stupid part of the stupidest thing: you never travel when you can't see the sky. Even when there are stars out—and there were—you can't see what kind of clouds are creeping up at night—and there were clouds creeping up. The sky, the night, the *everything* closing in on me.

I could have gone to other houses; there were houses, some with lights on. That didn't mean much anymore. From our kitchen window, we'd seen lights on all over; it didn't mean people were alive…and even if they were, there was no telling what they might do.

Pain throbbed in my head; my tongue bumped around in my mouth. I remembered the thing Simon had said, about drinking your own pee…and I remembered another thing he had said once, a long time ago when I was just a little kid. We were on a walk, and I was moaning about being thirsty—like about five minutes after we'd set off, probably. What was unusual was we didn't have the ten tons of stuff Simon normally took. (I can hear my mom now: "Do we really need to take all that?" and Simon would say, "Well, I'm the one that's carrying it." He was our Sherpa Tenzing. Whenever you wanted something, Simon had it.) Only on that day, he didn't. It wasn't a *planned* walk with maps and stuff; it was a stop-off from a country pub lunch—at which I'd begged for a cola and been given lemonade, like that was somehow better for you. That kind of thing happened a lot.

"Ru," Simon said to me. "I'll show you an old Sioux Indian technique."

Probably it wasn't an old Sioux Indian thing at all. Probably it was a bird-watcher's survival thing. But I don't think it was something Simon made up. Simon didn't make things up.

"You find yourself a pebble," Simon said, picking one off the ground and rubbing it clean on his trousers, "and you suck it."

He popped the pebble in his mouth.

"It stimulates your production of saliva," he said, rolling the pebble around in his mouth, "and makes you feel less thirsty."

I grabbed the nearest pebble.

"Stop it!" said my mom. "Don't teach her that! That could be dirty, Ruby. You might choke! What you need to do is imagine—what would you like to drink right now?"

"A cola," I said. "With lots of ice—and a slice of lemon."

I can remember even now: I added the part about the lemon to show how grown-up I was—but the cola? I chose that because they hadn't let me have one, and I knew for sure that if I had been allowed one, I wouldn't feel thirsty like I did.

"So you just imagine that's what you're drinking," said my mom. "You try that."

I stopped my bike on the moonlit road. I didn't drink my own pee; I felt like I had no pee in me anyway. I couldn't see a pebble, so I picked up a small, sharp lump of road grit. I wiped it a little and put it in my mouth. I rummaged in my bag and pulled out Caspar's MP3 player, fiddled with it in the dark. Music blared. For a second, I was going to skip the track, look for something I knew, when I realized it *was* something I knew. It was Caspar. No band playing with him, just Caspar and his guitar. I looked at the sky—stars disappearing, moon disappearing—and I biked on, listening to Caspar's sweet, smoochy voice singing love in my ear and thinking about an ice-cold cola with a slice of lemon.

When I got in, I gulped so many bottles of water I threw up. I threw up until there was nothing left to throw up but bitter, acidy stuff.

I had this terror moment of thinking maybe I was *sick* sick—rain sick—and then I pulled myself together. My head hurt, but I wasn't about to go see what—if anything—Simon had left that I could take for that.

I'd called his name when I got home. An ostrich thing. There'd been no answer. I did not want to go up there and see why. I knew why.

I remembered what my mom did when I got sunburned (which totally wouldn't have happened if we'd gone on vacation to normal places and/or they'd just let me get a decent spray tan, etc.). On the outside, you need to cool the skin; on the inside, what I had was dehydration. I mixed a bit of salt and sugar with some water, and I forced myself to sip, sip, sip it, even though my stomach was churning, and I wanted to gulp it and throw it up again at the same time.

I sorted the phones out, starting with mine. That meant going upstairs, to the attic, to my bedroom, where I hadn't been—except to grab stuff—for days. I didn't hang around then either. I didn't want to look at my stuff, my stuff that had to do with the me that had been—and my friends. Most especially the photos plastered all over the walls. Me and my friends. And most precious of all: me and Caspar—and Saskia, barging into the photo to lean on his shoulder, pouting.

Saskia, who might still be alive.

It was only then that I noticed the rain, coming down on the windows in the roof. Streaming down the windows in the roof. I hadn't even registered that it had started. I could have been out in it. I could have died.

"🦋 you," I told it.

I got my charger, and I went back to the living room, to the nest, and I sip, sip, sipped—the bird-watching DVDs playing over and over—as I charge, charge, charged everyone's phones with my charger, with Simon's, with my mom's. All those phones, lined up. All those people's lives—on the coffee table, in one long, neat row. People (like Simon) go on about people (like me) not being able to be apart from their cell phones. They're missing the point; it's not the cell phone—it's the life that's in it you don't want to be apart from…even when they don't work anymore. That phone is your diary; it's your photo album. Your memory is crammed into its memory. But with the handy option to delete.

The only thing I couldn't charge was Caspar's MP3 player, so I made myself switch it off. I wanted that battery to last. I'd already gotten a little messed up with some of the phones—whose was whose—which I felt kind of bad about. It didn't look as if anyone had any missed calls or unopened texts; though I also felt bad about snooping, I would have had a look anyway, at least to help work out which phone belonged to which person, but I couldn't guess their password locks. Only Ronnie's had no lock on it—yep, that's right: Mr. Conspiracy von Paranoia had zero phone security…but there was nothing: no calls or messages from the evening the rain had come, and nothing since. His last text was from Zak, from earlier on the day of the party. I won't say what that said. It was meant to be private. It was sweet.

Sometime or another, I fell asleep. I woke up because a phone beeped at me; I thought it was a message!!! Someone's phone was all lit up! I grabbed it; the screen said it needed charging.

Huh?! I checked the connection—nothing happened. *Huh?!* The DVD had been on, I was sure. It was off…so were the lights, which I was also sure had been on. I was half asleep, waking fast. I stumbled into the kitchen, clicking on the lights—only the lights didn't click on.

How stupid I am is that for a moment I thought that I'd somehow drained the power or caused something to short-circuit, from charging the phones. Thanks to Simon, I knew what to do; I dragged a chair from the kitchen to the fuse box in the hall. Thanks to Simon, there was a flashlight there. I grabbed it and switched it on. The beam shone across the fuse box. Nothing was popped out, but what did I know? Electricity's kind of a scary thing, but I jiggled stuff; I switched switches on and off. I climbed down from the chair. It was so, so, so dark.

Drip, drip, drip went the kitchen tap.

Oh! I had this gasping moment of panic.

I ran into the kitchen.

Where Dartbridge had been—its lights, its streetlights—there was darkness. The poisoned world had gone pitch black.

Drip, drip, drip.

The first thing you want to do when there is no light is to get light. I had the flashlight, and we had candles, we had matches, we had lighters. We had these things—candles, matches—by the fireplace, in the fuse box, in the kitchen drawer. In the bathroom, because my mom (and me!) liked to take baths by candlelight. I could get them… I stopped; I thought about the man in the big house, the supermarket men. I was thinking the way Simon said to THINK.

Better the dark.

I switched off the flashlight. I looked out the kitchen window. I watched and I waited. Not one house lit up. I got Simon's binoculars; I scanned for lights, for even the flicker of candlelight.

On the other side of the house, there was also nothing. The hill rose above our road, so there wasn't much of a view from the den window, but from the houses opposite, no light shone. You could still see the shape of Mrs. Fitch, though, lying in our front yard—then movement. (🦋! I panicked!) Another small shape, sniffing around her. Ruby: Mrs. Wallis's Siamese.

I ran to the front door. I opened it.

"Ruuu-by!" I whisper called.

The cat shape stopped her sniffing.

"Ruuu-by!"

I switched the flashlight on for a second—and in the beam of it, I saw her eyes light up in that scary cat way, and then she sauntered off, weaving silently through the garden gate.

"Suit yourself," I whispered. *Please don't leave me.*

I shut the door, locked, and bolted it. I went back to the kitchen. I watched; I waited. I got all obsessed, thinking I could see flickers of light, zooming in on houses with Simon's binoculars, watching, waiting…then thinking I had been mistaken or that maybe I'd caught a glimmer of light out of the corner of my eye. Zooming in on that, watching, waiting… The Sun and Moon… That guy could still be there. Watching, waiting…I dunno for how long—for hours. Somewhere out there, there had to be someone I could go to, someone to help. Someone kind.

It was still dark, just, when a very weird and horrible thing happened. I was still watching out the kitchen window when the cell phones all went off. All of them. There was this burst, this blaring, mental chorus of beeping, of alerts, of music, some customized—that crummy dance track Ronnie liked. I jumped out of my skin—and ran to get to them. It stopped, but I was already on them. I grabbed my phone first, hit on the messages, saw one from my dad, hit *call sender* before I'd even read it. Unlike times before when there was nothing, there was now a voice saying, "Network busy." I hit redial. "Network busy." I hit redial. Again, again, again. I tried my mom's phone; I tried Simon's; I tried Ronnie's. I tried them all, calling my dad. Network busy.

In between times, on the phones that were locked, I hit *emergency dial*, discovered it really won't let you ring any other number but 911.

911.

Network busy.

911. 911.

911. 911. 911.

911. 911. 911. 911.

My dad: Network busy.

I put them all on speakerphone. I would get through.

911. 911. 911. 911. 911. 911. 911. 911. 911. 911. 911. 911. 911. 911. 911. 911.

Network busy.

I tried my dad again—Network busy—then from my mom's phone I tried Leonie's mom's landline. It paused, like it was going to connect.

Buuuuuuuuur.

From our landline I tried Molly's parents' landline.

Buuuuuuuuur.

I tried Ronnie's parents' landline.

Buuuuuuuuur.

I tried to call my cell from my mom's cell.

NETWORK BUSY.

I tried every number I had on every phone I could get into the dial pad on. I tried them all, over and over and over… Until I got so desperate, I dialed the same on each one, over and over and over:

911, 911, 911, 911, 911, 911, 911, 911, 911; 911, 911, 911, 911, 911, 911, 911, 911, 911; 911, 911, 911, 911, 911, 911, 911, 911, 911; 911, 911, 911, 911, 911, 911, 911, 911, 911; 911, 911, 911, 911, 911, 911, 911, 911, 911; 911, 911, 911, 911, 911, 911, 911, 911, 911; 911, 911, 911, 911, 911, 911, 911, 911, 911; 911, 911, 911, 911, 911, 911, 911, 911, 911; 911, 911, 911, 911, 911, 911, 911, 911…

NETWORK BUSY

It was light when even that stopped. The lines went completely dead again. Nothing, not even a *buuuuuuuur.* I cursed myself for not having even tried to get the voice mails, but at least I had the messages. I looked at them, the messages on my phone, on my mom's, on Simon's, on Ronnie's. And you know what…what all of them, what they all said, maybe not the exact words, but pretty much what they all said was: ARE YOU OK?!

NO! NO, NO, NO!
NO! I'M NOT OK!

To my dad, I texted back, just in case it would get through:

Coming to you. Ruby x

I hit *send*; the message failed.

CHAPTER THIRTEEN

No problem: I had a plan.

Just in case I saw anyone I knew alive, I went up to the bathroom to fix my makeup. I got another fright then. Even in the dim light of dawn, I saw my eyes were small and red and puffy and piggy, serious bags underneath. The Caspar-kiss scab on my chin was much reduced and flaking off. OK, it had been itching, and I might have been picking at it slightly. The skin underneath was baby pink. I smoothed a couple wipes over my face, then plastered on the wonder foundation I'd rescued from Zak's, went in heavy with the mascara, and slathered my hair with the last of the glittery dry shampoo. The only way around the "Is it glitter or is it dandruff?" problem was to go for maximum coverage. I slicked on frosted pink lipstick.

I looked a little space-age babe, but that was OK. I didn't even pack. I just shoveled all the cell phones, Caspar's MP3 player, and my wallet into my bag. Good to go.

I suppose I could have stood in the road and screamed my head off until someone, anyone, came…but I'd thought about the man up at the big house and the supermarket gunmen. "Someone, anyone" was not a good idea…so I'd go to the police. That's what they're there for, isn't it, to help people? That's what they HAVE to do. Oh! Oh! Oh! I could picture it: how I'd tell them what had happened and about how I had to get to London, and how a policeman would say, "All right, no need to worry. We'll take you." They'd pretty much have to, wouldn't they? I mean, even if there were just a couple of them left, they couldn't just leave a girl who was only fifteen years old on her own, could they? They'd have to help.

I think I can pretty much say that was the last normal thing I ever tried to do.

When did I realize it was hopeless? When the garden gate clanged shut, and I heard all the neighbors' dogs start up? When that made me remember—dur—to look at the sky? (Which was OK; it was OK. I remember it as fine and clear—but you know what? Really, unless you live in some gorgeously rainless desert—when have you ever seen a perfect clear, blue sky? There always seems to be some little blobby wisp or smudge of something hanging around somewhere.)

Did I realize it was hopeless when I tried to whizz down the hill on my bike like I'd usually do, only I couldn't because—hey, remember?— there were cars and dead bodies everywhere? When I didn't see a single living soul the whole way there? Or perhaps when I got there? Yes, definitely then. There was a police car parked sideways across the driveway and a whiteboard notice propped against it; whatever had been written on it had slid to streaks of black and red in the rain.

I tried the main door. It was all locked up. A part of me I didn't much want to listen to had known it would be. The other part of me, the part that didn't know that, stared at that building—and realized. On the front of the police station and spreading around the sides, there was a wall of messages people had left. Most so rain blitzed you couldn't tell what they said—but the photos… On even the most rain blitzed, you could still make out faces, blobs of faces that had once been real people: snapshots from vacations, portraits from school, photo-booth photos, a photo that showed a bride and groom. I wandered up and down—people I didn't know, people I thought I sort of recognized, people I thought I definitely did.

Photos of people who were probably dead put up by people who were also probably dead.

I stalked back to the main door. Safe inside a glass case: their stupid police notices about terrorism and pickpockets and rabies and Neighborhood 🦋 Watch.

I kicked the front door.

How DARE they not be there? How COULD they not be there?

Worse than the frantic bark of a scared and hungry dog is the cry of a human, trapped.

If there'd been traffic on the road, if the world had been half-way normal, I don't suppose I would have heard them. But in the silence, I did. I did, and my heart lurched with dread. I pressed my ear to the door. I could hear men shouting for help…so muffled I felt like maybe I had gone crazy and was hearing things—but no. I could hear them.

"*HELLO?! HELLO?!*" I screamed, top of my voice, kicking that door, battering my fists against it.

When I stopped, I could hear them, more clearly then, even before I pressed my ear to the door and heard those voices—muffled—hollering "HEY! HELP! HEY! HEY!"

I didn't understand, did I? My heart and guts told me this was bad; in my head, I thought… I dunno what I thought: that maybe the police were locked inside?!

I circled around the building. Dartbridge Police Station isn't like some Wild West jail—it's a big, officey kind of place with tons of windows; none were open, but inside all I could see were desks… until I got to the back of the building, where there was a row of six small, high windows—not officey at all, but those kind of ripply glass bricks you get at swimming pools and stuff.

That "HEY! HELP! HEY! HEY!"…This was where it was coming from.

"*HEY! HEY!*" I shouted at the top of my voice.

At each window, the ripply shadows of human heads appeared.

"HEY! HELP! HEY! HEY!" they screamed.

"*HELLO?!*" I screamed back.

"HEY! HELP! HEY! HEY!" they screamed.

The ripply shadows of human fists battered at the glass.

The realization hit me. With a sickening, massive clunk. Those men weren't police; they were locked in cells.

I heard this rustle behind me. I turned. There was THIS THING. AND THIS MINI THING.

They were human, I suppose—roughly human in shape—but the whole of them, their whole bodies from head to toe were swathed in black plastic and masking tape. That's all I took in, that and that the big one had a really weird, lumpy, bulgy shape, and the little one was carrying some kind of enormous green gun.

I could choose not to say this, but I have said I will try to be honest. I fainted.

In romantic novels and stuff, women in corsets and big puffy skirts faint. They faint because…I dunno…someone has put a stitch in the wrong place in their needlework, or they've just realized they've got a crush on the pastor or something…and some hot guy (or the pastor, who turns out to be hot) scoops them up and revives them. With a nice strong cup of tea, probably, or perhaps a tiny silver thimbleful of French brandy.

I fainted in real life. I fainted because I'd had nothing to eat, next-to-nothing to drink, and because I was completely, totally, and utterly exhausted and freaked out. I think maybe my fear-fried brain took one look at those THINGS and thought, *That's it: lights out.*

I didn't swoon into my skirts. I went smack down.

CHAPTER FOURTEEN

It was like the worst of your most embarrassing nightmares about school come true. You know, when you suddenly realize you don't actually have any clothes on in the middle of math class, and everyone is laughing at you, and whatever you find to cover yourself with shrinks to the size of a Kleenex or goes see-through in your hands; or you suddenly need to go to the bathroom and all the toilets are locked, but it's coming out anyway, and you have to run everywhere trying to find a private place to go, but there isn't one; or you dream you're kissing some disgusting—like, really disgusting—boy you wouldn't ever EVER EVER want to kiss.

You know what I mean? The kind of nightmare you wouldn't even want to tell your best friend? 'Cause it's TOO weird and TOO disgusting? Even though you basically trust your best friend completely, but there's this fear she might laugh her head off and tell everyone? (And then they'd all laugh at you, just like how it was in your nightmare?)

When I woke up, I was in the recovery position—know what that is? It's how you lay people when they've just fainted or had some other kind of hideous thing happen—so they don't choke on their own vomit. I woke up with the side of my face stuck to a garbage bag and...and...I opened my eyes, and practically lying on the garbage bag in front of my face was another face. The bespectacled, spotty, nerdy face of…

Freak. Bespectacled, spotty, nerdy, nobody freak.

"Ruby?" he said.

His face was about half a nanometer from mine.

I gasped in utter horror, shoved him away, and sat up—too fast. Little fuzzy fairyballs of light danced in the air around the face of—

"Here," he said, practically drowning me as he sloshed water into my mouth.

I peeled the garbage bag off my face, snatched the bottle from him, and glugged; it was yukkily warm.

Sip, I heard my mom say. *Sip, Ruby.* For another few seconds more, I ignored her; then I forced myself to slow down. To sip.

I remember I looked at that bottle, and I could see backwash flecks floating in it—which couldn't have been mine, being as how I'd not eaten anything. YEURCH!

That is pretty much when I knew for sure that I wasn't having some weird nightmare/dream thing, but I really was where I was…with—

"What have you done to your hair?" he said.

Darius Spratt.

Unlike whatever they do in novels and stuff, making up all sorts of fancy names to make some kind of lit-err-arr-ee point, or even what they used to do, changing names to protect the innocent in newspapers and things, this name has not been changed. *Darius Spratt.* If that were my surname, I would change it immediately. And even if I couldn't or I felt like I shouldn't for some family reason—like maybe my ancestors had discovered a country (Sprattland) or at least an island (The Isle of Spratt), or left their tiny village (Sprattington), emigrated, and founded a city (Sprattsville, USA)—I would definitely, no way, not ever call my child Darius. I would call him, I dunno, Mark or Steven or something. Calling your kid that—Darius—it's just drawing attention to it, isn't it? It's just like putting up some massive arrow, pointing to the word S-P-R-A-T-T, so you see it in huge white letters, like the Hollywood sign.

SPRATTYWOOD

It amazed me, even then, even in the middle of the most massive trauma that had ever happened to me or the world—not the fainting, specifically, but the whole of the rest of everything—that I could remember his name, that I even knew who he was. I had never spoken to him before in my life. Why would I? He was the King of Loserville. No, not the king at all—that'd probably have to be Ross Ramsden, so massively a creepy loser that his only friends were teachers, and you could tell even they didn't like him much.

Darius Spratt was not the King of Loserville; he wasn't even the crown prince; he wasn't even a lowly serf. He was, like I said, a nobody nerdy freckly freak.

My knight in garbage-bag armor. HAHAHAHAHAHAH UUUUUUUR.

"Nothing!" I snapped in response to the hair question. Total nerve, nerd boy.

"Do you need something to eat?" he asked.

Urch! TONE. Tone like…like Simon's. Like asking a question when really there is no question. URCH. YEURCH. Like when really he was saying, "Young lady, I think you need something to eat. Right now!"

He glanced at the sky, removed the elastic bands (oh yes) from the tops of his bright yellow rubber gloves (they're all the rage this season) so he could get them off, and then tore (manfully—not!) through the garbage bag covering his weedy chest. He was wearing a raincoat under it anyway, and on top of that, there was a backpack;

he rummaged in it and pulled out a crumpled jumbo bag of peanuts. An open, crumpled jumbo bag of peanuts. Well, that would explain the backwash.

YEURCH! CAN YOU EVER IMAGINE ANYTHING MORE DISGUSTING?!

I scarfed a couple handfuls.

"Got any more water?" I asked, teeth sticky.

He looked at the sky again—as if it would have changed that quick! No cloud is that fast!—and then (manfully, not!) tore off more of his garbage bag armor until he could get to the backpack on his back. This he plonked down and opened, and pulled out a bottle of water, but not before I saw the bag was full—I mean, like, FULL—of water and boxes of medicine. Whatever. I snatched the water off him and glugged. Sipped. Glugged. Sipped. Glugged—Darius Spratt snatched the water back.

"Hey!" I said, getting to my feet. Little fuzzy fairyballs of light danced in the air, but not so many.

"Slow down," the Spratt said.

I snatched the water back and glugged more.

I saw the kid then. The Mini-Me Thing with the space gun…the gun that was one of those super-soaking, water-gun things. Plastic. It—she, as I was about to find out—was all taped up. Seemed like the breathing hole wasn't quite in the right place because the garbage bag around it sucked back and forth, and you couldn't even see her eyes, although there were little slits for them.

"Who's that?" I said in between glugs.

"I dunno," said Darius Spratt.

I lowered the bottle, and I looked at him like, *What?*

"She doesn't speak. I just found her." He thought for a moment. "She found me, actually. At school," he said and pointed.

He pointed like I didn't know where our school was—which

was, like, about three minutes up the road. I mean, of all the places I had thought about going and all the places I hadn't thought about and probably should have gone to, what had never, ever, not even for a trillionth of a millisecond crossed my mind was—

"*School?!*" I said.

(Tone. Note the tone. The whole world had…and he had…gone to *SCHOOL?!*)

Darius shrugged.

"Well, what are you doing here?" he asked.

I shrugged.

See, I think this is the worst thing you could know about me. Or one of them. It's worse than the guinea pigs. I would… I might… have just gone. If it hadn't been for bumping into Darius Spratt, I would… I might…maybe I would have just left those men. Maybe I would have done that. Maybe I was too scared to break into a police station and—

"There are people trapped in there," I said. "I'm gonna get them out."

Was I? Was I really?

He didn't shrug, but he made this noise, this "hn" grunt sound that was just the same as a shrug. It had no *tone*; it was just "hn."

"You *knew?!*" I said.

"Hn."

"Well, we can't just leave them!"

He didn't say anything then. Not even a *hn*.

"I'm going to get them out," I said.

I snatched the peanuts off him, scarfed some, then guzzled some water. I think, honestly, I was sort of hoping he'd say something—like come up with some really, really good reason why we should just go. He didn't.

"Right," I said. I looked around…er, yeah, like I was looking for some way to break in, and I wouldn't be able to find one, and then I'd have to go.

"I've got this," said Darius Spratt. He pulled a teensy hammer out of his backpack.

"Thanks," I said.

I took it, just hoping he'd go away so then I could too.

I stalked off and sized up windows.

GO AWAY, GO AWAY, GO AWAY. Every time I looked around, Darius and the kid were still there, following me.

"Look, just 🦋 off, will you? If you're not going to help," I said as I strode past him.

I got back around to the front door. I attacked it. It was some kind of special glass; the hammer bounced off. Who'd have thought it? Dartbridge Police Station has special anti-smash glass! With any luck, all the windows would be like that, and I could give up (with dignity). I stalked back around the building; Darius Spratt and the small black plastic one followed. I tried another window, and it smashed instantly, like normal glass smashes. And instantly—

"HEY! HELP! HEY! HEY!"

You could hear them clearly.

"A little more clearly," I want to say, but, really, it was totally clearly. There was no going back.

That window, it was too high up for me to just climb in on my own. I looked at Darius Spratt.

"HEY! HELP! HEY! HEY!"

"This is stupid," he said. "This is so stupid."

I was going to yee-haa and then some, because the way Darius Spratt said that, it was like a Simon way to say that—like, YOU are stupid—but he stepped forward and gave me a leg up. I could feel his feeble arms straining while I hacked away the remaining glass; then I hauled myself in, on top of someone's desk.

"HEY! HELP! HEY! HEY!"

I opened the window, and Beanpole Boy heaved himself in after me, backpacks and all, then turned and waggled a finger at the garbage-bag kid (GBK).

"You stay there," he said. "Anyone comes, you run. You hide. Go to the school. You know where."

I dunno whether the GBK understood that; she didn't move.

So there was this door to where they were, a door that was locked—a door that led to another door, with a nothing space, a bench in it, in between. On the other side of that, you could hear them shouting.

Locks have keys. Keys get kept places.

Annoyingly, it was Darius who found them—at the front desk, the place where you go to tell the police stuff, like *help, help the whole town's rioting*, or that someone's stolen your bike (which you'd forgotten to lock). Behind that was a ton of keys. Those got us through the nowhere space. When we came into the corridor of cells, those men started screaming.

The stench of bodies, dead and alive, was incredible. It hit your stomach as loudly as the screams, and the battering at the doors hit your ears. There was a peephole in each door, but I was too scared even to look. I think it would be fair to say that I was terrified. It felt like…if we let them out, we'd get torn apart—like they were wild dogs or demons.

I turned to look at Darius and saw my own terror on his face. We backed up into the nowhere room.

"We'll have to give them your stuff," I said.

He hesitated.

"They're just hungry and thirsty. They're desperate. We'll give them your stuff and then we'll let them out."

"They could be murderers," said Darius.

"What, all of them?"

He shrugged. "Hn," he said. "In here for a reason, aren't they?"

As much as I pretty much hate Darius Spratt, I can't claim I didn't agree with him. I can't claim I didn't want to just walk away; I wanted to run away—but then it came to me, the truth of it, that couldn't be denied:

"If we don't let them out, *we're* murderers."

Darius stared at the floor for a moment, then groaned and dumped his supplies.

In the door of each cell was a hatch. We unbolted them, one at a time, and hands snatched what was offered. You had to shut your mind to it, the stink and the shouting and the swearing—and then the fighting you could hear starting up in the cells as desperate men battled over bottles of water, over crummy bags of peanuts.

"Let us out of here! 🦋! 🦋! 🦋! Let us out!"

None of the keys would fit.

"For 🦋's sake!" shouted a guy through the hatch of the first cell. "Come on!"

His voice, it sounded so broken. So dry, sore, and broken.

"The keys won't fit!" I cried.

"🦋! It's a kid. It's a 🦋 kid. SHUT UP! SHUT UP!" he screamed louder and louder. **"IT'S A KID!!! SHUT UP!"**

That corridor of cells, it quieted down.

"The keys won't fit!" I shouted at the row of doors.

There was another outbreak of swearing until the guy in the first cell shouted them all back down again.

"Try the custody desk, hon—behind you, on the way in. Try there."

Darius nodded at me and went to look.

"Hon?" said the guy.

"My friend's gone," I said. The fear made my voice shake and stammer.

(Please note, that's how traumatized I was: I called Darius Spratt my friend.)

Darius came back right away with a bunch of what looked like keys to a giant's house—keys four times the size of normal keys.

"Did you get them?" said the cell guy, hearing their rattle.

"Yes…" I said.

It was quiet compared to how it had been, but from every cell, you could still hear it, this bubbling of swearing, cursing, desperation. It felt like any second, it would all go crazy again—and who knew what would happen when the doors were actually opened?

Darius cleared his throat. "Look, you've got to promise not to hurt us or anything," he told the row of doors.

It sounds so stupid now, him saying that. It even kind of sounded stupid at the time, and it made those men angry. The swearing started up again until the guy in the first cell shouted them down.

"I swear," he said, "on my mother's life. No one will hurt you."

Right then and there, I thought, *Your mother is probably dead. Like mine.*

There was nothing else we could do. Darius unlocked his cell.

There were five men packed in there; three of them didn't come out.

The one that had spoken to us stood there with his face all twisted up and twitching …I suppose he might have wanted to cry, but when you get dehydrated like that, you can't get any tears.

"Thank you," he managed to say. He leaned on the wall.

"Everyone's dead," I told him. "Everyone's dead."

I don't even know why I said that. I really don't.

That man, he kind of nodded, like he could believe it, like he already knew.

He held out his hand for the keys.

"I'll do the rest," he said. "You go."

We didn't argue.

"You're good kids," he shouted after us. "God bless you!"

"Don't drink the water!" Darius shouted back at him.

I guess Darius hadn't seen what I had seen. There was a drinking fountain in that cell. I can't think about that. They must have found out the hard way about the water.

We climbed back out through the window. The kid was still there, waiting. Some random scary guy, bloody—like fighting bloody, eyes and nose—burst out through the window behind us. He dropped down to the ground, nodded politely at us, and then ran.

"We should get out of here," said Darius Spratt.

You don't say, I thought.

As we ran around to the front of the police station, another guy staggered past us. I grabbed my bike.

"Don't you want to come with us?" blurted Darius Spratt.

"No!" I said. As in, *No way*. As in, *As if*. "I'm going to my dad's."

I biked off.

Toward home. I wasn't so nuts that I was going to bike to London, was I? I didn't know how I was going to get there. I had what Simon would have called "a slight logistical problem," which is what he said when I told him where I was going to go, and he'd point out that that would depend on me getting a ride from "someone" and that "someone" had other plans that did not involve driving me about like a chauffeur.

"We'll be at the school!" Darius Spratt shouted after me.

I looked over my shoulder at the two of them, just standing there.

"Bye!" I shouted, which I thought was very charitable of me, considering.

Charitable and also a further sign of how serious the situation was: girls like me don't even acknowledge the existence of boys like Darius Spratt. It's a basic law of nature.

CHAPTER FIFTEEN

I took the shortest route home, cutting across the top of the High Street.

That was some sight: in the late afternoon sun, it was a river of broken glass, glittering. I leaned the bike against a wall and waded in, just a little, just to see.

Things floated on that river. Bodies, yes, but other things too: toys, electrical stuff, books, candy, random items of furniture even… and shoes, clothes, jewelry. Makeup. Really good makeup. The kind I couldn't afford, even if I'd been allowed to buy it.

I told myself I needed some more of that dry shampoo anyway, and while I was looking for it, I just happened to wander into a couple other shops, just to see…and, er, basically…it turned into my own one-girl riot.

You know where normally you'd have to spend, like, about an hour trying testers on the back of your hand and umming and ahhing because you could only afford one lipstick so you had to get it right? I didn't even bother with the testers. I just took every lipstick I liked. You know how you'd have to choose which color to get a top in because no way in a billion years could you get both or all three or all four, no matter how good they were? How you'd have to put that jacket back because it was way out of your price range?

How your mom would go CRAZY if you bought that dress? How you liked those shoes, but you weren't really sure what they'd go with? How no way would you be allowed a bikini like that and no way, not ever could you get fancy, flimsy, floaty, flirty underwear? How you had to make do with one bottle of perfume? And only had one decent bag? And no no no no no way could you ever get, like, real jewelry, stuff that was actually silver or full-on diamante mega-bling, with matching earrings AND a tiara?

HAHAHAHAHAHAHAHAHAHAHAHAHAHAHAHA!

I GOT SOOOOOOOOOOOOOOOOO MUCH STUFF!!!!!!

(Even though: (1.) It was Dartbridge High Street, which, as you can imagine, is not exactly Camden Lock or Covent Garden or Oxford Street or even Exeter, and (2.) In some cases, I'd been beaten to it, e.g., the place that sold MP3 players and phones and tablets and stuff was cleaned out. I checked. Thoroughly.)

I don't care how awful it sounds. I didn't care then, that's for sure, and I don't much care now. For the first time since before it rained, I was actually happy—or distracted, I was going to say—but you know what? I think I really was happy. I had, like, a crazy amount of stuff—so much stuff I had to double back to loot bigger (and better!) bags to carry it in—and I think I would have gone on and on with it, never mind how I was going to get it home, if it hadn't been for The George. I'd forgotten all about it, and the air stank so bad anyway that I hadn't noticed the smell wasn't just bodies—it was a burned pub.

Wow. It was gone. There was a charred black hole where The George had been. Only its beams remained: black bones hanging above a tumble of burned-up rubble. That place, where I had known for sure that I was in love, it was as dead as any dead person.

It was hard to carry on after that. I did try. There was this one particular boutique-y shop, the one that had THE best stuff in it and was owned by an evil old hag cunningly disguised as a super-chic designer-model-type woman, who hated me and my friends and anyone who was younger than her—hated the way that sort of woman does when she realizes we could easily look better than her if we only had the right clothes—and who would blast us with death-ray stares and openly persecute us with "Can I help you?"-type questions that didn't mean "Can I help you?" at all but meant "Get out of my shop, you rude young girl" whenever we dared venture into her insanely expensive kingdom of exclusive style—which wasn't often but which was often enough for our hungry eyes to have gazed longingly at every item in there.

I emptied a rack of sequined items, grabbed belts that cost a year's allowance each and stuffed them into super-expensive handbags I didn't even like all that much.

Surrounded by booty, sipping a fizzy organic ginseng drink looted from the designer mini-fridge at the back of the evil old hag's designer shop, I sat on the church wall, practically panting. Not from the heat—and it was bakingly, dead-body-rottingly warm—but from the mad, dizzy-making thrill of the thing. I could take anything—ANYTHING—I wanted.

And I'd have given anything to have Lee there with me, so that it really would be actual fun. Everything was dreadful, but there was this. There was this—and no one to share it with.

I burped.

Except Saskia. See…what I knew was that where she lived was just behind the church. I hadn't even been there, to her house, but Lee had. I'd just go look, that's what I thought. I'd just go look.

Truth? I wasn't even sure how much I wanted to see Saskia, because I felt like there were things I might want to ask that I wouldn't want to hear the answers to. Not even how she had gotten away from Zak's exactly, but…hadn't I seen Saskia refuse that glass of water Sarah had offered? Had she thought about stuff everyone else was too freaked with panic to think about? Stuff that not even Barnaby knew? Had she thought about that stuff and...not even bothered to tell anyone? Did she just stand around complaining about wanting to go home while she watched everyone else die?

Her road, it wasn't nice. It was close to the hospital. Where normally there'd be parking for residents only, it was jammed...with the usual—cars, bodies. I'd dumped my stuff at the church because I figured I wouldn't be long. I'd just go look; if I couldn't find her immediately, I'd go back—immediately.

The thrill of the shopping thing got killed by how that road was, but I got this other buzz on: how you feel when you're looking for someone, how you just want to know... So I picked my way right down that road; then I turned, I crossed the street, and I picked my way back. I wasn't about to start shouting her name or anything, and I didn't even know how I'd know which house was hers...until I did.

In the living-room window, I saw the sweetest, darlingest, snow-white Chihuahua you ever did see. Wagging her little tail at me; scratching at the glass with her tiny, mighty paws.

I knew this Chihuahua. I had seen this Chihuahua. This Chihuahua had to be—she HAD to be—the one that belonged to Saskia's mom. Hadn't we all ooh'ed and aah'ed and cooed over her when Saskia's mom had come to pick us up from Ronnie's flop of a party?

She had been called Tiffany—or maybe that was Saskia's mom's name?

"Hello, darling!" I whispered at her, my heart totally melting.

I ran up to the front door. I rang the doorbell. I shouted through the letterbox.

"Saskia! Hey, Sask!"

Then, "It's me, Ruby!" I shouted when there was no reply.

I went around through the gate to the back.

Saskia's mom, plus a bunch of other people, were in the garden. They'd been having a barbecue—with a fancy buffet, that had gotten wrecked. Stuff spilled all over the place. Saskia's mom lying right in the middle of it all. Saskia's mom, plus dip. That had to be guacamole, right?

The Chihuahua scrabbled at the kitchen door.

"Sask!" I shouted at the door, banging on it. "Sask!"

I knew I shouldn't be doing what I did next. It's possible Saskia had just gone out—like me—and would come back and catch me smashing my way into her house…but it was also possible that she was lying inside sick or dead and that was what I'd say to her if she did come back: "I thought you might be lying inside sick or dead." There was this knee-high concrete Greek lady by the garden pond. She was a hefty girl but manageable. I got hold of her and heaved her headfirst at the kitchen window. Her head broke off. Only one pane busted. Double-glazed…they're a nightmare, aren't they? The glass is super-tough and even if you get in lots of practice—which I didn't feel I had time for just then—it's still a hard job. I cased my options, like burglars must do—wood-framed patio doors, single glazed, key in lock; the little darling dog scrabbling to get to me.

"Come here! Come on!" I shouted to her. I lured her back around to the den window. I teased her through the glass, then zoomed back around, and—CRASH!—smashed that bare-bottomed lady feet-first through the patio doors. She was perched on a blob of rock; neither the rock nor the lady's chunky legs broke.

Good aim, Ruby! (Can't wait to tell Dan how I'm practically a professional criminal!)

I shoved my hand in and opened the door.

"Saskia?" I called.

The darling dog came running. I scooped her up before her precious paws could get cut on glass.

"Saskia!"

Clutching the trembling pooch, I toured the house. It felt creepy. Saskia had two sisters, and I wouldn't have known for sure which one of those freakishly neat and tidy rooms was hers if it hadn't have been for the photos; on the wall, in frames…a ton of photos of Saskia—doing gymnastics, winning stuff, posing on vacation somewhere hot, in a bikini…and that same one of me and Caspar—only it wasn't of me and Caspar anymore; it was of Caspar and Saskia. I had been cut out.

Know what I also saw? That I only saw because I just happened to open her closet and the drawers in her dressing table? Saskia's stuff was gone. She had packed stuff and gone.

I could have left that dog in that house. I held her in front of my face. How could—HOW COULD—that boyfriend-stealing 🦋 leave that sweet pooch?

"Don't worry, Darling!" I said. "Ruby will take care of you!"

Petting and fussing over MY dog, I stomped back to the church, put my tiara on, grabbed as much stuff as I could carry, and crunched back up the High Street. I got my bike, put Darling in the basket, and crunched back down the High Street, detoured to load up with yet more ditched booty because I couldn't bear to leave it, and crunched home.

Me and Darling, we split right, through the library parking lot. I passed the big fighting man and the woman who had hugged and rocked and kissed him.

I felt…not a grief thing, exactly, but really, really solemn.

I stopped in Holywell Park, like me and my mom used to do when I was little.

There's a spring there, a holy well; that's why it's called that. In medieval times, they believed the water from it could cure lepers—but it couldn't. There was no cure.

Now, not even the most desperate leper would want to drink from it.

Mom said it was a fairy well. When we first came here and I was young enough to believe in fairies, we'd stop by on the way home from the shops and pick a flower—or just a nice leaf if there were no flowers—and leave it for the fairies. If the fairies were pleased with it, she said, they'd leave a flower too...and sometimes they left other things: pretty shells and stones, sometimes ribbons, sometimes little bits of jewelry my fingers ached to touch; sometimes they even left a poem.

It took me a long time—like, really, an embarrassingly long time—to work out that it wasn't fairies...partly, I reckon, because we never told Simon about it. He hated that kind of thing, not just because it was a kind of hippie thing (which is what it really was; Dartbridge types leaving offerings for whatever pagan-y water god they were into), but because he also thought all that sort of stuff—tooth fairies, Santa Claus, guardian angels—was...not just silly nonsense, but lies that should not be told to children. What a fun guy, huh?

The fairy well, it was our secret. Mine and my mom's. And that, I think, is really why I believed in it for so long, because it was something just for us. I believed in it because I needed to believe in it—like the lepers, I guess.

Just this last spring, I saw my mom at the well—with Henry. She was holding him in her arms, and I could see her whispering to him—about the fairies, I expect...and I...I felt this awful twisty stab of jealousy. A twisty stab of jealousy and sadness and a knowing that she wasn't just mine anymore; now she belonged to Henry too...and I did what I think is the most grown-up thing I'd ever done. I wanted to run home and cry. I know that makes me sound like a baby, but it was how I felt. ("She finds change difficult"; that's what my mom always said about me, so I wouldn't feel so bad about hating new stuff like Simon, like discovering I had a brother called Dan, like going to middle school, like finding out my mom was pregnant.) (Like trying to survive a global death-fest mega-crisis.)

I didn't run home and cry. I picked a flower, and I went to her, and we both told Henry all about the fairies. I leaned my head on her shoulder, and she gave me one of her special kisses, on my forehead, and stroked my cheek. And then Henry started bawling because I wouldn't let him eat my flower, and we went home.

I let Darling wander around on the grass while I looked for a flower. I found the perfect one: a single honeysuckle bloom, delicate and sweet-scented. I laid it down on the wall by the well—the other flowers there rain beaten, sun shriveled, and rotten—and I asked the fairies, please, to never forget my mom. To show how much I meant it, I left them my tiara.

CHAPTER SIXTEEN

I pushed my bike and my loot home. As I came up the road, it started.

I heard the terrier's howl cut through the silence. I couldn't ignore it anymore. The neighbors' pets. The 🦋 neighbors' 🦋 pets.

With a heavy heart, I left my darling Darling and my loot in the stinky house, and went out again to perform yet another charitable act.

On the way to Whitby the golden retriever's house, I took the crowbar out of Simon's backpack, which was still lying in the middle of the road where I'd dumped it. I went to Whitby's first because I liked him best. I knocked. I called out. The back door was unlocked: Whitby bounded out. He must have barked himself stupid because he could hardly get a sound out, but he almost knocked me over. He was mad glad, crazy to see me…and me, I can say the same about him. (All those years I'd wanted a dog, it wasn't a dog like Darling; it was a dog like Whitby. Actually, it *was* Whitby.) I braved the stink in his house to feed him—and, though animals seemed to be OK with it, I just couldn't give him water from the tap. I went back and got a bottle of fizzy water from Simon's backpack and gave him that. He lapped and scoffed and lapped and scoffed. And wagged and wagged and wagged his tail. He was ecstatic.

Then I had this massive guilt attack because I knew the kids that lived (had lived) in that house had a hamster, so I went and got that. I stabbed holes in an old ice-cream carton and loaded Fluffysnuggles, food, and bedding into it. When I got to London, I'd generously give that hamster to Dan. He'd love it.

I left the door open for Whitby, dumped Fluffysnuggles by Simon's backpack, and crossed the road to Mrs. Wallis's house. If I was thinking anything, it was that the joy of seeing Whitby was still alive might make up for whatever had happened to Clarence and Mimi, because I'd already noticed those grumpy little shih tzus weren't running up and down on the windowsill anymore.

The front door was wide open. Mrs. Wallis wasn't home. Clarence was dead, lying there on the kitchen floor; Mimi didn't look far off. I ran back outside and pulled another bottle of water out of Simon's backpack.

I poured out water for her, filled a bowl with food.

"Please eat, Mimi, please eat."

She drank, then ate a little, then threw it up. She lay down on the kitchen floor. She whined at me. I coaxed her with food. All the while, I called for the cat—"Ruu-by! Ruu-by!"—but she was a no-show.

I stroked Mimi. Normally you couldn't even get near her. I smoothed back her fur from her little face. It was the first time I'd ever really seen her eyes, her sad little brown eyes, and it made it a whole lot harder to think about leaving her…but I had to, didn't I? I backed out of the kitchen. Whitby was sitting outside the door. His tail was wagging. He had an arm in his mouth—a woman's arm—the raggedy sleeve of a flowery blouse still on it. Her fingernails were painted a plummy red and she wore some pretty rings.

"Whitby! No!" I shouted at him. "Leave it!"

He dropped the arm and lumbered goofily up to me, ready to

slobber how he sorry he was all over me. Revolting! I pushed him away. I left him sniffing at Clarence (I hoped he'd remember Clarence had been a friend and not chomp on him too), and I went across the road, knocked, called out, and tried to open the front door of the house where the terrier was now barking like crazy. The door was locked; the back door was locked. I smashed the kitchen window (single glazed) with the crowbar, and opened it. The terrier—whoa! Somehow it managed to leap up onto the draining board, skittering on broken glass, and scrambled out the window—to attack Whitby, who'd come up behind me with the arm hanging out of his mouth.

You really don't want to see that kind of thing: two dogs fighting over someone's arm. It did seem to help Whitby get his voice back though. I shouted at them—zero impact—then realized what a racket we were making. Plus, I hadn't even realized Whitby had followed me—which I thought was a bad thing. If he could creep up on me, anyone could.

Someone, anyone.

I decided I really, really had to go. I felt bad about it, like I ought to go look for more animals to liberate, but I just couldn't handle anymore charitable acts. I just couldn't.

CHAPTER SEVENTEEN

There's a reason people don't dye their hair by candlelight, just like there's a reason people don't put on fake tan by candlelight either. It is too hard to judge when you've got the color right—particularly if you don't actually bother timing it like you're supposed to. That night, after my own one-girl riot, and after I'd gone upstairs and cut Saskia out of the photo of me and Caspar (so it was now just me and Caspar, as it should have been) and stuck it back on the wall and kissed him and felt sad (like *inexpressibly* sad, to the point of any-second-now-I'm-gonna-scream-my-head-off-because-I-truly-can't-believe-this-thing-that-is-happening-is-happening sad), I had my own one-girl beauty session. All things considered, e.g.:

- The smell in the house was at a new unbelievable high. (Or low.)
- I filled up Simon's hideous pot with lemonade, but those flowers—they looked done for.
- None of the phones showed any sign of working.
- I checked the Internet again, then—dur—realized that although the battery in the laptop was still good, the broadband wasn't working.
- The whole of Dartbridge was still in pitch-blackness, and the slightest noise made me jump.

- I was too terrified to have any candles lit apart from one tiny one in the bathroom, and even then I made myself go and stand in the backyard and check and check again that you couldn't see any light.
- Though I checked and checked it too, I also couldn't see any light from any house in town.
- I nearly made myself sick again on a looted chocolate-spread scarfing binge.
- In the middle of the night, a plane flew overhead.
- I couldn't actually play any music because everything we had to play it on ran off electricity, so I had to go next door again to get the massive battery-operated, old-school boom-box ghetto blaster that Mr. Fitch heaved around the garden with him when he was weeding, so he could listen to brass-band music (which he said the plants liked too) (see what I mean about Dartbridge? Even the most normal people…), and it only worked with tape cassettes, and the only tape cassettes I had were…Mr. Fitch's brass-band music.

Yes, all those things considered, me and Darling had a busy girly night that was kind of almost fun…if you ignored the "global meltdown, everyone's died, I'm all alone, what am I going to do?" aspect.

In the morning, it wasn't even vaguely fun. I did, really, actually gasp with horror when I saw myself in the mirror. The makeup I'd messed around with that had smudged itself all over my face in the night was not the problem. That could be (relatively) easily removed; what might not be so easily removed was my streaky all-over orange tan, which clashed pretty badly with my red hair. I'd bleached my hair first; by candlelight it had looked a ghostly, scary white, so I thought I should go for it. Why, oh, why had I chosen *red*? My mom was right; it really didn't suit me… And I knew that, even though it was hard to tell when my face was ORANGE.

I had to wash my face—a lot—immediately. I knew what I would do. I would get Simon's backpack, and I would use every bottle of water or soda water or tonic water or whatever—whatever was left—to scrub and wash my skin and my hair. (I did kind of know even then that there would be nothing I could do about my hair; I'd put permanent brilliant red on bleached white—only way that would come off was shaving myself bald and waiting for my natural mousy brown to sprout. Or dye it black? Hmmm…)

I burst out of the house, didn't even look at the sky (should have). Whitby must have won the arm fight because he was lying outside our gate, still gnawing on his prize. I skirted around him and marched into the road.

Simon's backpack was gone.

No animal could or would take something as big and heavy as that. Only a person could have taken it. A "someone, anyone," perhaps. I felt fear crackle in my bones.

"LEAVE IT AND GET IN!" I hissed at Darling and Whitby, who were sniffing Mrs. Fitch and eyeballing each other, as if they were trying to decide whether to share a nibble or a fight. (My tiny girl—she is so plucky!) (My big huggy hound—he knows when to go gentle!)

I slammed the gate shut. I frightened myself it was so loud—and I looked behind me. I wished I hadn't; Mimi was sauntering across the road—behind her, the crazy terrier was loitering, like he just happened to be there.

"GET IN! GET IN!" I hissed at them.

I held the gate open. The terrier bounded in.

"LEAVE IT!" I hissed as he sniffed at Mrs. Fitch, then Mimi condescended to enter our garden. "Don't even think about it," I growled as she veered off the path toward Mrs. Fitch.

I held the front door open and all the dogs trooped on in like they lived there.

I took one more nervous look up and down the street, and then I shut the door.

I locked it.

Inside the house, the dogs were already not getting along. Whitby and the terrier had obviously failed to make up after yesterday's fight and were snarling at each other, debating whether to have another battle, which was making Mimi and Darling nervous and yappy. That's the way I saw it, but maybe they were just egging them on.

I might have gone veggie, but my mom and Simon were raging carnivores. There was meat in the freezer—thawing but OK. It smelled fine, not stinky. I shut Whitby in the kitchen with a chicken... I kind of thought it was only cooked bones that dogs can't eat—isn't it?—and from the way I'd seen him crunching fingers, I reckoned it was all right. The terrier I lured upstairs with a pack of stewing steak, and shut him in the bathroom. I figured Mimi and Darling would get along. I opened the door to the den, fragrant with my pee bucket, and I tempted them both inside with some lamb chops. As I walked away, I heard Mimi snap. I yanked Darling out and put her with her very own chop in Henry's little room...that he'd hardly even ever had the chance to use.

The crazy terrier got kind of growly when I went into the bathroom, like I'd come to steal his steak. I didn't dare shout at him in case he got barky, so I ignored him and stuffed a couple of the loot bags with the best of the booty. Then I went upstairs and stuffed another bag with more of my things—including all my photos—and most especially the photo of me and Caspar. I kissed it, ignoring Saskia's chopped head, which lay on the floor, pouting at me. I might have stepped on it on my way out.

Hard to know what to pack; hard to know what I was packing

for…but does it sound like I was organized? Like I knew what I was doing? I tell you, I couldn't think straight about what was going into that bag—let alone how that bag and me were going to get to my dad. All the night before, when I'd been supposed to be coming up with Escape Plan B, all I'd come up with was stuff like I prefer glitter to crackle-finish nail polish and super-moisturizing gloss lipstick to frosted.

I went back down to the bathroom; the terrier had scarfed all that steak and was collapsed out in a "come pet me, I'll be good now, honest I will" way. I ignored him; I pulled things back out of the bag, so I could fix my face and hair…as much as I could. I scraped the scary red hair back into a topknot (think volcano erupting on top of head) and slathered my orange face with looted foundation. The mascara and the lipstick made it worse: I looked plastic. I looked like a scary dolly. A Halloween bad-dolly special.

And while I was trying to make myself look half-human and failing, I was thinking, *What are you doing? What are you doing?! WHAT ARE YOU GOING TO DO?* And when I'd finished, when I stared at my own bad-dolly self in the mirror, she answered.

"I'm going to drive," she said.

WHAT?! I said.

"That's what Saskia did, isn't it?" she said. "How else do you think she got away from Zak's? Dummy."

I kissed the door to my mom and Simon's room.

I breathed.

"Bye, Mom," I whispered.

◦◦◦

BUT I CAN'T DRIVE!!! I thought, lugging bags down the stairs. *I DON'T KNOW HOW!*

Get a grip! I thought. *Be like Saskia. Be like Halloween Bad Dolly Saskia.*

I got all the phones and Caspar's precious MP3 player and Simon's precious laptop and put them—and the chargers—into a bag. Then I rummaged in Simon's jacket pocket and fished out the keys to our car. Then I picked up the crowbar.

I got everything straight in my head. I would keep it really simple, like steps you follow on the back of a box of hair dye. (The crowbar wasn't a step; it was more like the part you don't read on the back of the box, about what to do if it all goes horribly wrong.)

STEP ONE. I took a deep, calming breath and unlocked the door and went out into the road and loaded the bags into the car. This went OK.

STEP TWO. I went back into the house to get the pets.

This took longer than it should have.

Darling was easy because I'd done a mini-detour and picked up a pretty little leash and collar for her on the return leg of the looting expedition. I couldn't bear to go back to Whitby's house, so I went back out to the car, got one of my new belts, and attached that his collar. I did the same with Mimi. The crazy terrier was too crazy to be saved, my Halloween Bad Dolly Saskia self ruthlessly decided.

As I led my pack of dogs out to the car, Mimi pulled toward home. So I dragged her. She snapped at me when I tried to pick her up, so I pretty much yanked her up by her neck into the backseat of the car. I put Darling down with her, on Henry's baby seat, then loaded Whitby into the back with my bags. I went back into the house. I scooted the terrier out of the bathroom, down the stairs, and out the front door.

"Leave it!" I hissed when he went straight for Mrs. Fitch.

I opened the gate and he bounded out—then turned, waiting

to see what I would do. Wondering whether he was getting a walk, I expect.

Be like Saskia.

I shut the gate on him.

Then I went back inside and got Fluffysnuggles.

I stood in the hall…the house—the whole world—silent.

Drip, drip, drip went the kitchen faucet.

Don't start blubbing now, I told myself.

STEP THREE. This was supposed to be "drive off."

It went horribly wrong.

The terrier pranced after me as I walked toward the car.

Inside the car, the dogs had rearranged themselves. Whitby sat in the front passenger seat, panting his vile breath everywhere; Darling waited cutely in the driver's seat; Mimi sulked in the back. I scooped up Darling, put her on my lap, and put Fluffysnuggles down on the floor in front of the passenger seat.

I started up the car.

That engine, it roared into the silence like a jet, sounding a million billion times louder than the plane that had zoomed low overhead in the night. Loud enough to wake the dead, Grandma Hollis would have said.

The first thing I had to do was open my window, or I'd be sick from Whitby's death breath. Then I checked out the pedals, fiddled nervously with the gears. Only my dad had ever let me try driving his car; my mom and Simon went mental when I told them—even though it was on this totally deserted lane in Lancashire (*"He let you drive on a public highway!?!"*)—and completely, totally, and utterly refused to let me try in our car.

We kangarooed out of the parking space, bashing next-door-but-one's car. Whitby fell off his seat onto Fluffysnuggles. Darling didn't fall but decided the floor was a better bet. The engine screamed, and the car lurched along the road where my foot pressed down on the accelerator as I rummaged around and scooped her up.

"🦋 animals!" I shouted. It was the nervous tension.

Oh no. I turned off the engine.

"Two seconds," I muttered to the 🦋 animals, then got out and went back to the house.

See, now maybe you've been thinking what a nice person I am and how I must really love animals and everything. (Well, apart from the terrier.) You know what I had forgotten? The stupid guinea pigs.

I didn't even know whether they'd still be alive. I unlocked the front door and charged through the house and out the back door into the garden. I think guinea pigs come from Peru, and I guess life must get pretty tough there, because, although there wasn't a scrap of food or water left, Gimli and Prince Charming (don't ask; that's a whole other story) were very much alive and squealed their little heads off for food. I opened the cage and—

I stopped. It wasn't because I realized it would take too long to find a box or something; it was because the dogs were going crazy— the girls' muffled yapping; Whitby booming; the terrier, out on the street, going nuts. Either the ghost of Clarence had arisen and was scaring them to death, or another dog had rocked up and a fight had broken out, or—I ran back into the house, I yanked open the front door—

Or something had upset them.

Not something. Someone. Not anyone, either.

He was standing a couple steps away from me. The rich man, gray-haired. The terrier barged past him into the house, and it was that—that two seconds of the dog barging through—that gave the rich man enough time to lurch forward and stick his foot in the door before I could slam it shut. I shoved against that door with all my might. The terrier started up again, barking like a lunatic right behind me. *Behind me*, like he was backing me up, like I could actually do something.

"I only want to talk to you," he said. "I only want to talk to you."

That voice: primped and prim and proper, like his house.

His fingers wrapped round the door. What I could feel... It was like...you know when you're a kid and you arm wrestle a grown-up? How they let you think you stand a chance, but really they could beat you instantly? That's what it felt like. I was pushing as hard as I could, but I knew any second he wanted, he could shove back, and it'd be game over. So I did a Whitby. I sank my teeth into fingers. I bit him as hard as I could. He yelled and pulled his hand free—but his foot stayed in the door.

"I won't hurt you," he said.

I spat his filthy taste from my mouth.

DO SOMETHING! yelled my Halloween Bad Dolly Saskia self.

The crowbar was in the car.

THINK! yelled my Simon-ish me.

I had no instructions to follow. I looked for something, anything... The den door was ajar. I saw my pee bucket.

I let go of the door, dived into the den, and grabbed it.

He did not come in after me. He pushed the door wide open with his fingertip and stood back, nursing his hand. I stood there, in the hall, with my pee bucket.

The terrier quieted—but maybe not because the door fight was over, maybe because the humans were out-crazying it.

"Get-away-from-me," I said.

My voice so choked with rage and fear and hate it sounded like another person's—a dangerous psycho person's. I held up the bucket, like I was ready to soak him. I held it really tight to stop my hands from shaking. I gave it a little swish about, menacing.

He backed up immediately. He slipped out through the gate. He held on to it.

"I won't hurt you!" he said. "Please—"

"You killed him," I said.

"It was an accident—"

"It was a trap!"

"I was frightened—"

"We were thirsty. WE-WERE-JUST-THIRSTY."

"I know that. I understand that—"

"You murdered him."

I came at him then—more with rage than bravery. I strode down the path, and he turned and ran.

"Stay away from me!" I screamed after him. "Stay away from my house! *MURDERER!*"

I couldn't stop shaking. I kept thinking he would come back. I kept the pee bucket with me as I locked up the house. I kept the pee bucket with me as I went back to the car. The crazy terrier followed me. I couldn't leave him now, not when he'd stood behind *me*, barking at *him*. I opened the back passenger door. The terrier hopped in, saw Whitby, and growled. Whitby growled back.

"BE QUIET!" I yelled at them.

I opened the driver's door, scooped Darling up with one hand, got in. I put the pee bucket down, jammed it in next to Fluffysnuggles, put Darling on my lap, and shut the door. I put my seat belt on.

The keys were gone.

Not knocked onto the floor gone. Not "ooh silly me, I forgot I put them in my pocket" gone. Gone gone.

I looked around. He was standing in the road, a distance back, holding up the keys.

"I JUST WANT TO TALK TO YOU," he shouted. "I PROMISE I WON'T HURT YOU."

I undid my seat belt. I scooped Darling up, kissed her, and

swapped her for the pee bucket. I got out of the car. I didn't shut the driver's door. I stood right by it.

"I didn't know it was you and your dad," he shouted. He came toward me slowly, very slowly. "I was scared," he shouted.

I said nothing. Not even, "He's not my dad."

"Look, I'm really not going to hurt you," he said, moving closer, his stupid hands, his stupid evil murderer's hands, outstretched as if to prove it—my keys in one of them. MY KEYS.

"And I know you're not going to hurt me... I know you're kind... You fed the cat..."

He'd reached the back of the car now; he put one of his hands on it, as if to steady himself.

"I can see you really like animals," he said.

One step closer...

He took that step; his hand swept along the side of the car, the terrier jumped up barking like a lunatic, the man jumped back, and I chucked the pee into his prim and proper face.

I guess poop and pee and bleach sting when they get in your eyes. I bet they sting even more when you think they might be going to kill you. He yelled worse than when I'd bitten him. He dropped the keys; his hands went to his face. I snatched up the keys. The dogs—all of them—were going crazy. I scooped up Darling from where she'd crept back into the driver's seat, and I chucked her into the back of the car. I slammed the door, stuck the keys into the ignition, and kangarooed out of there.

Step Three really did last a long time. It was the slowest, crappiest escape in history. When they make the blockbuster movie, I want that changed. I want me to be in some kind of flashy sports car—red—no, white. No. Black. And my hair should be the blonde I wanted it to be, not a ghostly haystack, and definitely not Halloween horror. It should be an convertible sports car, my tiara glinting triumphantly in the sun, my skin zit free, kissing-rash free, and gorgeously sun-kissed (not ORANGE) (and definitely not plastic-coated). Darling would have to be with me, wearing a spiky, punk, leather-and-studs collar. My dog: small but super-mean.

Whitby could be there too, I suppose, but only if he's been washed and blow-dried, and has had a serious doggy oral beauty treatment. No scraps of dead people are to be stuck in his teeth. Mimi, the terrier, the guy I left howling in the road—they should just disappear. They're gone, not in this scene at all. For reasons I don't care to discuss right now, it'd be a lot better if Fluffysnuggles wasn't there either.

I still have nightmares about Step Three. In them, I am Halloween Bad Dolly. I drive a tank. I kill people. I am alone.

CHAPTER EIGHTEEN

The car stalled about a hundred times just getting to the end of our road. If that man had come after us, he could have walked, slowly, and still caught up.

The dogs—all of them—crouched down and shut up as we lurched our way to freedom. Even Fluffysnuggles was probably crouching in terror inside his carton.

I stopped at the four-way stop, like you're supposed to, and we stalled again and rolled backward down the hill. I braked and restarted and kangarooed straight out onto the main road—onto the wrong side of the road. That was deliberate; there was more space on the wrong side of the road. I managed the next half mile without stalling or kangarooing. I even managed to get into third gear and only clipped a couple cars, just a little... But I tell you: I did not like it ONE BIT.

No wonder people get angry driving! Even if they've been doing it for years and years, so they've stopped bumping into things and stuff and don't have to actually THINK REALLY HARD about how you do it, it's basically the most stressful thing EVER. Seriously, when I got to Ashton Road, I pretty much thought I'd be better off on a bike and, at this rate, it'd probably be quicker.

I braked at the junction, and I stalled. That was OK, in fact, because otherwise I'd have turned right, which would have led me straight into the giant car graveyard of town. Instead, I had a moment to think, so I went left. OK, I kangarooed left. On the right side of the road this time, the side coming into town was lined with abandoned cars. I was just building up to second gear when the crazy terrier decided he'd been quiet for long enough and launched himself at Whitby.

There was a massive boy dogfight right in my car, with me, Darling, and Mimi screaming and shouting like most girls do when there's a fight. (Unless they're in it.)

I told myself that's why I had to pull into the school. I flung open the door and the terrier leaped out—sneaky Mimi scrambled out too—and they both went skittering off while I hammered on the horn.

Call it a charitable act. Know that I was scared.

So, yeah, I hammered on the horn.

♦♦♦

Ever heard of a backseat driver? No? It's someone who sits in the back of the car and tells the driver what they should be doing, basically a know-it-all who should get out and walk. I felt like I was in shock from the whole three-step escape thing, and really I just wanted to be quiet for a while, but after ten minutes in the car with the Spratt, I was starting to lose it.

How they even came to be in the car was like this:

"Oh, all right. Hey," I said casually as the black plastic creatures emerged from the staff room. (Can you imagine that? He hadn't just gone to the *school*; he'd gone to the *staff room*.)

I bet that kid hadn't been out of her plastic wrapper all night, and Darius had re-bound himself. Did I mention that none of my steps had included putting on any kind of waterproof clothing? Um…no. I was just wearing what you would wear, jeans and stuff.

"Are you *crazy?!* It's going to rain any second! What are you *doing?!*" blathered the Spratt. "GET BACK IN THE CAR!"

Did I mention that I hadn't even looked at the sky? Um…no. I had vaguely registered that it looked OK and stuff, but somehow, in the meantime, it had gotten to be not OK. An army of little blobby clouds was advancing across the sky, rank after rank of them, lined up, marching. Altocumulus stratiformus, legions of them. The ones directly above our heads didn't look that scary to me (though, actually, altocumulus stratiformus is perfectly capable of sprinkling a little rain on you, just for kicks), but they must have been marching too slowly for the rest of the army because, behind them, the ranks were blundering into each other, massing for a full-scale invasion. I whipped Darling off my seat and got back in the car, plunking her in my lap. Darius and the kid got in too, squishing plastickly into the back, next to Henry's seat.

"What ARE you doing?" said Darius, ripping away the plastic from his face so he could better nag me.

Whoa. Me, Darling, and Whitby turned around to get a good look at the newcomers. Whitby, the big dope, seemed none the worse for his car fight and lurched toward them to say hello; the kid—and gutless Darius!—flattened themselves against the seats like Whitby was some sort of savage beast.

I grabbed Whitby's collar. "Stay!" I commanded (like I had some sort of control over him).

Yeah, and what are YOU doing? I thought. *Hiding in the staff room until teacher comes and tell you what to do?*

"I'm going to London," I said.

Annoyingly, Spratt didn't fall to his knees and beg to come with me—which would have been hard, sitting in the backseat of a car with Whitby within savaging distance, but you know what I mean.

"What for?" he said.

"My dad lives there," I said. It sort of hurt a little to say it out loud. I got hold of some random sob that wanted to come out, and I stuffed it back down.

He thought about that for a moment.

"Hn," he said. There was another tedious pause before, "I don't think going to London's a very good idea," he added.

Whoa No. 2. Now I was not asking whether he thought my plan was a good plan or not, but if there's one thing I've learned (the hard way) from going on "social media" and that, it's that you sometimes have to just hang on for one second before you blast off some kind of devastating response to rudeness and brazenness from someone you don't really know all that well—particularly if you want something from them, like an invitation to a party or something. So I buttoned it—though obviously mentally toying with various devastating responses, blending them with colorful choices from the tempting palette of swear words I like to have available at all times.

"But I suppose we might as well come with you for a while, then," said Darius after another age.

"Yeah, sure, whatever," I said. *You can't leave me.*

"Just until we decide what to do," said Darius.

"Yeah," I said, "'course."

Until they decided what to do? *They?* Did that GBK ever even actually speak?

And how they nearly came to NOT be in the car ten minutes later was like this:

"Maybe you're letting the clutch out too quick," said Darius when we stalled for the second time on the Ashton Road roundabout.

It was about the five hundredth helpful tip he'd given me in the last mile—after he'd whined about there not being enough room in the back and couldn't he just take out the baby seat—*Henry's* seat— and I'd said no. No way, no. And don't lean on it like that either.

"You need to change up a gear. Put it in second!"

"Do you want me to drop you somewhere?" I snapped. "Like here?"

"I'm just trying to help," said Darius.

"Yeah?! Why don't *you* drive, then?!"

"I can't," he said. That figured. Probably he still rode a bike with training wheels or something. "I'm not allowed to right now."

"*Allowed?!* Hello?! Allowed? Guess what, Darius Spratt—"

Saying his name shouldn't have mattered ONE BIT, but I knew as soon as I'd said it—like, YEURCH! He knew I knew his name.

"I'm not *allowed* to drive either!" I yelled.

The GBK rustled a little.

Not in front of the kids, huh? I stalled the car, flung open my door, and got out. I breathed for a second—for not enough time at all— and I knocked on his window and beckoned him. I beckoned him like one of Dan's gaming-fantasy–hero types challenges a victim to a fight.

He got out.

"This is not a good idea, Ruby," he said, looking at the sky.

It's fairly humiliating to have to say this, but the cloud army had kept up with us. It was as if we hadn't moved at all.

"What are you, my *dad?!*" I blurted. The weird thing was I meant Simon, and not my *dad* dad, who would basically never say something like that. No matter. I raged on. "I'm not *allowed* to break into police stations! I'm not *allowed* to break into shops! Or other people's houses! I am not allowed to STEAL DOGS and I am not ALLOWED to dye my hair RED."

Before he could get one word out about that, I finished my hissing, spitting rant: "In fact, I am not *allowed* to do anything!"

"I'm epileptic," he said.

What?! What? *You what?!* My mouth gaped open and shut, open and shut, like a goldfish. Beanpole Boy turned crimson.

There was this really terrible, awful pause. Then we both looked at the sky and got back in the car.

"I like your hair," he said quietly. "I think it could really suit you. The thing is—"

"I know my face is kind of orange, all right? I know," I snarled.

I started up the engine, and we lurched off down the road. Darius Spratt leaned forward to speak to me.

"So, the thing is I was going to ask if you have anything to eat or drink, Ruby?" he said. "It's just I looked in the back and…"

We stopped in Ashton village, on the pavement, right outside the shop. The door was wide open. When I took my hands off the steering wheel, they left behind serious driver's hand sweat.

We got out; the cloud army was behind us now. I gave the Spratt this big, fake smile, one I usually saved for Simon, on the rare occasion that he got something wrong—triumphant with a hint of withering smugness.

The shop had not been looted like the shops in Dartbridge; nothing was smashed. Stuff had been taken, but the shelves weren't stripped bare, and nothing had been left strewn about on the floor. No windows had been shattered by bullets; no dead people lay about. Probably the people who had come there had even paid for what they had taken because there were little piles of money left on the counter by the till.

Ashton village; that's the kind of place I would like to live someday, a place where people don't go NUTS and trash stuff and threaten to kill each other, etc., etc., just because the world is being destroyed by a killer space bug.

"Wait a sec," said Darius.

I dunno where he went, off foraging for more backwash peanuts, I expect. I didn't pay attention—like normally I wouldn't pay attention to newspapers either, but I got kind of *mesmerized* by them. It was just weird: Saturday May 23—all of them. There was some National Health Service scandal thing splashed all over the big papers, but the little ones all stuck to the main story: "BBQ BRITAIN SIZZLES" (with a picture of the outline of the country burned onto a giant, greasy sausage); "MAY MELTDOWN" (Retirees in swimwear). Then the news had stopped.

The magazines were still current, though. I loaded up with every fat, glossy, drool-worthy, style-soaked magazine I had never been able to afford, and some celebrity dirt-dishing mags I probably could have afforded but wouldn't have been caught dead buying— even though what was in them was, like, totally fascinating and you desperately wanted to know about it.

Darius came back. He had stuff. (Healthy stuff.) For a moment, he just stood next to me; I thought that in spite of the fact that he was Nerd Beanpole Boy, we were somehow sharing some weird moment, about how everything had stopped and seemed like it never would be the same again. I bit my lip; I kind of wanted to say something about it all, but I didn't know what.

"They didn't even get the weather right," said Darius.

"They never do," I said. I swear those Simon words came out of my mouth without even calling in on my brain. *I* didn't pay any attention to weather forecasts; I just moaned when it was rainy or cold, and was glad when it was sunny.

"Still, I suppose we ought to take some papers," he said. "To show our kids."

WHAAAAAAAAAAAAAAAAT?!

I looked at him in complete and utter horror.

"I don't mean *our* kids," he said, turning crimson again. "I mean *kids* kids…any kids…kids in the future."

"Oh," I said. If I hadn't been orange already, I think it would have been obvious that I had gone bright red too. Did he seriously think that I had seriously thought…that I would EVER…

"I mean, these papers might be worth something one day," he said. "But probably not… It's not like there won't be tons of them left. Dead people don't buy papers."

I looked at him again then, ready to tell him that was a horrible thing to say—YEURCH!!!! He was looking up at the top shelf, at the bare-boobed-and-bottomed smut-fest magazines even polite Ashton villagers must have read…and the stuff no one in their right mind would want to read, like *Trainspotters Monthly*, or whatever. He reached out and took the last—hey, probably the ONLY—copy of *New Scientist*.

"Oo, great," he said, eagerly leafing through it.

I mean really—REALLY—is there no end to the monstrous cruelty of the universe? I truly was in the company of a nerd. Possibly the last boy on Earth…and he was a nerd. Not a geek—geeks were useful and cool and kind of hot—but a nerd. A deeply unsexy nerd who had just thought I had thought—really, I can't even repeat it.

That snapped me to my senses; for the sake of the GBK, I scooted around the shop; I loaded fizzy drinks, chewy candy, cheap chocolate, chips, and bubblegum into one of their plastic bags. For the sake of shocking Darius Spratt, I also took a packet of cigarettes.

"Ready?" I said, grabbing a lighter and testing it.

"Yeah," he said. He closed that pervy science magazine and stuffed it down the front of his garbage bag. "Ruby," he said, "would it be OK to put the big dog in the back? It's just…I think…maybe it'd be better if the kid sat in the front."

"Yeah, sure, whatever," I said, casually loading a bottle of vodka into my goodie bag.

Outside, there was kind of an alarming sight. The cloud army had gained on us, advancing relentlessly. A fresh battalion was sliding into position below the others, massing overhead. Until you have to pay attention (or die), you don't realize that: how scarily fast some clouds move. When it feels like it, altocumulus stratiformus is particularly quick. It's a sprinter.

"🦋!" I said and dragged Whitby out of the front seat.

Darius helped the GBK to take his place, getting her to climb across the gap, so she wouldn't have to get out of the car, while I attempted to bundle Whitby into the back. The Spratt climbed into the backseat.

"Come on, Ru!" he had the nerve to shout at me.

The hatchback clunked down on Whitby's big dumb head; I wished it was Nerd Boy's. By the time I'd got into the driver's seat, Whitby was already blundering his way out of the back.

"Aw! He likes you!" I sniggered, as he tried to barge his way onto Darius's lap.

I didn't laugh when Darling scrambled out of my lap to get to the GBK—and that was before the snacks came out.

I dumped my bag of goodies down (on top of Fluffysnuggles), started up, and lurched out into the road.

"Help yourself," I told the kid.

It was no contest; she chose my selection of delights in favor of the whole-wheat things Darius had got. Fizzy drinks and chips and candy disappeared into the black plastic.

"Can't she take that stuff off?" I asked.

"We'd better wait until we're safe," said Darius.

That was news to me: I thought we *were* safe. My passengers didn't seem to notice how skillful my driving was getting. None of them. Darling rustled about on the GBK's lap and was fed tasty junk morsels.

"That's bad for her," I said.

"It's bad for her too," said Darius, meaning the kid.

From the corner of my eye, I saw the GBK do what I would have done. She fed stuff to Darling anyway, pretending it was an accident when it so wasn't. Whitby refused Darius's more wholesome offerings and poked his stinky head over the gearshift, so the kid could feed him junk too. I didn't go on about it.

What with the kid being mute and Darius being Darius and the world having been destroyed, the general conversation wasn't up to much either.

"So how come you're not dead, then?" I asked, by way of an ice breaker. You know, the kind of question you ask someone when you don't know what else to say. I'd seen my mom do it a thousand times, ask people, "So how was your trip?" or "So how do you know Mr. and Mrs. Such-and-Such?" Even if the answer was totally embarrassing—like "I live next door" or "Actually, I *am* Mrs. Such-and-Such"—it was OK; people'd just laugh and have another drink and ask the same question back.

My ice breaker, it was crap. The second I asked that question, the most horrible thing happened. I felt everything that had happened and everything I felt about it come welling up inside me. It felt like… like a tsunami coming, carrying everything—EVERYTHING— with it.

I felt myself choke. I turned the choke into a cough.

"Just lucky, I guess," he said. "You?"

"Same," I said.

I was driving. I didn't even know him; that tsunami, it had to be stopped or I would start blubbering so hard I'd crash the car and kill us all anyway. I—HAD—TO—GET—TO—MY—DAD. I drove on, steely eyed. Steely hearted.

"I was inside, studying," said Darius Spratt.

"*WHAT?!*" I shrieked.

I got into a gear confusion and the car swerved around a little.

"I was studying," repeated the Spratt when I'd shoved Whitby's head out of the way and discovered where third gear was. "You know, for exams?"

Did he think I was an imbecile? Who could not know about the horror of exams? It's just that—

"It was a holiday!" I screeched.

"So?" he said.

I looked at him then in my rearview mirror. He looked kind of like he was having his own tsunami issues. He glared up at me.

I looked away—back at the road, where I suppose I should have been looking all along.

Behind me, I heard him speak.

"I was inside," Darius Spratt said, "and my parents, my whole family, all our friends, all our neighbors, everyone, except me, was outside."

I didn't say anything.

I didn't say anything to Darius about Exeter either. When I saw the signs for it, when I saw where I could turn off, I thought about Caspar. I made a choice: I would go find my dad. Then I would look for Caspar. After everything I had seen, after everything I knew, I still couldn't quite put it in my head that Caspar wouldn't be alive. So I would find him after.

That's how it is, isn't it? I mean, really, until you know for sure that someone is dead, there's always—isn't there?—this tiny little flickery wisplet of hope. A cirrus floccus of hope. This tiny little lone brain cell—maybe connected by weensy fairy-silk strands to a tiny lone heart cell—that will forever believe that they could still be alive. And will never, ever give up believing that. No matter how much it hurts.

Even if that person is Saskia, right? Even if you never did much like them in the first place, that's what it's like. You just hope.

CHAPTER NINETEEN

I stomped on the accelerator more than I suppose you should. When we hit the highway, the driving was a lot easier. Less gear changing! Less braking! Less steering! There were cars stopped here and there; there were cars crashed, but most had pulled over, and I got really good at zooming around anything that hadn't.

I was driving! It was easy! The thing that had seemed so impossible, to get to my dad, seemed more possible with every mile. Easy: up the highway, get to Bristol, turn right onto the other highway.

The "what happens when we get to London" part was a little unclear—because it wasn't as if I'd ever actually driven to my dad's before, was it?—but I'd figure it out when we got there. Basically, it was all going swimmingly.

Ha ha ha ha. Do you think anyone will ever say that kind of thing anymore?

I felt as right as rain. I was on cloud nine. Ha ha ha ha ha.

And then the gas-indicator thingy flashed red.

I wanted to ignore it; I would have ignored it. It was not part of my plan. DUR.

"Ru," said Darius, leaning over my shoulder. "We should turn off, huh?"

He spoke quietly; the GBK had fallen asleep—I think; it was

hard to say for sure. She'd sort of slumped a little and the plastic around her mouth was sucking in and out in a steady sort of way. Darling, on her lap, had also crashed. Whitby snored on the backseat.

"No," I said. *And don't call me Ru*, I thought.

It was getting dark, but I wasn't going to stop. Didn't Simon always go on about how there were fifty miles left on empty?

I swerved around an abandoned car—harder to see them coming when you're zooming, and it's getting dark, and you can't work out how to switch the lights on, and you've just realized there's a bit of a major problem with your plan.

"Turn off," he said.

No, no, no, no! I would not! I could not! It was FINE. I got the lights on—just in time to show me that there was a body in the road. I swerved. I kept going.

"If you don't turn off, we'll run out of gas."

No!

"We'll get stuck on the highway."

No!

"In the rain," said Darius Spratt, leaning forward to tap on my shoulder.

Startled by this random assault upon my person, I turned to demand that he refrain from poking me and saw his finger pointing, practically in my face. I shoved it out of my face.

🦋. From the side of us a fat blanket of gray was rolling in low, tucking the land into a lovely space-bug-infested bed. (Stratus nebulosus—creeping up from the sea, I guess. It really likes to hang out there.)

I'd only been looking straight ahead, hadn't I? We'd outrun one storm only to have another sneak up on us. The car weaved about dangerously as I peered at it. All I could think about was what the clouds had been like being trapped in that car at the supermarket. I stamped on the accelerator.

Next exit, I turned off. We zoomed up on to a roundabout. I braked; I stalled. The GBK woke up; the dogs woke up. I restarted. I was so panicked I just drove.

"Ruby, where are we going?" asked Darius.

"Weston-super-Mare," I snapped, slamming my foot down on the accelerator.

I'd been there before, with Leonie's family. With any luck, we'd get to the pier and be able to spend the night in the video arcade. Brilliant! Except nothing would be working, I suppose…

"This is the wrong way," said Darius.

"*WHAT?!*"

"Wrong way!"

"🦋!"

I searched for a place to turn—for a while there was nothing but hedgerows—then there was a track on our left. I braked—

"*What are you doing?!*" squeaked Darius.

I reversed.

"I AM TUR-NING A-ROUND!" I bellowed.

We bumped backward along the track. I stalled.

The car would not restart. I did that thing I'd seen my dad do too many times in his old beater. I banged my hands on the steering wheel—but it was Simon I was thinking about. "It'll do fifty miles on empty." Yeah, right! I knew, instantly, the only reason he ever said that was to stop my mom from panicking. Simon, it turned out, did make things up—what a great time to find that out.

"Brilliant," said Darius. "Just brilliant."

I took my seat belt off so I could turn around and yell at him properly—and then I saw it: looming in the gloom, there was one of those plastic greenhouse tunnel thingies they grow stuff in.

"I'm going in there," I said.

I jumped out and slammed my door, then opened his.

"C'mon, Whitby," I said; Whitby, who'd been sprawled on Darius, trampled all over him to get out.

"Ruby, I don't think—"

I didn't hear what the Spratt didn't think because I slammed the door on it…but I can guess. As I said before, it's really stupid to go anywhere at night, even just hardly any distance at all—and especially when you do actually know it's cloudy. I knew that already; I just didn't care. NO WAY was I spending the night in that car.

I barged into the plastic tunnel and…I'm not all into gardening and stuff (OK, I pretty much hate it), but it was gorgeous. There were long metal tables filled with pots and pots of flowers; it smelled like heaven. My mom would have loved it. *And* it was deliciously warm. Perfect—no, better than perfect. There was a bank of switches by the door. I flicked them on—LIGHT! Beautiful, beautiful electric light! Flower heaven lit up in a rainbow of color.

Darius erupted from the car.

"TURN THE LIGHTS OFF!" he whisper-squealed.

He'd put his rubber gloves on; he yanked open the passenger door, picked the GBK up (and Darling and the water gun because the GBK had tight hold on them both) and dashed into the tunnel with her.

"People'll be able to see us for miles around!" he said, killing the lights.

"So?" I said, but I didn't put them back on. "I'm gonna get my stuff."

"I'll get it," said Darius.

Yeah, right. He dashed out and then came back in with the food and the drink and ONE random bag of MY things: makeup, when what I really wanted was a change of clothes.

"Don't!" said Darius, grabbing me by the arm to stop me from going back to the car.

Nerd Boy actually manhandled ME. I looked up at him with a snarl; his glasses had misted up.

"Please, Ruby. It's not safe."

The GBK rustled. He let go of my arm.

"OK," I said quietly. "OK."

It didn't rain ten seconds later, so it's not like Darius Spratt saved my life or anything…but it did rain. Such a soft and gentle rain you wouldn't even have heard it, probably, if you'd been inside a house, but in the polytunnel you could hear it: the tiniest pitter-patter. That would have been a lovely sound if it weren't for…well, you know: what was *in* it. The Spratt's whole-wheat survival kit also contained (cheap) flashlights, and we got paranoid for a while, checking and rechecking the roof; it didn't seem like it leaked anywhere, but it was so freaky, having just this thin skin of plastic between us and *it*. In the beams of the flashlights, you could see the tiniest slight shadows of rain, blurry through the plastic. Bloblets pooling with other bloblets, sliding sneakily down the sides of the tunnel, looking for a way in. The darker it got, the harder it was not to get spooked just thinking about it. It didn't help that there were weird crackly noises inside the tunnel; the GBK was following Darius around like a little rustly ghost.

"Can she take that stuff off now?" I asked him.

"Do you want to take it off now?" he asked her.

The GBK just stood there.

"Maybe if you take yours off first?" I suggested to Darius.

Honestly, I half expected him to have his school uniform on under the waterproof gear. It might have been better than what he was wearing. (Red corduroy trousers and a *Star Wars* sweatshirt that would have looked cool and retro—on someone else.) Next time we went anywhere near some kind of clothing stores, I was gonna have to force him to sort that look out—but the priority would be locating some deodorant: Darius Spratt stank. I caught a severe waft of it and—

WHOA! It was TOO weird! Hadn't Lee read an article about exactly this kind of thing to me? How you could take some boy who was HOT—really, totally undeniably HOT *to look at*—and a boy who was NOT HOT—really, totally undeniably NOT HOT *to look at*—and you could waft their sweat under the nose of a blindfolded girl and ask her to pick which one she liked, and it was scientifically proven that there is some crazy animaly sweat thing that meant if the girl couldn't SEE the boy the sweat came off, she wouldn't necessarily choose the hot boy. Her nose could actually force her to choose…

WHOA!

I forced myself to get a grip.

"You stink," I told Darius Spratt.

"Sorry," he said. "*Personal grooming* hasn't exactly been a priority."

"Well, maybe it should have been," I pointed out, because I was pretty sure that personal grooming comment had to be some kind of sneaky dig at me.

He peeled off his sweatshirt and offered it to the kid. His arms weren't feeble; they were wiry. He was wiry and gangly—but luckily there was no danger WHATSOEVER that I would have another random freaky animaly attraction attack because he was wearing a tank top. Like, really! And not some kind of a cool T-shirt tank top, but an underwear tank top, the kind your mother makes you wear when you're about FIVE.

It did the trick, though. The GBK sidled up to Darius, apparently immune to the *hideous* smell. I'd seen already how they'd worked out this communication thing, this little private language where Darius would say stuff and the GBK would move in a certain way, and Darius would interpret that…and he seemed always to get it right—though as the GBK didn't speak, it'd be hard to say for sure.

"OK," said Darius, like the kid had spoken. He cut (with his whole-wheat multifunction penknife) and tore the plastic off her.

In a weird way, I wished he hadn't. For as long as you couldn't see that silent kid, she was just a thing. What was under the plastic… it broke my heart.

Tearstains on her cheeks. I'd imagined a mini female Darius Spratt, but she was beautiful. A solemn-faced, sad kid. An Asian kid, maybe Indian? And beautiful, so beautiful. A skinny kid in leggings and a sun dress, with a mop-top of matted curls, a little bow on a clip half buried in them. Her face—it was studded with tiny scars, tiny scabby scratches.

"I think she was in a car crash," said Darius.

The car. My driving. She must have been terrified.

The kid shuffled closer to him.

"There was glass, little slivers of it, in her hair," he said, "but I think we got it all out."

Really? It didn't look like her hair had been brushed for a week.

The kid was looking up at Darius. Seemed like maybe she was older than I thought too—not six or seven, but eight or maybe even nine? Maybe. Maybe not. She scratched at her face, little fingers scab hunting.

"Don't," I said. "You'll get scars."

She wouldn't look at me. (But she did stop scratching.)

"I think she's a little bit scared of you," said Darius.

Huh?! Kids LOVED me.

"I mean, you sort of shout a lot," he said.

I felt so terrible I could have burst into tears on the spot…and that kid, she'd wet herself. You could see it on her leggings.

"She needs a change of clothes," I said.

I heard my own voice… It sounded dead and cold—when what was in my heart so wasn't. What was in my heart, it was red and hot and alive, and it hurt so bad for that little kid.

"We don't have anything," said Darius.

I took off my hoodie for her—the kid shied away. I nudged Darius, who offered his sweatshirt.

The kid just stood there…then she kind of wriggled a tiny bit, frowning.

Aaaah! *I* got it! So, old enough to not want to be seen in the nude? How old were kids when they started to care that? Dan was twelve now, and he still didn't seem to care sometimes…but he was a boy, and my brother and a show-off (when he felt like it). So when had I started worrying about things like that?

Darius seemed sort of awkward himself; he folded his lanky arms in front of his lanky chest.

"Turn around," I said to him.

We turned away to give the kid some privacy.

"Tell her it's OK," I said. "We won't look."

"Get changed," he told the kid.

Out of the corner of my eye, when she had done, I saw her nudge him and hand him her clothes. I took them off him and hung them from the table with plant pots to hold them down.

I turned around. You could see the kid didn't like that one bit, me touching her stuff.

"It's OK," I said. "We'll get them nice and dry…"

The kid in the *Star Wars* sweatshirt looked away from me. Not like I wasn't there…like she didn't want me to be there.

OW. And Darling seemed to prefer her to me? Yeah. Nicer to have someone quiet who pets you and gives you treats than a shouty ogre who drags you around all over the place and has thrown you into the back of the car. But I could win that kid over… Like I said, kids LOVE me. I could be great with them… when I wanted to be… So, I saw a massive roll of that stuff they cover plants with—fleece, it's called, like my mom puts on her most delicate, precious plants in winter. Right. I ripped off massive armfuls of the stuff.

"I'm gonna make you a nest," I told her.

She edged up against Darius. It was going to be hard work, but I WAS going to win her over. I chattered on—quietly—to the kid while I assembled a nest, telling her all about my brother Dan and how he could sleep anywhere because he always built himself a little nest just like Fluffysnuggles—who was safe in his bed and fast asleep already (I added quickly, because really I'd totally forgotten about him and had left him in the car). I told her how maybe we could build a little nest for Darling too, thinking that was bound to get her interested. It didn't, but I went ahead and made one anyway, chattering on about how maybe Darling would like a bedtime story and shall we tell her one and which one shall we tell her? I even put pretty pots of flowers around the nests.

NOTHING. The kid still wouldn't look at me; the kid still wouldn't say a word.

"So maybe Darius would like a story too?" I said.

"Hn," said Darius.

I eyeballed him viciously, and he came and sat down next to the nest. I sat down too, trying to ignore the waft of stink now that his pits were fully exposed.

(WHOA—NO, NO, NO—WHOA. NO. NO WAY. NO. If Leonie was still alive and if cell phones still worked, I would have texted her immediately to tell her the freaky animaly sweat thing was true—or not. The horrific, sinister enchantment of the Spratt's pits had to fall into the category of things that were TOO weird and TOO disgusting to tell to anyone, even your best friend.)

"It's bedtime," he told her.

She got into the nest and put Darling down in hers. Whitby tried to muscle in on the whole snugly bed thing, but I pulled him back, and he flumped down on the floor next to me. At least someone liked me.

I chose *Rumpelstiltskin*. I don't know why, because I could hardly remember it, so I kind of made it up a little. The miller's daughter became a princess and nothing too horrible happened to anyone—including Rumpelstiltskin, who said he was sorry and got taken on as a nanny because although he had seemed horrible to begin with and shouted a lot, he was actually really REALLY nice and very VERY good with children.

When I got to the end, I had a total Ruby genius moment.

"Well, now, I wonder what your name is?" I said.

I reeled off the name of every Asian girl I knew, then any old name at all: crazy names, pretty names, boys' names, pets' names, i.e., the kind of thing that would have any other kid in stitches—or at least force them to squeal out, "No! I'm not Malcolm!" or whatever. Even Darius joined in a little, starting with "Thingy?" and "Whatsit?" and then throwing in weird names that sounded pretty much like the sort of fantasy-hero characters Dan gibbered on about: "Are you Thorgarella, daughter of Kriksor?" That kind of thing.

Finally…

"You know what?" I said. "Until we know your name, I think we should just call you…"

"Rumpelstiltskin," muttered Darius.

I slapped him—then smiled sweetly to make it look playful, because the kid was there.

"Princess," I said.

I was pretty sure it couldn't have been her name, but I saw her little nose twitch and the tiniest of tiny nearly-a-smile smiles flicker on her lips.

"Night, night, Princess and Darling," I said and blew them both kisses.

"Go to sleep," instructed Darius.

The kid tucked herself up in the fleece; Darling—the traitor—nestled in with her.

If this all sounds kind of sweet to you, it really wasn't.

I felt awful. Really, really awful. That kid…that kid being like that, not being able to speak… In a weird kind of way, it got to me as bad as anything I'd seen—and it made me wonder what she'd seen and what had happened to her, because I sort of had the feeling that she could speak, but that whatever had happened was so hideous it had turned her mute. And…you know what else? It made me think of Simon, of all those years he'd spent trying to be sweet to me and me giving him back nothing but a snarl, not wanting to have anything to do with him. I'd had—what?—not even an hour of that from a kid I didn't even know, and I felt useless and frustrated and exhausted. And very, very sad.

So I couldn't leave it at that, could I? I insisted we sing. Darius said he didn't want to do that. The kid—obviously—didn't say anything, but you could tell she didn't want to either. So I sang.

Did I say already? I can't sing.

As soon as I'd got the first warbling word out, I knew I'd made yet another horrible mistake. Not because of the not being able to sing, but because the song was the song my mom sang to me when I was little, the one she wouldn't sing that night when she sat outside the door. "Dream A Little Dream Of Me." It was the song her mom had sung to her when she was little, that's what she always said. (My mom, she used to change the "me" to "Ruby." And like the whole thing with the fairies at the holy well, it took years before I realized the truth: the song wasn't actually about me.)

Every lovely, pretty thing in it felt wrong:

There were no stars. (YOU COULDN'T EVEN SEE THE STARS BECAUSE IT WAS CLOUDY AND IT WAS RAINING KILLER RAIN.)

There was no breeze. (THERE WAS JUST KILLER RAIN WHISPERING, "I WANT TO KILL YOU.")

There was no birdsong. (BECAUSE THE BIRDS WERE TOO BUSY PECKING OUT HUMAN EYEBALLS.)

The next part is supposed to be really sweet, about how you'll dream of the people you love. It doesn't say anything about "EVEN THOUGH THEY'RE PROBABLY DEAD." I couldn't go on. Not because I was worried the kid would dream about me (or that Darius Spratt would), but because I got all choked silent. I wanted my mom.

Genius, Ruby. You really are a genius.

The killer rain applauded me, drumming down harder on that thin plastic roof. Now everyone definitely for sure felt like crap; you could just tell. The kid had shut her eyes. She'd shut them like all kids shut them when they're just pretending to be asleep, like: go away. A lonely little tear squeezed out between her eyelashes.

Me and Darius, we divided up the rest of the fleece and wrapped ourselves in it (SEPARATELY). It wasn't cold, not really, but the fleece was comforting. There was this kind of awkward few seconds about where we were going to sleep—well, there was for me—but Darius just cleared himself a space among the flowerpots and laid down on one of the long table things, so I cleared myself a space on the table on the other side of the walkway. I made a little wall of plants so I wouldn't actually have to look at him, but I felt like I really wanted to talk, to talk like I'd talk to Leonie or how I did with my mom sometimes, before Henry was born. To just pour my heart out…but no words would come. We lay in the silence.

"It's a shame it's not a zombie attack, isn't it?" said Darius after a while.

"*Excuse me?*"

"You know, because if it was zombies—or vampires—we'd sort of know what to do, wouldn't we? Well, *I* would."

"*I* would too," I said.

He was right. We would have known exactly what to do. If only it was that simple.

"Or even aliens," said Darius after a while. "Then we'd just have to locate the mother ship and destroy it. Although I suppose the bacterium is an alien. A very small one."

"They don't know it's that space-bug thing," I said. "Not for sure."

"Yeah they do," said Darius.

Rain fell steadily on the roof, millions of little wiggly micro-murderers sliding down the plastic.

"Still, I suppose you've got to look on the bright side," said the Spratt.

"*What…*bright…side?"

The only—THE ONLY—thing I could think of was…that phone bill under my bed? That premium rate rip-off line I called? I am NEVER going to get into trouble for it. Somehow, it didn't exactly seem like a bright side.

"No more school," said Darius.

"No exams!" I said. Now *that* was good. First time that had occurred to me. Every cloud's got a silver lining. Ha ha ha ha ha.

"I didn't mean that. I was looking forward to them," said Darius Spratt.

DO YOU SEE? DO YOU SEE WHAT KIND OF A FREAK I WAS STUCK WITH? I sat up so I could get a better look at it too, the Darius freak, but it was too dark to make out anything more than the rough shape of it.

"You're kidding me, right?" I spoke at the shape.

"No. I've worked hard for two years for those exams. I was going to do civil engineering in college."

"Wow," I said and lay back down. "Great. That's just great." I didn't actually know what civil engineering was, but honestly…

"See, that's what I mean about school," said Darius Spratt.

"Huh?"

"It's full of people like you, isn't it? Clueless bullies."

"*What?!*"

"Well, you're more of a snob," he said and yawned. He ACTUALLY yawned.

"*Excuse me?!* I'm not a snob!"

"Yeah you are. You and your friends. You're, like, sooo super-cool, aren't you? Urh. That Caspar kid—he thinks he's James Dean or something."

I didn't know who James Dean was either, but I did not like the sound of that. I sat back up to glower at the shadowy blob of the freak in the darkness.

"My *friends* are all dead, Darius Spratt. So's my mom. So's my stepdad. So's my little baby brother. So is…*my boyfriend*, Caspar." I'd never called him that, "my boyfriend." I'd never had the chance to. I caught my breath. "Probably."

"Yeah, everyone's dead," he mumbled sleepily.

He rolled over and fell asleep…or at least I think he did, but he could have just been doing some more advanced version of the pretending-to-be-asleep thing.

I lay back down, my brain buzzing, fizzing, *infected* with rage and sadness.

CHAPTER TWENTY

I dreamed about my mom.

Does that happen to you? You dream about the people who have died—only they're still alive, and everything is lovely, or at least normal. And then you wake up, and you wonder how it can be that you saw them, that you heard them, that you touched them... They were there, and now they are gone again. And realizing that makes the hurt stab knife-sharp. I truly don't know what is worse: the nightmares or those dreams.

When I woke up and realized it was a dream, it made me sob. I struggled out of my tangle of fleece. The others were still asleep: Darling with Princess; Whitby, also a traitor, had crept over under Darius's table (probably attracted by the stink). I got up and—truth? I checked on Darius Spratt. I just looked, like you can't help but look at a person sleeping.

🦋. What if he really was the last boy on Earth?

I felt another sob come, and I like to think I wouldn't have gone outside if I'd have thought it was still raining, but the truth is I forgot to even think about that; I just pushed open the door and went out. Then I looked up. The sky looked weird: half of it milky and stripy (cirrostratus fibratus!), half of it yellowy and pale and sickly looking. The sick part was overhead. For a moment I thought some new and dreadful thing was happening to the sky, and I panicked about where the 🦋 the sun had gone. Dur. It was dawn; that's all it was. Me and the sun had gotten up together; it was dawn and it was cold. I rescued my fleece bed from inside the polytunnel, wrapped myself in it, and walked up the track.

There was a farmhouse at the top of it; it seemed like there was no one home, but I didn't go closer, and there were cows mooing somewhere just round the corner—which was great; no one would hear me as I howled my eyes out.

The milky stripes had burned away and the sun kept me company, kindly promising a toasty day, as I walked back down the track and opened up the back of the car. That was the first time I saw how mad my packing had been: there was nothing anyone would call sensible, apart from about ten thousand pairs of underwear. It was weird. Having dreamed about my mom, I felt like she was looking over my shoulder, wondering why I'd packed such silly clothes.

"Sorry, Mom," I whispered.

I changed—right there, on that track—into a looted dress. It was a silver sequiny thing from the evil old hag's boutique, a thing I'd never normally have been allowed. I felt better just putting it on—and, I swear, it was pretty much the most sensible thing I had, apart from some super-skinny skinny jeans I didn't much fancy the effort of squeezing into. I picked up one of the trashy magazines and went back into the tunnel to fix my makeup.

It smelled so sweet in there (despite a whiff of Spratt). The others were still asleep. Only Whitby opened a lazy eye but didn't even pretend to take an interest. I climbed back up among the pots and sat cross-legged in a sea of flowers, flicking through the gossip while I sorted out my face.

Yup, it was still orange. The post-make-out pink chin was pretty much gone. I felt kind of sad about it, even. Gone. My eyes looked piggyish, in need of serious work. I slapped on some moisturizer followed by a mega coat of foundation.

I was a blank canvas. I, me, Ruby stared back at myself in my compact mirror.

I need to get to my dad, I told myself. *I just need to get to my dad.*

I sighed…and in that sigh, I became aware of a small pair of eyes watching me—I looked. The kid shut her eyes.

Right, I thought. *Gotcha.*

I didn't look at her again. I went for it; I put stuff on my face—eye shadow, mascara, blush, lipstick—then I'd change my mind. I'd take it off again. I'd pretend I didn't know which color eye shadow I wanted, which lipstick went best… The kid got up and edged toward the table. *Gotcha, gotcha, gotcha.*

All the while, that place heated up. The warmth of it was delicious, like being on vacation someplace nice.

"Hmmm," I sighed at the purple eye shadow. I stripped it off.

"If only someone could help me," I said.

That didn't work.

I tried the gold eye shadow. The glittery, gorgeous gold. I had one eye done when I saw something flitter… I looked up and saw a butterfly.

"Oh!" I said.

I pointed at it, for the benefit of my audience of one.

This butterfly, this white-winged destroyer of cabbages, flitted about.

Out of the corner of my eye, I could see my audience of one watching it too.

And then a small thing happened.

There was a click, followed by a *DZZZZZZZZZZZ*—a soft buzzing sound from this box in the corner of the tunnel.

Darling pricked up her ears. Whitby got up from under the table and stretched, then slouched off outside to have a sniff around. Darling tried to follow, but the kid picked her up. My audience increased to two.

OK. I daubed my brush in gold. I was poised, ready to sweep it across my other eyelid, when I heard a funny gurgling sound above me.

I looked up. I saw pipes. In one half of a milli-nanosecond I got it.

Such pretty flowers.

"RUN!" I screamed.

PSSSSSSSSSSSHT!

I leaped off the table, sending pots of flowers tumbling and crashing.

"OUT!" I yelled at the kid, grabbing her and shoving her toward the door—I turned and I yanked Darius Spratt off the table by his tank top. Behind us, water showered down, a shimmering curtain of it moving in on us as—*PSSSSHT! PSSSSSSSSSSSHT! PSSSSSSSSSSSHT!*—one sprinkler after another burst into life, cool air kissing our backs as we ran.

As we reached the door, Whitby blundered into us.

"OUT!" I screamed.

Know what? I didn't hesitate. We burst out of the polytunnel and I went straight for the trunk to rummage for the crowbar because it felt as if we were being attacked, as if maybe someone could have set those sprinklers off deliberately.

"It's automatic," panted Darius, studying the sky. "It'll be automatic."

"*You don't know that!*" I screamed into his face, then carried on rummaging.

"There's a battery."

"*The thing in the box?*"

"Yeah. It would be on a timer, wouldn't it?"

My hands found the crowbar even as my brain decided the Spratt was right; those plants were perfect, and like Simon had said about the supermarket flowers, it was too hard to imagine someone thinking, *Hey, the world's in meltdown, but I think I'll just water the plants. Every day.*

"That water's probably OK too," said Darius. Satisfied that the sky was OK, he actually looked at me. "It's probably from a tank."

"Really? Well, why don't you go back in there, then?" I snarled. "And take a shower—because YOU REALLY NEED ONE."

Whitby bounded around like a puppy, cranked up from all the running around, thinking some brilliant new game was being played. Darling wriggled to join him, but the kid wouldn't let her go. For the humans, the trauma wasn't quite over. Everything in Darius's whole-wheat survival kit was getting rained on in that tunnel. Everything we had to eat and drink (apart from vodka!) was being watered with the flowers. The bag of phones was still in the car, but I'd lost my makeup—that was totally disastrous—and now the kid only had that mangy sweatshirt to wear. But the biggest calamity of all had fallen on Darius Spratt, who had lost his trousers. Dig the underpants, Grandpa.

"I got too hot," he said, going bright red.

I couldn't help myself; I snorted with mocking laughter.

"Shut up," said Darius, hiding his modesty.

I tried to control myself as I offered what I had. The skinny jeans were a nonstarter, so it was down to fancy frocks and floaty tops… or a silver sequiny stretchy miniskirt from the same line as my dress.

I cracked up completely when he put it on. How that kid managed not to laugh I do not know—you could see she wanted to.

"I am NOT walking around like this," said Darius.

Then I realized we sort of matched. I stopped laughing. I didn't want to walk around like that either.

I didn't want to walk around period; we needed gas, or we needed a new car.

"There's a farm," I said.

And Darius and the kid *couldn't* walk around, period. I had on brilliant killer-heel boots from the old hag's place; their feet were naked. The track looked damp. Drying, but scarily damp. (How much water do you need to touch your body before it'll kill you? Really, how much?) I rummaged around in my bags and plunked down the only spare footwear I had: jeweled flip-flops. The kid seemed to like hers (even though she wouldn't take them off me and had to have them replunked to her by Darius and even though they were a hundred sizes too big); Darius Spratt's hairy-toed feet squashed into the pair I gave him like monster's feet, oozing over the front, the sides, and the back. He looked at me helplessly.

"I am not going to carry you," I said. "I am SO not going to carry you."

"Hn," said Darius Spratt.

I wrestled a belt-leash onto Whitby—he was so giddy from trying to figure out the new game of running and flip-flop throwing, I could just see him taking it into his doggy head to have a little fun with a herd of cows—and we started up the track.

Remember that game you played when you were a kid? When you were only allowed to step on the light parts on the pavement, the parts that were dry, and you weren't allowed to step on the dark parts that were still wet from rain? And you'd have a race with your mom, and before you knew it, you'd be at the place—the library or school—that had seemed so far away? Monster-feet Spratt lurched from one light patch to another, then got stuck.

I had to hoist him onto my back. His arms wrapped tight around me. His hairy legs dangled. Donkey Ruby. In killer heels. Trudging along in a fog of *Parfum de Spratte*.

Whitby did go nuts when he saw the cows, and the cows went nuts when they saw us. I had to dump the Spratt in the farmyard because Whitby wanted to say hello to those cows so much he was going to pull me over—and they would have had no choice about the meet and greet because they were shut up in the barn. You could pretty much take that as a sign that there was no one home (or certainly not home and alive), but what proved that was the dogs: two collies chained up right outside the front door, dead. Those collies, by the door, there wasn't even a water bowl for them. I guess whoever had left them there hadn't thought it would be forever.

A better sight was that there was an old worn-out farm truck: open, keys in it. Great. I shut Whitby inside; the kid clutched Darling, so I couldn't do the same with her.

The Spratt picked his way across the farmyard and tried the front door: locked.

"Knock first!" I told him. "You've got to knock first and shout. Tell them we just want help."

"I don't think there's anyone home," said the Spratt.

I shoved him out of the way, and I knocked and shouted how we just wanted help—"And we're just kids!" I yelled—though the cows were making so much noise, it was probably pretty much pointless.

We stalked around the house and found that even the farmers had been having a barbecue. In this little yard, at the back, it was still there: half-cooked meat, rained on; bowls of salad, swimming in water; pecked-at soggy bread and chips. *BBQ Britain Sizzles.*

We had to go in through a window, then let the kid in through the back door. Inside, it smelled bad. Sweet, spicy bad. The fridge was a no-go area, with nothing to drink in it anyway, but they had a pantry with cans of stuff in it. Darius sat the kid at the kitchen table with a spoon and a can of peaches, and the kid sat Darling down on the kitchen table to sniff at a can of sardines I'd opened.

217

"You get scared, you bang your spoon on the table," Darius told her, and we went to see what we could get.

We hadn't even gotten halfway up the stairs before the spoon banged on the table. We rushed back in expecting some sort of horror, and instead found an enormous ginger bruiser of a cat sitting on the table, eyeballing Darling.

"Kitty just wants to see what there is to eat," I said, and, as Darling hadn't touched the sardines, I lured the cat off the table with them and shut it in the den. The kid watched, tight-lipped.

"Dogs don't like fish," said Darius, plonking a handful of dog biscuits that were way too big for Darling on the table.

I got a rolling pin and gave them a battering—the kid and Darling flinched.

"So she can eat them," I said softly, wondering how come everything I did somehow ended up with me seeming like an ogre when all I was ever trying to do was HELP.

Darling crunched delicately; the kid relaxed and spooned herself another peach.

Ever worn secondhand clothes? Ever worn them and wondered who they had belonged to? We didn't have to wonder; there was a couple dead on the bed. I decided I'd rather stick with sequins than the clothes of a dead Mrs. Farmer, but Darius didn't exactly have much choice.

"Can I get some privacy here?" he said, pulling clothes out of their closet.

There was no reason to go poking around; I was just looking for the bathroom to see if I could find something for Darius's pits. I opened a door.

She was lying on the bed. Her room was just like mine. Same mess of stuff she probably got yelled at for every day. Clothes jumbled on the floor with her school stuff: same books, same exams coming up. Same mess of makeup scattered all over the dressing table. Same wall plastered with photos of her and her friends… I wondered which boy she had liked. I decided it had probably been the dark-haired one.

I wondered if she had died before her parents, and had her mom to comfort her, or whether she'd died alone.

I felt cold then, shivery. I looked in her closet. I took one of her cardigans because I had to; I took a T-shirt for a Princess dress.

"Thanks," I said to her. I wanted to do something for her.

It takes a girl to know a girl. I picked out what I knew would be her best dress—this gorgeous lacy white frock she'd probably had to beg to get. I took it off the hanger. I held it by the straps and, careful not to touch her, I laid it on her body.

"That's a great dress," I said. "You look really pretty."

When I came out of the room, Darius, in jeans, was coming out of the bathroom, spraying stuff into his pits.

"Are you OK?" he asked as he ditched the empty can of man-spray and pulled on a checked shirt.

Before I could have some weird, random thought about him looking not too repulsive, really, considering, I blanked it by staring at his dead man's socks. I felt it again, that I really, really wanted to talk. It just wasn't the time.

"Here," I said, throwing the T-shirt at him. "You'd better give this to her."

"I'll get your skirt," he said.

"I don't want it."

"Ruby?" said Darius. "*Are* you OK?"

Shut up, shut up, shut up, I thought. I didn't know whether I meant him or me.

"Don't go in there," I said, closing the door to her room.

Apart from there being nothing much but the syrup from canned

fruit to drink, the house was good to us. Very good. It sounds awful—
well, it would have sounded awful to the me that used to be me—but
they had a big old stove like Zak's parents had, only even older, and it
was still on, so we made a massive pile of scrambled eggs and sat and
ate them in the stinking house of dead people. It was the first hot food
I'd eaten since...that stew Simon had made. Which was...

"How long has it been?" I said out loud.

Darius didn't ask what I meant.

"Six days," he said.

After breakfast, we got busy. First we fought. Darius, dead-man's
sock feet shoved in rain boots, wanted us all to get geared up in
garbage-bag armor, and I refused. I had to stand in the yard and
shout about how blue the sky was (it was!) before he'd listen. Then
I got on with things. I checked the truck, ignoring Whitby's boomy
barks (he wanted out) and the cows' mooing (I guess they wanted
out too). I started it up: over half a tank of gas. I didn't know how
far that would take us, but anywhere out of there was good enough.
We raided the house for everything that was useful—and I mean
everything: food, anything waterproof, more rain boots, garbage
bags, tape, blankets, tools—a whole bag of them, but no pointless
electric stuff.

Crazy, really. I thought I'd never get us stuck like that again with
no gas, and the way things were, it seemed like we could pretty
much go into any house or any shop and get what we needed. It
was just that...there's this fear thing, isn't there? Every time you go
in someplace, the fear that there might be someone, anyone there...
and the other fear, which is really more a fear of yourself, that you
are going to see something, yet another something, that will upset
you. *May Meltdown.* So it's easier—isn't it?—to stock up.

"We should let them out," I said to Darius, looking at the
shouty cows.

"Hn," he said.

"Well, we should, shouldn't we? It's not like any of them are gonna be murderers, is it?"

"Cows kill more people than sharks," he said.

"Keep out of the way, then, if you're scared."

"I'm not scared. I'm just saying."

I was scared too, but another thing I'd learned on Simon's country walks was how to deal with cows. Mostly they won't come near you anyway, so you should just ignore them and not crowd them… but if they're frisky or curious, you need to show them who's boss. You need to act big and stern and noisy. And if you're really worried, you should get a branch or a nice chunky stick. I got a mop from the house.

Darius brought the kid out to see. (The kid in her new Princess T-shirt dress that was a hundred sizes too big and a pair of rain boots that were a hundred sizes too big.) That surprised me—like, why would he do that?—and it annoyed me—like, are they just going to stand there and watch me mess it up? Afterward, I thought maybe he did it so she could learn something: either that cows could turn nasty and were best avoided ("See how they're trampling Ruby?") or a thing about handling animals ("See how Ruby nearly got trampled?"). In either case, it was not a great lesson.

As I walked toward the barn, the cows came barging forward. When I got right to the gate, they backed up a little, jostling each other, nervous. I eyed my escape route, unbolted the gate, swung it open, and clambered up onto the fence. The cows did barge out but in a fairly orderly manner—not quite single file, but almost. They were mooing with delight and pretty darn speedy for plodders. What I hadn't really thought about was where they would go, but they seemed to know exactly where they were headed. They all turned right and disappeared up a muddy track. Darius and the kid came to see. We walked up the side of the barn and watched the cows speed-plod into a field, fanning out to gorge on the grass.

There was another thing I hadn't thought about; they weren't lady cows, milking cows, they were boy cows. Young boys. I know two (Simon) things about them: (1) a lady cow will just come get you if she thinks you're messing with her calf, but if her calf has gone, she's probably going to be OK; but boy cows—young boy cows—like to hassle people, for fun; and (2) boy cows are only kept for meat.

So they'd been double saved, hadn't they? No starving to death in a barn and no one-way trip to Burgersville either.

The kid climbed up on the fence to get a better look.

"Now they're happy," I beamed. "Lovely fresh grass!"

Princess ignored me, but I knew she'd heard. Some random horrible thought about what it was they were chomping *on* bubbled up in my head: how wet the grass might be, whether…if that *thing* was in the rain and the grass drank up the rain and the cows ate the grass. Hey, I was veggie, what did I care? But lady cows…what about milk and—cheese?! Was there going to be no more CHEESE?! I popped the thought and carried on beaming. I even smiled nicely at the Spratt.

"We could just stay here," said Darius.

Huh? Instant frown.

"We'd have to go and get some stuff to drink, get some more food, but then we could come back and hang out here—just for a few weeks or something…until we work out what to do…"

"I *know* what I'm doing!" I said.

"No you don't. I mean, you don't seriously think your dad's still going to be alive, do you?"

CHAPTER TWENTY-ONE

I have only driven a truck that one time; it was old and more worn out than my dad's beater. It rattled your bones, it crawled along, it guzzled gas, and NO WAY would it have kept the rain out, not for one second. There was moss growing in the little grooves where the windows should have slid open; now you couldn't even slide them closed.

Oh, and it was really noisy. That was FINE, because basically I didn't want to speak to Darius Spratt EVER AGAIN.

He didn't even apologize. OK, the words "I'm sorry" came out of his mouth, but they were followed by the words "but it's pretty unlikely he's alive, isn't it?"

Kid or no kid, I went NUTS. I shouted so loud the cows got spooked and ran across the field. I said every nasty thing to him I could think of. I ranted and raved and stomped around. I think you could summarize what I had to say as "*HOW DARE YOU?!*" and I think you could summarize what Darius Spratt had to say as "I'm just trying to be realistic," which apparently involves not caring ONE BIT what anyone else feels.

It should have ended with me getting into the truck and driving off. That's what I felt like doing. It ended with me getting into the truck and starting up and just sitting there.

Please don't leave me!

Over the clatter of the engine, I couldn't hear what Darius was saying to Princess, but I had a bad feeling it was basically going to be her decision, whether they stayed or came with me. And as far as that kid was concerned, I was Rumpelstiltskin, wasn't I? Not my lovely made-up version, but the shouty, horrible real thing. If they decided to stay, I'd take Darling back—that's what I thought. Hey, I could even threaten to take Darling from her unless they got in the truck. I thought that too. I think I would have done it, I was that tightly wound, when the kid suddenly made this funny little shruggy gesture and trailed toward the truck…but not toward the passenger door. Apparently, I was too awful to sit next to. Apparently, I was worse than the memory of a car crash. Apparently, I was now more revolting than death-breath Whitby, whose rear end was already letting us know that the leftover scrambled eggs didn't really agree with him.

We rattled on in silence for a while. Every time I accidentally glanced at the Spratt, he was frowning. Seemed as if he was deep in thought about something; how sorry he was, that's what it should have been.

"ZERO POINT TWENTY-SEVEN PERCENT," shouted Darius.

"PARDON?" I shouted back.

"SAY THE POPULATION OF DARTBRIDGE IS APPROXI-MATELY TEN THOUSAND. I MEAN, IT CAN'T BE THAT MANY, BUT IF YOU INCLUDED THE CLOSEST VILLAGES IT PROBABLY IS. SAY THERE WERE TWO PRISONERS ALIVE IN EACH CELL, PLUS US… THAT'S TWENTY-SEVEN. TWENTY-SEVEN PEOPLE LEFT MEANS ZERO POINT TWENTY-SEVEN PERCENT SURVIVED."

I drove. I just drove. I was just a girl out for a drive on a lovely sunny day.

"SAY THE UK POPULATION IS SIXTY-THREE MILLION," bellowed Darius, "THAT MEANS...THERE'S APPROXIMATELY..."

An age went by. Like I say, I was just a girl out for a drive on a lovely sunny day.

"ONE HUNDRED AND SEVENTY THOUSAND AND ONE HUNDRED PEOPLE LEFT," shouted Darius triumphantly.

I gripped the steering wheel.

"DOES THAT SEEM ABOUT RIGHT TO YOU?"

"WHATEVER," I shouted.

"NO, BUT DOES IT?"

"NO! ACTUALLY, NO! YOU DON'T KNOW. THERE COULD BE TONS OF PEOPLE. THEY COULD BE HIDING. THERE WAS A GUY AT THE SUPERMARKET AND THERE WAS A GUY AT THE PUB."

I saw Darius open his trap.

"AND I THINK SASKIA MIGHT STILL BE ALIVE," I shouted.

And Caspar—and Caspar—and Caspar, I thought. I didn't speak it. I couldn't bear to have to tell about that, to hear what Darius thought.

"*SASKIA MILLER?*" he shouted.

"YOU KNOW HER?!"

Like, really, was he some kind of perv? How come he knew all our names?

"WELL, YEAH!"

I glanced at him. He smirked. Revolting. Apparently, like every other boy in the school, Darius Spratt liked her.

"AND THERE WAS A GUY WHO **MURDERED** MY STEPDAD," I shouted, to shut him up.

It didn't work. There was this intense waft of stink, which could have been Whitby's bottom or could have been Darius Spratt blowing off from the strain of calculating.

"A HUNDRED AND NINETY-FIVE THOUSAND, THREE HUNDRED!" he shouted.

"WHY DON'T YOU SHUT UP?"

"I'M JUST SAYING—"

"*SHUUUUUUT UUUUUUP!*"

Please, my heart thought, *please don't say another word I can't bear to hear.*

I knew we needed to turn off and find another car. Though I hated the thought that this might involve speaking to Darius, it'd have to be done. No way was there enough fuel in the truck to get us much farther.

I was so busy thinking about how awful it was going to be, having to speak to him, that I missed the first turn-off. I could have turned around and gone back, but I couldn't bring myself to do that, to admit I'd made a mistake. I was bristling about that so much we rattled past the next turn-off. That's when Darius spoke up.

"RUBY," he shouted.

"I KNOW!" I shouted.

He was quiet for a moment.

"I NEED TO GO TO A PHARMACY," he shouted.

"*WHAT?!*"

"A PHARMACY."

"WHAT FOR?"

Even as I said it, I knew. It wasn't just Darius's trousers that had been left in the polytunnel; it was that stash of medicine he'd had in his bag.

"I NEED MEDICINE," he shouted.

"ARE YOU GONNA HAVE AN EPILEPTIC FIT?!" I shouted, panicked.

"NO."

I glanced at him; he was crimson.

"I JUST NEED THEM. THAT'S ALL."

"WHAT DO I DO IF YOU HAVE A FIT?"

"I'M NOT GOING TO HAVE A FIT."

"YEAH, BUT WHAT IF YOU DO?"

"I'M NOT. I JUST NEED MY PILLS."

So the epilepsy thing was a total no-go sore spot, discussion-wise. Hello, Darius Spratt! Just like my dad's chances of being alive! I felt like pointing that out. Only thing that stopped me was that if I pointed that out, he'd probably end up saying again that my dad was DEAD. So I shut up…but I was boiling mad—and pretty scared that Nerd Boy would have some kind of fit on me.

Great, eh? But wait! It gets even better!

When we got to the suspension bridge in Bristol, the barrier was down. Being smart like I am, I backed up and drove across in the other lane. Not so smart; the barrier at the other end was down and I guess someone else had tried to leave through the incoming lane because they were still stuck there. Lovely choice: I could either reverse right back across the bridge or attempt to turn around.

Do you know how high that bridge is? Do you know what that drop is like? Do you know how, out of the corner of your eye, you can see seagulls swoop through the air and down UNDER the road?

Want to know something about me?

I DON'T DO HEIGHTS. I DO NOT DO HEIGHTS.

I revved up a little—OK, a lot—and—

"RUUU-BY!" screamed Darius as I jammed my foot down on to the accelerator.

Too late. That barrier just snapped right off. Easy.

(Probably a lot of people got panicky on that bridge, so they didn't even bother replacing the barrier with a decent one every time.)

You think that's the good part? Nuh-uh!

The pharmacy was already smashed open, the pills raided—but no one wanted the drugs Darius was after. He took what they had: two boxes.

"How long will those last you?" I asked, rooting through their (poor) selection of makeup for emergency items.

Darius shrugged. "A while," he said and swallowed down two big purple tablets with some babies' rosehip syrup.

I dabbed on some brand-you've-never-heard-of eye shadow, while Darius hunted for something, anything, to drink and found precisely nothing but more yucky baby drinks.

"Do you think you can drink this stuff?" asked Darius, examining a bottle of contact-lens potion. "It says it's mainly water…"

"Of course you can't!" I said, deciding against a plum-colored lipstick (that reminded me too much of the fingernails on a certain lady's hand).

Thing is, I was really thirsty. I almost would have at least tried that contact-lens stuff. Hadn't I told Darius not to put so much salt in the scrambled eggs?

We're nearly at the good part.

♦♦♦

We'd left the kid, clutching Darling, just outside on the street, instructed to bang the crowbar on the side of the truck if she got scared. You couldn't blame her for not wanting to stay in there, even with all the windows open; Whitby's bottom was out of control. So the kid banged on the truck…and she banged on it pretty hard because you could hear it above the noise of an engine, above the blare of music, above Whitby's big boomy bark.

But it was that, Whitby's bark, I heard first. Dumb, smart, big, stinky dog. Gentle smelly-bummed giant. He heard that car coming long before we did. He warned us.

Me and Darius looked at each other; I hate that, when you see your own in fear in the face of another person—how it had been with my friends at Zak's, how it had been with Simon. People just shouldn't look at each other when they're scared.

What could we do? We couldn't just leave the kid, could we? We had to go outside—and nothing to defend ourselves with if a some-one, anyone nasty was there…unless what? We threw sponges and baby bath toys at them? Pelted them with plum-colored lipsticks? The fear wasn't just crackling in my bones—it was jumping about in every cell of my body.

Parked next to our truck—and blocking us in—was a pink stretch limo. Oh yes. One of those party cars that are kind of tacky in some ways and in other ways you just want to get in. Music thumped away inside it, but you couldn't see a thing through the blacked-out windows. You could only see this boy driver (who looked about ten!) in a peaked cap that was way too big for him sitting in the front of the car and staring straight ahead, a bunch of wild-eyed kids packed into the passenger seat next to him.

Then the rear passenger doors cracked open like it was a spaceship—might as well have been!—and smoke and music and people piled out of it…but not just any people: super-cool people. Most seemed twenty-something—two fashionista-type trendy girls, a skater dude, some punky-looking characters, and an ultra-preppy boy, and even the oldest one—who looked as old as Grandma Hollis, but was wearing some kind of skintight leopard-print Lycra catsuit and a feather boa—looked desperately cool.

"Hello, sweetie!" one of the fashionistas cooed at Princess, trying to offer her some water from a bottle.

I sort of squared myself up—but not for a fight. It was weird, meeting that bunch of people, but I didn't feel afraid of them. I tried to come over all dignified and like I'd never been scared at all, not even for one second...while at the same time: (1) relieved I had a superb outfit on, because—no matter how weird my hair and makeup were, they would surely see I was cool too and (2) wondering how come the world goes mental and some people end up with people straight out of some mega-stylish style magazine, whereas other people end up with Darius Spratt and a dog with a stinky bottom.

They swarmed around Princess. It didn't even seem to matter to them that Darius barged through them to put his arm around the kid, and it didn't seem to matter to them that the kid wanted nothing to do with them and just stood there looking (impressively) hostile: a small, fierce thing in gigantic rain boots.

"Look at her little dog!" cooed the other fashionista, reaching out to pet Darling (who didn't even snarl).

The kid (even more impressively) actually raised the crowbar to stop the dog petter. Darius took the crowbar from her and held it down by his side, but I could see his hand all tense on it—and his eyes were as angry as the kid's.

"Do you wanna come with us?" the preppy boy asked Princess, and the others laughed as if that was a brilliant idea.

"Hey," I said, sort of starting to think that they were actually being pretty rude in some ways; it was like me and Darius Spratt weren't even there.

I glanced at Darius; he glanced at me. He was frowning—boy, was he frowning.

Then this...*other guy* got out of the limo. Unfolded himself from it. The guy was seriously tall. Looked like a Dartbridge tree-hugging crusty type, but cleaner and paler: skinny and scruffy and ratty blond dreadlocks poking out from under this country gent's flat-cap hat, the sort of wintery, tweedy, what-are-you-wearing-that-for-when-it's-boiling thing that made you feel hot (and thirsty) just looking at it (and wonder whether he sucked head sweat out of it, like I'd thought about licking pit sweat out of my raincoat). And I wouldn't have looked at the hat or at him at all except (1) he was actually pretty good-looking and (2) although he didn't speak a word, not to begin with, the way the others all acted around him it seemed like he was their king or something.

"Xar! Look! Can we keep her?" asked a fashionista.

"You picked the last one!" said a punky-looking boy.

"But she's so cute!" said the fashionista. "Xar! *Please?*" she whined.

"🦋 off!" shouted Darius.

Whoa. The Spratt swore!

It basically had as much impact as Whitby's barking. It was embarrassing. Not the way the kid was behaving, because she was just a kid and so you couldn't blame her, but the way Darius was acting…because it was really obvious—to me—that these people weren't about to hurt anyone. They weren't just going to *take* Princess. If I had any worry at all, it was that they might—they just might—try to take MY dog…even though MY dog didn't seem to be MY dog anymore.

King Xar sighed. He flicked his gaze over us: the Princess, the Spratt, and me.

"The girls can come," he said quietly. "Just the girls."

"And the little dog!" squealed a fashionista.

"You'll be safe with us," cooed Granny Lycra.

"You really will," the skater dude said to me, nodding calmly. "It's all cool."

I nodded back—in a deadpan but pouty way. He was hot.

"We're going to London," the Spratt said.

The nerve of it! *I* was going to London.

"Awwww!" King Xar's court groaned.

"But we've got such an amazing house! Just come and see!" said a punky girl. She pointed up the road and I admired her excellent silver skeleton hand bracelet.

"Ruby!" said Darius. As in, *Snap out of it!*

More nerve!

Being as how I wasn't ever allowed to go to festivals, I think I can honestly say that—apart from me and my friends, obviously—they were the most interesting and exciting bunch of people I'd ever been up close to, even if they were behaving a tad badly and had a giant tree-hugging dread-head for their king. If I'd just happened to bump into them on any day prior to the global meltdown situation, and if—say—I was with Leonie…you know what? I think I would have gone with them. Just to see. But it wasn't any day prior to. It was Day Six of.

"I'm going to London," I said.

"Awww…" sighed the court.

The preppy boy pinged a finger on the window of the truck; Whitby went crazy.

"Have fun," King Xar said to me through the din. For a second, he looked down at me, straight into my eyes, cocked his head just a little—like a dog does when it's trying to figure you out. I looked at my shoes. He laughed—a quick and quiet ha-ha of a laugh—then opened the door to the limo wide; who knows how they'd all crammed in there because it was rammed with bottles and containers of water.

"Come, children," he told the court.

Whining like disappointed kids, they piled back into the limo—and Darius—🦋 Darius!—reached out and grabbed King Xar's arm. Really, that whole manhandling thing was a very bad habit. Sooner or later someone (anyone?) was going to deck him for it.

"Where'd you get the water?" Darius demanded.

King Xar removed Darius's hand by his shirtsleeve, picking it off like it was a speck of something unpleasant. He got into the limo and shut the door. There was a pause, one of the blacked-out windows slid down. Granny Lycra popped her head out, with what was obviously a joint in one hand and a glass of champagne in the other.

"You need…to go…to the swimming pool," she instructed us—in a lazy voice, in between sips and puffs.

"Which swimming pool? Where?" Darius demanded.

It seemed like he was about to snap. He leaned in and put his hand on the window. Seriously, I thought the next thing he'd do would be to grab hold of her feather boa. Granny Lycra blew smoke into his face. The Spratt—oh my 🦋—coughed.

"We…don't know…where the swimming pool is," he said, mimicking the chilled-out tones of Granny Lycra.

On reflection, it was fairly—weirdly—a tiny bit impressive. At the time, I thought I'd die of shame in my killer heels. (I mustn't say things like that.)

"We're from Dartbridge," I blurted—and instantly wished I hadn't; the passengers tittered.

"Ooo-aaar!" someone inside the limo mocked, trying to sound like the kind of country farmer-type you just don't really get in Dartbridge.

The skater dude—who really was hot—leaned forward to speak to me. ME—not Darius. "Go into town, and follow the signs for the highway," he said, pointing.

"You…can't…miss…it," purred Granny Lycra, blowing another hit of smoke into the Spratt's enraged face.

The skater dude smiled at me (hot, hot, hot!), and then they both sat back, into the darkness of the limo, and the window glided up. The enraged Spratt pulled away his fingers—in plenty of time. He brandished them, embarrassingly, at the blacked-out glass, as if they'd wanted to trap him and he'd outwitted them. I could have died on the spot. (I mustn't say things like that either.)

"You…can't…miss…it."

That, unfortunately, turned out to be true.

"What a bunch of *jerks*," spat Darius as the limo pulled away.

I was just working out a scathing reply to that—something like "it takes one to know one," but without saying anything that might make it sound like I thought those people were jerks, because I didn't—when he started in on me.

"Ruby…" he said.

"No!" I said, working my way along the line of parked cars, tons of them…some locked, some unlocked…none with keys.

"But, Ruby…" said Darius.

He went on. He went on—and on—about how we really should get some water while we could, about how we couldn't carry on drinking junk, about how we wouldn't have to go breaking into places if we did, about how it'd just be a lot easier if we just went and got some now…on and on and on. I ignored him. I just kept on hunting for a car with Darius trailing behind me whining, and then I found a car—one of those massive family cruiser–type things— and I ignored him while we shifted all our stuff from the truck to the new car.

Only I wasn't really ignoring him. Skilled though I am in the art of blanking out all manner of stuff I don't want to know about, whether it's stuff in my own head or stuff coming out of other people's mouths, his going on about the water was quickly driving me nuts. It was like…when you really need to pee and your idiot (lovely!) friend tortures you going "guuuuuuuuuuussssssssh" until you feel like you're going to burst.

But I am Ruby, and I am tough. So I kept my dry-as-dust mouth shut.

Until I caved. The thing that tipped the scales was when he said we could maybe even get enough water to wash.

Now I'd already fully got my head around the baby wipes deal— you can do a lot (so much more than you ever could have imagined!) with them—but I'd seen my face in the mirror in that shop and had been shocked again at how orangey I looked (in spite of the foundation). It was the sort of major orange only serious, prolonged scrubbing *avec* soap will remove.

"OK," I said.

SO. THIS IS IT: THE GOOD PART… (THAT'S GOOD AS IN DEEPLY BAD, BY THE WAY.)

CHAPTER TWENTY-TWO

We followed the signs.

As we came down a long hill lined with smashed shops, you could see the city ahead of us: here and there little smudges of smoke rising almost straight up into the warm, still air, reaching up for—and getting nowhere near—the sweetest, teensiest clouds. Cumulus humilis, they must have been. They look like the little puffy clouds kids draw. Like the world is a storybook and no harm will ever come to you.

We weaved our way through the city center, saw a lady pushing a cart full of bottles filled with water. Didn't stop to ask. Didn't need to. The highway, it starts in the city center. One minute there are houses and offices and shops, and the next minute... It wasn't a highway like other highways are—not three lanes each side in the middle of nowhere, and you can't even tell where you are—it was two lanes each side and a ton of dead cars to get around. And even if we hadn't seen the sign hanging off the bridge saying "WATER" with a great big arrow pointing where you should go, we would have known where to go because there were other cars ahead of us, pulling in at the junction and people wheeling carts and lugging bags over the bridge above.

No one—no one—coming into or out of that city could have missed that sign:

WATER

←————

I couldn't get up the exit ramp because it was blocked with cars, so I went up the way cars came down onto the highway—see how smart I am? We couldn't get any closer, but that was OK; at the top of the slope you could see the pool. There was a line outside. It was very orderly; it felt OK.

We poured out every container we had. When we'd cleared out my mom and Simon's car, we'd grabbed everything and done it so quickly we'd even scooped up all the empty bottles from the Ashton shop. Then we'd cleared out the truck and done the same thing again. We poured out my looted bags, dumping ten thousand pairs of underwear into the back of the car. We loaded the bags with the empty bottles. Still, it didn't seem like anywhere near enough. I tipped the vodka out into the gutter, wondered what else we could use and…remembered.

At the farm, I'd picked up Fluffysnuggles's mint-chocolate-chip carton…I'd put Fluffysnuggles's mint-chocolate-chip carton on the driver's seat to pick up when we'd finished loading the farm truck…and…

I left Fluffysnuggles's mint-chocolate-chip carton on the driver's seat…at the farm.

I am a bad person. I am a very bad person. Please let someone have found Fluffysnuggles; please let someone have taken pity.

In the movie of this book—after the end credits, probably, when most people have left, weeping—there should be this extra little storyette. Just for the people who have stayed, weeping. Some random cows will wander out of the field. I didn't shut any gates, so they're bound to. These random cows will have a stroll around the farmyard; the bravest and boldest and most inquisitive of them will wander down the track. It'll get to the car; it'll poke its head inside. (I left the car door open too.) It'll knock Fluffysnuggles's mint-chocolate-chip carton to the floor. The carton will bust open. Fluffysnuggles and the cow will consider each other, nose to nose. Then, as the cow plods off to eat its way through a polytunnel full of flowers, Fluffysnuggles will climb out of the car. He'll drop down onto the track, sigh, and begin his epic journey home.

We left Princess locked in the car in the care of Whitby and Darling—or the other way around. That was how confident we felt; apart from the kids' drawings of clouds, the sky looked blue as blue can be. We wouldn't be long. We'd be close by.

As we joined the back of the line, this random boy, must have been Darius's age, came to check our bags. Then he climbed into the back of a Girl Guides' van and handed us these big plastic containers, two each. They were like the kind of containers Simon had once bought hard cider in on the way home from some awful walk, back in the time before Henry was born.

(The next day, my mom went around the house clutching her head and saying, "Never again." Until she explained it was the cider, I had thought—hoped—she meant we'd never have to go on another walk. Fat chance.)

And then we waited. More people came and joined the line behind us. We seemed to wait for a very long time.

First thing I noticed was: maybe Darius Spratt had been wrong about how many people had survived—because there was a lot—A LOT—of people there, shuffling in, thirty at a time. That's what I counted. (Yes, I can actually count, in fact.)

The other thing I noticed was it seemed like there were only four people "in charge" at the pool: that random boy outside; some random guy inside; this Girl Guide Leader woman, who paced around inside and out; and this girl, my age, also in a Guide's uniform, who was trying to make sure everyone stayed in line. The random bloke inside didn't seem too good at his job; you could hear him shouting "Stop!" when people tried to grab too much water, and if they didn't stop—which they often didn't—he shouted "Melissa!" and the girl pushed past us all and shouted STOP too. And if they still didn't stop, the girl pushed back past us all, and the Girl Guide Leader came in and shouted. Then they stopped.

Honest? I'd been in Guides. I can still remember the Guide Law—and when you think about it, if this disaster wasn't going to be the moment teenagers took over the Earth, power should have been handed over to the Guides. Why?

A Guide is honest, reliable and can be trusted.

A Guide is helpful and uses her time and abilities wisely.

A Guide faces challenge and learns from her experiences.

A Guide is a good friend and a sister to all Guides (but there probably would have been a vote to include a few other people on account of the global disaster).

A Guide is polite and considerate.

A Guide respects all living things and takes care of the world around her.

Being a Girl Guide is not easy. Probably there are religions that are easier…but I don't think there are any religions that are more fun or with as many different things to do. Still, I had to stop doing Guides, didn't I? I'd loved it…and then I hacked it out of my life in the hobby-ditching I carried out at the end of junior high. I should have done it at the end of the summer, but—DUR—I did it at the beginning. Leonie was still a Guide, going off, doing this and that. Tumbleweed blew across my social life…and, like my dad was to blame for it, that's when I started going on about going up to London all the time, about going on crummy vacations with Dad and Dan. (Crummy? That was the summer my dad let me drive the car!).

I think I never was a very good Girl Guide. But I did try. I tried. I had enough time to think all this. We had plenty of time. For the first ages, we were in line on the street. For the next ages, we were in line inside the building. We edged down the stairs. Step by step, we came closer to it: that pool, that lovely water.

People didn't really talk much. I suppose it was the sort of situation where people would normally have gone on about the weather; that was off limits, and what else was there? *May Meltdown.*

I didn't feel worried at all. Swimming pools, that was a thing I knew about. That's a thing kids do: lining up to get into a pool. The chloriney smell, the echoey sound, the heat. I remembered lining up in Dartbridge, holding my mom's hand when I was little. Then in elementary school, lining up with Leonie, giggling—all the way up until the brutal junior high hobby ditch—your towel and your swimsuit and your allowance in your bag, and just wishing they'd hurry up and let you in…

I wrapped and rewrapped that dead girl's cardigan around my waist, makeup melting in the heat.

"My wife is sick!" some fancy guy started going on. "Now look here, you people! My wife is sick!"

"Sick of you," some woman said.

We giggled; everyone giggled. That's what you do when you're waiting, excited, in the line for the pool.

And then…these sirens closed in. The way the steps went down to the pool, we had this weird view of the world; we could just see the legs of the people outside, so we had to crouch down and crane our heads to get a good look at the fire engine.

WOOP! WOOP!—WOOP! WOOP! the siren went.

The men that arrived on it weren't firemen. There were men you could see straight off were drunk, clutching bottles, clambering about…but there were other men, who looked just normal. Normal like normal people's normal dads.

WOOP! WOOP!—WOOP! WOOP! the siren went.

Us line people, we didn't budge. We stayed where we were. We heard the men had come to take water; they'd come all the way from Gloucester to get it. The people in the line said there wasn't enough water.

The arguing started up. The Girl Guide, Melissa, she looked at me. I saw that she was scared. Maybe she wished she was me, standing there in a sequiny dress and red hair and free to run if she wanted…and not her, standing there in a uniform with no makeup and this mass of people expecting you to be helpful and use your time and abilities wisely, etc.

Truth? I looked away. There. I've said it. I looked away from that girl. I couldn't stand it, but I should have looked back at her. Seems to me, maybe sometimes the least you can do for another person is to show that you have seen them. No matter how scared it makes you. The arguing got louder. Melissa, she went outside. What badge do they give you for that? Community Action? Water Safety?

You brave girl, Melissa, you should get Brave Girl—Advanced!

I should get Ostrich—Advanced!

I don't know how you know, how you just know in your gut that something really bad is about to happen, but I knew it. And I ignored it; I didn't get out while I still could because no one around me seemed to want to get out—until it was too late.

The fighting outside turned to scuffling. At knee height we saw it. We saw men running back and forth. We saw what feet and legs do when men fight.

KER-PLSSSSH!

Water jetted and streamed down off those windows. They must have turned on the fire hoses. We saw the first man fall. Everyone on those stairs did; we saw him fall and we saw him claw at the glass—at us: he was right in front of our faces. We saw…that he was bloody, but not bloody in a fight way, and we understood that the water in that fire engine, in the hoses that had been turned on, that were jetting everywhere…that water was bad.

A Guide has courage and is cheerful in all difficulties.

The people in the line panicked. Everyone wanted to get out and all the people who'd been lining up outside wanted to get in.

See how it was: there was already a load of people in there, in that pool, and there was already a load of people waiting on the steps. And then even more loads of people came in from outside.

Me and Darius Spratt, we had no choice. We got pushed and shoved and pushed toward that pool until we were stuck on the side of it, bunched in with all these other people and some of them still trying to fill up their containers when the screaming started up by the entrance and this people-ripple spread, and it had nowhere to go. It had nowhere to go. There was a fire exit down at the end of the pool; you could see the little white man sign above it, that picture of the little white cartoon man leaving, only no one else could. People battered at that exit door, but it must have been locked. All that could happen, all people could do was—*PLOOSH!*—the first person, just a kid, fell into the pool—but it was OK, because that water was OK; and everyone kind of got that and—*PLOOSH PLOOSH PLOOSH PLOOSH PLOOSH*—a whole bunch of other people jumped in too because it was the only place left where there was any space.

Me and Darius Spratt, we jumped in.

It was colder than a pool should be. I remember that. How cold it felt. But we glugged that water. Treading water and glugging.

There was this weird couple of minutes of thinking that maybe it'd actually be OK, that maybe all those panicky, pushy people would get a grip. I even got a grip myself; my makeup would have been done for anyway, so I had a scrub at my face with the dead girl's cardigan.

"What are you *doing?!*" gasped Darius.

"Mind your own business!" I spluttered back, half drowning.

Then there were more screams—bigger screams, closer screams—and this time there wasn't a people-ripple, but a surge. *PLOOSH PLOOSH PLOOSH PLOOSH.*

We all saw him: the useless random pool guy standing there at the top of the pool, people trying to back off all around him because he was bloody with the sickness. He had these keys in his hand and he tried to get around the side of the pool—to open that fire escape, I bet; he tried to do it, but he came too near people and someone shoved him away.

The useless random pool guy fell into the pool.

Panic exploded. People didn't care now; they wanted to get out and get out fast. Me and Darius, we hauled ourselves out of that water, nearly trampled as we scrambled to our feet…and…and the sickness spreading all around us… Like one minute it was just water dripping off someone and the next minute it was blood. The pool wasn't a pool anymore; it was a giant vat of invisible wavy-tentacled space micro-blobs: replicating, attacking, killing.

Where we'd come up, the other side of the pool, there was some big woman lying groaning, and behind her was this door with no little white cartoon man running, but it was a door, so I yanked it open—never mind the poor woman, not even thinking "the poor woman"—just enough so I could drag Darius in and what we got into was a closet—it was just a closet, a stupid closet full of kids' pool toys—and the door shut and it was pitch-black.

Other hands yanked at the handle and me and Darius Spratt, we pulled back on it as though our lives depended on it, which they did.

I thought I was going to die. That was it, plain and simple: I thought I was going to die.

I said my dad's address over and over and over again. Making Darius repeat it, over and over and over.

"If you get out of here, you go find my dad and you tell him."

Tell him what? That I had died in a closet full of floaty spongy pool snakes?

"Tell him I love him," I sobbed and made Darius say the address again. And again. And again.

"OK—your turn," I told him.

"You gotta take care of Princess," he said.

Ouph! I hadn't even thought about the kid once since things had kicked off.

"And," he added.

Whoa! A last request is a last request, right? It's not a last to-do list!

He spouted numbers. I was so terrified I didn't even realize to start with that it was a date of birth. *His* date of birth.

"Got it?"

"Yeah!" I said, even though it had gone straight out of my terrified head.

"I want you to find my mom."

"But—" He'd said his whole family was dead…

"My birth mother."

Someone yanked on the door, hard; we yanked it back.

"I was gonna find her, after our exams, and—"

The door got yanked again—before we got it shut, I saw his face for a moment in the light, and I saw that he was crying too, and when we got the door shut, the tiny pea-sized piece of brain in my head that still had any thoughts at all said, "You're *adopted*?"

"YES," said Darius.

I didn't know what say, so I said the numbers again.

"That's wrong!" cried Darius. "Look, you don't even have to remember it. Just go to the school, get it from my records."

"And then?"

"I'm not really sure," he said. "You need to find the adoption certificate."

"Oh," I said, already the pea in my head thinking that, as last requests go, it all seemed kind of tricky. "How would I do that?"

Someone thumped against the door, and we tightened our grips.

"I don't know how it works," blurted Darius Spratt. "I was gonna do it all online."

Our hands were locked together, straining on that handle.

"You can find out, can't you? You can try?" pleaded Darius.

"Yes!" I cried.

It was pretty much the world's worst and most complicated and most impossible last request—and I knew it…and he knew it. I knew he knew it. I knew he knew I knew it.

It was bad, what you could hear going on out there. It was very, very bad.

"Darius, if I couldn't do that," I said. "Let's just say if for some reason I couldn't do that…"

Someone yanked on the handle; our knot of hands held it shut.

LIKE WE'RE BOTH GONNA DIE RIGHT HERE, RIGHT NOW, IN THIS CLOSET, I thought.

"Is there something else I could do?"

AND MAKE IT EASY! I thought.

Darius Spratt was silent for a moment.

"Kiss me," he said.

THE CHAPTER OF SHAME—
TO BE DELETED

I kissed the Spratt. We were in a closet. I thought I was going to die. So I did the deed. He asked me to kiss him, so I kissed him.

I took one hand off the door handle. I grabbed his head for the purposes of ensuring a quick delivery, and I mashed my lips against his—like BOMF!—in the dark.

There. I had fulfilled his last request.

End of.

ONLY IT WASN'T!

OH, WHO CARES IF I TELL THE HORRIBLE TRUTH?

ME! I DO!

Someone yanked on the door; light flooded in for a sec, for long enough for me to see his face looked sad and grim and scared and weeping...and not at all how it was supposed to look (GRATEFUL) when I, me, Ruby Morris had just kissed him.

"You could say thank you," I said when the door yanker gave up.

"Oh, yeah, thanks," said Darius.

Thanks? I thought. *Thanks?!*

"I just kissed you!" I blurted...meaning I, me, Ruby Morris had just kissed...a SUB nerd.

"Yeah," said Darius. "Thanks. Or whatever."

WHOA. OH WOW. OH MY 🦋.

"Or *whatever?!*"

"I mean, you know, thanks. It was OK," said Darius.

"*OK?!*"

"Yeah…it was OK."

"*OK?!*"

"Yeah, Andrew Difford said you were an OK kisser."

"*WHAT?!*"

"Get over it, Ru. Now would be a really good time to just…get over stuff."

"*WHAT?! WHAT?!*"

"Actually he said you were lousy."

"Andrew Difford *said that…*"

"Yeah…he told everyone."

"He *told everyone…* He's a jerk; he's a total jerk. He's a gutless, lying, lowdown, blabber-mouthed, gossiping…a lousy kisser! He's a lousy kisser!"

"Whatever."

"I'm a wonderful kisser!"

"Hn."

"I AM a wonderful kisser!"

"Prove it to me, Ruby Morris," said Darius.

Someone yanked on the door. In the flood of light I saw his face, like mine: the fear and the hopelessness. The door slammed shut.

"Please," he whispered.

I took one hand off the door handle again.

I laid my hand, trembling with fright, on his face.

He took one hand off the door handle. He put his hand on my hand. Our fingers linked, steadying each other. He turned his head and, softly, kissed my palm. We stayed like that, for a moment. His lips, so still. The terror and the grief flowing between us. The power in our hands. Like we could make it all stop. No. Like this was all we had. All we would ever have. Our fingers squeezed.

His hand left mine. I grieved for it, instantly, in the darkness and the emptiness.

Don't leave me. Please don't leave me.

His hand came gently to my face, fear shaking in our fingertips, tracing tears.

It wasn't like the Caspar hot-tub thing. There was no BOMF. In the darkness, there was a kiss. There was a first kiss.

And because we might have had no time at all in the world, it seemed as if we had all the time in the world. We had all the time there ever was and ever will be.

CHAPTER TWENTY-THREE

You wanna know how I know the thing about no one living for longer than three hours?

That's how long we were in that closet for.

After a while, people stopped trying to get in, but we didn't come out until the whole world was silent, until all those people were dead.

We wouldn't have dared to…apart from anything else.

We shoved open the door. It would have been hard to have gotten out of there without stepping in pools of gore, but there were a ton of those little elastic blue plastic-bag things they make the swimming teachers and visitors wear over their shoes. We even put them on our hands, in case we had to touch anything, and we crackled out along the poolside, picking our way really, really slowly and really, really carefully through the hideousness.

All around us, inside that pool and outside, it was a scene of appalling horror. You really didn't want to look at it.

I also really didn't want to look at Darius Spratt's face. Further appalling horror.

Yup. I wasn't imagining it; in the middle of the nightmare of where we were and what was, this funny little goofy smile kept sneaking on to his face.

"Stop it!" I snapped.

"What?" he said.

Yup, there it was again.

Oh my 🦋. I was DYING from the sheer mind-melting horror of it. (I have to say that, the dying part.) (It's fully necessary and justified.)

"That!" I snapped.

What happened in the spongy-snake closet stays in the spongy-snake closet, that's what I thought.

I had this dreadful, dreadful feeling like somehow I'd been tricked, only I couldn't have been tricked, could I? He'd said kiss me, and I'd…

Oh my 🦋!!! It was too awful to think about…and in a way, it was just as well. Pretty much everyone at school must be dead *because if what had happened in the spongy-snake closet ever got out, my life wouldn't be worth living.*

I do realize that could sound terrible, but it is also true.

At least he wouldn't be able to say it was lousy. He wouldn't be able to say that.

I blasted the goofy smile off the Spratt's face with the mother of all death-ray "say one word and I'll kill you" stares and flounced off around the fire engine to get to the car. (The flouncing part wasn't easy; there was a lot of water and gore about.) Darius trailed after me.

The smile, which had crept back onto his face, melted away all on its own when he saw the kid. Princess was still in the car, sitting there, rigid. Darling was asleep on the driver's seat, so that seemed not right; the kid never seemed to want to let her go. I unlocked the trunk to let Whitby out—oh man! There was a stink!—and Darius opened the kid's door. She lurched out at him.

Kids—like Dan, when he was little—fling themselves at you, but I've never seen a kid do anything quite like that. She sprang at him like a wild animal, and she would not let go.

Meanwhile the bad things Whitby's butt had foretold came to pass…and were still passing. Set free, Whitby had a poop-fest.

"We could just stay here," said Darius, the silent kid fastened onto him.

The day so beautifully warm. Little cumulus humulis, still drifting about on high, making the world look storybook simple.

"We could go back into Bristol. We could find someplace. Just for tonight," he said.

Part of me really did just want to stop and rest. But in those storybook stories, in fairy tales, that's when it all goes horribly wrong, doesn't it? I had a quest on my hands; I had a place I needed to get to. It's important not to forget what you're supposed to be doing, isn't it? It's important not to let yourself get sidetracked and distracted. It is important not to give up or give in. It is important to be strong, even if you have never felt so weak and so tired and so sick of being afraid. Isn't it?

It was getting late, but there had to be hours left until night.

"I'm going to London," I said. "You two can do what you like."
Please don't leave me.

"It was just an idea," he said, prying the kid off him and practically forcing her into the back of the car.

"Yeah, well, I've had enough of you and your bright ideas," I grumbled. I handed him Darling, and he handed Darling to the kid and shut the door.

"Ru," he said.

I don't know what else he was planning on saying. I didn't want to know.

"Just get in the car, would you?" I snapped.

I opened my mouth to call for Whitby and got as far as "WHI–" before I saw him. He was guzzling water from a puddle near the fire engine.

Me and Darius Spratt, we looked at each other.

Now it seems so obvious, that the dogs were a risk. And not just a little risk but a MASSIVE risk. Even when I'd seen Whitby chowing down on dead people, I'd just thought, *Urgh!* I hadn't thought… And nor had Darius; you could tell by the look on his face.

"We've gotta get rid of him," said Darius.

"No!" I said, but more from the horror of the realizing it.

Whitby raised his head up, water dribbling from his chops.

"OK," I said.

Seeing us looking at him, Whitby bounded toward us. We both dived into the driver's seat and slammed the door.

"Get over on your own side!" I shouted into Darius Spratt's face.

He extracted himself and clambered into the passenger seat.

Whitby, the big dear darling old dope, didn't get it; why was the door shut? He shrugged his doggy shoulders and loped around the car, tail wagging, looking for a way in. He barked at us: *Hey, come on! Let me in!*

I burst into tears—then caught Darius Spratt eyeing Darling. Princess clutched her even more tightly and I spoke. I spoke for Darling, for me…and for the kid, I suppose.

"No!" I gasped. "Darling's fine! She's fine and we'll be careful!"

That Princess kid, she swung it all on her own. She looked at Darius with those big, solemn eyes, and she nodded. She actually nodded.

Seemed like that nod came out louder than anything I could have shouted.

The Spratt caved.

"Hn," said Darius. "OK."

It's not YOUR decision, I wanted to shout at Darius. Whitby, outside, had started to whimper…and the sound of his crying, it was awful, and I could feel I was about ready to totally yee-haa…

and then…something kicked in, just for a second, about how… I dunno. How it's so hard now to work things out, it's maybe be easier to work them out with other people, but how being with other people is dangerous as well as safer…because you have to agree all the time…because if you don't sort it out and you don't agree, a lot of things can go wrong. Basically, people can die.

I didn't think that then. Back then it was…so who did Darius think he was and he should just shut up because I'd gotten them out of Dartbridge, hadn't I? But he'd stopped me from going out into the rain to get my stuff, even though it hadn't really been about to rain or anything. And I'd gotten them out of that polytunnel and we'd helped each other out of that pool…so…it all seemed so complicated, and like *I* should just shut up.

My eyes were so tear-blurry I could hardly even see Whitby running after the car, barking. *Please don't leave me, please don't leave me, please don't leave me.*

I could hardly even see him until he was just a tiny dot, sitting in the middle of the highway, howling.

CHAPTER TWENTY-FOUR

As we zoomed toward London, Darius fiddled with the radio, skipping through miles of hiss in between repeats of the broadcasts that had not changed: "Stay home. Remain calm."

Yeah right. Someone needed to tell them that advice really wasn't working.

"Can you turn that off now?" I asked.

I asked it nicely the first time; the second time, because he'd ignored me, I said it not so nicely.

"Just a sec," he said, skimming through again.

So, third time: "TURN IT OFF!" I snarled and death-rayed him.

"So how come you don't want to know what's going on in the world?" he said, putting his naked feet up on the dashboard. Evening sunlight caught the hair sprouting on his toes. He'd used his window to hang his socks and mine out to dry. They flapped about together as we zoomed—with our clothes, still pool damp, drying on our bodies.

"I don't want to not know," I said, "I've just heard all that stuff before, right? What's the point?"

I wasn't exactly comfortable—in my clothes or in my head. I kept shifting about.

"Because they might be saying new stuff."

"Err. *Hello? Hello? Who might?* Have you not noticed? Everyone is dead."

The second I said it, I was waiting for him to DARE say something about my dad, but he didn't. No need. I was thinking it anyway.

I felt sick and like I needed air; I hit the wrong window button and our socks left us. I hit the right window button and stared out the window for a dangerously long time, breathing. Just breathing.

After that, we bickered about what music to listen to. The music collection in that car was a best-ofs bonanza (but at least it didn't include The Carpenters), and I've noticed that in a lot of cars. It kind of supports my theory about how stressful driving is; you couldn't cope with listening to anything interesting at the same time. I made him put some retro *Best of the '80s* CD on, and it flustered me instantly because every single song seemed to be about LURVE and kissing and such, but luckily I discovered I had an executive control switch on the stick you would have thought would be for the windshield wipers, so I kept skipping anything that sounded like it might be too slushy, which annoyed the Spratt.

"Oh, come on!" he whined when I did it yet again. "I was listening to that!"

He actually leaned forward and did a manual override on the CD player, skipping back to the lovey-dovey ballad. And he sang! The Spratt sang! And the worst and most annoying thing about the Spratt's singing was that the Spratt's singing was *good*. Not better than Caspar good; I will never say that.

"I don't like it," I said, skipping forward again.

"Why's it got to be what you want all the time?"

"Because," I said. "I'm the driver."

"So?"

The Spratt skipped back; I skipped forward.

"So we listen to what I want," I said. "Or we could always turn it off and play I Spy… That'd be fun, wouldn't it? I spy with my little eye something beginning with DB.".

The Spratt looked confused.

"Dead body?" I said. "Or maybe CC? Crashed car! Oh look! It's another DB!"

The Spratt went quiet. I felt mean, so I even though I wanted to skip the current track too because it seemed to be all about SEX (what was *wrong* with those '80s people?! They were obsessed!), I let it play. The Spratt lounged sulkily in his seat.

Honestly, what is it about songs, even crappy songs you wouldn't normally bother to listen to, that makes you hear every EXCRUCIATING word when you most don't want to?

But it gave me a brilliant idea. A Ruby genius idea.

"I hear, with my little ear, something people won't be able to sing about anymore," I said.

"Well, what does it begin with?" the Spratt asked.

"I dunno," I said, "but there's bound to be one."

The Spratt, I noticed, got a little less loungey. I could see his toes tensing. In the rearview mirror I saw the kid perk up, listening.

(More than that, I'd see her poke Darius a couple times, when a word was coming up. It turned out the Princess knew some of those songs.)

"LB! LASER BEAMS!" I shrieked.

I skipped forward.

"Why can't we listen to the rest of it?" cried Darius.

"Too bad!" I said. "Winner chooses!"

"Game on," said Darius, sitting up.

It was hilarious. It actually really was—once I'd carefully explained to Darius that it didn't even matter whether stuff still existed or not; it was just stuff that would OBVIOUSLY never be the same again. ("Look, it's really simple, dummy! No one's gonna sing about it being hot in the city again, are they, you idiot? It doesn't mean 'hot' hot, as in 'ooo, isn't it warm?' It means *exciting* hot. So: HITC—point to me—next track, loser!"

CB (cocktail bar!). M (money!). ST (steam train!). T (telephone!). PR (phone rings!). E (electric!).

Darius got grumpy about the electric one. Even though I was prepared to admit that you'd still be able to get electricity from batteries and generators and whatnot, I decided it was perfectly allowable because it was perfectly obvious when people sang about electricity they didn't mean electricity that came from batteries and generators and whatnot.

It came up loads of times, electric. Those '80s people were obsessed with that kind of thing too: electricity, atomic stuff, nuclear stuff... N (neutron!).

D (dime!). D (dollar!). I (industry!). T (tickets!). R (rent!)

We got silly (J! Jam! It doesn't mean that kind of jam! It's not about *fruit*!); we got picky (P! You can't have phone again—you just had phone!). We had this mind-boggling fight about whether FAM (four a.m.!) would still exist if all the clocks ran out or were busted, and people couldn't make clocks anymore and didn't care what time it was anyway because it wouldn't be like they had to go to school or work or anything, would it, and—anyway—what exactly is time?

(In a closet, at a swimming pool, it had ceased to exist.)

I.e., we had pretty much the kind of argument you'd have to go to Wikipedia to solve. Only we didn't have Wikipedia, did we? I (Internet!) never came up in any of those '80s songs. Not much of the stuff that was really important in our lives did. That's why it was fun, I guess... I mean, even though it was terrible, it wasn't really exactly completely *now*, was it?

"M!" shouted Darius. "Medicine!"

After a sec, he skipped to the next track, as the winner was allowed to do.

I had this thought. This thought about Darius and medicine and...

"So how long *will* those tablets last you?" I asked.

"Shut up, Ru," Darius said.

He laid his head against the window. OK, so everything had gotten weird. OK, so better not to ask.

"Hey," I said. I reached out and poked him. I should have just said sorry.

"B," he said.

"B?"

He didn't even look at me; he just said it: "Braces."

My braces aren't the kind that come out. They're glued onto my teeth. How would I ever get them off now? I was going to be wearing braces for the rest of my life. I was going to be sitting in an old people's home eating canned fruit, fretting about the weather, and...still wearing TRAIN TRACKS.

"Sorry," said Darius. "I'm sorry."

Some band squawked on about lurve.

"This is crap," I muttered, trying to eject the CD; the car swerved.

"I'll get it," said Darius. He took the CD out. "What do you want to listen to?"

"Not that."

"This?" said Darius, holding up some best-of classical music thing.

I thought he was just joking, so I said yes to annoy him.

He wasn't joking.

Actually, it was better not to hear people singing *about* stuff (like LURVE, for example), and the swoopy, sad violin music was a much better soundtrack for my mood, which had returned, completely, to deeply brooding and tragic.

And then I screamed.

I screamed because a car zipped past us. A little red sports car, traveling so fast I never even saw who was in it.

After that, I was too nervous to be tragic. I kept looking in the rearview mirror. Over the next hour, there were three more cars. I saw two of them coming. The first one, a silver car, tooted as it cruised past, a guy in it, alone.

"Honk back!" said Darius, craning out of his window.

I hesitated, then I honked. I don't know whether he would have heard. He didn't stop.

Some way past the Chippenham turn-off, I saw another car gaining on us from behind. This one didn't zoom past; it came up steadily.

"Look," I said.

"At what?" said Darius.

"That car. Behind us."

He turned.

"Hn," he said, sitting back round.

Hn?! We were being followed! I glanced at Darius. Another penny dropped with a massive clunk.

"Where are your glasses?" I asked.

"Polytunnel," he said.

"Oh my 🦋. Can you actually see anything?"

"A little. Not much. Look—I can see things close up. I can see you, all right, so stop making that face. It's not my fault, is it?"

"I Spy!" I squealed. "No wonder you didn't want to play I Spy!"

"Nothing I can do about it, is there? I can't just walk into an optician's and get a new pair, can I?"

"*Can't you?*"

"No! They're *prescription* glasses."

"What? Are your *eyes* sick too?"

"No! It just means you need someone who knows what they're doing—just like *you* and your braces!"

Tchuh! No wonder he wanted to stay at that farm! He'd have made us all hang around there until he got the guts to go back into that polytunnel and get them! No wonder he wanted to hang around in Bristol! If he was as blind as a bat he could hardly roam around, could he? But he had, hadn't he? He'd roamed around with me! He'd put ME in danger!

"Get the crowbar," I said.

"Ru—"

"Just get it."

Darius sighed and took off his seat belt.

"Don't crash," he said to me as he clambered into the back.

"Yeah, and don't call me Ru. Do NOT call me Ru," I said. "Not ever."

Uh. I realized he had to be rummaging through a ton of my underwear to find that crowbar. I had no time to be mortified. That car grew larger in my rearview. Darius clambered back, brandishing the crowbar.

"Don't let them see it," I said… Then, "No, do."

That car, it came right up behind us. Then it swerved right to overtake…but they didn't overtake; they came up alongside.

🦋, I thought. 🦋!

Darius leaned across me—he squinted, then he waved. I looked over…There was a family in that car: a mom; a dad driving; two kids in the back, a girl, a boy…all of them waving like crazy—and smiling. Smiling!

"Honk the horn!" said Darius. "Honk it!"

I honked.

"Pull over!" said Darius.

My heart was in my mouth, but I did it. I pulled over and I stopped.

They pulled up ahead of us and reversed.

They got out. The mom did, and then the dad. You could see the kids in the back, unbuckled and leaning over the backseat to see us.

"Stay here," I said.

Me, I got out and sauntered to the front of the car like one of Dan's carjacker characters. A real tough guy. Was deeply annoyed that Darius got out too—and without the crowbar. The Princess got out of the back, Darling in her arms. See how much authority I had?

The mom stepped forward; the dad held her back.

"Are you OK?" said the dad. Accent…Welsh?

Are you OK? That could mean a lot of things under the circumstances—like, Are you sick? Or, What the 🦋 are you doing driving a car? Or, How come you're just a bunch of kids on your own? Basically, it was probably pretty hard to believe that we were OK.

"Yeah, we're fine," I shouted. No need to shout—we were on the world's quietest highway—but somehow my voice came out like that.

I have come to realize…that when I get stressed, I get shouty. I was like that before all this happened, a little, but after the rain fell…I suppose I got a lot more like that. I do know that about myself. I do. I just can't help it.

"We're going to Salisbury," said the Dad. Welsh, definitely Welsh.

So?! I shouted in my head.

"What's in Salisbury?" asked Darius.

"There are big army bases there," explained the mom. "There's help."

She looked at the dad, who nodded.

"Do you want to come with us?" she asked.

This wasn't like being invited along by King Xar's court. I felt this pang, this serious *owwwww* ache for my mother. This ache to be taken care of, to not have to worry about another thing.

"We're fine," I said. Another tsunami, held back.

"Ru—" said Darius.

"You can go with them if you want to," I said.

Please don't leave me.

"It's OK," Darius told them.

Could he make it sound a little less like he was being abducted against his will?!

"We're going to London," I said.

"To find her dad," Darius added.

Oh! You could see just what a good idea they thought that was. And how likely they thought it was that my dad would be alive.

The mom looked at the dad, her face full of worry.

"If you change your mind," said the dad, "you'll need to turn off at Swindon. There'll be a sign."

"Your dad might be there already," said the mom. "It's where everyone will go."

"I don't think so," I said. "He'd have come for me first."

The dad nodded. Kind of sadly, maybe, but definitely like if he was my dad that was what he'd do…only…somewhere deep inside me a little voice said, *But your dad didn't come for you, did he? So what do you think that means, Ruby Morris?*

"I'm Sandra," said the mom.

Then she really did rush forward. I think she wanted to hug me, but I kind of stepped back, so she grabbed my hand instead and shook it. There were tears in her eyes.

"I'm Ruby," I said. Her hand was warm and soft, and I didn't want to let it go. "This is Darius," I said—the dad was already shaking Darius's hand.

"Dar-ius," said the mom, shaking Darius's hand next, while the dad, Mike, shook mine. "That's unusual," she said. She turned toward the kid…who stood there, clutching Darling. "Hello, lovely," she said. "And what's your name?"

The kid just stood there.

"This is Princess," I said. "And Darling, my dog."

My dog. That's MY dog. That's MY dog, I thought. And I knew it wasn't anymore. I knew that kid needed that dog more than I did. And I needed Darling a lot.

"*Princess*, is it?" said the mom, crouching down to try to coax a smile from her.

"We don't know her real name," Darius cut in. "We found her."

"She found him," I said. "She doesn't speak."

"Oh! You're a *shy* princess," crooned the mom, and you know what? The kid let her stroke her cheek. "That's Ethan and Holly," the mom went on, putting her arm round Princess and waving at her own kids. Ethan and Holly waved back.

The mom gave Princess a squeeze and stood; the tears that had been in her eyes escaped down her cheeks, and she wiped them away.

"Well," said the dad, putting his arm round the mom, "we should get going…"

With his gaze, he pointed out why. *I spy with my little eye something beginning with C.* The cutesy little cumulus humilis clouds were running, chased by their bigger, meaner brothers and sisters. Fatter clouds, puffed up with death. I'm not great at telling them apart, cumulus mediocris and cumulus congestus—which is a shame, because one can suddenly pour down; the other just looks like it might.

"Are you sure you don't want to come with us?" the mom asked. She looked at the dad.

"We could just take the little one if you liked," said the dad gently.

Aaaa-oooo!

Inside, I howled like Whitby. I howled like Whitby…because I felt like I was a little one. I felt like I wanted them to take ME.

"Do you want to go with them?" Darius asked the kid.

The kid looked at him.

"She's not sure," said Darius.

"She should," I said quietly, to Darius.

I've got to tell you that I felt pretty awful right then. I thought it would be best if the kid went with them, and I pretty much figured the kid wouldn't want to leave Darius, and—groan—truth was I didn't want Darius to leave me. I mean, I did, and I didn't. Mainly I didn't. Groan. Yeurch. Groan.

"Why don't you think about it?" said the dad. "We'll drive with you as far as Swindon, eh? See how you feel then?"

I looked at Darius. He shrugged. He looked as cut up about it all as me.

"OK," I said.

◆◆◆

We got back into the car, and we drove on. That mom and dad and kids stayed in front. Me and Darius, we didn't speak until I turned around to just look-see how the kid was doing.

"She's thinking about it," said Darius.

And that was it; that was all anyone had to say.

I was middle lane, just following the mom and dad, when—whoa! The last car that passed, the one I didn't see coming because I was so gloomed out, appeared from the opposite direction—fast lane, our side of the highway. They were zooming, flashed their lights, tooted and slowed down…but we had already passed. I didn't stop and back up; the mom and dad didn't either. They slowed for a moment, as though they were thinking about it, so I did too. Then we went on.

That's how it is, isn't it? Every time you see another person, you've got a choice: run or talk. Unless the fear decides for you. We'll never know what those people wanted to say to us, what they might have wanted to tell us. With the next people we met, there was no choice.

I was lost in a trance of gloom when the kid—the kid!—leaned forward and jabbed me. I whipped around in shock—the car swerved—the kid was pointing. I looked. On a bridge over the highway, there were two men in white onesie suits and masks and sunglasses. Both held massive guns—*machine guns?* One held a walkie-talkie.

"*Darius?*" I breathed.

Urh. Dur. He couldn't see, could he?

"There're men on the bridge," I whispered.

One of them waved us on. We zipped beneath them.

"What kind of men?" asked Darius.

"I don't know, do I?" I hissed—as if they could hear.

He made me describe what I'd seen and insisted they had to be army. They were wearing bio-suits, he said. I knew that; I'd seen crime things on TV, on the news and on drama stuff—also on the Web, when Ronnie had shown us "real footage" from an alien spaceship crash. I'd just never seen people in bio-suits carrying guns. Clipboards, maybe, but not great big *machine guns*. Even as I told him he couldn't possibly know that, that they had to be the army, the cones began to herd us in.

CHAPTER TWENTY-FIVE

The whole world has gone crazy, and still…you follow a bunch of cones.

The cones said *No, you can't leave here*, at every exit we came to. And we obeyed. Cones mean order. Cones mean someone is in charge. But who?

Then the cones appeared on the road too; they funneled us in… in and in and in until we were squeezed into the middle of the road. The highway that was supposed to take me to London stopped right there. Up ahead, they'd set up camp under the bridge, blocking the whole road, both sides.

They were waiting to greet us: four, five, six, seven men in those same white suits and masks, all carrying…machine guns.

"Hallelujah!" said Darius, squinting through the windshield.

That isn't what I was thinking. I was thinking, *Oh my God…*

Sorry, Mom…but this thought, this one thought, I won't replace with a 🦋. I can't; if I did, you might think I mean some other word. In most cases that wouldn't matter; in this case I feel it does. I thought it not because I believe in God (I don't, I think, not after all this), but because what was inside me was such a jumble, it sort of made me wish there was something outside me that could help. So it wasn't even swearing, really; it was for real.

An instant jumble of fear and shock; that's what I felt. Let me name the parts of it:

1. I truly had not believed that there would be anyone. I had not thought that there could be any sort of serious organization, any real order, left. (Apart from Girl Guides.) That shocked me.

2. Though I got why those men would be wearing bio-suits, that shocked me too, and it was frightening.

3. But it wasn't as frightening as those men having guns.

4. A little like a teacher catching you outside the gates during school hours, I also immediately thought—and no *kind of* about it—that somehow these people would not just let me go on my way.

5. So I felt, immediately, like I was in trouble.

6. And that it might be better to run.

7. But that if I did they might shoot me.

8. And, if I ran, I'd have to run alone.

There is another thing, a thing that won't quite sit right in some kind of list. A thing that was bigger than that moment, bigger... and more scary and more shapeless than anything else...and it was something like...was this how things were going to be? Men, with guns, loading people onto trucks. Men, with guns, telling people what to do. Was this what the world was going to be like from now on?

The fast lane of the highway was basically a parking lot. At our end of it, I saw the red sports car, ditched. I saw the silver car that had had that guy in it, ditched. And I saw the men that had been in them sitting in the back of an army truck under the bridge. A man in a bio-onesie sat with them. His mask was off, his gun laid across his lap; he was smoking and chatting with the men in the truck.

These people—everyone—seemed relaxed. Like this was somehow *normal*.

The mom and dad, they'd stopped in front of us. They'd gotten out and were chatting with the men; they pointed at us a little. The mom and dad got the kids out, shooed them over on to the army truck, heaved luggage out of the car, beckoned us.

I looked at Darius, realized he probably couldn't exactly see what was going on.

"They want us to come," I said, my voice ice.

"Let's go, then!" said Darius.

He helped Princess out of the car.

"C'mon!" he called, heading straight for those men.

I got out of the car. I'd been driving barefoot since we'd escaped from the pool. I opened the trunk and hunted amongst the ten thousand pairs of underwear for the only shoes I had left, the jeweled flip-flops I'd lent Darius. That mom, she came over to me. I know what parents look like when they're about to go on about something, so I got in there first.

"I have to find my dad," I said to her. "Please take care of them."

We looked over to see Darius lifting the kid into the back of the army truck. The mom nodded slowly, like she meant it. The most shocking thing was I realized I meant it too. With all my heart.

I put the flip-flops on. Before she or my stupid heart could get another word in, I split.

The Please Don't Leave Me Girl left. Girl Gone. Gone Girl. I didn't stop to ask anyone anything; I didn't take anything—not one thing. I just ran.

"Oh! No! Wait!" shouted the mom.

I guess she hadn't expected that I would just take off. That's the way it's got to be with parents sometimes: strike first. Otherwise, they're just going to bombard you with should-dos and shouldn't-dos and before you know it, you'll be not-doing.

I crashed through the jungle of weeds at the side of the highway and scrambled over a wooden fence. "RUBY!" shouted Darius as I busted through trees and bushes. I sort of expected Swindon to be right there, but it wasn't; what was there was a small field, then more trees.

"RUBY!"

SHUT UP, DARIUS! I thought. I glanced around to death-ray him, but it was pointless. Mr. I-Spy was just shouting my name into space, not even looking in the right direction. Princess, in the back of the army truck, rose to her feet, staring at me. That mom, who'd obviously blabbed to him, stood clutching his arm.

I sprinted across the field. I thought I was going to get shot at, that at any second bullets would whizz. Instead, what came was:

"STOP!" blared a soldier's voice on a megaphone. "COME BACK…WE ADVISE YOU TO COME BACK…*RUBY*, WE ADVISE YOU TO COME BACK."

Great. Now I was being nagged by the British Army—AND they knew my name. I blamed Darius instantly. If I ever saw him again, I would be forced to punch him.

I hit the next band of trees and pushed on into it…another field on the other side—but bigger—too big to run across, too exposed. I stayed in the trees. I'd follow them around the field.

"THIS COLLECTION POINT WILL OPERATE FOR THE NEXT TWENTY-FOUR HOURS."

And I'd still be there too, the way things were going. The trees got shrubbier and tanglier; brambles grabbed and scratched at my legs.

"I REPEAT: THIS COLLECTION POINT WILL OPERATE FOR THE NEXT TWENTY-FOUR HOURS."

I hit the corner of another field; a short run and I'd get to another bunch of trees. I made a break for it. Harder to hear the megaphone shout now, but still, I caught it:

"THERE IS ANOTHER COLLECTION POINT IN HYDE PARK, LONDON."

They knew my name; they knew where I was going. Probably the Spratt had blurted out everything he knew about me, kissing incidents included.

"I REPEAT: HYDE PARK."

In my mind, my fist collided with Darius Spratt's nose.

It took me longer than it should have to find a car. For a start, Swindon wasn't where it was supposed to be. If they're going to put a sign up for a place, it should at least be there. After that field was another field, and after that field was a lake.

Let's just pause for a second here, because I did. Imagine it: sweaty girl with a stitch in her side, all out of breath and scratched and frightened and angry and *thirsty*.

I mean, I don't know whether I would have drunk from a lake even before everything got poisoned, and I certainly wasn't going to now, but…it looked so cool and sparkly and inviting, as if you could just dive on in. OK, or at least dangle your legs in it a little, just to cool off.

See how this world is ruined? How the things that were so beautiful are hateful and wrecked? Shimmering blue dragonflies dancing over a pool of death. A pair of swans a-swimming on it.

I paused for a second to curse it all.

I bent down to pick up a rock. I wiped it, but it still looked dirty. (Little tentacly bugs waving, "Hello, Ruby! Eat us!") I flung it in the lake—and watched it trash the reflection…of big fat clouds that looked like they meant business. I looked up and cursed them too and ran, skirting around the lake, hating the entire world.

Across a golf course, there were houses—fancy houses—so that's where I headed, sprinting across fancy, clipped, golf grass toward the sunset. The beautiful sunset…running at it as if I was running to catch up with the sun itself.

That's all you ever want, isn't it? If you're not snuggled up somewhere safe and dry with plenty to drink and eat, you just want the sun to stay, for night not to come, for all clouds—even sweet and innocent ones—to 🦋 clear off.

That fancy housing development, it was a very locked-up place: cars, doors, windows—even sheds—were locked. I had no tools with me, saw no handy-sized rocks lying around, couldn't even see any Greek ladies to smash windows with. I got more and more angry and frustrated—and desperate…and thirsty—I was so thirsty!— until I came across MG man's house: front door open, garage doors open, car inside, him lying dead in front of it.

A smarter girl than me—a girl like Saskia, for example—would have gone straight into the house, I expect. I went for the garage.

Thank you, mister, I thought, when I saw the keys in his cool little sports car. I started it up; I saw there was nearly a whole tank of gas…and I would have taken off, but now that I knew I had an escape route, the urge to run eased off the tiniest, tiniest bit—which let the urge to drink grab hold. Grab hold and choke me, screaming in my face that I needed to drink and drink NOW.

I paced at the garage door. From the looks of MG man, he'd died the way Simon had died; he hadn't been rained on, but there was a mess round his lips that the flies liked.

The thirst thing, which had gotten seriously angry, was killing me so badly I did it. Like a psyched-up Dan gaming warrior launching into mortal combat, I roared something terrible at the world and sprinted for the front door.

It was the first time I went in somewhere without knocking or shouting. I couldn't have cared less whether the whole fancy neighborhood was hiding in there, drinking sherry and discussing how *simply awful* everything was. (They weren't.) I just barged in, went straight to the kitchen, and ransacked.

It was all junk, but it was brilliant—because there was something, at least there was something. I grabbed a bottle of cordial. I swigged it—disgusting—and kept looking. The fridge was cleaned out, but there was an unopened carton of melted chicken stock left in the freezer and an orange in the fruit bowl that looked just fine. I didn't even peel it. I just ripped it apart with my teeth and gored it dry while I rooted in the cupboards for something, anything else, to drink, the chicken stock churning in my stomach. Too much salt. And too dark now. Silly Christmas candle on the table; I'd seen that, hadn't I? Silly Christmas Santa candle and matches—I lit matches. Santa burned; nothing else left to drink…apart from…I had a pharmacy flashback and sped up to the bathroom.

You wear contact lenses, don't you? I know you wear them, I thought, pulling everything out of the bathroom cabinet.

MG man didn't wear contact lenses. I looked at the toilet. I thought about the water sitting there in that cistern. I thought about all the poisoned water sitting all over the house, locked in pipes. *Drink me.*

Santa, his head burned off, crackled.

I looked at the toilet again. I considered the advice of the Royal Society for the Protection of Birds. "The RSPB does not recommend…"

And nor do I. But I will say that drinking your own pee is probably not anything like as bad as you might think. I mean, it is bad, but…

Refreshed—as much as I was going to be in that house—I had a

burst of sensibleness. I looked out the window. I studied the sky…
only I couldn't see the sky—could I?—because it was dark. Cloud
dark. That's what clouds do; they cunningly make the night even
darker than it should be, so you can't see what they're up to.

It wasn't raining, though, was it?

The old me—who wouldn't have even looked and thought in the
first place—had become a new me, who did look and think. But I
was the even newer version of the new me; I didn't just look and
think and decide, *Hey, it's not raining—let's go!* The newest version
of the new me thought, *Nuh-uh!*

Even though it was just a quick dash to the garage and the car,
I got geared up; I did a Darius Spratt special and taped a thousand
garbage bags over my body, I shoved my feet into Mr. MG's walking boots and taped them over too, where the gaps were. If he had
an umbrella, I couldn't find it, so I got a baseball cap and taped
together an Indiana Jones and the Temple of Garbage Bags rain hat.
Finally, I turned my hands into black plastic paws.

Brilliant. Good to go, Ruby, good to go. And I was going.
See, the newer version of the new me still didn't want to stay in
that house. I snuffed out Santa—mid-belly, his buckle starting to
sizzle—chucked him and the matches in a plastic bag, and—

BOMF! I slammed the door shut behind me—like you
do—and—

SCREECH!

Seems wrong if this comes across like something out of a cartoon. There wasn't anything even remotely cartoony about it.

A millimeter from my face, rain streamed down.

🦋 poisoned rain.

🦋🦋🦋 poisoned 🦋🦋 rain, teeming with a million billion
microscopic killers.

(So, definitely cumulus congestus then.)

I flattened my back against that front door, the measly little porch above. One frightened hand crept around behind me and went to open that front door. That front door wouldn't open. The porch I was under was so narrow I was too scared to even turn around and yank on that door—but that wouldn't have made any difference, because the door was well and truly closed. Closed, shut, slammed shut—not going to open ever.

I tried to get Santa relit. My black plastic paws fiddled around, panicking; I dropped matches, I nearly set myself alight, and when I got one struck and managed to keep hold of it, I saw it: this little single glistening bead of rain hanging from the brim of my Indiana garbage-bag baseball hat. I dropped Santa and the match. I reached behind my head, grabbed the back of that hat, and flung it into the darkness.

Then I had this really bad few minutes thinking I could feel my hand wet, burning, bloody under the plastic… Because that's the thing, isn't it? That, really, a bunch of garbage bags and some sticky tape…would you trust them? Even before I'd dumped the hat there was NO WAY I was going to go wandering out in that rain. Garbage bags, waterproof gear; the only use they might—might—have is that they'd maybe buy you a few seconds. Who would risk longer? You may as well parade around naked if you think that stuff is going to save you.

For ages, it felt like, I stood pressed against the door in that porch. If the wind changed, if the wind picked up, if the stupid measly porch LEAKED…I would have been done for.

Not good, Ruby Morris, not good. NOT GOOD. Rain streamed down right in front of my face.

"*It's you and me now,*" I whispered at it. "*You and me.*"

Sooner or later, rain always stops. It stops, but it's laughing at you.

I can come back any time I please. Perhaps the second you step out from under this porch.

When it did stop, I waited. I got Santa and I relit him. I watched drips fall from the roof of the porch. I didn't wait for as long as I should have. I just waited for a while. I waited like I could trick the rain…or trick myself into believing it could be safe.

Without giving myself or the rain any kind of warning, I launched myself out into the dark, roaring something terrible.

It had been good, then, that I had looked at the garage first. I knew what was there. I stuck Santa on the roof of the car. I heaved and shoved the dark lump of MG man out of the way with a garden fork. I snuffed Santa out. I got into the car; I started it up and I got the 🦋 out of there.

It was the journey from hell.

Going to Zak's and back on the bike, that was easy in comparison; on the way there, I'd been too freaked out and frantic to think about anything, and on the way back, I'd been too shocked to really understand what a dumb thing I was doing. Plus, I was somewhere I knew. Now, I had no clue. There was a road map in the car and still I had no clue…but if there hadn't been a map, I'd have been sunk from the start. I'd probably still be driving around…wherever it was I was.

There was no light in that car and I had to keep stopping and lighting and relighting the Santa candle to work out where I was. Apart from Oxford, it was all places I'd never even heard of: Kingston Bagpuize; Monks Risborough; Great Missenden. *Were they making these names up?!* Who had ever even *heard* of them?! And—no *probably* about it—I should have found a different car. When I'd seen that car, a tiny part of me had thought…I dunno, how cool that'd be, to drive it. How cool it'd be to turn up at my dad's in a sports car.

Yes, an MG is a sports car, but it's a really, really ancient one; not zoomy or souped up at all. In the *Ruby Morris Guide to Disaster Survival*, a book I hope I'll live long enough to write, I will have to include a special chapter on picking cars.

There was no light and there was no CD player. All I had was the rattling boom of the engine and, below that, the rattling boom of my own heart. Bodies, dumped cars, burnt-out stuff, smashed-up stuff—I zigzagged my way through all that; and as far as I could tell I was zigzagging, period. Left turn, right turn. Stop the car, light up Santa, check the map. Right turn, left turn. Stop the car, light up Santa, check the map.

What I suppose I should have stopped was me. Plenty of places to do that. Endless plenty of places to stop and hole up for the night. Plenty of places to have at least stopped and found a better car. And something to eat. And something—please—to drink. But no. All I could think was, *I'm going to see my dad.*

Last match gone; Santa, stuck to the dashboard, burned down to his boots and went out.

It took a thousand hours before I got somewhere I recognized. I knew I'd gotten to London—houses and apartments closed in—but it wasn't until the road rose up into an overpass that I knew for sure(ish) where I was. I saw that building with a gigantic bottle on the side of it that poured sparkling neon liquid into a neon glass. Only it wasn't pouring anymore.

Like me, the MG was groaning with thirst. Probably I couldn't have gotten much farther anyway… It's just that I wouldn't have chosen to stop right there, on top of that overpass. The road, which had gotten more and more difficult to drive along, was finally completely blocked. I grabbed the map and I got out.

It wasn't raining anymore, but you'd think, wouldn't you, that I'd have at least tried to look at the sky first. You'd think, wouldn't you, that I'd have realized I needed to do that by then. Not me, no. I stepped out of the car, then I thought that thought, then I looked at the sky. I saw stars, tons of stars.

Stars, beautiful stars…how you never, ever saw them in London, where the sky was always a dirty orange…and a moon, full—like an O.

Like an O!…O! *Look! No clouds!*

NO CLOUDS. BRILLIANT.

No way down off an overpass; no way other than forward. (Because no way was I going back.) So that's what I did. I walked on; if I couldn't get around the cars and bodies that were in my way, I clambered over them. *I'm going to see my dad; I'm going to see my dad; I'm going to see my dad.*

When the road came to ground level again, I started trying cars. I tried cars even when there was no point in trying cars. I tried cars that were boxed in. I'd stopped thinking straight. All I did was keep on walking. I saw things, I heard things, I saw people. Live people. I kept on walking.

I realized I was at Euston Station. I turned left. That was how to get to where my dad lived: Kentish Town. Soon be there. I walked… I walked; I didn't even bother trying for cars, I walked…faster and faster…until I ran and I ran. *I'm going to see my dad.*

I don't know what time it was when I found his apartment. It was pitch-black, had been for hours. Only the O! of the moon and the stars, twinkling. The door was open; not *open* open, but open— unlocked. I burst in.

"DAD! DAD! DAD!" I screamed. "*DADDY!*"

He wasn't there. I was an empty person in an empty house and just to make good and sure there was nothing at all left inside me, I lay down on his bed and cried out every last tear I had.

CHAPTER TWENTY-SIX

Like I was already learning how to tell stuff from bodies—about the way people had died and how long they had been dead for—these days I can tell stuff from houses. There are the obvious things—how much of a panic the people were in, whether they'd been out looting stuff—and then, most importantly, there's whether someone else like me has been there and how recently. There are so few of us left that it's rare we cross paths, and it's always a shock when it happens. It's usually in the kitchen that you find the signs, by looking closely at how dried up stuff is and what is rotting. There is, for example, a whole disgusting rainbow of molds that come along at different times. If you find food frosted with white fur, I'd say that house has had a visitor in the last week, depending on how thick the fur is. Even if there are just some crumbs on the table, press them—if there's just the slightest tiny softness to them, you should get out of there immediately unless you're feeling brave enough to stop and chat.

In the morning, at my dad's, it was the start of that learning how to look and to pay attention. Not how I'd looked at Saskia's, which was just snooping, or in the poor dead farmer-girl's room, but looking closely and thinking.

When I woke up, I felt really ill. Ill in my heart and my head, but *ill* ill too: the pounding headache and killer thirst of dehydration. Dad had nothing to drink, so the first thing I had to do was get out and work my way through the neighbors' houses looking for something, anything, to quench my thirst. I looked through the window; I saw a dazzling day. I stripped off my garbage-bag armor and I went out.

I found the usual.

I came back and sat in my dad's bed and wasted precious body fluids on the production of tears and snot at the same time as I sipped in life: grapefruit juice from the neighbors, mixed with a little sugar and salt. Puke-tastic.

It was there, sitting in that bed and feeling like a one-girl megadisaster, that I started to notice stuff. His closet was open, and it looked half-empty. He was kind of messy—like me—but there were small piles of clothes left on the floor, rather than a general scatter. The clothes looked clean and smelled clean, so I deduced the piles were not pre-laundry sorting heaps. I checked the drawers in his dresser; stuff was gone. Looked like he'd packed, and not in some kind of frenzy but thoughtfully (for my dad).

Same story in the bathroom; no toothbrush, no toothpaste, none of the usual stuff you'd expect to find. I hadn't thought to check when I'd gone looking for something to drink, but now I wandered outside up and down the street. I couldn't see his car—but the parking, as he always said, was a nightmare, so it could have been miles away. I went back in and checked coat pockets—no keys, and in any case, the jacket he always wore, his tattered favorite, was gone.

In the kitchen, my numb, dumb head buzzing, I sipped on the puke mixture while I analyzed the trash, worked out what *he'd* had to eat and drink. Looked to me like, if he hadn't been pigging out, he could have been holed up for a few days. Like us, he'd snacked on canned fruit—but the crucial thing was the freezer. Normally it'd be crammed with all sorts of random stuff. Any little piece of food left, he'd throw it in there. It was the land of frozen mysteries— 'cause most of that stuff was my dad's experimental cooking and pretty hard to identify. Stuff had gone from it, that was for sure, but the stuff that was left, the melted stuff, was in bowls and pans, some in the fridge too. All of it was heading toward being disgusting (although most of it probably had been in the first place).

It was a revolting sight—that filled my heart with joy and hope. It meant—it had to mean, surely?—that he had still been alive when the power went down. That he'd realized stuff would melt and make a mess, so he'd put it in bowls—and left it in the freezer and the fridge where it'd at least keep cool for a little longer. I looked at what was left; I looked at what was festering in the trash; I looked at what was festering on plates and in the sink.

What I concluded was that my dad had not been killed when the rain had first come (and my dad had worked out that the tap water was bad), that he had been alive when the power went down. If it was the same in London as it was in Dartbridge, that meant, up until three days ago, my dad was still alive.

I don't think he ate much from that freezer. (I don't blame him.) He had packed his bags, carefully, and gone.

He wouldn't have gotten far. He couldn't have. It made my heart ache to think that…one of those thousands of cars I had passed in the night must surely have been his. He would have had to have gotten out and walked, like I did. He would have walked, and he would have found another car. He would have gone to find Dan first, I suppose. That made sense; Dan was in London. I just didn't know where. He would have gone to find Dan and then…

Three days ago… Why hadn't he come to get me?

Because he would have gotten stopped, I thought.

He'd have gotten stopped, like me, at Swindon. If he'd had Dan with him—maybe Kara too—he'd have taken them to the army base. I didn't like those men with guns one bit, but I could kind of see how someone with a kid would feel like that'd be the best bet, that they'd be safe, I suppose (from other men with guns). Maybe… maybe he thought that's where I'd be too. That's probably what he thought. That's what I told myself, *That's probably what he thought.*

My head hurt even more from thinking it all out. I had not wanted to believe that Darius Spratt could be right before, and now I certainly absolutely couldn't and wouldn't think my dad was dead. I refused to believe that something awful must have happened—no matter how many times I'd seen by then—and would see again and again—how easy it was for people to die in this new poisoned world. The way I saw it, what I had to do was simple. I didn't even have to go all the way back to Swindon either. All I had to do was get to Hyde Park.

I kind of knew my body was even more done-in dog-tired than the day after biking to Zak's. Probably my body was even more done-in dog-tired than it EVER had been in my entire life, but I didn't care. It didn't bother me. Only the thirst did. Seemed like every smashed-in shop I passed was robbed of everything, but I found two packs of home-freeze ice pops and swigged the plastic tubes of colored, sugary water as I went. I cut up, over the park, and saw how the city was.

Sitting up there in the park, among the barbecues surrounded by dead people, I wondered, *Had London ever been so quiet?* Like Bristol, you could see smoke from fires rising…so somewhere in that city maybe things weren't so quiet. The only sound came from the buzz of a lone helicopter, one of the kind with two sets of propellers, that crawled its way across the sky like some nasty big fat insect and set itself down somewhere green.

I didn't get depressed about what had happened to the world. I worked out where I was in it. I matched up what I could see with MG Man's map book. I was on Primrose Hill. The helicopter was in HYDE PARK; I REPEAT: HYDE PARK. All I had to do was get there. It didn't look so tricky. I'd just cut through Regent's Park. Easy peasy.

One thing: …the day was lovely. The sky, it was blue. It was blue except for the cloud I hate most. There is no reason to hate it; it isn't going to rain on you. It doesn't even mean rain is on its way. I hate it because I remember I noticed it that day, and now I know its name: cirrus uncinus. High streaks of thin, wispy clouds…with claws reaching down. A demons' sky. Ghost demons. Coming to get you.

I speed-walked down the hill. Wasn't it so weird? It was so weird, wasn't it? Don't panic, Ruby, don't panic; it's all going to be fine. This place that would have once been full of people, now so empty… so empty…

"I spy," I started up with myself, "something beginning with R."

Road—clogged with dead cars and dead people, the me that was frightened said.

I refused to say W (*Water! It's poisoned! It's poisoned!*) as I walked across the bridge over the canal. "I spy, with my little eye, something beginning with Z," I got in quickly, before the me that felt frightened could butt in. It didn't do much good.

ZOO! Zoo! And what about the poor animals?

Hadn't I been past London Zoo so many times with Dad, me on my own with him, or me and Dan with him, begging to go in? We were always on our way to somewhere else. It was the same this time: I had to keep going.

"I spy something beginning with…F."

FB! Flower beds! Your mother loved flowers! Your mother is DEAD. Your dad is—

"T!" I said, to shut myself up.

I stuffed my empty box of ice pops into a trash can and started on the next box.

Trash! Trash! Trash!

"Another T!" See how pretty they were, the trees? How the light shone through them?

G! G! shouted the me that was frightened. *G!*

There they were: two giraffes snacking on trees. Giraffes in the middle of a London park. Some *kind* someone, anyone must have set the animals free.

It was, I think, the most amazing and beautiful sight I had ever seen—or ever will see. I'll never get to Africa, but I have seen that now: giraffes, right in front of me, snacking on trees.

Oh wow.

Even though I had to realize immediately that I had no phone to snap "selfie with gee! raffes" on, no Web to post it on, and anyway all the people I wanted to tell about it were dead, my heart—which had been sunk deep in my chest, worrying and scared—lifted up.

Oh wow.

Chomp, chomp—rip—chomp; it was so quiet I could hear their gentle little mouths working. Tails swishing—just a little—big brown eyes looking—just a little—at the human girl passing by.

I had these thoughts—strange but not scary—about how maybe there'd be so few people left now that the animals would set up a human zoo and bring their animal children to stare at us and tell them in Animalese to shush and not frighten us, and give us cell phones to play with and feed us on canned stuff and bottles of cola. Yikes! And try to get us to breed! Imagine spending the rest of your life trapped in a cage with Darius Spratt, being forced to try to like each other.

On the other side of the park, I walked down a long city street toward Hyde Park. Whenever I passed a clothing store, I thought about the state my dress was in—ripped up, filthy—and how the boots that weren't my boots were: tatters of plastic bags hanging off them. They didn't even fit me, had rubbed my feet into blisters. But mainly I tried not to think about anything. I am so very good at that. It's a skill, actually. It really is. You probably know that. One day, all the people who have survived should have the Ignoring Things Olympics. If I am alive, I might win...but I have a weak spot.

OXFORD STREET

Look, it wasn't like I could hear helicopters in the park; it wasn't like it was about to rain; it wasn't like I didn't have HOURS left, probably, to get to the "COLLECTION POINT IN HYDE PARK. I REPEAT: COLLECTION POINT IN HYDE PARK."

It was like...I'm fifteen years old; I only just turned fifteen years old. My clothes were in tatters, my feet were bleeding, rubbed sore. My face was naked. I looked like a mess; I felt like a mess.

I crunched over broken glass into the valley of temptation.

Ten minutes. Just ten minutes. Dad would understand. I could get something for him. Ten minutes. Five.

CHAPTER TWENTY-SEVEN

I picked the biggest and best department store I could find, strode on in through a shattered window, and I shopped until I dropped.

There were other shoppers in there. First one I saw, I froze in panic. She just nodded at me, said "Hi," and carried on browsing.

Next one I saw, I nodded at, said hi.

Third one I saw, in men's ties, I just ignored. Not in a nasty way—we were just browsing. We had no reason to speak.

I got my dad a really good tie, a bunch of really good ties. Silk ties. I'd never seen him wear a tie, but…

A long time later, I sailed out of a changing room in exactly the kind of insanely gorgeous super-expensive designer frock I wanna wear to the premiere of the never-to-be-made blockbuster of my bestselling book—and froze. There was someone hogging the mirror, twirling about, this way and that, in an incredible dress—in a hideous color: orange. Don't you just hate orange?

"What do you think, darling?"

I thought it was Naomi Campbell. I pretty much knew it couldn't have been, but that is what I thought. She made everyone I had ever known, every person I had ever seen, including every person in King Xar's court, look…shabby and ugly. Apart from my mom, if you know what I mean. This person, she was THE most gorgeous thing ever. Wondrous to behold. Glowing with extreme loveliness and beauty. If she'd had a wand, I would have sworn I had surely met a fairy godmother, one I wanted for my very own.

So she had seen me. Also she wasn't a she. She was a he.

There was a guy in Dartbridge who wore women's clothes, but he just looked like…a guy with a beard wearing women's clothes. This person, THE most gorgeous person I had ever seen in real life in my life, looked…AH-MAY-ZING. He/she had been on a makeup binge too, but he/she was a lot better at it than me. Great, GREAT sweeping eyelashes. Shimmering, perfect lips.

I could have bolted. I looked around. There was this couple, miles away in the underwear department; the guy sat flicking through a magazine while the woman pondered sexy-looking corsets. But other than that, me and the most beautiful person on Earth seemed to be alone.

"Maybe a different color?" I said.

He/she gave me a long, hard, pouty stare—but a much better long, hard, pouty stare than I could ever do—then looked back at him/herself in the mirror.

"Hmmm, you're probably right," he/she said.

He/she picked up her enormous (DESIGNER!) handbag, hoisted it on to his/her slender shoulder, and skimmed, with elegant manicured nails, through hangers.

I looked to see where the emergency exit was, where the little white man was running now.

"What do you think about this?" he/she said, holding up something: a green shapeless thing that could have looked brilliant on, or could have looked—

"Hn," I said.

"Isn't it?" he/she said. He/she released the item from her fingers; it dropped to the floor.

"I'm Diana. From Knightsbridge," she said, extending her hand to me.

There was something so—SO—elegantly *sophisticated* about her, I just couldn't help but take that hand. I thought that—maybe—it trembled slightly.

"I'm Ruby," I said. "From Dartbridge."

"*Enchanté*," breathed Diana, gently squeezing my hand.

She let my hand go and flitted, like a beautiful butterfly, to another rail.

"Diana?"

"Yah?" she said, wandering off to look at shoes.

I wanted to talk. I—randomly—wanted to talk. *No, Ru*, I told myself. *Not now.*

"I have to go," I said.

"Sure," she said, jamming a shoe onto her foot.

"I'm going to Hyde Park," I said.

"Sweet cakes," said Diana, gracefully flinging the shoe across the floor, "you don't want to go there."

"Why not?"

"Army, darling. Army."

She flitted on to another display. Me and my bags of loot clumped after her.

"I wish they did half sizes. You just *know* they won't. Why does NO ONE do half sizes?"

"What's wrong with the army?" I asked.

"Uh!" said Diana, like the army was the worst thing she could think of. "What's *right* with them?" she fumed, trying to get her foot into a shoe that was too small. "They've been rounding everyone up, haven't they? What are they doing with them?"

She flung the shoe across the floor.

"Helping them?"

"Yah, right! How come it's all come-to-mamma now? I mean, *sweetie*, think about it! These people—the army, the gov-ern-ment—didn't even bother telling people…anything. Not one word that would have saved a body's life!"

The angrier she got, the more her accent kind of bounced around. These words crept in that sounded more like the kind of South London gangsta-rapper thing Dan tried to do; only with Diana, it was like that was what she was trying not to do.

She looked up at me. She sighed a mighty sigh.

"What else could they do, I suppose? I expect that's what they'll say, anyway. There was hardly going to be enough bottles of bubbly to go around, was there?"

She delved in her designer bag and handed me a glass (DESIGNER!) bottle of fizzy water.

"At least now there's plenty," she said.

I'd been too busy shopping to notice how thirsty I was. I opened it and drank it down.

"For as long as it lasts," added Diana with another sigh.

"Oh! Sorry!" I said, thinking I'd deprived her.

"No, no, no," she said, waving my words away with her beauti-fully manicured hand. "Plenty more where that came from…for now. What I meant was," she said softly, "it won't last forever, will it? And then what, eh?"

I burped. "Pardon me," I muttered. I hadn't thought about this. I hadn't thought about any of this. Only about the Spratt and his pills, about my train tracks—and even those things I hadn't exactly *thought* about, not really.

"Doom…" she sighed. "Hey-ho. I'll tell you what, we simply shan't talk about it, eh? We don't want to go getting ourselves all miserable, do we?"

"No…" I said. "Diana?"

"Yah?"

"My dad's there. At the army place."

She fixed me with her fairy-godmother gaze, magicking everything.

"I'm sure it's all perfectly charming," she said. "I'm sure it'll all be fine."

"I will say one thing, though, sweetie," she added, examining a crocodile-skin-look red ankle boot. In spite of the magicking, I kind of wished she wouldn't say another word, but she chucked the boot aside and advanced on me. "I think we need to do something with your hair."

Huh?! One minute we were discussing the hideous mess the world was in, and now the hideous mess of my hair.

"I mean, if you're going to do red—and, frankly, I think you may need to have a rethink on that…" she said sternly. "Do you mind?" she asked, and before I could say that, yes, actually, I did mind, she'd liberated my hair from its elastic band. "IF you are going to DO red, you need to **DO** *red*."

Before I could protest, she mussed up my hair and steered me to a mirror.

"Uh," she sighed, gazing at me with me. "What DO they teach you in—where is it you said you were from?"

"Dartbridge," I said. "It's a little town in—"

"Shh! Sweetie! Concentrate! Absorb!"

Diana dumped a ton of stuff from her handbag and did stuff to my hair.

I really, seriously, did not recognize myself. I'd already tinkered about with makeup so my face didn't look so scratched-up-with-hints-of-orange, and now, there I was, in an amazing dress, with amazing hair, looking amazing.

"Shoes," muttered Diana. "You need the right shoes."

I had quite a fantastic pair of platform sneakers on already.

"I should go," I said.

"What are you?" asked Diana. "A four?"

"Five," I said. "But—"

"Wait!" commanded Diana, stalking dramatically back into the land of shoes.

She found what she was looking for and put the box in a bag for me.

"They'll be perfect," she said and air kissed me. "Mwah! Mwah! Go knock 'em dead, sweetie."

"Thank you," I said.

"*De rien!*" said Diana. "*De rien!*"

"Thank you," I said again. I didn't know what else to say, so I kissed her—for real—on the cheek…because she was beautiful, because she had made me look amazing, and because, if I could ever have a fairy godmother, I would wish for one who looked just like her. Just *looked*, mind; the general somewhat bossy attitude was a little too much. My fairy godmother would have to dote on me, be forever gentle and kind.

"You take care, girlfriend," she whispered.

A big, fat tear slid down her beautiful cheek, right through the lipstick mark I'd left where I'd kissed her.

I left. I wasn't going to cry and wreck two hundred dollars' worth of makeup. I had no reason to cry anyway. I was going to see my dad.

In the next ten minutes, when I stepped out from designer world and crunched back down Oxford Street into real life, I went from feeling like I looked a million dollars to feeling like I looked like kind of a twit. Kind of a Darius Spratt. Glamour plus army does not go.

There was this makeshift, razor-wired army post and polytunnel-type space tent in the middle of the park. Men in white bio-suits, masks, guns. No one shouted; no one waved. They couldn't *not* have seen me. I waddled up to them in my dress, weighed down with bags.

"All right, love?" said one of the men.

He opened the wire, and I went into their compound.

"I need to get to Salisbury," I said.

"Well, you've come to the right place then," he said. "Take a seat."

There was a handful of other people like me there too, sitting on plastic sheets on the grass. Most looked like they'd also got sidetracked on Oxford Street, dressed up to the nines in whatever took their fancy, surrounded by millions of shopping bags. One woman wore a ton of diamonds. I mean, I really think those might have been real diamonds—they kind of looked different from the bling I'd picked up—and she kept clutching her neck, checking her ears.

A few of those people nodded vaguely at me. Mainly they just stared at the floor or at the sky, waiting.

I didn't know what else to do, so I did what they were doing. I waited. *I'm going to see my dad.*

CHAPTER TWENTY-EIGHT

M e and my two million bags of designer loot sat in front of them, this woman and this man—in normal clothes—sitting behind a desk. The woman had a notepad. The man had a laptop. The army had electricity.

I waited for a while while the woman muttered stuff to the guy and folded her notepad so she had a clean sheet of paper.

I didn't mind waiting. *I'm going to see my dad.*

The first helicopter ride I ever had didn't lasted very long. We got dumped in another park—somewhere beyond the traffic jams, I suppose—put onto a bus, then dumped in this stinky hangar with a ton of other people, where everyone had spent hours and hours shuffling forward and backward in this long (stinky) zigzag line. Reason for the shuffling about was quite sweet, really; every time a new bunch of people arrived, those in line already let anyone who was old or sick or had little kids go to the front. Quite sweet—and totally rage-making. Some people lost it; some people shouted—or muttered to anyone they thought might listen—about who they were and why they were there and why they should be at the front of the line. I kept my cool though. *I'm going to see my dad.*

When it really was my turn, the door slid open, and I stepped out into the light. It was blinding, dazzling, after the darkness of the hangar, and it wasn't even proper daylight; it was plastickly blurred through some kind of army polytunnel that led from one building to the next.

"This way," said a soldier, and I followed his voice, blinking, into the next building, into a room—the room where the woman and the man sat. Two soldiers stood at the back—but slouching, like they'd had a long wait too.

"Do you want a drink?" the woman behind the desk asked.

There was one small plastic cup of water on that table.

"No thanks," I said, even though I was dying of thirst. *I'm going to see my dad.*

The woman asked questions; the man typed my answers into the laptop. It went OK at first: name and address. I got my own date of birth wrong first time they asked—not because I was so impatient and excited, which I was, but because I went into fib autopilot. It's just what you do, isn't it, when someone in authority (like the shopkeeper you're trying to buy beer from) asks you to confirm the date on the fake ID that's not even yours. (Lee, darling, will it even matter now if I say it belonged to you?)

I corrected myself, and they carried on.

Was I accompanied? Did I have a parent or other relative with me?

"No," I said. "But I think my dad's here."

"And your mother?" the woman asked.

They made me tell them; they made me give the names and dates of birth of my mom, of Henry, of Simon. Of the "members of my immediate family" I knew for sure were dead. Henry's date of birth, I knew. Mom? Simon? I couldn't get it right; I knew when their birthdays were—the dates and months—but which year? I had to tell *them* how old they were and let them work it out.

"Sorry, I'm no good at math," I said.

That woman, she sort of smiled at me.

"So, you're not good at math…but are you good at other things in school"—she glanced down at her notepad—"Ruby?"

I shrugged. I couldn't think why she'd be asking something like that. What did that matter?

"You just need to answer honestly," she said. "This isn't a test."

Funny thing was that *that* was exactly what it felt like.

"I do OK," I said. "I mean, I'm not all that good at that much. I do OK in English. I like art."

"And outside school? What do you like to do?"

Why was she asking me this stuff?

"Same like anyone," I said. "Just hang out with my friends, I guess."

"No hobbies?" she asked.

"Not really," I said. I definitely didn't want her asking about those guitar lessons.

And then she asked a bunch of other questions. These got really specific. Had I come into contact with any infected water? Had I come into contact with anyone who had come into contact with infected water? Had I eaten any fresh fruit or vegetables? Had I drunk any fresh milk? Eaten any fresh meat?

"No," I said. Confidently. I wasn't stupid, was I?

The man hit a key on the laptop, like he'd been hitting a single key on the laptop for the last ten minutes. All those questions and he hadn't typed anything I'd said in; he'd just hit a key.

"Thank you, Ruby," said the woman. "You can go."

All the way through that test they said wasn't a test, I'd held on to my shopping bags. I stood up.

"Can I see my dad now?" I asked.

"He's not here," said the woman.

CHAPTER TWENTY-NINE

Short chapter, that one was. Short and bitter. Bitter like the acidy stuff you throw up from your stomach when there's nothing left inside you to throw up.

I was led out into another room. They fingerprinted me; they photographed me. I'd seen that stuff too, on TV. The flash of the camera made me snap out of it a little, and I tried to ask about Dan, about Grandma Hollis, about Nana and Gramps, about Auntie Kate about Uncle James…about the Spratt.

"They're not here," said a soldier.

"Turn," said the photographer.

"But—" I said.

"Turn!" barked the soldier.

The photographer glanced over his shoulder at her.

"Turn," the photographer said, more softly.

I turned; he snapped my picture.

"But—"

"You're all done," the photographer sighed.

I'd heard them. I heard them like I heard Darius say my dad was dead. I heard them and I refused to believe. All dead? Not all dead. All done? Not all done.

◆◆◆

They led me out into another yard through another army polytunnel and dumped me on another bus.

"You took your time," said some rude woman as I plunked myself and my bags down in the first free seat.

I was numb. I couldn't think where my dad could be. I don't mean that I was actually thinking about that, about where he could be; I mean I just couldn't think. I couldn't think, and I felt as if I could hardly move.

I only remember two other things about that wait on the bus. Two other things:

1. We were there so long people chatted to the soldiers on the coach—who weren't real soldiers, it turned out, but "reserves": people who were soldiers on the weekend and stuff, for a hobby; people who were maybe accountants like Simon the rest of the time. (Can you imagine? *Surrender or I'll miscalculate your taxes! Sorry, Sarge, but we've had to cancel the invasion because someone has spotted a rare species of bird nesting on the battlefield,* etc., etc.)

2. Looked to me like those army people had taken all the water. Trucks pulled up, supplies got unloaded into a hangar. Food—yes—and about a million bottles of water, and a truckload of huge plastic tanks in which yet more water sloshed. One plastic cup, they'd offered me, one measly plastic cup. I bet it was the army that had cleared out the supermarket in Dartbridge. I bet it was.

I wished I'd drunk that measly plastic cup of water because that bus was only half full, and it seemed like it'd be days before they filled it up. It was an age before the next person got on—the next two people: this girl in a headscarf who was lifted out of her wheelchair and carried on to the bus by this guy. This guy who was her dad. I'd felt sorry for her the second I saw her, not because she was in a wheelchair but because her dad looked like some kind of religious type, beardy and serious and smocked. (There was a girl in my class at school whose dad was a pastor, beardy and serious and smocked, and she got no end of teasing and hassle for it.) I'd heard them in the line, a couple people behind me, the dad going on in some foreign language and the girl getting so annoyed with him she burst out in English, "Dad! *Abo!* Please! It's not as though I'm sick, is it? Please don't make a fuss!"

Me and my bags shifted back a seat before the dad could ask me to and the girl could tell him again not to make a fuss. I did not want to hear that.

Do I even need to say how much I wished my dad was there, making a fuss?

After that, they seemed to decide that was enough people, even though the bus was only half full. One of the soldiers did a head count like it was a school trip or something, and they shut the doors. Then they opened them again to let this other guy on board—a doctor, must have been; white jacket and stethoscope and a look on his face like he'd just had to tell someone they had a week to live.

"Hey, guys," he said, flashing an ID at them. He said "Hey, guys" like Simon would say it. *I'm just like you, really I am.*

We drove out through a different exit, a different set of gates. There was another small gathering of people outside them, like there had been when we arrived. They were angry; they were shouting—I couldn't hear what. I didn't much care. Same as when we'd arrived, soldiers in bio-suits cocked rifles at those people so they could get the gates open. This time it was to let the bus out.

We went down a road; we went down another road. We stopped outside another camp. The doors opened.

"Cheers, guys," said the doctor-man again as he got off.

I looked out the window. There, lining up outside a building in the camp, I saw Darius Spratt.

I didn't want to punch him.

"DARIUS!" I screamed, hammering at the window. "DARIUS!"

I saw him turn. I saw him look. I saw him not see a thing.

"DARIUS! DARIUS! DAAAAAAAAAA-RIUS!" I tried to storm off the bus, but the two soldiers blocked my path.

One shook his head at me.

"Please!" I shouted at them. "That's my friend! Please!"

That's how desperate I was; I called Darius Spratt my friend.

Second time—AND LAST.

Their faces were stone.

"He can't see me! He can't see a thing! He's lost his glasses!"

"Just sit down, love," said the other soldier.

"Please!"

"For 🦋's sake," said the woman who'd been rude to me, standing up…but she wasn't saying it at me—she was saying it at the soldiers.

"Come on, buddy," said a guy, getting out of his seat. "Show the girl some pity."

"Yeah," said another guy, standing, "show some 🦋 pity!"

That soldier, the one who'd told me to sit down, he cocked his rifle.

"SIT DOWN!" he said.

And that's what everyone did. Everyone. You don't argue with a gun, do you?

I sat there shaking—with rage, I think. I wished I had a bucket full of pee to chuck in their faces. I wished my Halloween Bad Dolly self would come. I wished I could be Saskia; a girl like Saskia would know what to do.

"What's your name?" asked the SIT-DOWN! one.

"Ruby," I said.

The other, quiet soldier muttered something and went out and said something to the ones guarding the gate.

They looked at me, my hands pressed to the window mouthing, *Please, please, please!*

Eyes got rolled, but one of the guards sauntered across the yard, got blind Darius, and brought him to the gate.

The SIT-DOWN! soldier nodded at me over his gun—I sprang up out of my seat, down the steps, and "Darius!" I screamed, and I ran for that gate and flung myself at it:

BOMF!

He was there. He was right there. My hands panicked. They sort of grabbed through that gate at Darius—and his hands, Darius Spratt's hands, they panicked back.

I felt tears sting at my eyes and Nerd Boy went all blurry.

And I thought...and I thought...that Darius was all I had left. And that was how it was now. That was just how it was.

"Ruby!" he gasped, all choky-throated, like maybe that's how it was for him too.

"Darius!" I sobbed. I couldn't help myself—no more than I could help how my hands grabbed. I was ready to talk now; I was ready to tell him how it had been. That it had been bad, Darius. And I would hear—and I would listen—to how bad it had been for him. I would listen. We were all we had left.

"Hey, Ru!" said a familiar voice.

BOMF!

My hands fell away from Darius Spratt.

"Hey, Sask," I said.

There she was, looking just fresh and perky and as if everything was normal.

"You look amazing!" she said. "*Are you OK?*"

"Yeah...yeah...I'm fine," I said, swiping tears off my face.

I couldn't have looked that amazing because I saw, on the back of my hand, that my tears were mascara black. I had to look better than her though. I had to.

"Oh my 🦋! It's just been so totally awful, hasn't it?" gushed Saskia.

"Yeah," I said, smoothing my hair, smoothing my dress, smoothing myself.

"Is your family—"

"Yeah," I said, before she could go on about it.

"Mine too," said Saskia.

There was an awkward moment, during which I could have said I knew that, about Saskia's family, because I'd seen them spread around the back garden with the guacamole, and that—by the way—I'd broken into her house and seen the photos in her bedroom and taken her mom's dog, which she had cruelly abandoned, etc., etc.

"Luckily, I found Darius!" she trilled. The way she said it reminded me of that American Mom character she'd played in their spoof washing-detergent ad. Perky? Super-perky!

She slipped her arm through his.

"We're *engaged*," she said.

This explosion of a laugh filled my cheeks and half spat out through my lips.

It was a joke, right? It had to be a joke.

Like her arm was a hook, the Spratt-fish dangled limp on the end of it.

I couldn't help myself; I looked at Darius Spratt. This weird, wobbly, pleading smile slunk onto his face.

"Ruby," he whispered, staring straight back at me.

What had happened in the spongy-snake closet was not staying in the spongy-snake closet; it was flashing before my eyes.

My brain could not process the unimaginableness—the unimaginable, unbelievable, outrageous, horrific horribleness—of such a thing. My jaw dropped open from the weight of the words of horror and disbelief that filled it. YOU *WHAT?!* I wanted to shriek. *AS IF!* I wanted to shriek. I could have shrieked those words and about a trillion other things, none of them nice. I spoke one. One word.

Oh, I am so proud of myself for that one word. I—truly—am RUBY the GENIUS.

"Congratulations," I said.

"Ru!" whispered Saskia, almost managing a giggle. "It's not, like, *for real* or anything. We totally just had to! They keep kicking people out of here and—" She gasped then. She actually gasped. "Ru-by!" she shrieked. "Do you, like, *LIKE* him?"

The quiet soldier lost it. "Come on!" he said. He *sighed*... Like this, the most mortifying and appalling and...*soul-wounding* situation on Earth was the most boring situation on Earth. He grabbed my arm and he pulled me back to the bus. I did not resist. Someone had to stop it. Someone had to stop...all that.

I don't mean that, about the soul wounding. It just felt like it was at the time. It was an extreme time. During which extreme things happened. I was very traumatized and confused.

"My dad is alive," I shouted over my shoulder at Saskia, and at Darius Spratt. "MY—DAD—IS—ALIVE."

Saying that? It was better than swearing. It was the best and the most triumphant thing I could say, the best and most triumphant thing anyone could ever say: YOU ARE WRONG AND I AM RIGHT.

It's the best feeling in the world, isn't it? Being right.

"Where are they taking you?" Darius shouted.

I didn't answer. I shook the quiet soldier's hand off my arm, and I walked with dignity. I didn't answer because I didn't know. I didn't answer because it was an outrage that he should even—

"You take care, Ru!" he shouted. "You take care!"

OK. That was too much. *Don't call me Ru. Do NOT call me Ru.* I turned, I grabbed hold of every swear word I ever could have thought of, and I—

"Come on," said the SIT-DOWN! soldier, pulling me onto the bus before I could lash the Spratt with my burning rage.

As I made my way to my seat, I noticed something. Those other people on that bus, they looked at me funny. They looked at me funny as if…they felt sorry for me? They thought I was stupid? Surely not that they—seriously—thought a girl like me would ever have ANYTHING to do with a boy like Darius Spratt.

I did an emergency rummage in my head.

"That boy," I announced to them all, "is a lousy kisser."

"SIT DOWN!" yelled the SIT-DOWN! soldier.

I glared at them all and sat down.

My heart—bristling, bleeding, bruised, confused, messed up good and proper—shut itself up, tight…and *right*.

I checked my makeup. It was pretty bad, unfortunately. Worse than I had thought. Amid the swipe and smudge marks, mascara run-off streaks fell like black rain from my eyes.

We passed other gates to other camps. I was so busy fixing my makeup (it's a very calming activity, I find) I hardly noticed much, but some didn't even look like they were army bases how you'd think they'd be; they just looked like housing developments behind high fences—you even saw people there, with kids…out playing, because it was sunny and dry.

"House like that'll do me," said the woman who'd been rude, loudly.

"Probably have to share it," said a guy.

"No way," said another woman.

But that wasn't where we were going.

When we finally stopped, it was getting dark.

We pulled up in the middle of this pretty little village.

Sweet little cottages crowded around a sweet little village green filled with sweet little dead people. And a maypole, around which pretty ribbons fluttered in the breeze.

"This ain't right," the rude woman said.

"Shut up," said another guy. "They know what they're doing."

They did know what they were doing. I'd been dumped so many times that day I should have known too. I was being dumped. Again.

They herded us out.

"What the 🦋 is this?" said the rude woman.

They got that girl's wheelchair out of the bus; I remember how cool it looked, decorated with a million stickers. Her dad carried her off the bus and put her in it.

"Now what?!" demanded a guy.

The SIT-DOWN! soldier cocked his rifle again. Didn't he just love doing that?

This bawly brat in his mother's arms started to cry.

"The army is not able to accommodate everyone at this time," announced SIT-DOWN! soldier.

I saw then that maybe he wasn't so tough; I saw his fingers all nervous on that gun. It looked like maybe he was going to say something else; maybe he was supposed to say something else, but, really, what else was there to say?

"You have 🦋 got to be 🦋 kidding me!" said a guy.

"You are NOT leaving us here," said the rude woman.

"You 🦋s!" screamed the woman with the bawling kid as the soldiers got back on board.

They hadn't switched off the engine; they were positioned just right to go.

The abandoned (half) busload of people didn't even try to get back on board. The soldiers got back on, and they pulled away.

All day long, I hadn't looked at the sky. I hadn't needed to; it had been sunny, and then I'd been at the army place, and I didn't think—for one moment—that I'd get dumped... The wind had picked up, and it looked crappy: a jumbled altocumulus sky, the kind that changes every two seconds and is almost impossible to read. It's the kind of sky you only go out under if you have to, and you'd better be quick about it.

Like going on about dead bodies—which, incidentally, do NOT go zombie gray when they start to go off. They go GREEN; they go GREEN with white mold spots, and their lips shrivel, and their mouths rot so everyone looks like LIPLESS MAGGOTTY-MOUTHED SPOTTY ZOMBIE ELVES. BUT NORMAL-SIZED. PEOPLE DON'T SHRINK. THEY JUST GO GREEN. **GREEN!** Yes, like not going on about that, I also do not want to go on about the way people behaved—I just want to say that I was brought up to think that if something awful happened, PEOPLE WERE SUPPOSED TO HELP EACH OTHER, NOT GRAB ALL THE BEST SUPPLIES, THREATEN PEOPLE WITH GUNS, MURDER PEOPLE, CHASE PEOPLE, ATTACK THEM WITH POISONED WATER, OR...OR GO OFF WITH PEOPLE THEY WEREN'T SUPPOSED TO GO OFF WITH.

OR DUMP PEOPLE IN THE MIDDLE OF NOWHERE WHEN IT'S OBVIOUSLY JUST ABOUT TO RAIN. PROBABLY.

"STOP!" STOP!" I yelled, chasing after that bus.

Amazingly, they did stop.

Look charming, look contrite, look…desperate. That's how I felt: desperate.

"Please!" I said, grabbing at the open door. "There's been a mistake!"

I didn't know what the mistake was, but I knew there must have been one. (And not mine, surely!)

That soldier, that SIT-DOWN! soldier, he came down to that door, and he looked at me; I looked at him. I thought I saw a flicker of something human in his eye. Something human, but maybe only some flicker of shame. And so he should be ashamed for what he was doing.

"Go to Salisbury," he whispered.

Was that supposed to be some kind of *joke?!*

"I'VE-JUST-BEEN-THERE," I hissed. Maximum cobra-strike sarcasm.

I'll remember you, I thought, staring him straight in the eyes. *I'll remember you.*

"To the cathedral?" he whispered, like I was stupid or something.

I felt like I *was* stupid or something. "*What?!*" I said.

"GO-TO-SALISBURY-CATHEDRAL-IN-THE-CITY-OF-SALISBURY," he said.

He definitely thought I was some kind of an idiot.

And then they shut the doors. And then they drove off. Yeah, they left us.

CHAPTER THIRTY

I would have just gone straight home; I wanted to just go straight home.

There were a few really ugly few minutes when everyone who'd been thrown off the bus stood in the middle of that pretty little village and raged. That wasn't the ugly part: the ugly part was when people realized there was no point raging. Then people just split. Some went for houses, some for cars; some teamed up and some headed off alone. A kind guy helped the woman with the bawling kid. The rude woman, amazingly, went off with this frail old lady—but probably only because she seemed to be deaf and could put up with the rudeness. That left me, some guy with Down's syndrome (like Ronnie's brother had), another old lady, the wheelchair girl, and her dad standing on the pavement.

I split.

Ten minutes later, I was back with a car. Think that's because I'm a nice person? It's not. I'm the kind of person who leaves a hamster in a car, who forgets to feed guinea pigs—every day, for two years. Why I went back wasn't really because I couldn't ignore them (like I'd ignored Melissa, the Girl Guide girl). It wasn't even that the thought of those people left there would chew deep into—and feast upon!— the massive guilt I already felt about a whole load of things I couldn't even exactly name because I couldn't even exactly think about them (like Melissa). Those people left on the pavement, they probably would have been OK. I'm sure they would. Why I went back, really, was because some creepy guy from the bus who said he was an artist had been following me around, trying to get me to go with him.

Safety in numbers, that's what I thought, as I hammered on the horn to summon my new passengers.

That girl, she smiled when she saw me; her face lit up and she grinned at me like I was her best friend.

Please, please DON'T, I thought.

"Hello! I'm Sagal!" she said, beaming at me as her dad helped her into the passenger seat.

"I'm Ruby," I said in a dead voice.

The dad, who had climbed into the back with the others, asked Sagal a question; she said "Ruby" and he gabbled on again. The only word I understood was when he repeated my name.

"Abo—my dad says to say thank you and to tell you that you are not useless after all," said Sagal.

Whoa. From somewhere deep inside me the spirit of yee-haa arose.

"YOU *WHAT?!*" I said.

Before I could stop her, Sagal translated that.

It seemed to be an accurate translation—even the tone of her voice and the steely gaze matched—and her dad, looking fairly cross, launched into a long speech.

She grinned apologetically at me as her dad droned on.

"Does he want to drive?" I whispered.

"He'd love to, but he has no UK license," she whispered back. "It's against the law."

Oh, for crying out loud…

It's international, I guess, cranky parents droning on. What's less widespread as far as I know is us actually bothering to listen. Even though Sagal had to translate, she asked questions too; we both did. You kind of didn't want to believe it, and at the same time...you totally could. And you weren't really allowed not to, because everything the dad said, the old lady (Margaret) agreed with. Even the guy with Down's Syndrome—his name was Peter—agreed: "Listen to what you're told, Ruby!" he said to me.

(And how the 🦋 had Peter ever made it to the army place on his own?)

(And 🦋 🦋! I hate that I can even remember these people's names! I hate that.)

So, the *Ruby Morris Summary* of this one would be:

It wasn't as simple as people being old or disabled or having screaming kids, for example. Plenty of people who were old or disabled or who had screaming kids hadn't been put on the bus and dumped. And plenty of people who weren't any of those things had been put on that bus (like me). What we all had in common—and this is the horrible part—was we had no skill that the army wanted; we weren't even the daughters or the sons or the husbands or the wives or the grandmas or the grandpas of people with skills that the army wanted. Or the fiancées.

Oh yeah, I got that part. I swerved about when I did. Then I composed myself.

Sounds outrageous, doesn't it? But you couldn't argue with it. (Sagal and me, we did try: "Yes but," we said. "Yes but.") Yes but... I'd spent so long waiting in that hangar I practically knew the whole life stories of the people who'd shuffled back and forth around me: a blind man who spoke Russian; a nasty, shouty man who was an electrician and his nasty, shouty wife and nasty, shouty kids; this weeping and wailing woman who was a chemistry teacher. None of them were on that bus, were they?

Nerd Boy. They'd definitely have wanted to keep Nerd Boy. If they'd had any sense, they would have wanted to keep Saskia too—not even just because she was pretty darn bright, which she was, but because she had a skill I was starting to realize was essential in this new world. She was...*devious*, that's the word. She was a human polyextremophile.

Don't do anything I wouldn't do. That doesn't leave much, does it, Saskia Miller?

Sagal was just a schoolgirl, year below me. Know what she was good at? Cooking! Her dad was a community worker of some sort. Know what he was good at? Talking to people...in Somali! Margaret was just a nice old lady who said she didn't get out much, but seemed to get out and do more than I did, and Peter said he liked techno music and swimming.

We were not worth saving. We were no use to anyone. We were useless.

I said something pretty bad about the army that Sagal didn't translate.

"It won't be their fault, dear," said Margaret. "They'll just be doing what they've been told. It'll be that ❦ man's fault. I wish I'd never voted for him. I'll not be doing it again. I only hope the Queen's all right."

Once we'd hit a main road, it was OK getting to Salisbury (THE-CITY-OF-SALISBURY), just the usual avoiding smashed-up and abandoned cars, dead bodies, that kind of thing. Yes, the driving was OK; I was not. Once I'd realized what Sagal's dad was saying was true, I pretended I had to really concentrate on what I was doing so I didn't have to speak. My head felt in as much of a mess as the sky: raggedy thoughts forming, changing, swirling about, bumping into other thoughts, getting mixed up with each other; new thoughts splitting off, puffing up, turning darker and darker. Thoughts infested with wriggly little space bugs, tentacles waving.

I didn't know how I'd find the cathedral when we got there. I didn't need to know. On the outskirts of the city, there were signs. Signs saying "welcome." Signs written on bedsheets like people do for crummy village festival...then a trail of balloons to follow. Bunches of balloons tied to lampposts. This way to the party!

Sagal's dad started singing—not loud, party singing, but some soft warbling song that sounded so sad I was glad I couldn't understand the words to it.

"That's lovely, that is," said Margaret. She caught the tune and hummed along a little. Peter added some pretty impressive beatboxing.

Sagal rolled her eyes at me, giggling, but you could tell she was excited too.

"That way, Ruby!" she shouted every time she saw another bunch of balloons. "Over there!"

That was how we found our way to the giant parking lot that surrounded Salisbury Cathedral. Basically, it was like how a shopping mall is just before Christmas. A sea of cars packed around it. Only it's enormous, Salisbury Cathedral, isn't it? It's taller than any shopping mall (but with less stuff to buy). Light—lovely electric light—shone out from huge windows.

"Stop!" yelled Sagal's dad as Peter stepped straight out of the car.

I peered out through the windows. I got out too. I waved my hand up at the sky: a raggedy mess of sunset orange and black clouds, above us one small gap in which the sky looked an unpleasant shade of green. (Like...you know.)

Truth? I hadn't known for sure that it would be OK when I stepped out.

"It's OK," I shouted. "It's OK."

Now see, what you must have realized and what I didn't even get was that as well as the mess in my head, I was whacked out from tiredness and half nuts from thirst.

"It's OK!" I shouted. *I* really wasn't.

I don't want to make a habit out of fainting. Before the whole global meltdown end-of-the-world thing, I hadn't fainted once, not in my entire life—and there had been plenty of times when I could have (kissing Caspar McCloud, for example). I didn't faint outside that cathedral, not exactly. I just went really weird and dizzy. Sagal's dad got the wheelchair out, shoved Sagal in it, and shoved me on top of her, and bumped us along between cars and across grass to the doors of the cathedral.

Some lady shoved a bottle of water into my hands.

The next thing I can truly say that I clearly remember was me sitting in a pew, looking at the great ribby stone bones of the ceiling, having some crazy thought that I'd been swallowed by a great ribby stone beast, and then realizing I hadn't and that Sagal was next to me in her wheelchair, holding my hand while someplace nearby this candlelit choir of the useless droned out "Amazing Grace."

There were groups of people dotted around all over the place, talking, sorting stuff, ladies taking down names, people handing out survival goodie bags, people handing out blankets, people handing out maps of the city.

People consoling people.

And I do mean "people." This looked like no kind of church I'd ever been in. EVERY kind of person was there.

Sagal's dad was deep in (heated, translated) conversation with another guy, who looked a little like him, and a woman in a head scarf and a Christiany churchy-looking man and some random guys—one of whom lit up a cigarette and puffed on it until this stressed-looking mother with a baby on her hip told him to PUT IT OUT. He put it out.

Sagal handed me another bottle of water. I glugged it down.

"What are they going on about?" I asked

"Stuff," said Sagal. "Why this happened, that kind of thing."

"It doesn't matter why it happened," I said.

I wanna go home, I thought. *I wanna go home.*

That's what I thought.

Like, really, this place was nothing like the army place. No one was hassling anyone with tricky questions; anyone who arrived was given food and water. (Peter, who "arrived" twice, scored double rations.) But to me, even though I felt like it shouldn't, the whole thing sucked. No—not that. It was all really lovely and everything (although I did wonder why they couldn't have picked somewhere more cozy)…but really:

1. It reminded me in some weird way of the school carnival. Like any minute now, I'd get told I had to make cupcakes or sign up for a turn running the raffle. (Not good!)
2. What I had felt when I first saw the army men? About "was this how the world was going to be?"…I kind of felt that again. (Not good!)

"Oh 🦋! He's so embarrassing!" whispered Sagal, rolling her eyes about her dad.

"At least he's here," I said, getting to my feet. I swayed for a second.

"Oh! Sorry! I didn't mean…" said Sagal. She smiled sadly at me and pushed another bottle of water and the kind of whole-wheat snack bar Darius would adore into my hands.

I chomped; I drank. I looked at the bottle, half the water left.

I listened to the singing. Hymns—they always sound bad, don't they? They always sound...so drony. My dad says that. He works in the music industry—which sounds really cool, but he hates his job. He always says how he's just a "glorified accountant" and stuff, but he knows about music. I'm useless at it, but even I can tell when something sounds bad. My dad? He wouldn't have stayed in that cathedral for a second. Not with that racket.

"I'm going home," I said.

"Abo! Abo!" I heard Sagal shouting as I walked out down the aisle.

They caught me at the doors. Literally: Sagal grabbed ahold of my dress.

"Ruby! Please! Don't go!" she said.

Please don't leave me.

Her father, he looked at me.

"Where will you go?" he said in English.

"Home," I said. "*You speak English?!*"

"Of course," he said.

"He just doesn't like to because he thinks he's not very good at it," Sagal said. "That's how people are; if you don't speak perfectly, they think you're stupid."

"Like me," I said.

Sagal's father gabbled something else, then he took hold of his daughter's hand and made her let go of my dress.

"He says no. He says anyone can see you're not stupid," said Sagal. She giggled, a little shyly. She looked unsure. "He says...you just look like trouble."

That dad, he smiled at me. It was a nice smile. A dad's smile.

I walked out, straight out, into the crazy-skied night.

"He says," Sagal shouted from the door of the cathedral, "that your father would be very proud of you."

◦•◦

I had no map. I guessed. I zigzagged; I went wrong.

I had to ditch the car and get another one.

I got out at Stonehenge. Time before the rain, you couldn't even touch those stones. I was in a big starry patch of sky, so I went for it. I smashed into the gift shop and I swigged my drink and snacked on chips sitting right on top of one of the stones.

Imaginary snap No. 2. Selfie with stones.

I went wrong again; I went right again. I ditched my car again. I found another one. It was not like the MG journey from hell. I was not frantic to get where I was going. I was just going there. I was just going home.

Even when dawn came and the rain started, I didn't panic. When I finally got to our house, it was pouring. Nimbostratus.

Welcome home, Ruby. Welcome home.

That's what the rain said.

Why, thank you, I said, and I lay down on the backseat of the car, and I went to sleep.

CHAPTER THIRTY-ONE

S hort and oh so sweet.

Later that day, when the rain stopped, I didn't have to break into my own house because someone who knew where the Ruby Emergency Key was had left the front door open. Not *open* open, but open.

The house stank.

There, scrawled on the kitchen wall in permanent marker that would never, ever come off was a message from my dad.

Ruby—Where are you?! We are going to get Grandma. stay here! Back soon!

Love Dad and Dan

Dan had drawn a little smiley face after his name, and they both had left a trail of kisses.

CHAPTER THIRTY-TWO

That was nearly three weeks ago.

My dad didn't come that day, and he didn't come the next day, or the day after that. My dad hasn't come yet, but he will.

To start with, I didn't want to leave the house again, not ever, because I was convinced my dad would turn up at any second. Even the first time, later that day, when I had to go to the Fitches to look for something to drink, I left a note. I also left the window open because of the smell, and when I got back, the note had blown off the table, so now, every time I leave the house, I write where I am going, what time I am going, when I will be back and WHAT DATE IT IS on the wall.

My dad, he never did that, did he? There was no date on the wall.

Meantime, because I've got no one to talk to, I started writing this. I didn't think I'd get this far, but there you go.

I was going to call this *The Disaster Diary of Ruby Morris*, but that sounds too cute. It's just not that kind of story, is it? I think I'll just call it *H2O*. I always did hate the rain, even before it turned into a killer. And *H2O* sounds so much more Hollywood, doncha think?

Can't you just see the trailer? Can't you just hear that guy's growly voice…as my face (deadpan but pouty) stares out of the window at:

H2O
IT'S DRIPPY. IT'S DEADLY.

Then, to dramatic music, we have a fast montage of everything that's happened (cutting out the Darius parts). We end with me giving my dad—who's weeping with joy at the sight of me—a hug and a gentle reprimand about time-keeping issues. I ruffle my grinning brother's mop of hair—and he has to let me because he's so happy to see me. Then I turn and passionately kiss Caspar. Who did (somehow) survive.

I've got the perfect dress; I've got the perfect Diana shoes. There is no longer even the tiniest hint of orange on my face. My hair has gotten a little weird and brittle, but it is an excellent jet black…and I've swapped that runny mascara for one that definitely stays put no matter how much you sob. (I've tested it.) I'm premiere good to go!

Meantime, there's reality.

I found this book next-door-but-one's kids had, all about clouds. This, I am studying. It seems simple when you look at the pictures; when you step outside, it's tough to spot what's what. I am getting better at it. I have to get better at it.

And that's about it, really.

I know! Just to check whether you've been paying attention, like I would listen to your story, if I ever met you, I'll give you an essay question…like: *In what ways should Ruby have behaved differently? Discuss…* or *In what ways will everything now turn out OK? Discuss…*

OK, scrap that. I'm just kidding! (I don't want to think about ANY of that.)

Let's have a multiple choice instead. I love multiple choice! You don't even have to know the answer to stand a chance of getting it right.

QUESTION: When *should* you give up hope?

A) Now. Immediately. We're all doomed.

B) Give it another couple of weeks.

C) Never.

I suppose there might be an option D), but if there is, I can't think of it.

Mom, I am still breathing.

● ◆ ●

I am Ruby Morris. This is my story. Any day now, my dad will come.

Also, although I'd rather die than… Although I basically never want to see him again as long as I live, Darius Spratt has got a ton of my stuff. Including *my cell phone*.

H2O Discussion Guide

A NOTE FROM VIRGINIA BERGIN

I chose the subject of water because it is essential to life…and yet waterborne diseases kill about 1.8 million people every year, and 783 million people do not have access to clean water. So for a lot of people, the situation described in *H2O* already exists.

According to the last set of UNICEF figures, 18% of the world's population is aged 10–19, so, by my calculations, that means there are at least 140,940,000 Rubys and Dariuses and Princesses trying to survive…right now.

1. What would *you* do if deadly rain fell?
   a. Is there a character in the story whose actions you identify with?
2. Would you be concerned about animals? What about your own pets?
3. As a character, Ruby has a lot to say for herself, but what do you think about the way she behaves?
4. *H2O* is told from Ruby's perspective. As a reader, how did you feel about this?
   a. What are the positives and negatives of reading a story written in first-person point of view?

    b. Did you trust what Ruby has to say, or did you sometimes doubt her?

    c. Were there things in the story you felt you might have understood better than Ruby did herself?

5. Why do you think Ruby is writing this story?

6. What do you think the army and the government would do if a situation like this really happened?

    a. Is that different to what you think they *should* do?

    b. What would *you* do if you were in a position of power?

7. Overall, how do you feel about the way different individuals and different groups of people behave toward each other in *H2O*?

    a. Are there any encounters you particularly liked/disliked—if so, why?

8. *H2O* is science fiction, but do you think there is an environmental message in the story? Does it reflect any current environmental issues we face?

9. Has *H2O* changed the way you feel about water in any way?

10. Why do you think this book is called *H2O*? (And not *Water*, for example.)

11. What do you think will happen next?

12. Ruby made me put this in: When should you give up hope?

ACKNOWLEDGMENTS

I would like to thank:
My family.
Steve Geck, Kate Prosswimmer, Jillian Bergsma,
and the team at Sourcebooks.
In the UK, Rachel Petty
and the team at Macmillan Children's Books.

Also thanks to:

Jackie Pridham, for being truly wonderful.
Hilary Hunt, for being Hilary Hunt.
Louise Lamont, for being my agent.
Donovan Hawley, for trying to be sensible. Sometimes.
Gary Sugden, for reading and thinking and being honest.
Erik Tarloff, for putting up with me. A. D. Cooper, likewise.

And Helen Summers, for knowing and for waiting.

Thank you to Dr. Matthew Avison (University of Bristol) and
Dr. Helen Smalley for kindly giving excellent scientific advice, which
I tried to heed as much as I could. Sorry about the made-up bits.

Also to Brendan Boyce, for explaining the finer points of mass civil unrest.

The Guide Law reproduced by kind permission of Girlguiding, the UK organization for Girl Scouts.

Finally, thanks to my consultants: Ruby T, Stan, Aidan, and Luke.

THE END WAS ONLY THE BEGINNING.

Don't miss Virginia Bergin's

CHAPTER ONE

I was sinking.

That's how it is when you're all alone and there's been a global apocalypse and you're just hoping your dad is going to show up like he said he would but there's no sign of him so what exactly are you going to do if your dad doesn't come and every day you try hard not to think about that because…

Everything's going to be OK

is what you have to keep telling yourself but some part of you or maybe it's all of you thinks it isn't going to be OK so you try not to think at all but you can't stop thinking because pretty much everyone is dead and you've got nowhere to go and no one to go anywhere with and anyway who wants to go anywhere when THE SKY IS RAINING DEATH?

Yes, in an apocalypse-type situation, it's very easy to think bad things. In fact, there's SO much time for thinking, it's really easy to slide way beyond even regular apocalypse-type thinking into TOTAL COMPLETE AND UTTER DOOM THINKING… because there's about a million days when you're stuck inside because it's raining killer rain or it looks like it's going to rain killer rain or you just can't face another day in the library.

Yup, that's how bad things got: I broke into Dartbridge Public Library. Studying up on clouds (I know twenty-four different types!) didn't seem like it was going to be enough to get me through this thing. (Through it and into what? That was a whole other question, one best not asked.) My specialist areas of study were:

1. The self-help section. Oddly, there didn't seem to be that much on feeling a bit gloomy because human life on Earth as we know it has been wiped out—but you could tell people meant well. Ruby usefulness rating: 4/10.

2. Microbiology for people who quit biology at the end of eighth grade, weren't really all that interested in science, and weren't any good at it anyway. It's baffling and creepy. Ruby rating: 1/10.

3. Car maintenance for people who would have dropped that too if they'd tried to teach it to us in school (which they should have done). I would not have chosen to study this, but something happened. I'll explain later. Ruby rating: 10/10.

4. Survival manuals. Frankly, I could have learned most of this stuff when I was in Girl Scouts, but I tended to opt for the cake-making side of things (the benefits seemed more obvious at the time). However, not even the SAS (the Special Air Service = very, very good-at-surviving-stuff British Army crack force), who have handy tips on surviving a nuclear bomb going off right next to you, seem to have been able to have imagined this particular kind of disaster. Or maybe they did, but when people saw the chapter on how the army would abandon anyone they had no use for and we'd all be left to fend for ourselves, they complained that it was an outrage and a lie and the SAS were forced to take it out.

(Even though it was TRUE.) Nevertheless, Ruby rating: 7/10 (because you never know).

5. Oh, and…one particularly sad and lonely day, I had a quick look at cellular telecommunications. There are no phones and no Internet anymore, so I was just curious, I suppose, about how difficult it'd be to build and run a thing like that. (Quite difficult, I think. Judging from the diagrams.) Ruby rating: 0/10.

My cell phone is at the top of a list of all the things there'll be no more of (currently 402 items long with the recent shock addition of chocolate spread; I was scooping the last fingerful out from under the rim of a jar when I realized supplies *will* eventually run out).

There are no people on this list. Their names, the names of the dead, are written on my heart. My small, sad, human heart. Hurt so bad it will never cry again.

Don't get me wrong. I cry. I cry plenty. I howl! But my heart? It is all cried out. It is silent.

I don't do pets anymore either. Apart from the risk that a single sloppy lick from a puddle drinker could kill you, they're nothing but heartbreak and trouble…and they're ganging up. There are probably small, mean teams of guinea pigs and rabbits, but the dogs are certainly hanging out together—I've seen packs of them roaming—and I've even seen *loose affiliations** of cats. Not Ruby,

---

* A very useful term: here's how I learned it:
TEACHER: So, although Molly Stevens is your friend, you're saying you don't know why she's not in PE?
ME: Well…
TEACHER: Just try to answer the question, Ruby.
ME: I wouldn't exactly say we're friends friends…
TEACHER: So… (sighs) despite the fact that I see you in each other's company every single day, you're claiming you're not… (sighs again; does little quote-mark wiggles with exasperated fingertips) "friends" friends, you're saying you're just loosely affiliated?
ME: (Pause) That would be correct?

though—that's Mrs. Wallis's Siamese; she doesn't affiliate herself with anyone. She's still hanging around in a strictly unaffiliated sort of way, and she seems to be doing OK, though I sincerely hope her well-fed appearance has got nothing to do with the disappearance of Mrs. Wallis's shih tzu Mimi (last seen absconding from a car in the school parking lot and running in the direction of home), or indeed with the disappearance of Mrs. Wallis herself.

There is a shorter list of things I'm glad there'll be no more of, currently twelve items long. Exams come top, which I never would—"come top of the class," geddit?—so that's why they are *numero uno*. This list is a lot harder to think of stuff for, so it's brilliant when I do come up with something. The last time I thought of something—"No one can stop me from drinking whatever I like whenever I like!"—I drank to celebrate. I hit my mum's gin.

I remember standing, swaying, at the open front door, watching the rain pour down. I think I was talking to it. I wouldn't have been saying nice things.

When I woke up the next morning, alive, I crossed the drink thing off the list.

The thing about going a little crazy is it's hard to realize that's what's happening.

I stopped going to the library. (What do the SAS know? They're buffoons!) I stopped doing anything much, other than things I absolutely had to do—and even my grip on those got a bit shaky. I'd get up and think, *I must clean my teeth*…and it'd be bedtime before I got around to it—although bedtime itself got a little flexible. Sometimes it happened in the middle of the day; sometimes it happened all day. And sometimes, when it was supposed to be bedtime, because it was the middle of the night, it didn't happen at all.

One such night, I shaved my hair off. All of it. It seemed easier to do that than wash it. Easier, even, than trying to find a can of dry shampoo with anything left in it—when in any case, just like chocolate spread, supplies *will* run out eventually, so why not face facts? That's what I imagine I was thinking...when really I don't remember thinking anything much, just picking up my (looted) battery-powered lady shaver...and watching grubby clump-lettes of (dyed) black hair fall.

It should have been the head shaving that alerted me to how serious my situation was. Bit of a clue there. But all I ended up doing was adding the result to one of my other lists: the list of stupid things I've done.

That one's not written down either; it's just burned on my brain. It hurts.

My shaved head looked like a small, fuzzy globe, a planet...inside which strange things happened. Below the spiky surface, dark, wordless thoughts massed, rose, and sunk. Popped up again, doing the backstroke. Giggling. Or hidden deep in the goo of my mind, screaming messages that bubbled up, garbled.

All day, every day, all night, every night, my head simmered with nonsense. Sometimes it boiled. Until finally, there didn't seem to be anything very much left inside my head at all. Boiled dry, I guess. I don't think the thoughts had words anymore. First off, even the sensible, normal ones got texty: "I must clean my teeth" became "clean teeth." Then it was just "teeth." Then, when the words had pretty much stopped altogether, it was probably just "🦷."

I was lost on Planet Ruby, where weeks and days and hours and minutes and seconds (there were some very long seconds) got muddled—and dreams and reality got muddled too. And nightmares, but they were pretty much only about as awful as what was real.

And it might have all gone on and on like that until I really did walk out in the rain (then it would stop), but finally SOMETHING HAPPENED TO ALERT ME TO HOW SERIOUS MY SITUATION WAS...

I crashed a Ferrari. Totaled it.

I was flooring it, coming around a bend (up on Dartmoor, I was about to realize), when I hit a patch of mist, part of which turned out not to be mist but a sheep, so I swerved and—

SCREECH!

KA-BLAM!

BOUFF!

The airbag thing smashed into my face. Only somehow my own hands had gotten involved.

OK, I know how. I like to do this fancy cross-hands thing when I'm turning corners. So, yeah, my own arms got biffed into my face by the airbag.

I sat there. Punched face screaming. Dazed—double dazed, because you want to know a terrible thing? I wasn't even sure about how I'd gotten there. I mean, I must have thought I should get out of the house for a bit—to go on an I-need-something-to-drink mission, most probably. (Supplies always seemed to be running low, but that was probably because time was running weird: one minute I'd have plenty of cola or whatever, and the next minute I'd be draining dregs and panicking.) But since I often thought I should do something and didn't do it or thought something had happened when it hadn't actually happened, I was seriously shocked to realize that this crash thing, apparently, *had* really happened. Though I only knew it for sure because IT HURT. OWWW. ARRRGH. OWWWWW.

WAKE UP, RUBY! WAKE UP!

The car was wrecked; I didn't even have to try to start it again—which I did—to know that. It had made out with a wall. They didn't like each other. Not one bit.

I got out of the car. My eyes were already stinging like something nasty had been flung into them. I put my hand up to my bashed nose and felt blood. I looked at the blood on my fingertips; then I squinted at the thing that would like to eat that blood.

Mist's a funny old thing, isn't it? Basically, it's just a cloud that's hit rock bottom. A cloud (stratus nebulosus, doncha know) that can no longer be bothered to get up into the sky. It drags its sorry self along the ground. Funny? It's hilarious, really: Is it going to kill you, or isn't it? How much of it—*exactly*—would have to settle on your skin before…

I could see that mist swirling and swelling toward me. I should have gotten back into the car and waited it out…but I have an *emotional issue* about being trapped in a car—particularly, in this case, one that had just SMASHED into a wall; probably anyone left alive in Devon would have heard that crash. Some scary someone-anyone could have been on their way to investigate. So—add this to the list of stupid things!—I didn't wait. I ran.

All I could think was: *it* was coming after me. *But I could outrun it.*

I bolted across the moor. I scrambled up—up—up. Up rocks. Up-up-up. Up-up-up. Stupid-stupid-stupid Ruby. Up-up-up.

Until there was no more up.

I knew I was at the top of Hay Tor not because I'm, like, really keen on long, rambling walks in scenic landscapes, but because there was no place higher to go; anyone who lives in Dartbridge knows this place because you can see it for miles around—when it's clear.

I stood on the rocks, where there was no place up—**no** place, no other or further or higher place—watching the mist rise around me, puffing itself up like it was just remembering it could be a cloud that could get on up into that sky and rain.

I wiped at my throbbing nose, saw blood on the back of my hand. What if it could *smell* it? What if all those little wiggly-legged bacterium ET microblobs could smell my blood? What if they were all now paddling away like mad, waving their little tentacles, letting out little microsqueals of joy at the scent of breakfast?

I didn't know how that would be, having that *thing*, that disgusting little blood-gobbling, world-murdering *thing* get me slowly.

Bad? Very bad? Unimaginably, excruciatingly bad?

And lonely.

I was going to die alone on Hay Tor. My body would be pecked at by crows, nibbled on by sheep bored of grass. Foxes would come and have a good old chew on my bones—maybe drag a few back to the den for the cubs. Someone someday would put my rain-eaten, worm-licked, weather-worn skull on top of the highest stone, and Hay Tor would get a whole new name: Stupid Dead Girl Hill.

I stood. I roared.

No, that's just what I'd like to say I did.

I lost it.

I stood and I whimpered, and in the mist in front of me through stinging, weeping eyes, I saw the shadow of a someone-anyone. Fear crackled through me.

No one moved.

And they'd die if they stayed there, swallowed by the mist—and I felt my arms waving and I heard my own wrecked voice shouting, "COME ON!"

And the shadow-being waved back. She waved back.

And I saw she was me and wasn't real at all.

And I sat down on the rocks, weeping.

And the shadow girl sat too…and melted. She went away. Almost as quickly as she had appeared, she disappeared.

I knew what she was. I'd seen her in the cloud book. A rare thing—called a "Brocken spectre," when you see your own shadow in a cloud. Enough to spook anyone out. More than enough to spook me.

The mist went with her—the shadow ghost of me—burning off in the sun, until I was just a stupid girl with a punched face, sitting alone on Hay Tor.

Wake up, Ruby Morris.

ABOUT THE AUTHOR

Virginia Bergin has had about a hundred jobs, including working as a writer on TV, online learning, and corporate projects.

She lives in Bristol, England, and has visited the U.S. once, traveling by train from Schenectady, New York to Clearwater, Florida, in search of long-lost relatives.

H2O is her first novel.